No Ice,
No Slice

NO ICE, NO SLICE

HUGO TANG

authorHOUSE®

AuthorHouse™ UK Ltd.
1663 Liberty Drive
Bloomington, IN 47403 USA
www.authorhouse.co.uk
Phone: 0800.197.4150

© *2014 Hugo Tang. All rights reserved.*

No part of this book may be reproduced, stored in a retrieval system, or transmitted by any means without the written permission of the author.

Published by AuthorHouse   04/04/2014

ISBN: 978-1-4969-9256-7 (sc)
ISBN: 978-1-4969-9275-8 (e)

This book is printed on acid-free paper.

*To those loved,
and to those lost.*

*'Love makes the world go round?
Not at all. Whisky makes it go round twice as fast.'*
Compton Mackenzie

零

My name is Harry Chen: nearly twenty-seven years young, part-time entrepreneur, part-time alcoholic. As an early birthday present to myself, I purchased some discount ingredients and created a cheeky cocktail or three. Entrepreneurial alcoholism.

I'd like to think, however, that there are more strings to my pint of Strongbow than just a keen, lean eye for business, and a penchant for recreational drinking. In fact, I think every person needs at least three words to be fairly 'summed up.'

Take Dylan for instance – my second in command. To the unwary eye he seems like an ambitious, capable individual, accomplished to be the assistant manager of such a large venue at his tender age. Ambitious. Capable. Accomplished. Or so you'd think. The average customer doesn't hear the typical conversations we share (or more accurately, I have to endure), this afternoon at the club being no exception.

'Why give up your life of freedom for one girl? There are so many women out there,' proclaims Dylan. 'The sea is chock-a-block with fish, ripe for the sticking. You wanna lose that for *Gemma*? Show me the Harry I've always heard about. Harry the ledge, when you were at your last club getting all the gash, innit.'

'Ledge? I'm no legend. But your belly would make a pretty decent ledge.' I poke his potbelly. 'You're wrong about the sea. Sustainable fishing. Take what you need, and I need Gemma.'

'Engagement this year, kids the next. Before you know it you'll be in your rocking chair with your false teeth and your blue balls.'

'You haven't thought past the Wham, Bam, Thank You Ma'am.'

'Woah, I don't thank them buddy, they thank me,' he replies, brushing some imaginary dirt off his shoulder.

'Look, I need you to repair the rip in the sofa next to the DJ booth and stamp each complimentary drink voucher before 8pm. There are hundreds here. More work, less preaching.'

'I didn't know I was a seamstress in a past life. Let me get out my emergency needle and thread. You have a wifey now, get her up here to fix it.'

'I want the vouchers done for 7pm now. And why should Gemma fix the sofa when it was your shagging that ripped it?'

'Never get down on one knee for a girl that won't get on two for you! I better be invited to the stag do, that's all I can say,' he smirks.

'I truly wish that was all you said. Any advances on 6pm?' I ask, and he finally reaches over for them. 'Choosing women is like choosing cologne. I've had my fair share of testers to know that I've found the ideal scent,' I say, trying to humour him slightly; at least until my drink vouchers are validated and the sofa gets shoved in a corner so I can't see the rip.

'Another pile of tokens. When will Barney realise that giving away drinks doesn't gain us loyalty? I never used to have to do this. We might as well become a registered charity.' His defiance towards me not satisfying enough, he has to have a go at *my* boss too. Though he does have a point.

'Get these jobs done, get the bar and club ready, make us a grand tonight and your drinks are on me this Sunday,' I say, using the promise of free booze as a motivational tool. 'I won't let a Monday ruin an otherwise perfectly good Sunday.'

The first five days after the weekend are the hardest.

'About time you got the drinks in! Definitely your round,' he screeches, following my successful carrot dangle. 'At least all the fanny out there is mine now. No chasing skirt for you, playboy.'

'It always seems to be my round.' I don't recall Dylan ever buying a drink.

'Hey, what would you rather be? An old pervert's sex toy or a gypsy caravan slave?' he asks, and it wouldn't surprise me to find that he's been both.

Lewd. Inappropriate. Embarrassing.

*

You could fully analyse someone, exploring their very being in countless adjectives, describing their each and every idiosyncrasy in tremendous detail. Each word added providing more insight in to what a person is all about, their character and appearance, their personality and peculiarities, their qualities and quirks. Marvellous as that may be, sometimes there just isn't the time, or inclination, to do so. When you summarise someone in an instant – in a nightclub, perhaps – you make an assessment of them from your initial reaction, like on a blind date. You probably only have time to pass three judgements. In daily life we make these 'micro-judgements' all the time and we often don't even realise we're doing it.

When we absentmindedly channel hop over reruns of *Jerry Springer*, as he invites another home wrecker on to the stage, we all make our preliminary judgements before the guest has even had the chance to stick their finger up at the audience and call everyone 'compulsive lying bastards.' If someone offers to take our picture on holiday, so that Gemma and I can be in the photo together, I make a rapid assessment as to whether or not this guy is going to run off with our camera and whether or not I'd be able to catch him. Then there are those we walk past in the street, or those sat in cars next to us in traffic. Even those stood in front of us in the check-out queue at Morrison's, where we inadvertently find ourselves spying on their purchases, gaining a brief glimpse in to their lives, and fridges.

We all make our three word assumptions in everyday life whether we intend to or not. They are often observant, but there are occasionally times when our preconceptions have been entirely wrong – when we misjudge people from the start. The three words we choose for ourselves would be very different from the three chosen for us by another. I would consider myself not only an entrepreneur and a drinker, but also a fiancé. My work, and my relationship to my bride-to-be Gemma define me, and I enjoy enhancing these experiences with a tipple or two, often. However, Gemma would change my three word synopsis from 'Entrepreneur, Drinker, Fiancé' to 'Workaholic, Alcoholic, Best friend.'

'Best friend,' which is two words (although this is my system so I can bend the rules), isn't to suggest that she sees me as more of a pal than as a fiancé. What we share goes beyond social expectations of a cohabiting couple taking the next logical step, but more like swans or golden eagles that mate for life: they share an affinity and a connection, or so *National Geographic* would have us believe. She is my best friend who happens to be wearing a ring on a particular finger.

This is my basic view on how we interpret one another and is my roundabout way of saying that I don't just work too much and drink too much, but also do just enough to warrant a wife-to-be, who, if given another three words, would describe me as 'Impossible, Irritating and Sweet,' not to totally discredit myself at the end there.

What would your three words be? That's for everyone and anyone to decide, all the time.

*

'You should have proposed to her like I suggested man,' says Dylan, interrupting my stock-take for the third time in as many minutes.

'Have you done those bloody coupons yet?' I politely enquire.

'You arrange to meet Gemma at a quiet café. I run in with a fake gun and I'm wearing a balaclava. I grab the pair of you and throw you in the back of a van...' he regales me yet again, failing to accept that I've already proposed to Gemma and that she's already said yes. Without anyone getting kidnapped. 'She'll be crying and screaming, but you tell her you love her and at least you'll die together,' he continues with delight. If only he had this imagination for his work.

'Original, I'll give you that, but she'd be in hysterics. I'd have traumatised her for life,' I say, just as I said the last four times he tried to convince me to hire the Ford Transit.

'That's the whole point. When I pull the van up to a scenic spot, with a picnic laid out, with champagne and the ring, she'd be shocked and certainly never forget it!' His plan gets more outrageous each time he tells it.

'You stick to the sofa repairs, and I'll stick to my engagement proposal, which was ages ago, by the way. Maybe save your hostage plot for the divorce, Dildo,' I say, knowing how much he hates being called 'Dildo', and having to fix sofa arms, it would seem.

1

New Year's Eve is just around the corner and, quite frankly, it can stay there. An interesting time to have your birthday, to say the least. By interesting, I mean shit.

I do share my birthday with some distinguished company though, and it has been said that people with unique birth dates tend to go on and accomplish great things. Look at the esteemed list: Anthony Hopkins, Ben Kingsley, Donna Summer, Henri Matisse, Alex Ferguson, Heather McCartney, the list goes on. All born on New Year's Eve. Considering I can't act, sing or paint and I know nothing about football, this is where the similarity ends. At least I'm still in with a chance of marrying a Beatle.

Things could be worse though. Yes, I've had to babysit Dylan for most of the week to get the venue ready, and yes, no one apart from Gemma has remembered it's my birthday in a few days, but at least there's always a party to go to, even if I do have to host and work it. Bar staff are on double time, so there's no way Barney's ever going to give me the night off, seeing as I'm salaried.

I've never been a fan of ushering in the New Year and as this is my twenty-seventh attempt to enjoy it, I am well-versed in how it is likely to play out. There will be no shortage of scraps – after all, what better way is there to bring in the New Year than out on the street covered in blood? I will more than likely run out of change and glassware and, without a shadow of a doubt, question why I put myself through it every year. I can't imagine this happens to Anthony Hopkins whilst celebrating his birthday.

I'd also never receive two lots of presents, with my birthday being so close to Christmas. What I do get, however, is forty texts from people I've never spoken to, probably for good reason, not content with simply wishing me a prosperous New Year, but soliciting me to pass it on. I shouldn't have to be invasively badgered on my birthday by someone who hasn't even remembered it and texts *en masse*. The only redeeming quality to my New Year's Eve outweighs all its shortcomings by a scale of magnitude. There is always one thing to look forward to:

My Midnight Kiss with Gemma.

Gemma Goodman: Fiancée. Compassionate. Mine.

This might not seem much to most, but before Gemma came along I never had someone to kiss at midnight, and now I'll never have to go without one.

Gemma is caring and kind and thoughtful of others, traits I was in serious short supply of before I met her. She was the benchmark for what I wanted to become, as my wayward path was in need of redirection: meandering through a fondness for drink, women and other drugs. I don't necessarily agree that 'opposites attract,' but I do feel that Gemma and I fill in each other's blanks. We stick as a team and wouldn't get anywhere fast without the other.

Our 'honeymoon period' has had time to wear off, yet the fondness and love is still very much there. The romance and the butterflies perhaps aren't what they once were, but these feelings have been replaced with an overwhelming sense of purpose, security and an end to a lifelong yearning for family. But right now I want to strangle her and, failing that, I wish she had let me stay at home.

'Stop being a prude, Gemma. I didn't know you were too posh to use a public toilet.'

'I'm not being posh, you're being a knob. There's no way I'm peeing in there,' she replies fairly, because she isn't posh and I am being a knob, even if only a harmless, floppy one.

'Go in, pinch your nose, pull your panties down, job done.' A relatively easy task from a bloke's perspective, considering I wouldn't need to sit down, require bog roll or have to put my bag and coat anywhere.

'We need to find another one. You'd think gardens like these would have better facilities,' she says, a point I shall remember to bring up with the town planner the next time I see him.

'You're absolutely right. In between fixes, the junkies should flush and put their needles in the appropriate waste receptacles. It was your idea to come here Gemz,' I say, even though up until this point I was fairly enjoying, or at least making the most of, our wander through the Abbey Gardens, which seems moderately junkie-free today.

'Don't *Gemz* me, Harry. You're not helping. Next time I'll just come by myself. I thought it'd be nice to spend the one afternoon you're not working out and about together. I thought wrong. I'd rather pee in a bush,' she hisses, finding a reasonable alternative to her soiled toilet seat dilemma. She even does the annoying rabbit fingers thing when she says her name back.

'Your face is a bush,' is the best I can offer.

'You smell like a bush,' she says in clever retaliation.

'You *look* like a bush.' Not as good as my first offering.

'Well, you act like a bush,' she says, laughing to herself.

'You *are* a bush,' I say, laughing at Gemma.

'Well, *you* are a bush,' she says, conceding the battle.

'Already said it, fool!' I reply, having won at this little game we play. You'd think she'd be better at it, the amount of time she spends with children. Especially this one.

She relieves herself in a bush while I stand guard for wardens and crack fiends and we're friends again. See, it isn't all smiles and rainbows; like most couples we have our arguments, and they usually start with working too much, resenting day trips together and finding nowhere to pee.

Soft. Warm. Gentle.

Her, not the sensation of peeing.

When Gemma isn't doing all the normal things like peeing in bushes and losing at eye-spy games, she is pretty weird, like me. She cries during RSPCA adverts, makes up her own lyrics to songs, puts way too much Ribena in her water and the smallest pipette amount of milk in her tea. She gets a 'gazebo' and a 'gondola' mixed up and claims to have watched every Disney movie ever made, an achievement helped in large part by her profession as a nanny. She looks after little Millie, who insists on calling each evening to say goodnight.

She also deeply believes that we all have a guardian angel watching over us and is always looking for signs to confirm her conviction. She has one toe stubbier than all the rest on her right foot and she does a great dolphin impersonation too. Gemma would kill me if she knew I told people all of this. In the simplest of terms, she's the only person peculiar enough to put up with me.

2

When I'm not looking forward to celebrating the day that my mother purged me into the world, I am the manager of a large bar and nightclub, but you probably gathered that. We are based in the dreary town of Bury St Albans, which I think is named after some bloke called Albie who was buried here (in the town, not the bar) and for the most part I enjoy it. I've been running this venue in the east of England for over four years now, despite it only ever being a stop-gap. The gap that required stopping is only getting larger by the day. I'll be stuck here forever – until I'm buried next to that Albie chap.

The pay isn't great, but it's enough to get by and even meant that Gemma and I could move in together. We found a small maisonette that we can just about afford between us. I refused to go through an estate agent (much to her frustration) because I have a thing against funding the middleman when I don't have to.

Gemma and I share our home with our animals, the most important creature comforts of them all. We keep saying that we can't accommodate any more, but every Christmas and birthday/New Year, I am half expecting another furry friend, in spite of our inability to care for them all. Keeping in mind that our house barely contains the two of us as it is, we have Spike the springer spaniel, Cottontail the rabbit, Nibbles the dormouse (Gemma would never forgive me for leaving one of our animals out, so please excuse me as I name them all), LambLamb the lamb, who looks more like a deer, Kiwi Bear the koala, even though koalas are neither bears nor from New Zealand, and their leader, Pandi the panda.

As unoriginal as they may sound, these are their real names. You can only imagine the madhouse of a zoo our home must constantly be, if it wasn't for the fact that all of these animals are stuffed. But we love and nurture them nonetheless. Before you judge, it is common in Hong Kong, where I grew up (just not all the way up) for grown men to have houses, dashboards, key rings etc. full of soft toys and animal charms. Whether this is due to being more in tune with feminine sensibilities or a cultural thing (there is less prominence placed on appearing 'manly'),

I have always loved cute cuddly things, which is a sentiment shared by Gemma. Why do I get the feeling that these offspring are paving the way towards an actual baby?

I fell into bar work by accident, although 'plummeted' is a better way to describe it. It was never my childhood dream to withstand drunken abuse from the drinking classes and slave every cursed hour under the sun (or rather the moon) to pay the occasional bill.

My main motivation was to get away; to get away from what was expected of me. More specifically, to get away from my father and all that he represented, if I was being honest. More specifically still, to *spite* my father, if I was being a bit too honest. He considered a career in the bar trade to be a complete cop out.

My father: Stern. Traditional. Disappointed.

Like most Chinese fathers, he had the highest expectations for me. He wanted me to be an architect, a doctor or a lawyer. The most I can accomplish is designing a drink containing Dr Pepper in a reasonably lawful manner. He wouldn't consider this entrepreneurial. As his only child, I was going to be a bitter ginseng pill to swallow, of that there was no doubt. Looking back, I realise that he only wanted what was best for me, but I wanted what suited me best.

The venue I run is The Bomb Bar. It holds about sixty people and has a nightclub up above, holding a good four hundred. I'm lucky to have over a hundred in at any one time, so if we could sell off some of the capacity we would. Barney has tried to sublet on countless occasions, asking me only last week what I thought about turning part of the building into a laser tag centre.

To help me run the venue, I have my promotions manager – Richard Priory by day and DJ Snoopy by night. Committed. Outlandish. Popular.

When Barney decided that it was essential for us to open seven nights a week, we soon realised that we needed another party DJ and I asked a friend of mine, Timo Mandara, to join our ranks. Intelligent. Sincere. Pacifist. He goes by the moniker of DJ Man-Dem and instantly became pivotal to our business. He is a very tall, skinny, jet-black, homosexual Kenyan, raised in a posh English all-boys school but somehow fluent in American lingo and dressed like a gangster rapper, never without his fitted baseball cap worn over a durag. You couldn't make it up.

On Saturday nights when Snoopy is out flyering and Man-Dem is entertaining the bar downstairs, our club DJ upstairs is the locally respected Stevie Mac who has a prime-time breakfast slot. Talented. Enigmatic. Expensive.

All in all, we have a pretty remarkable team. We're a bit like the action-packed cast of the blockbuster movie *The Expendables* – well, without the guns, the fight scenes and the steroids, but just as many tattoos and cheesy one-liners. A band of misfits that shouldn't be teamed together and a dynamic that most definitely shouldn't work, but does.

Barney would have to be Bruce Willis; cool, calm and collected. In the film he is known as 'Mr Church' which is fitting because Barney has faith in his team and never does much work on a Sunday. If Bruce gained four stone and started wearing thick specs, they'd be twins. I would be Jet Li for obvious ethnic reasons and Dylan is Mickey Rourke, fat and doesn't do a lot. I wish our very own Mr Church paid five million a job.

The name 'The Bomb Bar' is derived from the act of dropping liqueurs into energy drink. Bombs are the poor man's crack cocaine, they're just so more-ish. Not wanting to be a one-trick pony, we created numerous inventive ways to drop your bomb. Every time someone ordered four bombs or more we would create a 'train', which is commonplace in many bars now, but we must have been one of the first to catch on. All you do is line the glasses of energy drink in a row with the shots resting on the rims between the gaps. The longer the train, the more dramatic the experience.

Across the country, you can walk into pretty much any bar with a youngish demographic and order a bomb – Jägermeister being the most popular. If only our grandparents could hear us now, requesting round after round of German bombs to drop into our unsuspecting energy drinks.

During what is meant to be a formal meeting between Barney, Snoopy and me about a new Wednesday night music policy, our discussion soon turns to Jägerbombs. Snoopy and I jokingly start naming other potential variations of bombs with silly names, such as Sex Bomb, Bombaclat and James Bomb, much to Barney's frustration. This continues for several minutes, Barney continually trying to get back to business.

'We seriously need to do something that brings in money. Not just during the night, but beforehand too, otherwise –' Barney starts, before finding himself bombarded with bombs.

'Stink Bomb!' I interrupt, realising I'm being rude, but too inebriated to stop myself.

'Very good, but is there any way we can get some money in sooner without having to –' Barney endures, with a lot more patience than I'd have.

'Bomb-Bomb-Bomb-Let-Me-Hear-You-Say-Way-O!' Snoopy interjects, having enjoyed the other half of the missing brandy. 'Or Who Let the Bombs Out?'

'Let's write a list of all the people we know that could sell tickets for us. They can get 50p a ticket and if we get enough –' Barney begins again, speaking to himself like a schizophrenic.

'The Bomb Shelter! We light the sambuca in a wine glass and then instead of sucking the fumes out like a Gas Chamber, we drop the flaming shot into energy drink,' I explain, as carefully as I can despite the excitement behind my Eureka moment.

'Guys, we've got a lot to get through and –' Barney pleads, getting nowhere.

'We could let people *Bomb Blast* any bomb of their choice! Instead of dropping a small shot into a glass, they drop a whole glass into a jug. We could charge twenty quid for it and groups of four could pay a fiver each. We get their money quicker, before they leave to The Havana,' I continue. We should definitely try one now. The Havana Club is our biggest competitor. By 'competitor,' I mean bitterly hated rival.

'*Twenty quid* for one drink? I like the sound of that Mr Chen!' Barney says, suddenly interested in our separate ongoing conversation. 'How about Mr Bombastic?'

Barney agrees to put our music policy discussion on hold for another time and we write down the names of every bomb combination we can sell. Once our brainstorm is complete I create a menu called 'Drop The Bomb.' There are some good ones such as 'The Costa Bomb,' which drops Jäger into Champagne, but the one we will become renowned for, is the infamous 'Nuke Bomb.' Lethal.

Putting the menu together is a laugh, but in all honesty, and for the first time in my career, I am starting to worry. We might not be quite the registered charity Dylan describes us as, but before The Havana opened its doors we ran this town. Maybe not to an Olympian level, but our town-running was at least of Commonwealth Games standard. Our new opponents have begun to overtake and the taking of our wealth is most uncommon to us. Simply put, Drop The Bomb is the next vital pass of the baton and it mustn't be dropped.

Bombs Away!

3

On our debut night for Drop The Bomb, the response is incredible. All the students are back from university and the crazy concept is right up their street. We must have a good forty people in the bar at the start of the night, which is decent for us at the weekend, let alone during the week. Snoopy is thrilled to have such an enthusiastic dance floor, and his microphone work is exceptional.

On several occasions you can tell that Snoopy is desperate to slander The Havana Club and tell the crowd not to go there, always just stopping himself. As much as I don't want to mention our competitor's name, I do hate The Havana with a passion. I would happily see that despicable venue burned to the ground. Its owner is an abomination and its staff abysmal. It should really be called The Palava Club. Every night our customers leave in droves, all at once, like a mass exodus. We can go from an unbelievable atmosphere, to a barren wasteland in a matter of minutes, tumbleweed knocking my drink over. People in this little town are sheep and The Havana is their shepherd. They might graze in our bar for a short while, but they know where their barn is and it isn't with Barney.

The Havana Club is owned by Sammy Fisher, although everyone calls him Mr Fish. A suitable name: he is a slippery, cold creature, and (painfully), our customers take his bait. They go to him like those useless salmon that travel millions of miles to get back to the wretched river they were spawned from, or whatever Attenborough was on about.

But tonight, we are a success. All along the bar, a bomb-train is being lined up as soon as a bomb-circle is being knocked down. Lisa, who is back behind the bar with us while on break from university, is amazed to see the difference in the place from when she worked here a few months ago.

'I can't believe how many people are here! It's as busy as it used to be. We've run out of Apple Sourz. Any more in the cellar?' she asks, serving four people at once.

'I'll have a look,' I squall, over the noise of our excitable throng. I wish I could split this horde across the week instead of being empty one day and rammed the next.

As I get to the cellar, the last thing I expect to happen happens.

The fucking *fire alarm* goes off.

How? Why?

Of all nights, why does it have to be when we have a house packed to the rafters? I rush back into the bar and the sound is deafening. The DJ console automatically cuts out when the alarm is activated and everyone is looking at one another in disbelief, some finding the situation incredibly amusing. They start to pick up their belongings, making their way to the door.

I run to the alarm panel in the reception room and frantically start to button-bash. There are only a certain number of things that could trigger the alarm. Someone smoking in the bar or toilets, but I would surely have noticed; the DJ over-using the smoke machine, but the mist hanging above the dance floor is thin; or someone breaking the glass on one of the red emergency points. Sammy. I bet he has sent someone in here to sabotage our debut night. Is there no limit to that arsehole's audacity? Mr Fish has me hook, line and sinker, the bastard crook, swine, stinker. He wants to swim in polluted waters and I'm not sure I can stomach the poison.

I give up on the panel just as Barney pushes me out of the way to enter the code, which he makes a point of pointing at, written right there on the wall below the screeching white box. I'm grateful that Barney is now on the case, far more capable at dealing with costly crises than I am. I rush towards the bar to tell people that it's only a drill and that the music will be reset in a matter of minutes. They've made up their minds. It is time to Copacabana all the way to The Havana. I faintly hear Dylan on the front door begging people not to leave – the desperation in his voice doesn't fill me with confidence. I glance over at Lisa. Stiff. Lost. Mumbling. She is talking to Mandara about someone walking off during the chaos without paying for their drinks.

'Don't worry about that. Wait, how much was it for? No, fuck it. Did you see anyone hit a red box thing on the wall?' I interrogate, at such a speed she looks at me as if I'm speaking Tagalog.

'Harry, I'm sorry. It was... *me*. I hit it with a bottle by accident.' Lisa looks like she is bracing herself for a serious backlash, but what's done is done.

'I thought it was someone from The Havana. I was convinced. What is wrong with me? Let's get some flyers back out there, yeah? Lisa, go with Man-Dem,' I say, allowing her to help in the damage limitation to compensate for her mistake.

'You wanna come flyering with us once I get the tunes back on?' Mandara asks, encouragingly. Snoopy and Barney are arguing in the DJ booth and they don't need me getting involved. We have snatched defeat from the jaws of victory.

'People know if I'm flyering, we must be dead. Sends out the wrong message; bit like a fire alarm,' I say. 'What the fuck is so great about The Havana Club?'

I don't want Lisa to respond to this question. The answer, if she even has one, will be too difficult to stomach. A question that I ask myself more than any other. They don't do anything that we don't, yet they are supremely successful where we are not. Tonight was a one-off for us, whereas they are always on to a winner. In truth, I don't think I'll ever figure it out.

'I'm sorry, but accidents happen,' Lisa replies defensively, as she draws me a beer from one of only four working fridges.

'I know all about accidents, don't worry,' I say, morosely. I can't hear the word 'accident' without thinking about my father. I've messed up yet again, as he said I would.

His alarm bells had been ringing well before mine.

Two years ago, on the fourth of April, my father passed away, or at least that's how it was described in the email. 'Passed away' sounds far too gentle for the way he was taken. It would be more accurate to say that my father was stripped and torn from us, although I suppose there was no more 'us' to strip and tear him from, considering my mother had left him some time ago and seeing as it didn't take me long to follow suit.

My father and I never had the closest of relationships but, for what it's worth, I was devastated by the news. Not because I had lost a lifelong friend or that we shared any kind of genuine bond, but because he died before we could reconcile our differences. Before I could say I was sorry for everything, especially for the disappointment I had become.

My devastation was selfish. As selfish as the motives behind everything that I did that caused us to require reconciliation in the first place. My father was never one for 'feelings' and definitely didn't own any soft toys. He was a man of very few words: not because he didn't know any (as he happened to know many, being proficient in three languages), but because he simply didn't have any for me. He was a man of action and though I never fully understood what he did for a living, he was forever harping on about 'cause and effect.' I didn't quite understand that either.

I don't know if he would have done a better job at expressing himself to me in Cantonese or Mandarin, but as I spoke next to nothing of those, we agreed on silence. Maybe it's an inherently Chinese thing, or perhaps it was just his nature, but everything he did say to me was literal, direct and painfully to the point.

I never even called my father 'Dad'. I tried calling him by his first name once, but he smacked me in the face, so I settled on 'father,' which seemed much more formal, but intentionally impersonal. My father and I had countless problems. He was as argumentative and stubborn as I was adolescent and self-seeking. I think time would have healed most of our wounds, apart from the most recent and deepest, which was his unreasonable and unjustified contempt towards Gemma, whom he had never met.

He had already decided he didn't like the most special person that I've ever known and undeniably the best thing that's ever happened to me before he even knew her name. My father somehow got it into his head that he wanted me to marry a Chinese girl, a bigotry that defied logic. His marriage to my British mother had ended so miserably, I think it was a blinkered case of type-casting. Looking back on it now, it was like something out of *East is East*, the Chinese version. He felt he made the mistake of marrying an English woman and didn't want the same for me. He was willing to never speak to me again over it, and he succeeded. The beleaguering hypocrisy left me exasperated enough. Then I read the report that followed his death:

Two males died and 14 were left injured after a minibus collided with a container lorry at approximately 4pm near the Kwun Tong Interchange. The police said that the driver of the minibus, Wong Li Ho, 44 and passenger Robert Chen, 54, were killed instantly. The injured were taken to a nearby hospital. The immediate families of the deceased have been contacted.

I wasn't contacted. My aunt had to email me about it. I was living halfway across the world, which meant I no longer qualified as being 'immediate.' I passed up the chance at being the next of kin; I was the one who passed away. The police released a statement saying that the bus driver misjudged the speed of the lorry while overtaking on a slope and that the incident would cost the taxpayer several thousands of dollars.

Looks like I'm short of a few Bob in more ways than one.

4

'There are way too many bombs on this menu,' says Barney, shaking his head in the most jagged of manners, like there's a glitch in the Matrix. 'It takes too long for people to decide.'

'Took me ages to design that,' I reply, even though he is absolutely right. We got carried away and just wanted to have an item for each original name we came up with.

'It looks really good, but you'd have an easier time if there were fewer drinks to remember.' I know full well that reducing stock is at the forefront of his mind.

'I'll have some new ones for the weekend,' I say to Barney, who at least has the grace to look regretful over asking me to redo a menu I have only just finalised. 'I told Harley to put a splash of energy drink in with the bombs so that we don't give as much away. He called it *staining*!'

'Staining, I like it. Can't wait to see the new menu,' he says, genuinely wondering what piece of creative panache I will produce next. I can't help but feel that Barney has been somewhat of a father figure to me, despite there being just four years between us. He really does look out for me and I appreciate it. 'We need to limit each page to ten. I trust you'll make the right choices.' By 'right' he means 'cheap to make'.

How can I decide what to keep when there are so many? I'm a hoarder by nature. It'd be an easier decision if we hadn't concocted hundreds. All this recent thought about my old man makes me wonder what would make the cut if I had to compile a list of Top Ten moments that my father and I shared. I saw something similar on an episode of *Lost* once and thought it was cool.

I think I'd seriously struggle to do it. The pivotal moments aren't necessarily good. The memories that stick with you aren't always going to be sat around the Christmas tree or the celebration of a winning goal at a family fun day. I'll give it a go though:

10. My friend Midas Murray stayed at my house for the weekend when we were in our first year at secondary school. On my old estate in Hong Kong there is a local club house with a few facilities: restaurant, swimming pool, squash court and a snooker room. I asked my dad if Midas and I could play some snooker and, happy to get us out of the house, he gave me his membership card and some money for drinks.

After playing for about forty minutes, we lost interest in the game and started swinging the cues around wildly as if they were light sabres. While we were chasing one another round the table with our hunting spears, I picked up a piece of chalk and tried to hit it with the cue as if it were a baseball. Midas took on the role of pitcher and with the almightiest of swings, I missed the chalk completely and ended up smashing the clock on the wall with the follow through. I jumped at the sound of the crashing glass and without thinking, started picking up the shards and placing them in the bin. We headed to reception, gave them back their snooker balls, grabbed my father's card and treated ourselves to iced lemon teas before cycling home.

Some hours later, while playing video games, I was called from my bedroom by my father. He sat me down at the dining table and asked if there was anything I wanted to tell him. I said that there was nothing I could think of and tried to head back upstairs to take *Bomberman* off pause. He gave me one last chance to own up without repercussion. When he realised that I was showing no signs of cracking, he dragged me outside. Throwing me into the back of his car, we drove to the club house in silence.

When we arrived, he had all the staff gather round. He asked me, both in Cantonese and Pidgin English, if I had broken the clock and, out of embarrassment, I just shook my head. Without my confession, he told the reception staff to explain to me why I was a 'no good liar.' The hands on the clock had stopped at the exact time the glass got smashed and all they had to do was check it against their booking form, which revealed our membership card number.

My father had to pay $400, which would have been over £30 back then, and he went ballistic in the car home. He told me that if I had owned up, things could have been a lot easier for me. I fear I still have a fair few clocks to break.

9. It had nothing to do with my mother leaving, though my Head of Year and the school councillor thought otherwise. It was really just your run of the mill teenage rebellion and trying to show off to a mate that I could do it.

I still remember the name of the CD to this day – 'It Takes A Thief' by Coolio. Appropriately titled, considering what I intended to do with it. I didn't recognise a single song on there and I had no desire to own it. It was the first CD I saw when I walked into the store. I was sixteen and untouchable.

I mooched around the shop, circling the rack, first pulling off the security tag, then the cellophane sleeve. The security cameras were watching everything I did, but I was unassailable and it made no odds to me. It was only when I went to take it past the beeping pillars that I realised I wasn't quite as invincible as I first thought. A guard held up a badge and told me that I was to follow him to the office. My heart descended deep into my bowels. On the escorted walk, tapeworms were ripping away at the beating flesh of my racing ticker.

I was asked to empty my pockets and the CD was quickly identified as stolen. He asked me if I wanted to view the footage of my failed shoplifting attempt, but I didn't want to see it. Watching it would be like playing back a sex tape you've filmed and starred in – a role that seemed a good idea at the time, but unfortunately turned out to be disappointingly amateurish.

I remember the song playing throughout the store on the day it happened. It was an Enya track called 'On My Way Home.' Even when I hear it now, it takes me back to that HMV. I remember the guard telling me that half get sent on their merry and the other half head down to the station to be processed. The fifty-fifty didn't end up working in my favour. I was not on my way home. When the police arrived, two uniformed officers were given a copy of the footage and the Coolio CD, to seize as evidence. I was put in handcuffs and taken through the shopping centre and down to their meat wagon.

I cried the entire way to the police station, my life as a career criminal failing at the first hurdle. Many people go through a shoplifting phase, not so many get carted away in a Chinese police van, antagonised by cops and subjected to racial abuse. My Cantonese wasn't fluent, but I knew enough to know that they were ripping the piss out of me. Foreign or otherwise, I deserved the ridicule.

The irony of the album title was lost on the police, the only part of the language barrier for which I'm grateful. Had I been in England, they'd have stuck the crime report up on their notice board and sent an email around the department. They probably would have let me off for giving them something to laugh about. Things are looked at differently over here in the UK. When you have fourteen-year-olds carrying knives and kicking people's heads in because they wouldn't agree to buy them fags, a pinched CD isn't as big a deal.

I was put in a holding room and left to wallow in my self-pity before they demanded to know my father's mobile phone number. Turns out this was a bit more severe than a broken clock. Those next few hours were the longest of my life. It was near enough one in the morning by the time my father arrived and he had come straight from work out in mainland China. He would normally have made it home in forty minutes, but he had to pass our house and travel a further two hours to get to me. He glared at me through the glass. I would have rather served six months in a juvenile hall if it had spared me *that look*.

My father spoke to the superintendent for what seemed like ages before they brought me out. I remember apologising but he had no interest in anything I had to say. My mug shot and fingerprints were taken and I had to sign several statements. It was 4am when we left and my father still wasn't speaking to me. He took me back through the plaza to head to the taxi rank, stopping at the front door of McDonald's. The gates were down and a young guy was mopping his way out. My father asked him if it was possible to get any food for his son and, after some persistence, the chap gave us the remaining cold cheeseburgers that were going to be thrown out and my father offered him some money through the gate.

I publicly humiliated him and wasted what was left of his very limited down time and he still didn't want me to go hungry. I never thanked my father properly for going to all the trouble, but learnt the most valuable of lessons. If you love someone, you stand by them.

8. Shortly after my mother moved out, my father gave me a stunning Hamilton watch. I came home to find it on my computer keyboard one day, and he never mentioned it. It is the only watch I have ever worn since. It feels like it was custom made to my liking and I knew it was of real quality as soon as I tried it on. Despite it being the thought that counts, I went online immediately to ascertain its worth.

It set him back five thousand Hong Kong dollars, which at the exchange rate then would have worked out at about £400. I was astonished. As I got older (or more cynical) and started living in a country that used one less digit to value its currency, the novelty of the once cherished gift wore off, even though I continued to wear it.

I began to believe that my mother had been replaced by something to simply adorn the wrist and that this particular something happened to tell the date and the time, allowing me to see just how long she had been gone. In my ungratefulness, I thought that it was his way of buying my love and purchasing my forgiveness, which wasn't for sale in any tender.

*

I can't think of anymore at the moment, but I'll come back to this. It's rather therapeutic actually.

5

Sometimes I wish Barney had just opened a humble coffee shop. Running two levels under the one roof is strenuous enough, even more so when tiles are falling off it. The building is listed (I have no idea which list) and has been around for ages: from the state of the wiring and plumbing, possibly from the beginning of time itself. It isn't in the best condition, but we make our repairs, lick our paint and try to keep it in decent enough nick.

The site has been notorious for changing ownership, countless times in fact, and has had so many different uses that people find it hard to keep up. Someone once told me it was even used as an abattoir, which, judging by some of the patrons that drink here comes as no surprise. The premises started as a car dealership (as soon as the wheel was invented), and then became a bathroom fitters. Once that closed down, the bar that opened afterwards ingeniously called itself Taps! (their exclamation mark, not mine). After that, it became a cocktail bar called The Animus and then a pub called The Embers. More recently, it was a nightclub called Extreme, although from the sound of it, there was nothing extreme about it. 'Moderately Average' doesn't quite have the same ring to it though.

On each of the walls throughout the venue there are famous quotes relating to alcohol. We looked at having them applied by a professional vinyl firm but the cost was too much for Barney's liking. The type of customers we attracted would only try to pick away at certain letters to leave crude words. If they didn't do it, Dylan would. Instead, Barney requested that I cut and spray the countless stencils from cardboard. I know them all off by heart, my favourite being the Ernest Dowson near the fire exit which reads 'Absinthe makes the tart grow fonder.'

The business is governed by a board of directors, the most hands-on being Francis Barnaby, or 'Barney' to his friends. Funny. Survivor. Thrifty. He holds the largest stake and, before hiring me, was single-handedly running the entire place. The only person Barney truly answers to is his pregnant girlfriend Charis, ten years his junior; the age gap not lending any favours to the stereotype of nightclub owners. Either way, they are a very sweet couple and everyone is fond of Charis. Lovely. Patient. Expecting.

Barney has a sharp eye for numbers and is forever trying to break things down to their smallest parts.

'I don't get it, Harry. Bury St Albans is only a market town, but apparently it has a population of forty thousand people. According to Wikipedia anyway,' he starts, and there is no guessing where this might be going. 'There are four clubs in Bury, so that's ten thousand people each. Only one in seven people are likely to visit a nightclub on a regular basis, so we should have at least fourteen hundred patrons on any given Friday or Saturday.'

'One in four people are lightweights and don't make it past the bars,' I say, trying to make him feel better about our lack of trade, despite what Wikipedia says. I might even edit the online Wiki article to cheer him up.

'That still leaves me with one thousand and seventy-one and a half people at the end of a night,' he says, lost in thought.

'The point five of a person will be someone half-cut.' I find Barney's powers of deduction brilliant and my lack of arithmetic shocking.

'Imagine if we didn't have you and Harley behind the bar, think how little we'd be making then.' Counting his blessings better than I can count our customers.

'I'd never tell him, but he's too good for this place.' Doing Harley more justice than our venue, but Barney doesn't deny it. 'We're very lucky.' Harley Evans, our amazing flair barman. Confident. Steadfast. Loyal.

Harley is the most laid back, cool cat there is: a calmness that only comes from experience; composure built off the back of working at countless venues, over hundreds upon hundreds of shifts.

When Harley isn't slaving away here, he has his very own (and considerably more successful) business called Wensum Maintenance Limited, a registered company name he has let Barney use in the past, mostly to provide false invoices, seeking compensation to cover any vandalism caused in the club. Many a drunken culprit who lashes out at a toilet cubicle door or plasterboard wall doesn't know (or remember) the extent of the damage they've caused. Hence the overpriced bill, plus VAT, plus call-out charge, plus materials.

Harley's willingness to help me at every turn is extraordinary. Whenever I envision a new concept that will improve the venue, he is a sounding board for all my schemes, adding an informed opinion to anything I have planned. A builder by trade, he has experience in all disciplines of handiwork and repair. He said that most of the work he does during the day is as a 'snagger.' This is someone who gets people's houses ready for sale, which makes him perfect for sorting out our crumbling building. There has been many a time when Harley has come in on his day off, usually at 9am, despite only leaving the club at 4am, to help me construct a wall, a banister, a stage, anything. When I say 'Help me,' he does the majority of the work and I go to fetch the sausage McMuffins in the morning and the KFC family bucket in the afternoon.

The work that Harley has done for us goes beyond what we actually see him do. All the wood, nails, tiles, grout, that he goes out of his way for in his own time is always with his own money. The shopping list is as long as the Screwfix catalogue. We reimburse him when we can, asking for a diesel receipt too so that we aren't physically taking the piss from his bladder. Barney has stuck the occasional £100 into his pay packet, but most of the projects are in an attempt to make more money, money that we no longer have.

There have only been a few occasions when I've been able to show my appreciation. He once did a job in Norwich and had to pop into a house to drop something off. For the brief moment that he left his Nissan Navara pick-up truck, some jammy pikey made off with his tool bag. If you had a task that needed doing, Harley had the obscure and clever utensil for the job in his magical sack. Harley was gutted. Who wouldn't be? Something had to be done.

I went to B&Q the following day and purchased a large utility bag. I bought a sturdy-looking spirit level and an assortment of screwdrivers, blades, hammers – everything that your self-respecting builder should have on his belt. I slipped a couple of extra bits into the side pockets in the hope that the clerk wouldn't notice (a trick that Harley once taught me himself, by sticking the plasterboard tape in between two bags of plaster sat on the trolley) and proceeded to the checkout. If only they sold bags of plaster at HMV. Knowing that I was bound to have missed some key essentials, I asked the lady at the till to stick £100 on a gift card for good measure, and probably a measuring tape.

Later that night when Harley came to work, I told him to collect some paperwork from my desk. Despite it being several thousand miles in trek, he willingly agreed to make his ascent up to the stratosphere of my seldom-used office without protest. Ask Dylan to perform the very same task and expect a tut, a humph and an, 'If I must, dickhead.' The only paperwork was an envelope containing his gift card attached to his brand new bag of tools. I'm sure the message in the card said something like 'Try not to lose this one,' and if it didn't, I wish it had. When Harley came back downstairs he was at a loss for words, and I could tell that he was most grateful for my gesture. No words needed to be spoken, as I found myself speechless each time he constructed something out of nothing: a cocktail lounge, VIP room, friendship.

Although we don't meet up outside of work, Harley often forwards me outrageous and highly offensive text messages to keep me amused. They usually follow a world catastrophe, the death of a celebrity or some other sinister revelation in the news. Where he gets them from I don't know, but we reckon there are people out there just waiting for a landslide in Romania or an earthquake in North Korea so they can release their comedic gold on to the cellular nation.

Harley is forever the joker. He is notorious for catching me unaware whenever I'm pulling a pint. If I get distracted chatting to a customer, he will push the tap back and let me stand there like an idiot, pouring an imaginary pint of air for however long it takes me to realise.

I found it endlessly funny that Harley always thought his father was Arabic. He was proud of this fact as it made him appear different – rugged and worldly. He pictured himself crossing the sweeping sand dunes, mounted on the back of a camel, impressing Princess Jasmine on his ship of the desert. In his mind, he was a modern day Prince of Persia. Until he found out a few years ago that his father is actually Indian. He told me that his mum is a 'nutter' and 'wouldn't let a little thing like the truth get in the way of a good story.' Once I knew his actual ethnicity, the ammunition was readily available and I missed no opportunity to fire an onion bhaji insult or similar.

I asked why his surname was 'Evans,' which doesn't sound particularly Indian, and he said that was the name of his mum's 'latest squeeze.' When I asked what it used to be, he refused to tell me, saying that he'd never hear the end of it. It was only when I started calling him 'Patel' that he eventually gave in, provided that I promised not to tell anyone. Bhati Gupta. With my late father being of Cantonese descent, the Far East Asian assaults on one another are rife. I am related to Jackie Chan and can catch flies with chopsticks like Mr Miyagi. He is immune to the Delhi Belly when he enjoys his mandatory diet of vindaloo and Cobra beer. We play on every stereotype, karate kicking and bhangra dancing the night away. As neither of us look or sound like your typical Indian or Chinese guys, we often put a series of questions to girls standing at the bar. They are oblivious to the hidden connotations.

'In the highly unlikely event that either of you girls are ever asked out on a date, would you want to go for a Chinese or an Indian?'

'Chinese every time! So yummy,' one of the girls might reply.

'Egg roll and dumplings in your mouth,' I follow up with, reinforcing my victory.

'I love Indian, I like it really hot,' her friend might say. A draw.

'Leaves your bum sore in the morning though, right? The Chinese portion is far too small,' Harley may add, to outdo my crudeness. I think at one point we even kept a tally.

Harley finds me equally amusing, although he hates it when I pressure him in to dazzling the crowds with his flair routine. He used to enter competitions, where he'd throw the bottles about like he was the true star of *Cocktail*, but Harley isn't one to show off. The last time I asked him to do it (to try and keep a group of girls from leaving) I got an unusual response. 'What do they say in that film *Harold & Kumar*? Just because you're hung like a mule doesn't mean you have to do porn!' All the more relevant, considering Harold is Chinese and Kumar is Indian.

Having worked at so many different venues, Harley has some stories that are second to none. He once sent a saucy text to a 'bit on the side.' It was raunchy and explicit and definitely not what you'd want your actual missus to read. In his haste to get back to waiting customers, he sent it to his long-term girlfriend Kristina by accident. She would realise instantly that the message wasn't intended for her and this would land him in a universe of trouble.

While he rushed around the bar, nervously waiting for the furious reply that his text was bound to prompt, his phone vibrated mid-serve. Panic-stricken, he could barely bring himself to open it. He reached deep into his pocket, sweaty palms clutching at the Nokia that had failed him. The doomed text read: 'You have insufficient credit to send this text. Your current balance is 4p, please top up and try again' – or miraculous pay-as-you-go words to that effect.

Phenomenal.

It was moments like these that Harley and I shared each and every weekend that made coming to work that much harder once he told me the devastating news.

6

It seems like the start to any other shift. I am still bottling up the fridges even though we are due to open in forty minutes and I haven't even thought about getting the floats together for the tills. In my defence, this isn't down to my lack of organisation, but Barney's late arrival from the cash and carry, with coins and stock in tow.

I had wanted to get home hours ago, to shit, shower and shave and maybe even iron a shirt for tonight, but that window has closed, as it has a tendency to do. The only consolation for me is that Harley will be here any minute. He always turns up half an hour before he is due to start and I nearly always rope him in to doing something that Dylan and I have neglected to get round to. We really should start paying him for that extra time, but we probably won't. No sooner has the thought of Harley's assistance crossed my mind when he enters, shouting his customary racial remark.

'Oyster Sauce! How are ya?' I am amazed that he manages to produce a new Chinese-related moniker each and every time. I'd prefer being called 'Eurasian Sensation,' but somehow I can't see that catching on.

'Mango Chutney, my man! Come help me bottle up. The cases are lined up and good to go in.' Not my best sobriquet to date; his was better.

Without even taking his coat off or styling his hair (his usual arrival ritual), Harley comes behind the bar and pulls up a beer crate to sit on. He opens the fridge door and starts filling the shelves just the way I like them. I am quite particular about distance from fridge walls, labels immaculately centred and facing front, pulling the cold ones out to stock rotate etc. – a fixation I have that only Harley knows how to fix. I look over and wait for him to speak. Each week he ponders something in great detail during his long drive from Norwich and normally can't wait to ask for my opinion. He can be mulling over something simple, like why grape-flavoured and cherry-flavoured products taste nothing like their original fruit counterparts, or something complex like why men can't pee inside women when we shag them.

Today, he isn't chuckling to himself before he speaks.

'You were right all along.' Harley is about to tell me that unprotected sex can indeed lead to herpes.

'So I *am* right some of the time! Try telling that to Gemma! What was it then?' I ask, quite pleased with myself, even though he could be referring to a multitude of things that I wouldn't want to be right about.

'The lumps on my neck you told me looked weird; you were right.' Awkwardness squirms across his face. This definitely falls under the 'things I wouldn't want to be right about' category.

'What do you mean I was right about the lumps?' I reply, even though I know exactly what he means. I am stalling, wanting to enjoy a couple more seconds of life without my once fleeting concern being confirmed.

'Hodgkin's disease. Or what used to be called Hodgkin's disease. Now they call it Hodgkin's lymphoma. I finally got checked out,' he says, avoiding my stare. He is wearing a face that doesn't quite seem real, as I have never seen it look so unhappy. He looks like a woman who has just been peed in. There is a slight smirk to the corner of his mouth, which I put down to the uniquely uncomfortable topic, but his eyes, looking over my shoulder, tell a different story.

'Shit. I thought you were going to say it was cancer. At least it's not cancer, right?'

'It *is* cancer you dick!' he exclaims. 'How cool having a disease named after you, though. I wish I had a disease named after me. Inflammation of the cock! Wow, look how upset you are. I pull a sad face and you start to cry!' He is either in denial, in shock, or a total arsehole for winding me up over some perfectly harmless warts on his neck. 'The doc checked my balls for lumps too. It only got awkward when I ran my fingers through his hair.'

'Seriously Harley, this isn't funny.'

'I know it isn't funny. I'm the one with the fuckers on my neck,' he cackles.

He speaks as if I'd told him to check a dodgy wiper blade on his pick-up truck or that there was a button missing on his coat, rather than a series of cancerous protuberances on his body. I decide that I really didn't want to know the horrible truth.

'When did you go? I would have gone with you. Fuck, man.' I try to produce a facial expression that matches my inner feelings of lamentation. My face doesn't do justice to the injustice I have heard. The most earnest response I can rally to the news of my dearest friend having cancer is 'fuck, man.'

'Don't be a fag! If I wanted my hand held I'd have called Mandara,' he says, before peering over the top of the bar to see if Timo has arrived yet. 'I went the other week for a basic diagnosis. I've been *staged*, where they do blood tests and shit, but the actual results take a while. Kristina was going to come, but she had plans. Once treatment begins she'll have to drive me though – she'll love that!' He jokes about a homosexual handhold rather than cursing at God from a tile-less rooftop in the rain. I can't believe that Kristina didn't go with him. Gemma would have carried me to the hospital if she had to. I'm also not sure I necessarily agree with how he's dealing with this, but everyone copes with things in their own way. If his is to cushion himself with light humour, then who am I to judge? I've never had to face anything like this, so how would I know?

'How are you so calm?' I ask, although I have no idea what he may be like amongst his family or when he's at home. He could be (and probably is) in absolute bits. I almost hope that he is, as I don't think it's healthy for him to be so cavalier about something this grave. He would argue that he's hardly the epitome of health in the first place.

'What's the point in worrying about it? Won't make it any better. Think of all the sympathy pussy I'm going to get,' he says laughing. I laugh too; the most forced laugh I have ever had to conjure. I don't want him to be making jokes. I don't want him to be talking about sympathy pussy. I want him to weep hysterically into my shoulder. I want him to do that so he knows it is okay to do that and that I will be here for him.

The bravado must be an act. He is seeking treatment; willing to endure whatever the hospital says he must. This surely requires a certain degree of acceptance, right? Does our friendship oblige me to push for sincere dialogue? Or does a good friend respect privacy, joking as we always have done to keep spirits lifted and energy positive? If I'm as good a friend as I think I am, surely I would know?

The very least I can do is insist we pay him for that extra half an hour.

*

'Give us a nugget for the Pringles machine,' Dylan demands, but I'm not really paying attention. I am still struggling to come to terms with what Harley told me last night. I haven't had the chance to speak to Gemma about it, for her to sort my head out for me.

Surrounded by at least twenty uncompleted tasks, this does not strike me as a suitable time to sit and have a snack. 'How many of those do you scoff a week?' I ask, the most civil response I can offer.

'Shitloads. But I get the plain ones,' he replies, stating a seemingly obvious oversight on my part.

'Makes it one of your five a day then, does it? You can have a pot once you're finished in here.' I bribe my petulant child of an employee with Pringles. Not quite the results-based incentive scheme I envisioned when I took him on board, but here we are.

'I'll get started then. Just gotta go spend a penny first.' He walks into the gents' toilets and a putrid stench soon starts to fill our already smelly nightclub. I'm certain he's spent at least a pound. Dylan needs to start eating soap.

Dylan the dogsbody, getting fatter and slower by the minute following his binge diet of Pringles and Irn-Bru. Constant supervision is required, which is simply infuriating. Today, however, he is covering the cleaning so that I can take Gemma out for lunch. Once Dylan has dropped all his shrapnel down the bowl, I head home to fetch the missus.

When we arrive back in town, our journey to the restaurant involves a brisk walk around the side of the club. Dylan is smoking one of his Richmond Superkings on the front step. His choice of smoke is an unnecessarily long cigarette. He has chosen these to achieve the maximum duration of smoke break possible. He beckons me with a frantic wave. Gemma in hand, we stride over to say hello, visibly hoping that this unexpected diversion won't take long.

'Gemma, check this! You know your mate Stacey? And that Belinda girl? Well, I shagged them both last night, one after the other! Not as in, like, a threesome, but as in one first, then the other later,' he says, most excitedly. We don't close until 3am and don't ever leave before 4am, but I still wouldn't put it past him.

'You're disgusting!' replies Gemma, indicating that this isn't the best time to high-five.

'Nice to know you've been productive.' I doubt any cleaning has been done.

'They pop the morning-after pill like aspirin,' he says, chuckling to himself, my customary sarcasm lost on him once more. Gemma doesn't dignify him with a response. Wise decision.

'Stop spending all your time trying to take someone to bed; look for someone you want to wake up to,' I sigh deeply, for brownie points. 'You'd shag a washing line if it had knickers on it.'

'Steer clear of the knickers on my washing line, Dildo,' instructs Gemma.

'In school you might have called them *cooties*, now they're known as *STDs*,' I reply. Gemma tugs at my hand. 'Now, if you'll excuse us, we need to feed the little appetite we have left.'

'So that's what you and Dylan talk about all day, is it? All the people you've shagged,' before letting go of my hand. Thanks Dylan, thanks a lot.

After our meal, I head to the club to give Dylan a hand setting up for the night's trade. As soon as I arrive I notice that he's chatting to a girl, his hands on her hips. This won't be the first time Dylan has let someone into the building while we're closed and from the way they're standing, I highly doubt she has come from another venue to borrow some line cleaner or to swap some change. The girl looks reasonably attractive, a four and a half maybe, i.e. not bad, but you'd clearly be settling. Fairly bland: definitely vanilla.

I leave them to it in the hope that whatever they're doing is approaching conclusion, but as I return with the mop and bucket, I am astounded that Dylan still hasn't called his not-so-secret tryst to an end. These affectionate hands of his have seen a serious lack of work. I could be mopping around their feet and they wouldn't budge. I boil over and move in on them.

'Right, that's it! You, missy, see your lover boy here?' I yap, which makes them both jump. 'He will be the most drunken, disappointing three minutes of your life. He won't call you a taxi and he will ignore you the next time he sees you. He's also about to be jobless!' She looks Timid. Harmless. Distracting. With that, the girl turns to leave, struggling with the bolt on the door before bolting.

'Harry, man! The *best* three minutes, more like!' Dylan thinks that this is all one big joke. 'She's my favourite door whore. That's Belinda from the Fox & Hound.' I hope that she wasn't actually here for line cleaner or change.

'What's a door whore?'

'Chicks that only shag bouncers! I've shown her my door badge. I've got something for her to bounce on!' He grins so profusely that he looks like the Cheshire Cat, about to be the victim of a Chelsea Smile. 'What's the difference between a Fox and a Hound?'

'What?' I wonder why Belinda even bothers with this guy. He probably feeds her Absinthe.

'About nine pints!' Belinda should change her name, change her number and enter some form of witness protection programme.

'If you want a leg up in this industry, you need to stop trying to get your leg *over*. Please, I'm begging you.' Dylan exhausts me. He is the reason people need holidays. In his case, I need a six-month holiday. Twice a year.

'I've done everything you asked me to do already, haven't I?' he heckles.

'You've fixed the till drawer then?' One of the many jobs on his forgotten to-do list.

'Let me just get out my electrical engineering degree, shall I? I'll tell you what I will do. I'll hold my dick under the hand dryer and warm up Belinda's dinner,' he says defiant.

'I'm the only sarky one in this relationship, Dildo,' I say, defeated. Did I mention that my dog was constantly on heat and needs castrating?

After a lengthy phone call in the office, arguing with Lisa about her allocated shifts, I return downstairs to the club, hoping that Dylan has the place ready and good to go. It somehow looks worse than when I left. Lying sprawled out on the sofa, Dylan looks really out of it and I daren't imagine what he's been up to since I've been gone. The strong stench of cannabis is a slight clue.

'Are you fucking high right now?' I fume. 'How high are you?'

'No, it's Hi, how are you! I'm, dunno mate, no,' he says, trying to be clever.

'Time and a place. This is most certainly not the time!' I explain, reaching for the steam-less mop bucket that never got used.

'So the place is good? Nice!' he says proudly, as the vacuum hums away, wasting overpriced electricity.

I am dumbfounded that he is actually taking praise from this. Forever the ambitious achiever. He is meant to be my number two. I now know why they refer to something else as a 'number two.'

'I'm high as a kite, man. Being flown from the highest building. I'm stood on a ladder on top of the building, wearing stilts!' he sings in a flurry of delight.

'Fuck off, Dylan. Slugs are snails that sold their houses to buy drugs.' Slugs are notorious for destroying plants and leaving a trail. Marijuana and smoke.

'Life is like beer, best enjoyed chilled,' he says, cocky as ever. 'All you want me to do is work. Why should I change the habit of a lifetime?'

'You're so lucky Barney isn't here.' He only behaves like this for me. 'And I don't like gherkins on my burger.' I'm looking forward to seeing Dylan in his golden arches uniform.

'Question for you; would you rather have your left hand and no legs, just stumps, or no nose, one leg, *both* hands, but with your thumbs missing?' His bizarre questions seem to end most of our quarrels.

'The second one. Wouldn't have to smell this club or your bullshit. Still be able to punch you without thumbs,' I reply and despite my frustration, I do like his random conundrums.

7

The bar has been open every day in December, apart from Christmas Day itself. Even then Barney suggested a Christmas lunch for staff, friends and family before opening to the public, but there were too few takers to make it worthwhile. I have been given Boxing Day off to spend with Gemma and we decide to have a night out together, starting off in The Spitfire. They buy ice from us each weekend, because unlike us, they tend to have more customers than cubes.

Gemma and I agree to meet at 8pm, as she wants to drive to her friend's house to get dolled up. She uses the designer bag that I bought her to pack her new hair straighteners (she's done pretty well out of me this Christmas) along with an assortment of makeup and a choice of two outfits. I call my friend Big G and ask him to pick me up, so that I don't have to worry about leaving my car in town overnight.

Gemma plants me a peck on the cheek and heads down the stairs to her car. As I play some Mario Kart, Big G beeps from below the archway of the house, which sounds like a fog horn on a cruise liner. He has arrived early, so we can go grab some food before our night out. Lining our stomachs doesn't sound like a bad idea.

'Anything but Chinese. I spend enough time delivering noodles as it is,' he says, proving just why I love him. He works every hour God (or The Golden Dragon on Northgate Street) sends and is still willing to chauffeur me on his one night off. I couldn't ask for a better designated driver. Big G. Big. Ginger. Reliable.

'Could they make my favourite dish? I want char-siu pork sitting on top of sticky rice, instead of mixed in. Write that down.' I'm hungry just thinking about it.

'I can get Mr Ho to run you a foot bath as well if you like.'

'Your 'Authentic Cantonese' food is catered for the Western palate. They call it 'special' fried rice, but there's nothing special about it. Sort it out G, what the fuck,' I say, Big G taking the brunt of all the food faux pas made by the Chinese chefs across Britain

'I just deliver it! Anyway, where should we eat? The Fox & Hound does two meals for a tenner and they're open – I drove past on my way in,' he suggests.

'Sounds good. Gemma's gone round her mates' to slap on war paint, so we've got plenty of time. We have to be at The Spitfire for 8pm,' I reply.

'Dylan keeps asking me to do their pub quiz. Unless there's a question about cars or DubStep, I don't think I'd be much use,' he says.

'Which mate? Stacey with the big jugs?'

'I wasn't really paying attention. I couldn't wait for her to leave so I could stick the console on and play some games,' I say, amused that all Big G ever thinks about is cars, DubStep and tits.

'Mario Kart?' He knows me so well.

We soon arrive at the Fox & Hound and sit ourselves down by the window. I pick up a menu and it's not only two meals for a tenner, but you get a pint as well, which is a right result. Big G goes for the steak and I go for the spaghetti (which is pretty much noodles). Big G heads to the bar to order our food and I shout out our table number and tell him to make mine a pint of Kronenbourg, exploiting the most from the £10 deal. As Big G waits to be served, I wonder if he will chat to the brunette sat next to him. Cute. Unattainable. Solo. There is a greater chance of him spilling our drinks over her and stepping on her foot than striking up a conversation, but to my utter astonishment, he turns to her and asks if she's waiting to be served. Good lad, I didn't think he had it in him.

She says, 'No.' My impeccable lip-reading skills are wasted in my current line of work. He then asks her if she fancies a drink, which is *really* good going. Get in there my son. Another 'No.' Oh well, nothing ventured, nothing gained and once again, he's gained nothing. Despite her turning down his offer, they are still chatting away and Big G even plants himself alongside her. I couldn't be happier for him, unless of course he brought my beer over. We have a fair bit of time though, so for the sake of Big G being able to pull something other than a muscle in his right hand, I give him his window of opportunity as I stare out of the window.

'Big G-Unittt! WASSUP, me ole mucker?' It is Dylan. Sounding very drunk and having royally cock-blocked Big G. Can't we go anywhere without seeing this guy? It's bad enough I have to see him at work.

'Dylan, hey man. You couldn't get us a sirloin and spag bol for over there, could you? Kind of in the middle of something here,' says Big G, as he points in my direction. I try to offer encouragement in the form of secret body language that suggests he should persist, but from the puzzled look on his face, he thinks I'm suffering from an epileptic fit.

'Get your own food, you cock. You brought me ole China with you. Hey Harry!' says Dylan, the most pissed I've seen him in a while. 'The cock and the cockle-picker! We're getting on it, yeah? On it til we vomit!'

'Just stop.' Big G is embarrassed by the company it would seem he keeps.

'Hey, who's this cute liddle thang?' asks Dylan, slurring near enough every word. 'I'm Dylonius, assistant manager of the Bomb place. Yeah, you want a drink, baby? I know the bar girl here, she'll sort us out.'

'No thanks,' replies the blushing brunette as she shifts awkwardly on her stool.

'They say you are what you eat, which is strange, because I haven't eaten any sexy beasts today!' Dylan laughs, managing (or assistant managing) to offend everyone in a matter of minutes, including Belinda behind the bar. She can hear his pathetic and rather cruel advances towards our now extremely uncomfortable random brunette.

You can tell from Big G's posture that he is wishing the ground would open up and swallow Dylan. Despite giving his name a Spartan twist, there is nothing magnanimous about Dylonius.

'My taxi's here, bye,' she says, leaving her drink half-full. Blushing. Unattainable. Clever.

As gutted as I am for Big G and as frustrated as I am with Dylan for being Dylan, at least there is something for me to drink. The girl glances back round to give Big G a discomfited but sweet smile, whilst trying to avoid Dylan's ogling. Her innocent, somewhat disappointed look suggests to me that if Dylan had done us all a favour and not been born (or at least stayed at home), poor Big G might have been sharing that supposed taxi.

'I bet you've been banged more times than that taxi door!' howls Dylan. He should wash his mouth out with that soap before eating it.

Big G follows the girl to the door, but only with his eyes. She walks across the road in the light drizzle of the early evening and there is no taxi. Big G musters the courage to talk to a girl and Dylan manages to ruin it.

Dylan is now trying to summon Belinda over for another drink, which I highly doubt he is going to get. He has a better chance of wearing it than drinking it. Big G looks enraged that his serendipitous encounter has been called to a halt and grabs Dylan by the collar, asking him why he is the way he is. I'd put it down to six pints of lager, a distinct lack of aspiration and not enough hugs as a child. Big G looks like he is about to show us all why it's called Boxing Day.

'Let's get our food, get this twat some tap water and head to The Spitfire where we'll get you some proper female attention,' I say, in full knowledge that this episode will have knocked the little confidence he has. 'Pass me that chick's drink man,' I continue, trying to straighten everyone back in to line, including myself.

'Mark your territory. Pee on her next time! You'll just have to add her to the wank bank!' says Dylan, a bank that Big G is well acquainted with, no doubt making multiple withdrawals daily. 'She was frigid. I saved you if anything, you moody fucker.'

Perhaps not the sincerest of apologies, but it will have to do. Probably the most sense we're going to get out of him all night, so we embrace it by not punching him. Dylan refuses his water, which he refers to as 'council pop,' and jokingly asks for a 'pint of death,' which is a dash of every single item that a bar stocks thrown into a pint glass, sometimes even the drip trays. This is the guy who's in charge when I go on holiday.

With the possibility of a good night out salvaged, Big G hands me her drink, which I hope is a double. It's half-full, or half-empty, depending on how you're feeling. We finally get round to ordering our food from a different member of bar staff, with Belinda having retreated to the back room, and who can blame her. I try to savour the brunette's left-over drink of vodka and orange (sadly only a single) and silently hope that she doesn't have gonorrhoea or chlamydia of the mouth because, if she does, I should have given the drink to Dylan, who has those diseases already. 'I hope this is spiked,' I say, a little too loudly.

'I wish someone cared enough about me to spike my drink. Quite a compliment if you think about it,' says Dylan. 'You're the one I'm willing to do hard time for, less with good behaviour.'

'You've given that way too much thought.' Dylan is my right-hand man. He would make a better left-foot man, as all I ever seem to want to do is kick him.

'Give it ten years, Ping-Pong. Once all your game has dried up, you'll be spiking drinks too. One in the drink, one in the pink and a chink in her stink!' Dylan is verging on a half-empty glass to the face. 'There was that one local girl, wasn't there? She was found the next day on the pavement with her clothes on back to front.' I know he's going to be asked to leave. 'She couldn't remember it, but no one had broken her doors in.' People start to stare at us and it isn't with the intention to date rape. I want to explain that he's a lovable rogue and means nothing by it, but I would love to see him dragged out of here.

'Glad to know my pearls of wisdom are sinking in,' I say, uninterested in every respect.

'Pearl necklace!' shouts Big G.

'Police reckon the dross that drugged her weren't keen cause she was on the blob. Tampon dangling and everything,' Dylan lingers, when all I want him to do is spare me the remainder of this story. 'Saved by the ole vampire's teabag.' I wish I could spike his drink so he doesn't have to come out with us.

We are soon tucking into our food, which hasn't taken long to cook (microwave) and I get the booze in like it's going out of fashion. How the Americans suffered through prohibition I will never know. I'd be off to Cuba every other day for my Mint Juleps and Mojitos. Fuck The Havana Club though. If I went to Cuba, wild horses or donkeys or whatever it is they use couldn't drag me there. Cuba's a bit of a trek for a pint of lager – but the Isle of Man, maybe.

The food is surprisingly good and with our plates cleared and Dylan unfortunately in tow, we bring our empties back to the bar and head for the door. We walk to Big G's car and I call 'shotgun' so Dylan has to sit in the back. The way he was behaving, I doubt Big G would let him sit up front anyway, probably wishing he had a child seat in the back, or an actual shotgun. The air in the car is muggy with the three of us in it; Dylan breathing heavily and smelling like a brewery. I feel bloated after my beer and bolognaise and ask Big G to 'splash the ash.' He reluctantly hands me a cigarette. Dylan asks for one too but we ignore him and bop to the beat of DubStep instead.

We are five minutes early and The Spitfire is packed. I pop in to see if Gemma has arrived and wonder if there is anyone else out that I might know. The manager is behind the bar, along with a few of the other smartly dressed bar rats, who are rushing around making money, which we won't see any of tonight. I ask him if he's had Gemma in yet but he's more concerned with his drink order than the whereabouts of my typically late fiancée. I head out to the car to wait for the girls arrive.

Half an hour passes and Gemma still hasn't shown up. I call her mobile but it goes straight to answer phone. Her voicemail is typical Gemma. She says 'Hello? *Hello?* I can't hear you. Are you there? Ha ha! Got you! Leave a message, sucker!' I fall for it every time. I notice that Dylan is having a snooze, so Big G and I start chatting about the girl that he missed out on at the pub.

'I'll never find love. You have Gemma and this berk has Belinda, a girl he doesn't even want. When is it my turn?' Big G is wearing his heart on his sleeve, making an awful mess of his cufflinks.

'You always find love when you least expect it, Ginge. Let's see who's at the club, okay?' I propose, even though I know that if Big G wasn't looking for it, he still wouldn't find it. 'Gemma will hook you up with someone nice.'

'I hope it's Stacey she's out with.' That would be ideal. Single. Ditsy. Easy.

'Dylan and Belinda are a couple? Either way, we'll have a nice fat kebab at the end of the night. You love a bit of Alsatian,' I reassure.

'Ha! Not gonna get pussy-whipped like you, gook,' says Dylan from somewhere in the back, his eyes still closed, his head still slumped and definitely still an arsehole. '*I'm* going to smash Stacey! Again! If you had to choose between having sex with an actual dog or eating a doner made of dog, which would it be?'

'Shut up, Dildo,' says Big G.

'Maybe you'd get some minge if you made an effort. Use some aftershave. No Armani, No Punani!' says Dylan, who looks a complete state himself. 'No Spray, No Lay!'

'I'm gonna kick your head in once we're out this car,' replies Big G. My money's on the huge ginger one.

'You work for us and don't even get paid for it! If you were a manager like me you might get some vadge,' says Dylan, putting the 'cock' in cocky.

'We've waited long enough,' I tell the gang, raising their spirits and one of Dylan's thumbs.

We pull up at our club, which should only take thirty seconds if a crow was to fly us, but thanks to the poorly planned one-way system, we are driving for a good ten minutes before we arrive. It would be faster by Shanks's pony, but these boots aren't made for walking.

They are for kicking sobriety in the ass.

8

As soon as we enter The Bomb Bar, I am hit by the smell of stale carpet beer and reminded that I spend enough time at the venue as it is. When we get to the bar we are all really glad to see Harley. We exchange elaborate handshakes and, using my staff discount (which means free when Harley is serving), I order six Glitter bombs: Goldschläger (a Swiss cinnamon-schnapps) dropped into energy drink. Customers often ask me if Goldschläger is the one that has the bits in it that cut your throat, getting you drunker quicker. It's a misconception, but I never contradict someone who believes it. Why burst their bubble if it keeps the squaddies and jack-the-lads buying them? Even if the soft, malleable gold isn't nearly sharp enough to burst anything.

Big G asks if he got anything nice for Christmas and Harley jokes that his Indian household only lets him celebrate Diwali. He then tells us that his paltry bar wage only affords him Bhatura bread and water and that he's still waiting on his Christmas bonus. You and me both, mate! A flurry of Chinese, Indian and Ginger insults are swapped while Dylan and I raise our bombs together, the only set of bombs Harley is to pour that aren't stained.

I promised Gemma before she set off that I wouldn't allow myself to get roped into working should it get busy and, apart from listening to Mandara moan about how old our equipment is, I intend on staying true to my word. It's an amazing feeling to be stood this side of the bar for a change. Harley has everything under control: the perfect barman for tonight's proceedings. He won't charge me for a single drink and is the ideal understudy.

Just as I order a responsible soda and lime for Big G, arms are thrown around my waist. It's Gemma, and she's wasted. I give her a hug before she runs off, as she has a tendency to do. When she's drunk she's like a magpie, distracted by anything shiny.

I look around at our room of loyal regulars and at the staff, past and present. Despite the countless problems I face in working here, I revel in this sense of belonging. I am so ingrained that the thought of ever leaving this place would seem like a sin. My replacement family.

All my eggs are in this flimsy basket. The eggs are definitely those of caged hens, from the 'reduced to clear' section at Asda, but they are *my* eggs. This collection of assorted friends, colleagues and cocktails is my omelette.

I insist on paying for Gemma's drinks in case Barney says something, before going for a wander. I walk out to the smoking section and she is sat on a bench surrounded by Charis, Dylan and Big G, who were only moments ago trying to enjoy their night out.

Gemma is crying hysterically, mascara running down her face and holding a lit cigarette. She only ever smokes 'socially,' which means: when utterly wrecked. Big G darts me a look, suggesting that I should head back inside and not make my presence known. I ignore his warning and ask Gemma who did this to her, whatever 'this' might be. Gemma struggles to stand and throws her ciggie at me with poor aim.

'Fuck you Harry! Your sket is here. I hate you!' Gemma screams in drunken fury.

'What you on about? What the fuck is she talking about guys? The only sket of mine is you, stupid woman. Come here and talk to me,' I reply, oblivious as to what I've done wrong.

'That slag that fancies you is in here. I slapped her in the toilets. She's the one you want to be with, isn't she? You bastard!' shouts Gemma.

'A girl in the toilets? *Seriously*? I live with you, I love you and you're a fucking embarrassment, do you know that?' I reply sternly. Not my best form of delegation to date.

With that, Gemma jumps up and tries to kick at me, looking more Ukrainian Cossack dancer than Jet Li. I stumble into the fence, while the others hold her back. They are concerned that she'll do herself some serious damage, or more importantly, our confused bystanders, who are enjoying tonight's entertainment of Can-Can and Kung Fu.

As Gemma is forced to sit back down she grabs a glass and throws it, hitting me in the knee. I am thankful for Barney's decision to switch to polycarbonate earlier in the year. My patella even more so. Dylan and Charis try to console Gemma. Big G seizes my arm and ushers me into the bar. I try to explain that there is no other 'sket' and he knows I am telling the truth. I haven't tested cologne in years. 'Handbags at dawn, forget it,' he says, trying to dumb down the situation.

Harley looks over at me and gives me a nod of approval.

'What are you smiling about, Poppadom?'

'I saw some girl run out of here crying. Barney's gone to make sure she hasn't called the police. Crying girl running from a toilet, I knew you'd have something to do with it!'

'It wasn't me!' I yelp, and everyone in the bar is staring at me.

'That's what Shaggy said when she caught him on the counter,' he jests. Touché.

'Do we know this girl?' I approach the bar to avoid prying eyes.

'I've seen her in here before. The one always making song requests at the booth,' he replies, not shedding any more light on our mysterious phantom home wrecker. I've probably seen her on *Jerry Springer*.

I look around the room and Mandara and Snoopy are stood by the DJ console, gawking at me. Mandara is offering a look of puzzlement, Snoopy one of commiseration. They have no idea what's just taken place. That would make three of us, then.

I say my goodbyes to Harley, which involves one high-five, two shots of sambuca and a few racial slurs back and forth, before Big G drives me home. He urges me to stay and plead my case, but I've had enough of her hysterics.

When we reach my matchbox of a house I ask Big G if he wants to come in for a beer, but he says he'd rather not, saving himself from an epic rant about how much of a bitch my woman is. I rummage through my pockets for my clatter of keys, relieved to hear the jingle. I give Big G a drawn out handshake as compensation for the fare and fall out of his car door.

He puts the full beam of his lights on so that I can see the keyhole, which seems smaller than I remember. I thank Big G and wish him a Happy New Year, failing to mention the not so Merry Christmas. I now know why the crazy, drunken Oasis singer is called Noel. I manage to get the door open as Big G screeches off to the sound of his blaring subwoofer. What a Gary boy. I climb up the narrow steps to our equally narrow house and slump on a cushion on the floor. Gemma will be on her way home now. I can explain to her that there's no other woman. Some heated make-up sex will allow us to put this silly misunderstanding behind us.

Dream on.

Three hours have passed since I saw her last. Gemma staggers through the door having nearly snapped her key in the lock. Not impressed.

'Where the fuck have *you* been then?' I shout down the stairs.

'I was with Barney and Charis and everyone. Where did you go? I couldn't find you,' Gemma slurs, cheerfully.

I can't believe this. She has totally dismissed what happened. I march down the stairs to find her in the bathroom leaning over the toilet bowl, the contents of her clutch bag sprawled over the floor as she attempts to undo the last five hours of drinking. Gemma always refuses a drink during the week. She tells me that unlike the alcoholic I have become, she only ever 'drinks to get drunk.' Well this is the proof, I think, as I stare down at her now purged pudding.

How is this binge drink format any better than my constant continual? I mean, look at the state of it. This is the climax of tonight's event; a climax I had hoped would come in a different form. I simply spend my week on a pissed plateau. I lovingly hold her hair back and stroke her neck nonetheless. There is a fine line between merry and messy; it can be as little as a sip for some. She often tells me that my eyes are bigger than my stomach. It would seem that her eyes are bigger than her bladder. As I sit amongst Gemma's strewn possessions (a scatter of lip gloss, chewing gum and a mini mirror with a crack down the front), I realise that I wouldn't do this for anyone else.

Just when I think Gemma has vomited the last of her Cheeky Vimto, the puke process starts all over again. To be fair to the girl, it has been a while since she last called God on the porcelain telephone, so I continue to whisper shush noises. I know we are going to be sat on this cold floor for some time yet. If only the last four to five drinks hadn't happened. We would be merrily drunk, turning into Gordon Ramsay in the kitchen, before making a complete mess, failing to wash up, and then falling asleep before we can get our kit off.

I pull her grubby heels off and the menacing stilettos look like a contraption for torture, designed for the binding of feet. Her knickers are halfway down her shins, head in hole, body hugging the latrine. If this isn't a Kodak moment, I don't know what is. I take her mobile out of her handbag and snap a couple of sassy shots. Definitely one for the grandkids. Despite the flash bouncing off the toilet water, she is powerless to say or do or middle finger anything about it. With her phone in my hand and her face down the loo, I find myself clicking on her message inbox. I run down the list of recent recipients and there is nothing out of the ordinary. Someone who becomes accusatory is usually guilty themselves, but I can give my bog brush of a blondie the all clear.

I wipe Gemma's chin and try to lift her up. No chance. Instead, I roll her on to her back and drag her to the foot of the stairs. She looks like a wobbly, wankered wheelbarrow. Not wanting to risk further carpet burn (again, not the way I expected her to receive them), she groans as I pull her from the floor.

'Come on, a few more steps and you'll be snuggled up in bed. You can do this,' I encourage, knowing that if something sounds too good to be true, it probably is.

'Fuck you,' she grunts, as ladylike as ever.

'Let's not start that again, can we go upstairs, please.'

'You are shit, you are. Your club is shit. You're just shit.' There are two definitions of Karma: (i) throwing a banana peel in Mario Kart and skidding out on it on the following lap or (ii) buying your partner drinks, fuelling her drunken antagonism, and paying the price for it. I have been the victim of both today.

'That didn't stop you from spending the whole night down there without me though, did it?' I don't know where this conversation is going, but I don't like it.

'Everyone is leaving. No one wants to go to your shithole anymore. Even you left!' she advances. The gloves are off, revealing raptor-like, razor-sharp claws. Drunken girls' words are sober girls' thoughts.

'You think you could run it then, do you? I only left cause you were being a cunt!' The venom in her words has forced a hateful reaction from me. She must have been drinking Snakebite & Black at some point.

'Who do you think you are?' she screams, at the top of her lungs. The sharp increase in volume catches me off guard. '*Everything* you say fucking irritates me right now!'

I don't think I'm anybody. Before The Havana opened its doors, I did. I ran this town. I near enough owned it. I was the bee's knees. Now, I'm barely a wasp's ankle. This slanging match continues for a good fifteen minutes before there is a loud bang at the door. In the haze of our hostility, we didn't realise how much din we were causing and how thin our feeble walls are. It is bound to be the young mum next door and we've woken her baby.

Fuck.

We silence ourselves and freeze. After the knocking stops, I storm upstairs and she swiftly follows, stumbling on four of the twelve steps. As I turn, ready to tell her what I thought of that pathetic excuse for an ascent, she raises a hand to hit me but misses.

'Where is this coming from? Why are you doing this?' I scold. We're going round in circles and it's making me dizzy.

'Why don't you just fuck off? Go on, jog on! Things have changed. I can't stand to look at you,' she vents. The first reasonable thing she has said all night. Things *have* changed. But I don't see what I can possibly do about it. And I'm not jogging anywhere. Harley hasn't asked me to do the Race for Life or whatever it's called, so why should I jog for her?

'What's so great about what you do then, Gemma? You're a glorified babysitter. You act like a child yourself. Look at you!' I shout, knowing how seriously she takes her childcare and development work.

She shoots me a glare that implies I should go and die a thousand deaths, before throwing herself down the stairs a lot quicker than it had taken her to throw up. There is no satisfaction to be had from belittling the love of my life, but medusa leaves me fixed to the spot. I hear her scurry around the bathroom, picking up her mountain of crap from the floor. Expecting her to slam the bedroom door, relegating me to the sofa, I am surprised to hear her leave the house altogether. Moody. Unstable. Juvenile.

Where could she possibly be going mere minutes from daylight? Her mum's house is a half hour walk from here, longer still when barefoot and drunk. I don't pursue her: it would accomplish nothing. If I follow her now she will only expect it every time we have a row. In fact, I will *never* have this argument again. Forget this infantile cow, I don't need her.

I grab my suitcase from under the bed, throwing my clothes on to the floor. I sift for anything of worth. I salvage only four shirts from the pile of Matalan and TK Maxx. I take my car log book, as well as a photograph album from my father. Harry Chen doesn't have to put up with this shit. I begin to work myself up into more and more of a rage. I head to the kitchen and pour myself another drink, though it really won't do me any good. I throw open the drawers and find a box of porcelain chopsticks, kept in an ornamental box. They were given to my father at some conference from the former Chief Executive Officer of Hong Kong – the equivalent of our Prime Minister. My father handed them to me with great pride. There is no way I'm going to leave them behind, only to be binned by this trollop.

I look around our front room for anything of sentimental value. Books, DVDs, appliances, they can all be replaced. I look at the photos of us that line the units and windowsills and think what a waste of ink and three word assessments that was. I start to pull away at the shelves and cabinets, throwing everything on to the floor, more for gratification than for search.

With my suitcase awash with shabby clothes, family photographs and my father's governmental chopsticks, I turn on my laptop so that I can change all my passwords. The prospect of her cyber sabotage is too great to leave until the morning. The thought of our excruciatingly slow internet dongle fills me with as much dismay as Gemma's detestable words, but it urgently needs to be done. As I wait for the screen to load, I decide that I could probably make better use of time by throwing her stuff out of the window, or peeing in the milk. The longer I sit and wait, the wearier I feel, so I bang the table repeatedly to make it load quicker.

With passwords changed and security questions altered, I sit in our now trashed living room and take a swig of my drink whilst calculating my next move. I picture her walking all the way to her mum's on Belabor Court in her handkerchief of a mini-skirt, undies still halfway down her legs and sick all down her front. How the mighty have fallen, both her and me.

With no intention of ever returning to this house, I spit on the floor, but it comes out as a drool. I wipe this away with a cushion, throwing it over my head and down the stairs, taking the lampshade with it, which knocks over the novelty piggy bank that I got her. It has the writing 'Boob Job Fund' on the front in purple lettering. She is forever complaining about how she wants larger breasts, for 'self-confidence' and 'wardrobe' reasons, and not for the male attention. No, of course not. If I had paid the four grand for her new breasts I'd want them back, even if I had to pop them out myself. I empty her money tin all over the table. I take the gold and silver, leaving her the bronze. I'm all heart. What tits can she expect to buy with this?

Before I can finish separating my denomination of choice, my eyes start to close, the handfuls of coins heavy in my cupped hands.

I pass out drunk.

The only tit around here is me.

9

I wake up to a text saying 'We need to talk.'

These dreaded four words haunt every man across Great Britannia. The only other four words ensuring the immediate shrivelling of manhood are 'I think I'm pregnant' and 'The defendant is guilty.' I know what 'We need to talk' will entail. It will involve me apologising for being a complete and utter fool. It will involve me taking back all the rotten things I said last night, many of which I hope she can't remember. But most importantly, it will involve me explaining why I let my twenty-one year old fiancée walk for miles wearing next to nothing. I think I'd settle for the unplanned pregnancy.

A heated spat with the missus never seems of much consequence at the time. A bit like thinking stealing the odd bit of PicknMix wouldn't hurt. It destroyed Woolworths. I frantically try to recall what texts I may have sent. I fear the worst and will most likely have to apologise for my phone being drunk too. If only I was on pay-as-you-go like Harley. I think it's fair to say I overreacted just a tad.

My entire body is suffering from the effects of last night's antics. All I want to do is trap my hangover in a medieval set of wooden stocks and throw a greasy spoon breakfast at it, with extra fried bread. The *last* thing I want to do is sit here, waiting for Gemma to scold me. Having to eat my words will be as unpleasant as eating 'special' fried rice. My head is throbbing. When David Attenborough isn't talking about salmon he should be narrating my hangovers.

I reply with a warm and reassuring text that reads, 'Okay.' Gemma will now be on her way home, undoubtedly still over the legal limit. Last night she parked at her friend's house, which means her friend is bound to know all about our fight. Let the rumour mill commence once more.

I hear Gemma at the front door and she lets herself into the house. If I was a locksmith I would have changed the locks on her last night too, considering the mood I was in. I'm really not sure if I am mentally prepared for the court style proceedings that are about to ensue. There will be considerable objections, hearsays, and moves to strike as we determine who was wrong and who was more wrong. I only hope that we can settle out of court and she calls me to her chambers.

As Gemma climbs the stairs I brace myself for her reaction once she acknowledges the full trail of destruction I created after she walked out. I smile at her sheepishly, but she doesn't smile back. The room is deadly silent, as if we are waiting apprehensively for the foreman to read out the verdict.

Gemma sits down next to me, still wearing her clothes from last night and unfazed by the mess. I shuffle closer, attempting to wrap my arms around her. She pulls a face of revolt and gently pushes me back. I try to recuperate by slinging the sofa throw over the top of us, but she is in no mood for getting cosy. I feel awkward following this double rejection.

'I'll go slip into something a little *less* comfortable, shall I?'

'Stop! You never take anything seriously. Ever. Am I a joke, Harry? Cause you're the joke,' she says, looking flustered and rather attractive. Now probably wouldn't be a good time to try it on. There is something about the dishevelled, tired and up-all-night look that makes her seem all the more beautiful.

'The jokes you tell are normally funny.' Move to Strike.

'You used to be so full of motivation. Do you think you can become a success again?' I feel incredibly liable for something I didn't even know I was doing.

'Yesterday, I can't even get hold of you. Then when I do see you, you're already well on your way without me. Next thing I know you've turned psycho, all paranoid over some stranger who, I *promise* you, I've never even met,' I try to explain. The brief synopsis I've provided sounding surprisingly preferable to the night I actually endured.

'My dad is concerned.' I knew he would have something to do with this. 'I want someone who can look after me. It seems like you're a dead end.' Not that any explanation is necessary, she is making perfect sense. I was once the rising star and the talk of the town. Now I am not.

'A dead end? Ouch. How long have you had that one in the holster for? Your reputation isn't on the line?' I question, to the point of exasperation.

'I'm your girlfriend. Of course it reflects on me.' Gemma looks drained, the night of vomiting and vehemence not quite fully flushed away. It would also seem that I've been demoted from fiancé to boyfriend.

'This is the part where the caring *fiancée* says 'We're going to get through it together.' You think I won't be able to provide for you? Things aren't going great at the club, but I've got an income. Have as many sandwiches as you like with the bread I intend to win you,' I say, stupefied. She doesn't seem impressed. She prefers ciabatta.

'I need time to clear my head. I hope you understand.' I honestly thought the worst-case scenario from 'We need to talk' was a prolonged stint in the doghouse and a serious lack of angry make-up sex. Not the love of my life wanting to abandon me.

'This is bullshit. What's this really about? You were para last night, full of false accusations, why aren't we talking about that?' I protest. Objection!

'Let's just cool it.' Her bitch-switch has been flicked to the position marked 'ON' and the button has stuck.

'But I love you. And I know you love me...' my voice trails off. 'Don't string me along, Gemma,' I add, surprised by my maturity, even if I do sound pathetic.

'I know you love me. And I love that about you. Maybe things will change and you can be the boss again?' she asks, in a subtly flirtatious way. Like she used to when we were first dating, a look I haven't seen in years. This look, that would make your average warm-blooded male hot under the collar, is instead leaving me mystified.

I stare at Gemma blankly, bewildered that the last few minutes of conversation have apparently made little to no impact on her. Is she still drunk? Because I am sober as a judge right now. I'm quite sure a judge would consider her plea of insanity.

'This is bollocks!' I tell her, my maturity evaporated.

'Whatever. I fucking give up,' she says, in the most unhelpful manner.

She has thrown down the gauntlet, so hard that the internet dongle loads.

Case closed.

She has forgotten this connection that we share, this home full of intertwined possessions and our extensive family of cotton-based children. I can't have them witness a messy divorce and our subsequent battle for custody.

'I'm gonna pop out to see my dad. I'll pick you up a saveloy or a pie from the chippie on my way back. I'm sorry.' Her hand strokes the back of my head, as if I am a sick animal to be nursed back to health, or put down.

But Gemma was uncharacteristically proving to be an animal herself and that animal would have to be a vulture. Vultures never attack healthy animals, but wait until their prey is wounded and dying before planning their advance. My reasonably thick hide has been beaten down and breached by larger scavengers: the loss of my old man, Harley's health, the rapid deterioration of the club. Now it is her turn to gorge.

My soul mate is going to desert me and I don't know why. I don't know how it's reached this point so suddenly. I am certainly not in the mood for a saveloy, a sausage roll or any other kind of greasy treat she intends to distract me with. I am actually quite relieved that she is leaving though, as I need a chance to take stock of all that has happened.

Can I become a success again? I honestly don't know. The author David Brinkley once said 'A successful man is one who can lay a firm foundation with the bricks others have thrown at him.' Well, Gemma has certainly thrown an almighty brick and it has smacked me right in the face, broken my nose, claret everywhere.

Gemma picks up her bag, turns to the staircase and doesn't look back. She is off to join her father, her co-conspirator. Brinkley's quote isn't on a wall in the club, maybe it should be.

I can't wait here clock watching. I can't sit in this house a moment longer. I can always reheat the pie later. Gemma and her dad will be busy comparing notes on my general lack of worth. Let them get on with it. I need to be around friends and I need some perspective. The only person for that is Barney. I make my way down the stairs, debating whether spending the limited free time I have afforded to me by the club, *at* the club, is the right thing to do. At least I can get a drink.

I slam the doors to house and car behind me, and pull out of the drive. What will I say to Barney? The poor guy has enough on his mind, but I need his advice. He knows the venue is underperforming and doesn't exactly need reminding, which will be unavoidable if I tell him all that Gemma has said. In truth, he has developed a deep resentment towards the venue. I just hope he's there now. I wouldn't be doing this merciless job for just anyone. I do it for Barney. The poor guy tells me to achieve a 'work-life balance.' I'll have to look that term up some day.

When everyone is out enjoying their weekend that is when we are at our busiest. When everyone is at work, we are planning and plotting, cleaning and conspiring, fixing and flyering. Gemma doesn't appreciate any of this and thinks we're all just getting pissed and having fun. We do a bit of that too, sure, but it's mainly hustle, bustle and a great deal of worry. By the sounds of it, operating a successful business is more important to Gemma than having me around, as of late. Either way, I need to sort my act out and rebuild my brand. Gemma feels that the performance of the club reflects on her, something I never considered. If there is anyone that has the cunning to adjust perceptions, including hers, it's Barney. He's always been a bit of a Del Boy but he only wants to live what he calls 'a comfortable life.' If Barney is Del Boy, I've unwittingly become his Rodney.

Barney has found endless ways to get us out of trouble, even if only through temporary measures. Some of his endeavours to evade creditors have been truly remarkable and some just plain old school. One of his most common tricks is to post out unsigned cheques, which 'buy' him some time. Problem with this ruse is that he can only use it once before they cotton on. He changes his voicemail more frequently than anyone I have ever met. There is forever a new message saying 'On leave until Thursday or 'In meetings until 6pm.'

Barney has become notorious for his 'unexpected' leaves of absence. The day that he specifies as his return to work will conveniently tie in with a cheque clearing from a hire fee or after a big event we forecast to turn a profit. I once walked in halfway through a conversation between Harley and Barney about manipulating the jiggers, which are the thimbles that we use to dispense measures of spirit. All jiggers must be government stamped, signifying their compliance with HMRC.

'The Weights and Measures guy just assumes it's going to be twenty-five mil, right?' asked Barney.

'They see if it has the CE mark and that all the bottles have UK duty stamps. Why?' Harley is no stranger to odd questions from Barney, undoubtedly involving a scheme.

'What if we were to heat up some metal and drip a couple of mils into the jigger? It might only be two or three mil smaller, but serve two hundred people and we've saved ourselves a whole bottle of spirit. Do you think it would be possible?' asked Barney, expecting Harley to know the answer, considering his vast experience in ironmongery, blacksmithing and steel forging.

'Clever. I like it. You can heat it in a crucible and cool it to set like anything else. No one would ever know. We could get hold of some UK duty stamp stickers on the internet and buy our booze from the Albanians in Soham.' Barney has successfully moulded another financial fiend in Harley, although he is Indian, and therefore typically stingy to begin with.

'Or we could get the bar ready and open up,' I suggested. 'Let's not resort to smelting just yet!'

On one occasion, we received a faulty barrel from our supplier. Barney called customer services and an engineer was dispatched to assess the damage, who soon confirmed that it was defective. They eventually agreed to issue us with an additional keg, on top of the replacement one, to be sent by courier the following day. Barney saw an opportunity. He took the engineer's job-sheet to a supplier in Badwell Ash, from whom we often bought cases approaching their sell-by date and blagged that the keg was purchased from them a fortnight ago. He told them that not only would he be expecting a replacement, but a reimbursement for the engineer's call-out fee. He was happy to accept stock or credit. He said that if they didn't follow through he would no longer purchase from them and his custom wasn't something they would want to lose. They allowed him to take a new keg and provided an additional case of cherry-flavoured shots, which Harley will tell you taste nothing like cherry. Barney said he couldn't bring the faulty keg in with him because it would have leaked out into his car, but that they were welcome to send a courier down for it. They never did.

Derek Trotter was turning into quite the matchstick man. On our next trip to our wholesalers, Barney brought the barrel with us and after a quick word with the manager they allowed us to exchange our faulty goldmine for a working one. Barney had transformed eighty-eight pints in to three hundred and fifty-two pints, in three days.

Barney has countless ways to save money but, as Harley often points out, at what stage does it compromise the overall quality of the venue? Perhaps it has been this constant cutting back that has made us fall out of favour with the town, and consequently Gemma. When it's WKD Blue in the fridges one week, then VK the next, then VS, then, I don't know, *Blue Sludge*, people start to notice. It is commonly said that 'money is the root of all evil,' but I beg to differ. *Lack* of money is the root of all evil. If 'opportunity makes the thief' then Barney's distinct glut of opportunities is going to make him a full-on criminal.

'You think this Pepsi is too sweet?'

'All the post-mix tastes good here,' I reassuringly replied.

'No, have them lower the dispense. If we halve the sweetness we can get twice as much. And don't forget to take the Diet Pepsi box off the Pepsi line before the engineer gets here, otherwise he'll start asking all sorts of questions,' said Barney, slowly chipping away at my self-respect.

As soon as I was off the phone, he handed me a letter that needed posting. He told me that it was a cheque for the next instalment of rent. The cheque was both post-dated and unsigned.

Barney would buy third class stamps if he could.

10

I unlock the door, which isn't to say that no one's inside. Barney is stringent with the locking of entry doors, as 'You never know who might be trying to get in,' the 'who' meaning bailiffs. I hear them before I can see them: Barney is shouting at Dylan, a familiar sound that tells me I have arrived at my home away from home.

'Hold it steady! Why are you wobbling so much? Put your weight behind it!' Barney bellows in Dylan's general direction, as he can't quite see his face behind the large plasma screen they are detaching from its wall bracket.

'Harry, help me, quickly, this shit is heavy,' exclaims Dylan, clearly struggling with his half of the forty-two inches. You rarely get a 'hello' in this place before you're asked to do something.

I kick my shoes off and hop on to the sofa, reaching out to support the precariously dangling flat screen. With the fragile plasma now carefully suspended, Barney begins to pull out the leads. With my face firmly pressed against the side of the display, I glance around the room. Apart from a mound of paperwork, tell-tale of a serious review of our accounts, the place looks great. Dylan must have been on an air freshening, deep cleaning mission. Even the tables look polished. I decide that if I go into the gents' and the toilet water is blue, I'm buying Dylan a drink. This has to be one of the best looking venues in town (the others aren't great) and no one, not even my own partner, could argue otherwise.

'Don't tell me it's broken. We don't need another piece of equipment on the blink,' I say, which probably could have waited until the edges of the telly weren't digging into everyone's respective forearms.

'It's going on eBay,' he replies, matter-of-factly.

'Barney reckons it'll fetch two hundred and fifty squid. No one's going to pay that,' says Dylan, which Barney must find equally unhelpful.

'Four hundred for the pair then,' snaps Barney, conceding that he may have been slightly over-zealous. He doesn't seem too happy, not that 'happy' is a word usually used to describe someone having to sell off company assets over the internet. I just hope Dylan doesn't have an issue with four hundred, because Barney doesn't sound like he's in the mood for anymore riling.

'I'd take one off your hands if I had the dosh,' I say, offering the most pointless of condolences.

'We need to change the look of this room. These tellies look too dated, too *eighties*. We want the room darker, to build atmosphere, don't we?' Barney's feeble attempt to make the matter of TV removal anything but the need for money. My heart sinks for him, an increasingly familiar feeling. 'Dylan, write down the model number if you can find it.'

'You could always ask for two-fifty and see what bids you get?' I say, trying to be more helpful this time. I should have stayed at home after all. Barney will have me pulling out light bulbs to stick on Gumtree before I know it.

'Good idea! How are you, Harry? Didn't expect to see you down here today. Everything all right?' Barney asks kindly, considering his preoccupation. He would probably rather that I hadn't walked in when I did, although he doesn't let on.

'Just wanted to see you guys really. Had a nasty talk with Gemma.' As if I don't see enough of this lot as it is.

We place the telly down on the sofa, which isn't ideal because now he can get a good look at me.

'Things could've gone better last night. Give it a couple of days and you'll be fine. What was the conversation about?' Barney says, optimistically. You know you're among good friends when a personal question doesn't have to be followed by 'if you don't mind me asking?'

'Her slapping that girl I bet!' cheers Dylan, without looking around, still searching for his model number. 'I wish I had seen it, proper lesbian action.'

'About us, and her bastard dad. And the club,' I say, ignoring Dylan. I said the last bit quietly, making it all the more curious.

'What about the club?' Barney's defence mechanism kicks in like a shot. Not a nice shot, like peach schnapps, but a foul-tasting one like sambuca.

'She said things aren't like they used to be. As if she needs to tell me that!'

'You do everything you can. Perhaps she's having a bad day? I'm sure she doesn't mean it.' Barney has a profound understanding for both

Gemma and myself. I feel incredibly rude bringing all this up, but I knew I would from the start.

'We need to think of something big.' I sound as vague as she did. I'm pleading with Barney, as if there's a giant 'success' button up in the office that he hasn't told me about, that he could push at any time of his choosing.

'What did I tell you about getting engaged man?' says Dylan smugly, 'Forget sustainable fishing! Become a trawlerman, like me!'

'Shut up!' Barney and I snarl, near enough in unison. We're on the same wavelength. Most people do have a tendency to want Dylan to shut up though.

Barney always wants to have a formal meeting about the nitty-gritty, whereas I prefer to get stuck in. I tell Barney that I am finally free and his eyes light up, as if I've lit a Catherine Wheel on Dylan's freshly vacuumed floor.

I ask Dylan to rearrange some of the furniture so we can sit down and talk shop. We haven't a moment to spare, despite Barney calling for one of these every week. All of us have a vested interest in things going well at the venue. Barney wants to keep his doors open; I want to please my fiancée and Dylan doesn't want to have to carry, unscrew or pack anything else that needs to be flogged. Just as we're about to begin, there is a bang on the fire exit, which Dylan runs across to open without first asking who it is. Barney is about to erupt, but it's only Mandara and Snoopy. As they walk in they both seem surprised to see me and I start to feel that I'm missing out, with everyone gathering down here when I'm meant to be off.

'You're just in time! Big staff meeting. Dylan, coffee,' says Barney, with vigour.

'What's with the TV? I spent ages connecting that shit up,' replies Mandara, who looks puzzled.

'Never mind that, took it down to clean. Take a seat Mr Man-Dem, quick!'

'What's going on?' Snoopy looks at me with trepidation, as if we've been called into the Headmaster's office without the chance to get our stories straight.

'We need to turn this club around. For countless reasons,' I say, though only the one reason resounds in my mind. Snoopy looks relieved that this get together isn't anything more serious than keeping our livelihoods from impending doom. 'We need to do something drastic,' I continue, easing myself into what is going to sound like incongruity.

'I don't care what it is. Hire the club out for conferences, zumba sessions, a beer festival, flipping antenatal classes! We'll take anything, but it needs to be profitable.' Barney is going to start talking about his one-to-three ratio any minute now, I just know it.

'What are you not telling me?' questions Snoopy, completely ignoring Barney. So much for the easing in. Snoopy never misses a beat, due to us spending so much time together. He is looking inside my brain and extracting information and I don't feel like I have much to hide, so I come out with it.

'Gemma is giving me shit, okay. Do you want me sleeping on your couch, Snoops? I can't see her unhappy. When she's unhappy, she makes pretty damn sure I'm unhappy.'

'Oh,' says Snoopy embarrassedly. He didn't know this meeting was posing as marriage counselling and, as much as I love him, he isn't really one to talk about relationships. His mind reading is way off the mark, considering we are talking about the touchy-feely world of love in what is normally man time, bromance, boy space.

'This is about a little something I like to call our jobs,' insists Barney, who doesn't seem impressed that our crisis meeting is being hijacked. He's worried that we'll all start shouting the names of random bomb variations at him.

'We need to do £1 drinks, Barney. All drinks, all weekend. I'll get some promo girls out there with wristbands, Mandara on the early set and I'll headline, it'll be packed out,' Snoopy suggests, with the emphasis on the headline set. Snoopy may be our promotional manager, but before this title was put in place he had always been a DJ. The one thing every DJ has in common is the desperate compulsion to build up their name.

'The Council would have a fit, but maybe if we worded it carefully. *Selected drinks* only,' Barney replies.

'It has to be on everything and it has to be free entry. They won't go to The H Club if they can get drinks for a quid here,' Snoopy retaliates.

'This is a step back for us,' says Barney, despite *Blue Sludge* lining the top shelf of the fridges. It's probably a bottle of Blue Sludge that Dylan's painted the toilet water with.

'We'll just leave it then, shall we? Half of something is better than all of nothing. I can't continue playing to an empty dance floor,' Snoopy nips.

'How about we trial a session called one-two-three? We do £1 drinks on the Thursday, £2 drinks on the Friday and £3 on the Saturday. Would you be happier with that?' asks Barney, trying to ease the mounting tension.

'Not good enough. Havana does £2 drinks on a Saturday to anyone with a VIP card and they spread them around like the clap. We should've sold membership cards when I first suggested it. It'll look like we're copying them if we print some now.' Snoopy's disgruntlement is really starting to drag me down.

'Selected drinks. Free entry until 11pm. You can headline,' Barney says with reinforced conviction, '...but usually we need £3 back for every £1 spent.' There she blows.

Snoopy looks surprised by Barney's submission but not overjoyed. He may have won the battle, but has yet to win the war. Someone is also going to have to inform Stevie Mac that he won't be playing this Saturday. This is the first time he has ever been dropped from a set.

'What about Stevie?' I ask. The backbone of every promotion we have carried out for months on end, who could easily be getting paid twice as much somewhere else.

'We can't do rock-bottom prices, free entry for most of the night and three DJs on the line-up. It just won't work,' says Barney, a statement none of us can challenge. Snoopy shrugs. He has gotten what he wants; the rest is someone else's problem, namely mine. This is what I asked for, after all – a drastic change. I drop Stevie or Gemma drops me.

'Sammy Fish will offer Stevie a Saturday spot if he catches wind of this.'

'There is no way Stevie would play for the bloody Havana Club. I'm going to start on the promotion. What you up to Harry? You staying down here, planning things from your side?' asks Snoopy, happy to head off since he got what he came for.

'I'm gonna hang about. Don't want to be at home,' I say, which is the only reason I ended up down here in the first place. Snoopy and Mandara bid their farewells and head towards the fire exit.

'Try to sort those hair straightening machines for the toilets, Snoopy! Girls spend half the night in the ladies' room, they might as well be parting with a quid or two,' shouts Barney, just before they leave. He turns towards me to discuss the next item on his agenda.

'We have to sell the ice machine,' he says despondently. 'It produces one million ice cubes. Each ice well holds a thousand cubes and we have four of them. That's 980,000 too many each weekend, once The Spitfire takes their bin liners.' My GCSE maths cannot confirm this.

'We'd have better luck building an igloo,' I add.

Snoopy is headlining this weekend, promoting something that everyone is going to love. I have to cancel our long-term and committed Stevie Mac who has never been anything less than brilliant and Barney now feels compelled to sell his enormous ice machine. Dylan never bothered to make the coffees.

I should have been a DJ and bought a coffee machine.

11

Barney and I are sat on the sofa scrutinising the new slideshow that Mandara has put together for the screen behind the bar. Apart from spelling 'karaoke' wrong, he's done a pretty decent job. Shame there aren't any customers here to see it. We opened at 8pm this evening. Four hours have passed and not a single penny has walked through the door. It's always the same at this time of year; everyone is spent after Christmas and saving themselves for New Year's Eve.

The slideshow doesn't make any mention of Stevie Mac, our loyal DJ. He handled the news fairly well when I broke it to him. I tried to explain that it was a one-off but he didn't buy it. He saw this as a sign of things to come.

'I have Sammy Fisher at the front door, the smelly Havana trout. Should I let him in or tell him to fuck off?' asks Dylan. I just hope he didn't take that tone on the front door. Or do I?

Barney stands up straight, posture dramatically improved, and nods at Dylan.

Mr Fish's surname is as smelly as his attitude and the arrogant tosser only seems to get pissed on power. Sammy Fish. Competitor. Childish. Chubby. He slithers over to the bar and scans the room, seeing quite clearly that there are no customers. I too find myself anxiously looking around, waiting to see what his reaction will be. The big Fish is in our small pond. If he is secretly delighted that our fish tank is empty, which I can imagine he is, he does well to hide it. He waddles over to shake Barney's hand, who in turn offers him a drink of his choice, on the house, which really does stand testament to his character.

This greasy halibut empties our venue every single weekend without fail. And yet here we are, treating him like some kind of honoured guest. He asks for a Kahlúa and Orange and insists on paying for it, making it harder for me to hate him. Barney refuses to accept the money, so Sammy hands it to me. I am much closer to the till and quite happily oblige. I have targets to hit and most of my previous goals have fallen short because of this flounder before me.

I decide to let the grown-ups talk and leave them to it. I head up to the office to tinker about on the computer and promote our big weekender. If Sammy is here, he can't be smashing it out online, so I may as well be.

I have never been to The Havana Club and I hate all that his aquarium stands for. I hate that our patrons feel a life-or-death compulsion to go, and I hate the rum it's named after. However, I did part-time there some years ago, back when it was a Drum and Bass hall called Verity, owned by Snoopy's step-dad. It was a dive. The place was filthy and stunk to High Heaven, or Low Hell, whichever smells worst. Everyone was off their nut and the drug-taking became so commonplace that the doormen sprayed WD-40 in the toilets so that any powder placed on the surfaces would cause nosebleeds to those chancing it.

Verity even used to sell nitrous oxide balloons (which the ravers named 'sweet air') for a fiver a go. Snoopy told me that they used to make more money from the balloon sales than from the alcohol sales, so they were laughing from the gas alright, all the way to the bank. We would refer to the ravers as 'tree huggers' as they often frequented outdoor parties in fields. These illegal raves are clamped down on by police as they are completely unregulated and no one would ever report a crime or an overdose, in fear of having the party shut down and equipment confiscated. Such horrible and uncontrollable events.

And now we host them upstairs in the club every Friday.

We created an umbrella brand called 'Funk'd Up Fridays' and allow these promoters to come in, set up shop and wreak havoc on our venue. The 'music' they deafen their loyal followers with is utterly dreadful, but the doped hippies love it. On occasion, we have to resurrect zombified crack fiends. Someone who has taken ketamine can find themselves entering what is known as a 'K-hole.' This excessive substance abuse causes the individual to lose all sense of perception and although aware of conscience and self, is in no state to act properly within it. This serious 'tripping out' leaves us with a useless lump of a problem that only stands to scare off our 'normal' punters and highlights that we have a drug issue.

The sound systems often show up with three or four vans full of gear, despite being told not to bring too much kit. The speakers that I help them unload (to hide as soon as possible) will often be covered in mud from the last field it was used in. The rigs are powered by their own separate amps, meaning that the sound can't be limited – a legal requirement for nightclubs in the UK. Therefore, we are constantly telling them to turn the volume down and, more importantly, to soften the bass. This often leads to dissent, as they have little regard for authority.

We have received numerous complaints from our neighbours, some more threatening than others. One resident in particular, Mr Morrissey, who has a name I thought would appreciate music, really took his complaint to the top. In all honestly, I don't even blame the old codger. Even the real Morrissey wouldn't like this music we blast down the street, because it isn't music, it is noise. Mr Morrissey and his wife keep a decibel meter by their bed and a log sheet for recording disturbances. They coincidentally found that a pattern was emerging that seemed to revolve around Friday nights between 8pm and 3am. The Morrisseys are well into their sixties (age, not era of music) and if I had to endure the same suffering each week, I'd call the Council's Environmental Health Office too. Just last Friday, Barney spotted the Chief-EHO's car outside their house and warned me over the radio. Barely able to hear Barney's instruction, I signalled to the ringleader of the suggestively named 'Chemical Intakers' to cut the music.

I remember darting down the stairs and bumping into a couple of flower powers in their scraggy Doc Martins and Tarzan's hand-me-downs. When I got to the front door, Barney was talking to Brian Reeve. Tall. Tired. Treacherous. He looked like he'd been dragged from his bed, much to the anger of Mrs Reeve. I made my way over, waving to Brian as if we were lifelong friends and as if I'd been expecting him, which I probably have been, knowing it was only a matter of time before we got sussed. Acknowledging my arrival with faint recognition, Brian continued his dialogue with Barney.

'This is protocol, Francis. You gave me every confidence that you could resolve these issues. You clearly aren't in control of the situation,' Brian said authoritatively. As much as he is bound to enjoy his senior title, secure pension plan and magnificent Mercedes (funded by my council tax) I could tell he certainly didn't take any pleasure from this responsibility.

'We've carried out all the work on your Risk Assessment. The fire exit doors now have thick wooden boards attached. The residents' concerns were isolated incidents,' Barney said, knowing that 'isolated' meant one day per week as opposed to per calendar year.

'I've been called out here *tonight*. They expect something done about this once and for all. I don't like phone calls in the middle of the night. My wife wants to kill me,' Brian said (I knew it! The wife being mad thing, not our imminent closure). I prayed that for the next half hour the Chemical Intakers could keep their fag-stained fingers off the controls. 'Let's take a walk.' I had no choice but to follow. If I disappeared back inside, it would have been blatantly obvious that I was off to cut cables and hide hippies.

Barney didn't look at me the entire time we were out there. I would have only added to his unease with my nervous shifting and erratic everything. These grass-smoking, audio-bullying, techno whores were booming us into bankruptcy. Brian placed his hand on the fire exit door. He ran his palm down the large stencil artwork on our new sound barrier that Harley installed only a few days earlier. I wished Brian was admiring our creativity, but instead, he was feeling for vibrations.

'Not as loud as I was expecting,' said Brian, the best news we could have hoped for, all things considered. The reefer-toking ravers kept the volume down. I wanted to buy them all a 'bifta' for their troubles.

'It's the Morrisseys. They don't like the thought of living next to a nightclub,' said Barney, covering his tracks.

'The Havana is way louder than us,' I libel. My breath must have reeked of alcohol. I should have taken a swig of Crème de menthe before coming out – the barman's mouthwash.

'You can expect a series of checks in the near future,' said Brian. Before I got the chance to probe, the wooden doors suddenly started to shudder. So near, yet so far. If only we had taken the conversation back across to his car once he had finished molesting our fire exit.

'What's that noise there? I felt some movement,' said an increasingly concerned Brian, ear pressed against the door frame.

'Might be a certain song, they're all different aren't they?' A shaky attempt at decoy.

'Pipes. Someone's flushed a toilet. Old building, that's all,' said Barney. Pushing his luck, he asked Brian if he wanted to head up to the club to have a look for himself, which made me wonder if Barney values his toes. Brian could turn to leave reasonably satisfied, but Barney verged on shooting himself in the foot. If Brian took one look at the clientele and the size of the speakers they had brought in, we would have been branded rogue traders and shut down, finished.

'No, I'll let you get back to work. I shall report my findings and be in touch. I like the artwork on the door by the way. Different,' said Brian. Phew.

We briefly told Dylan about our lucky escape and then headed upstairs to the club together. Had we known this event was going to be so busy we would have hired some portable air-cons. The cooling units also act as dehumidifiers and extract moisture from the air, namely sweat. When the basins that collect the sweat get full, it is my glamorous job to pull them out, carry them across to the toilets and pour the contents down the pan. There have been a number of times when I have carried the containers, full of raver sweat, through the club, only to have the same revellers stick their hands deep into the bucket and splash their faces with it, thinking that it's normal water!

These strange creatures that we rely on every Friday are hard work and high risk, but we have little choice in the matter. I often ask Barney why they couldn't be fans of something nice, instead of psych trance acid house bullshit. As much as I dread the awful screech, we are aware that it's the sound of the pound. Funk'd Up Fridays are far more lucrative than anything else we have tried, but the risks are insurmountable. Barney says 'Who dares, wins,' and we have certainly been daring with this lot. The floor is trembling from their bass bins, which one of the sound junkies proudly told us were '18k Martin Audio Void LabSubs' – enough to power Glastonbury.

Barney and I took the back staircase and walked down to the vacant Bomb Bar, staffed by Lisa. It was clear that she hadn't had much to do, as she was texting away on her phone.

'They need to turn it down. Bits of plaster have been falling from the ceiling.'

'We're on for six grand,' said Barney. 'The entire industry is done for, might as well take what we can.' Who loses, dares.

On the Monday morning that followed, the Chief-EHO Brian Reeve – Prig. Killjoy. Gloom – took a Noise Abatement Order out on us. A breach of notice would simply involve having any sound audible from outside the building and would almost certainly see the club shut down. I even had Harley fit more sound board, far denser (and more expensive) than your typical plasterboard. Harley brought his beautiful Staffordshire terrier with him and she shat all over the carpet. I told little Pippen not to worry because she wasn't the first bitch to take a crap on the floor in the club. Thanks to Funk'd Up Fridays, this was unfortunately true.

The only reason any of this is relevant is that Sammy Fish, stood here in our venue, has started to do these very same events at The Havana Club. Without an Abatement Order. Not only does he take all the decent partygoers, now he wants our scummy raver crowd as well. His club has so many different rooms he could pull it off, too. The outcasts of the clubbing world do have some redeeming qualities. The tree huggers spend every penny they have in pursuit of getting wrecked – *obliterated* even. They also visit specifically for the music, so we're sure to have them for the entire night (or at least until they get kicked out) because they're not going to find the ear-crushing noise anywhere else. Until now. The H Club has muscled in on the scene.

I head back down to the bar after an unproductive promotional session (the internet bill hasn't been paid, so I played Solitaire instead) and Sammy the sea urchin is still here. He buys round after round of shots, showing off his wads of cash. He certainly drinks like a fish, a fat one like a grouper. He turns to play on the Deal or No Deal fruit machine. As I watch him stick a couple of quid in the bandit, I am half expecting him to win the £70 jackpot and leave with that money too.

Just as I've written the entire night off as a total failure, Mandara takes over the decks to give a shout out to a couple of girls who have arrived. They look like they're celebrating a birthday (the big flashing '18' badge and massive shot glass round her neck being a slight giveaway), whilst Snoopy is left chatting with Sammy. The birthday girl comes over to the bar to fill her titanic canteen of a shot glass. She barely looks old enough to come to one of our under-eighteen nappy nights, so I commend her on her brilliant disguise. Who is going to question someone with a badge? She's probably only fourteen and stole it from Clinton Cards earlier today.

I still can't believe he's in here. I should really make an effort to show how professional I am, so I stride over. I would never let something as trivial as cut-throat competition to the death compromise my ability to make polite conversation. As I approach them, Snoopy puts a fag in his mouth and heads off, which means it'll be a bloody one-to-one.

But instead of making small talk with me, he plods over to buy the girls a couple of drinks from Barney before saying his goodbyes. He shakes everyone's hand except mine – I am snubbed by the manky manatee. I hate this guy as much as when he swam in. Slippery Fish.

12

At the end of our particularly dull shift, (apart from the gate-crashing of one Mr Fish: Prick. Prick. Prick), we power down the bar and leave Dylan to set the alarm and lock up. As soon as we get in my Beemer, Snoopy is whinging about Barney's reluctance to price all drinks at £1.

'I'd do things so differently, I really would.'

'What? Barney agreed to do some £1 drinks and even dropped Stevie Mac! *You* should have called Stevie, not me. I love the guy,' I profess.

'We could smash this town if there weren't so many fucking restrictions! Every time I come up with something Barney is there to shoot me down,' he exclaims, having drunk far too much tonight.

'It's his name on the licence. If something goes wrong, he's the one up shit creek. Will you let him use you as a paddle?' I ask as we approach his stop. 'I need to see if Gemma's home. She's been staying at her dad's recently and I wonder if she's ever going to come back.'

Why is nothing ever easy? Goodnight Snoopy, you barmy beagle.

*

6.34am. Fuck. Ante meridiem, not post.

I have slept in. Again.

My head has only just landed on planet pillow and it's already time to re-orbit the club for the early morning beer delivery. With less than three hours sleep, it's back to work I go. I might as well have taken a duvet with me yesterday. Barney is going to kill me. Damn you, amaretto. My alarm track is 'Forever' by Drake, which seems quite fitting, really. I am always either at the club, or late for the club, and it really is starting to feel like *forever*. Surely signing for the delivery should be Dylan's job.

I roll over and, much to my surprise, Gemma is lying next to me. I've missed her and she must have missed me too. She probably tried to wake me up but I'd sleep through anything, a song by Drake being no exception. I brush her hair away from her face and she is now wide awake and staring at me, through weary but beautiful green eyes. Even in her fatigued, faded and makeup-less face, she still manages to look gorgeous. The only gal I know who doesn't need her beauty sleep.

'I know, I'm sorry. I'm late again. Will you be here when I get back?' I whisper.

'Just go, mind the ice. I'll be here.' She is surprisingly sweet, considering she has only had twenty of her forty desired winks. We still haven't spoken properly since our row. 'Love you Harry, you smelly ole thing.'

She is delirious from sleep, but hearing her say that she loves me feels amazing. With that, she rolls over and reaches for Nibbles. She shouldn't have favourites when it comes to our children, but Nibbles has been around the longest.

'You make the bed look so comfy. Look after Pandi. Love you.' I say, hating my job as much as she does.

I clamber towards the kitchen, hoping there is something in the fridge to wake me up. There is a third of a bottle of Chardonnay, a can of energy drink and some milk. She'll need the milk for her cereal, so I'll have to settle for the wine. With my bottle of Burgundy grapes, I stumble down the stairs and into the bathroom. I throw open the cabinet doors to grab the mouthwash. I wish it was Crème de menthe.

Making a dash for the car, I slip on a concrete slab and go arse over tit onto the drive. What a great start to the day. If I miss the delivery, this French farce will have been for nothing. I steady myself and spit the oral acid on to the floor, much of it landing on my shoes. If only I could have just woken up earlier and brushed my teeth like a normal, civilised and sober human being. The car is completely frosted over and the mechanism is frozen stiff. It's time to take it old school. I dig deep into my baggy pockets, pull out my lighter and crouch behind our brown wheelie bin, which is intended for vegetating foliage, even though we don't have a garden. I wonder if I can get a discount on my council tax. I spend way too much time with Barney.

Squatting like a Chinaman, I hover the flame of my lighter, which is painful to spark with cold hands, over the end of the key. I am careful not to burn the plastic or my frost-bitten fingers. A thin veil of smoke surrounds the metal and in this moment I am showcasing equal measures of resourcefulness and idiocy. With the car key now smouldering (as hot as I can get it without needing to claim on my third party fire and theft), I pray for a miracle. To my utter astonishment it actually works, although I did turn the lock with far more vigour this time. The car reluctantly awakens, its engine wishing it had a snooze button too. I am amazed to find that the inside seems even colder than outside.

The radio comes on and I am happy to hear the familiar repartee of Stevie Mac, chatting about the miserable weather. My dear friend Stevie; also victim to the 'late night' versus 'early morning' battle, even if his late nights will no longer be spent with us. Wine, fags, a functioning vehicle, Gemma back where she belongs, Stevie on the radio (thankfully not playing the song 'Forever') and only forty-four minutes into my delivery window. With my eyes stinging from lack of sleep, I persevere through the treacherously icy roads. It's never the drinking that causes my hangovers. It's the waking up that does it.

I rush through two red lights in quick succession and pray that I don't hit an early morning jogger or dog walker. That would be horrible. I'd never make my delivery. Fourteen minutes to seven. Barney is going to flip. Heads the supplier wins, tailgating, I lose.

I follow the one-way system, chancing it by taking a presumed shortcut that is designated for 'Taxis Only.' As I turn up the side street, my bald tyres violently struggle to keep on the straight and narrow. I desperately try to steady the steering wheel. Do I turn into the bend when slipping on ice? Brake? Probably neither. I do both. The car assumes a mind of its own. I am powerless to stop it. As I pass The Nutshell, Britain's smallest pub, I lose control and brace myself for the crash. I grab the steering wheel with white knuckles and grit my teeth in panic. Time seems to stand still and my mind is rendered incapable of thought. I have no reaction at my disposal other than a silent gasp as my body fills with dread, every extremity paralysed. Fuck. Travelling at only three, maybe four miles an hour, the front bumper of the car smashes into a metal black bollard, making a harrowing sound of metal meeting metal. The hand painted and regal bollard is now wrapped around the front of my headlight. The sound of shattering glass and bent bumper is almost as bad as the sound of a lorry full of stock driving away undelivered.

My icy incident wouldn't even result in a failed MOT. Nobody needs two headlights, surely. MOT stands for Mighty. Oriental. Tit. If it wasn't for that bollard I would have driven into The Nutshell, making Britain's smallest pub even smaller. In my haste, I failed to realise that the grit lorry is too large to fit through this narrow street. Without any taxis being out and about to melt the snow, I just melted my hopes of making it into work on time. Missed delivery aside, I am lucky to be alive, because that was a close one.

I slowly back out on to the main road, using the steering wheel, gears and pedals as little as possible. All I need now is someone to come up behind me and beep. Back to the original route, I race (just not as fast) round the one-way, hoping that the front of my car isn't beyond repair. The roads are my labyrinth and the club is my Minotaur, although I am far from Theseus and my BMW sails are definitely still black. On the approach, there is no lorry to put my worries to rest. I park up in the lay-by, turn off the engine with a sigh and assess the damage to the front of the car. My worst suspicions are confirmed: the framework is horribly disfigured. The car looks as bad as I feel. I reach for the bottle of wine and kick the door closed. I'm surprised the wheels don't fall off and the tank doesn't explode.

I manage to force the door to the club, after much frustration. I try to deactivate the alarm in the dark, which resembles a game from the *Crystal Maze* with an 'automatic lock-in' if it's not done quickly enough, but it seems to be broken. Typical. Lo and behold, a failed delivery note has been pushed through the letter box. I check the delivery time. The draymen were here at 6.54am. I have missed them by a matter of minutes. If I hadn't decided to play bumper car dodgems with a big metal post, I would have made it.

I rifle for my mobile to text Barney and break the bad news, but I've left the phone at home. If bad things come in threes, I don't know how many hat tricks I've achieved this morning and it's only just gone 7am. I walk through to the bar and fumble around for the fuse board to turn the house lights on. Cracking my hip on the side of the pool table, I head through to the front of the bar, finishing off the last of the cheap wine as I go.

'HOLY SHIT! What the *fuck* are you doing here?' I strain. I am more frightened by Dylan's unexpected presence than I was when my car was ambling towards the bollard. 'I thought you were locking up behind me last night.'

Dylan is still wearing his suit from the night before, minus the tie, with his shirt hanging out. He looks far scruffier than when I last saw him, mere hours ago. He looks like he's been drinking from the moment I left. He is sprawled out across the sofa, looking a lot less comfortable than he would have done before my angry arrival. There are a number of empty glasses surrounding him, many with empty shot glasses in them. My guess is that Dylan has worked his way through our Drop The Bomb menu four times over. There is also a pint glass with a carton's worth of fag butts festering in brown murk. If Barney knew that Dylan was not only on site after hours unsupervised, but smoking *and* drinking, there would be hell to pay. I'm not prepared to put coins on his eyes for the boatman.

'I passed out, innit. Why are you up so early? There were no taxis so I bunked here,' he says, rubbing his eyes. 'I was gonna clean the bar this morning so you didn't have to come in. You want a drink?' He hasn't shed any light on his real reason for still being here, as I offered to drive him home last night.

'No I don't want a drink! It's seven in the morning! You were here this whole time and we still missed the delivery? Barney is going to kill me.' My moral high ground unconvincing, considering I am holding a wine bottle in my hand. My high horse is more of a Shetland pony.

'Delivery? That's today? Oh shit! That must've been what all that banging was about. I thought it was Belinda trying to get back in,' he says, revealing the missing piece to the puzzle.

'Belinda? Drink at *her* pub and make *her* miss their fucking delivery.' I wish my car had driven into him instead.

'That's not a bad idea,' he replies, and I'm sticking the car in reverse to finish the job.

'Our delivery is the same time every week.' I notice the ash all over the bar top.

'What day is it today?' Dylan is the very reason I drink.

'Your mum must have fucked a hedgehog to produce a prick like you.'

'Bel wasn't even drinking, it was just me. You don't understand –' he says, but I'm not listening. I continue with my tatty ivory tower.

'Things go in one ear and out the other. Mind like a sieve. No, not even that: a colander.' Having watered and planted his seed, Dylan now leaves me to clear up his weeds. I finally have a use for my brown bin.

'She wanted to stay, but I wouldn't let her,' he replies. 'I only had her in here cause I was lonely.' And by 'lonely' he means 'horny.'

'You'll be lonely sat down the job centre on your tod.' I'll need more mouthwash because I can taste the spite.

'I'll call them up and ask them to deliver again. I'll go and pick it up from wherever it came from. Here, look, I made you something,' he says, making me feel guilty for my outburst.

'Yes, you will pay for the redelivery.' Barney would expect just that. 'You're on thin ice and I've slid on enough ice today, thank you very much.' Dylan's usefulness as a scapegoat is his greatest attribute, outweighing most, if not all, of his otherwise sub-average traits.

'I'm new to this, bro. I've only ever been a doorman, I can't do what you do. You make it look so easy.' Flattery really does get you anywhere. If anywhere is a supplier depot.

'What you made me then? It better be good,' I say, jokingly.

'Over here. I did it when I was waiting for Belinda.' He points at a print-out he has stuck up behind the bar. It reads:

THE LANDLORD'S PRAYER

Our lager, which art in barrels, hallowed be thy drink.
Thy will be drunk (I will be drunk) at home as it is in tavern.
Give us this day our foamy head, and forgive us our spillages,
As we forgive those who spill against us.

And lead us not into incarceration, but deliver us from hangovers.
For thine is the beer, the bitter and the lager.
Forever and ever,
BARMEN

'Like it? It's the bible, innit,' he says, impressed with his copy and paste efforts.

'I love it. Let's have that drink, bro.' I am warmed by his peace offering.

'Fancy some Jameson's Scotch?' He has clearly taken a liking to it.

'Jameson's isn't a Scotch, it's from Ireland, and I think you've had enough of that for the both of us. How about some of that Grappa we confiscated from that weird guy on Friday?' That's if he hasn't caned all of that as well. 'But only if we recite the Landlord's Prayer, okay?'

'I've got shot glasses!' he says, producing some orange ones from Halloween, unused because Barney said they were too big and we'd be giving away too much stock. Stock that Dylan was only going to drink anyway. 'Would you rather muff out Carmen Electra with a yeast infection or get shagged by Katy Perry's mum with a strap on?'

We prop ourselves at the bar as he struggles to read his own poster. He pours our shots of awful box wine, spilling more on the bar top than into the glasses. Dylan decides to propose a toast to missed deliveries, and I, to smashed cars. Still four hours from noon, we realise that these are the moments we'll look back on and despite our doomed attempt at a productive day, over before it's even begun, we toast and drink and enjoy. Gemma and Barney are going to kill me, but I'm finished feeling sorry for myself. What's done is done.

I bet Stevie is playing 'Good Life' by One Republic right now. He's not wrong.

13

Somewhere in between figuring out how to get stock for the evening and haranguing my assistant manager about his general existence, the landline rings and Dylan makes no attempt to answer it.

'You're not getting the phone in case that's Belinda too?' I shout, before picking up. 'Hello, Battersea Dogs' Home.' That was old the first time it was said, at the dogs' home itself.

'Harry, I tried calling your mobile but Gemma answered.' Snoopy sounds surprisingly awake considering he is never up before four in the afternoon.

'Shit, was she angry?'

'Nah, she's fine, we had a quick chat, she's cool,' he says, much to my relief. 'Listen, something's come up.' I instantly begin to scan my memory banks for any possible plans I may have made and subsequently forgotten.

'Oh, what's that then?' Hopefully whatever's come up will explain what would have only resulted in a let-down.

'Things haven't been going well at the club.' A painful understatement, considering the missed deliveries, missed phone calls, missed sleep and missed missus. 'As I keep saying, we've been missing crucial opportunities.' And missed opportunities.

'Tell me about it. I missed the draymen today so we're not going to have half the stuff we need,' I say loudly, for Dylan's benefit more than Snoopy's.

'I don't mean that, I mean everything,' he says, putting me right back in front of the depressing bollard again. I've had a shit morning. If I wanted to continue feeling shit, I would have left my car wrapped around a pole and sat in the snow.

'It's been naff, man. Any new ideas for the weekend? Could do with a good take and soon.' I hope that Snoopy can pull a rabbit (that lays golden eggs) out that hat of his.

'It's bringing me down. Barney never commits.' A real sense of distress enters his weary voice and I'm trying to imagine what Barney may have done to upset him. 'All last week I tried to have a serious discussion with him. Every time I collared him he was bartering with the council to reduce his rates. Before that, when I wanted to run some dates for events by him, he was on the phone telling the bank to change the wireless card machine for a wired one, to save money.' He sounds exasperated, as anyone would do trying to describe a day in the life of the wily Barney.

'He's trying to cut costs. We should be thankful we don't have to spend all week having difficult conversations like those,' I say, though this one is starting to head in that direction.

'My passion is to entertain. That's what I do best. That's why I got into this line of work.' I don't like where this is going. I close the door to the reception booth behind me so that Dylan doesn't hear what's being said. 'The stuff Barney is doing isn't helping my reputation as a DJ and it's getting worse and worse.'

'Do you want me to talk to Barney? This isn't anything that can't be solved.'

'I've already spoken to him. He said that I might be out of the job next week,' he replies, spitting out his words as if he was shouting out a drink promo to an empty dance floor.

'You would have caught him in a bad mood, mate.'

'Fuck that,' he says, his most aggressive contribution thus far. 'I don't want to be told that I'm out of the job, Harry. I don't need to be hearing that shit, do I?'

'I don't know what you want me to say, Snoopy?' I moan, trying to sound understanding, even though I have enough trouble within our ranks in the form of Dylan. I don't need Snoopy becoming an issue too.

'I want you to come with me.' I didn't take Snoopy for someone that needed back up to talk to someone as unintimidating as Barney.

'Barney's in later. Come to the club and we'll find a way to budget whatever it is that you need,' I say, maintaining a professional stance that I hope he will appreciate. 'He'll be fine, trust me.'

'I want you to come with me to The Havana.'

He carves and slaughters, slowly and quietly.

Without any warning, I have been stabbed in the back, Caesar style. The words hang in the air like one of Dylan's lager farts: overpowering, with bits in it. I don't know what to do. I don't know what to say. With

Snoopy I've always known where I've stood and have always been able to speak my mind. I'm starting to wonder if perhaps he's actually *out* of his mind.

'What do you mean *The Havana*?' I ask, a concept so foreign that even Harley and I would blend in as locals compared to it.

'Sammy offered me the manager's job,' he says, with no regret. It's as if he wants me to congratulate him. 'It's more money, more freedom and a better title.'

'Just like that? You're going to up and leave? Snoopy man, you can't be serious. We've been doing everything to fuck them up and now you want to go and *run it*?' I challenge. 'You're just going to ditch us?'

He mentions 'title' as if it's a determining factor. I would happily allow Snoopy to call himself the manager here, gladly relinquishing the designation. I already call him my 'promotional manager,' which has perhaps compounded the problem – too many chiefs and not enough Indians. Despite employing Harley.

'Barney and his club are on the way out. I've spoken to Sammy and he wants to rinse the town,' he says, truly buttered up and bribed by the greasy haddock. 'He's the side you want to be on.' Sammy infiltrated our squad, right in front of me. When they were chatting at the Deal or No Deal machine, it looks like Snoopy took the banker's offer and dealt, despite not knowing what our final box contains. I just hope our box isn't a blue.

'There is no way I'm leaving and you shouldn't either. Please listen to me. You can't do this. Hang up, ring me back and let's try this one again.'

'It's already sorted. He's arranged a new flat for me, and a car, too. You don't get anything like that where you are now. At least think about it.' He has already distanced himself from us by highlighting that where I am is somewhere he is not.

'I don't need to think about it. Barney is your friend, and so is everyone else that works here,' I snivel, but deep down, I know his mind is made up. Snoopy has always been immovably stubborn. 'You will be against us. Sammy is looking for a war, all or nothing.'

'Don't be part of the nothing. I won't let him stitch you up,' he tempts, as if his phone call is an act of kindness. The way he's talking suggests that this has been in the pipeline for a long time, and I wasn't privy to any of it. It was going on behind my back, which is now up against the wall. I rub my hand against my head, as if this is imaginary. I'd rather miss a year's worth of deliveries than have to take this call again. 'Sammy is a nice person once you get to know him.' Basically: he is a complete tosser, but I'd get used to it.

'The Havana is our *enemy*. You think moving there will change that? Undo the past?' I plead and this is the last of it, the dregs at the very bottom of the barrel. I have no argument left in me.

'I've asked you to come and work for me and it's the smart choice. Pride comes before the fall,' he says, cockily. I never once called myself his boss or his manager, yet he is now offering me the opportunity to work 'for' him. He hangs up, but he doesn't ring back.

Deceit. Deceit will come before the fall.

If we are *The Expendables*, Snoopy definitely isn't expendable.

All of the nights we shared, plotting our success. The countless shifts we worked together, some we enjoyed, most we simply suffered, but as one. The unforgettable lock-ins we hosted together, the stories we shared and the memories we were creating. The thousands of shots and glasses and bottles we raised together in cheers. The lifts I gave him to and from work. The lift in confidence he gave me when we were in full flow at the club, when we were in our element. The lift we were taking together to the top floor penthouse suite of sweet success. Now my lift is stuck in between floors, waiting for a maintenance man that will never show up. Snoopy has taken the stairs.

I can't even bring myself to call him 'Snoopy' anymore and have decided to refer to him only as Dick. I *hate* him, nearly as much as I hate someone that comes to the bar and orders tap water. He has gone from being my closest friend to my arch enemy in one fell swoop.

Snoopy is dead to me. For enough money he would deceive himself.

14

'You can't be serious, Barney. It isn't going to work,' I say, uncharacteristically, as I am open to most ideas. I even looked into that laser tag thing for him. 'Just because New Year's Eve is on a Friday this year, doesn't mean it has to be a Funk'd Up one. We haven't even advertised!'

'I had no intention of hosting another bloody rave, but with Snoopy gone, we need something. I had to accept.' He has a valid point. A building full of dirty, noisy greebos is better than an empty, quiet and clean one. 'I tried Stevie Mac, but he's already booked somewhere else. We've hosted Cranium Crushers before and they did pack the place, to be fair. The venue they had pulled out last minute.'

'And why did they pull out? Because they realised that Cranium Crushing isn't the best way to bring in the New Year.' Yes, they did pack the place last time, but it wasn't without incident. They blocked all the toilets, which flooded the club, and stole the DMX lighting effect controller. 'We want something classy, not a scene from *Trainspotting*.'

'We don't have a choice,' he says. 'I'll make it up to you, I promise.' Dick has single-handedly given me the worst birthday present of all time.

'This isn't your fault.' I stare vacantly at the screen behind the bar, still advertising Dick's set tonight, which he'll no longer be playing for us.

'Thanks, Harry. I know how much Gemma hates the Funk'd Up stuff.' He's absolutely right. She can't stand it. She calls it 'ping-ping-whoop' music. 'Maybe get her down here earlier? By the time they're in full swing, she'll be too drunk to care.'

'Considering our last piss up, I don't think starting earlier is the way forward,' I reply – the steps we've now taken back makes moving forward too much of a trek. 'I'm going to have to tell her. She won't be happy though. She has all her friends coming down for my birthday –'

'She'll be happy because you're here and her mates will be happy because she's here,' he interrupts, trying to put me at ease. I'm not sure it will be quite as simple as that, even though it should be. 'We'll give them loads of bubbly, to keep them sweet. And the money from the promoters – half of it's yours. A bonus.' I think I'd rather pay to *not* have them here.

'I can't take your money, but I will have some of that bubbly,' I say, as the telly catches my eye again. We're going to have to turn this screen off. If I see Dick's name up there one more time it won't be fit for the bin, let alone eBay.

'It might not be so bad,' he says, which is true. They've only got the toilets to block this time because they already own our DMX thingy. 'It's just one night, right?'

'Yeah, one night,' I say, disheartened that my birthday *and* New Year's Eve – what is meant to be the pinnacle of the year – is being dismissed as just any other night. 'I'll find a way to break it to her. I hope for my sake it doesn't end in something else breaking, like my legs.'

'Gemma is cool, she'll be fine.' Describing her like that doesn't wash. She isn't going to be 'cool,' like the other side of the pillow, or a gentle breeze. I'm not saying that she isn't cool, because she is, but she is a complex type of cool, like the freezing point of mercury. 'We won't have to pay Snoopy now. Think of the money we've saved!' I want to ask Barney if he's part Chinese too, the penny pincher.

*

The phone call to Gemma could have gone worse. She knows way more swear words than that. Being woken up this morning didn't leave her as 'cool' as Dick described, or at least not with me. I called her from the bar landline and she was nice as pie, until she heard my voice. When I told her about the Skull Fuckers, I was glad to be on the other end of the phone or my cranium would have been truly crushed.

After eventually managing to convince her to come down earlier, I cancelled our receptionist for the night, as there is no longer a door take to be had. She handled the news better than Gemma did, even though she's £50 out of pocket and now has the night off with no time to make plans. Thankfully, if she knows any swear words she waited until I hung up to say them.

Dylan and I spend the rest of the early evening cleaning, whilst working our way through the Grappa. He isn't thrilled about having to spend the night resuscitating rebellious grungers; his attitude towards the unexpected event more lukewarm than cool.

'On the screen it says Snoopy is playing tonight, but he isn't.' Dylan *is* fit for the bin. 'Barney didn't seem very angry about Snoopy leaving.'

'Barney sees it as ten more cases of stock that you failed to open the door for.'

'Would you rather be really, really happy but everyone thought you were a total nutcase – like, mentally unfit – or never happy, but considered sane?' I have no idea which I'd choose. The first option pretty much describes every pothead we can expect in the club later and the second one is likely to describe us, the staff, stuck behind the bar.

'Next!' I am reluctant to think about how I feel or want to feel, at a time when my mood and mental state seems to be completely dictated by others.

'Okay, let me think. Would you rather everything in your life happened twice as quickly, or at half the speed?' This question seems even more stupid that the last. 'Belinda wishes it happened at half the speed.'

'Jesus, man. If you came as slowly as you cleaned, she would be the happiest girl alive. People would think she's a nutcase,' I say, thankful for his silly questions, distracting me from the disappointment of tonight. New Year's Eve will regain its disenchanted status once more. 'You alright? Your questions aren't nearly as vulgar today.'

'I bust my nut in her didn't I, got it all out my system,' he says, and we're right back in the gutter again. 'Do you want a wrong one? Cause I've got loads.'

'I don't doubt that for a second, or half a second, however fast your life might be travelling.' Part of me wants to hear a cringe-worthy one, but I can't encourage him, even if they are becoming a bit of a guilty pleasure.

*

Gemma and her friends show up at 9pm and are the first to arrive. Barney has only just got back from the wholesalers with the stock and the fact that they are open on New Year's Eve is the first stroke of luck we've had all week. The Cranium Crushers have also shown up and unloaded their myriad of speakers. This counteracts my stroke of luck, with a scratch of misfortune.

Harley and Dylan are frantically loading the fridges. I give Gemma an apologetic hug and comment on how great she looks. I greet her friends, but none of them wish me a happy birthday. Instead, they opt for looking around disinterestedly at our lifeless bar. Faces. Like. Thunder. Where the fuck is Mandara with the music? Embarrassed by their lack of enthusiasm, I give Gemma a kiss and get back to work. In spite of his rapid speed, all of Harley's labels are facing forward, as if he got a ruler and a spirit level out. I bet Dylan's bottles are upside down and back to front.

'She's gonna kill me when these tree-hugging vegans upstairs turn their system on,' I whisper. 'Without Mandara's music down here, there'll be nothing to distract them from the crumbling ceiling.' There is only one thing that will serve to entertain the girls: some classic Harley charm. 'Can you look after Gemma's mates' for me? Chuck a bottle about, mule.'

'Not a problem, Chop Suey. What's on the menu then?' he asks, struggling to stand. I've been so self-absorbed that I haven't even asked Harley how he's feeling. 'Coupla nice ones here, buddy. I like the one in the short skirt.'

'Very funny. Gemma doesn't need your advances. She's in a mood with me as it is.'

'How are we, girls? Who am I kissing at midnight then? You look up for it,' he says, pointing at Stacey, who seems delighted at the prospect and the girls laugh. Only Harley could get away with comments like that: Dylan should be taking notes. 'You look like a four-pinter, which isn't too bad. You got here early to claim first dibs, I like your style.'

His tongue in cheek vibe has them lined up along the bar, lapping up his company. He's just a nice guy to be around. Because of him, they no longer think this is a shit place to be. He'll have one of their tongues in his cheek within the hour. Barney tells Harley to 'always appear available,' which he says is from the film *Coyote Ugly*. Trust him to watch a movie about trying to get people to spend money at a bar. I hope he doesn't expect us to dance on the worktop in hot pants.

'You're not a four-pinter Gemz,' I say and she grins at me. 'You're *fourteen!*'

'Shut it you,' she says, before blowing me a kiss. 'Where's our drinks then, buster? I'll need to be pretty drunk to be snogging you later.'

'We've auctioned off Harley to Stacey for drink money,' I say, and she pretends to rummage for her purse. 'Barney said that you gals can have all the free champagne you want.'

'Really?' says her friend Kelly, followed by Stacey, followed by Harley.

'Yes, really! It's not the cheap stuff either,' I reply, even though it's the cheapest stuff we do. But it does come in an attractive bottle and they'll never know the difference. Barney has been very gracious, but I know it's because keeping pretty girls here is the only way to get the lads to stay for that extra drink or two, the drinks that Harley and I will insist they buy for them.

'You're a sweetheart,' says Gemma, and the animosity and tension from the past couple of days has subsided. I'm back in her good books, which I can't wait to read tonight. 'Can I have some sugar syrup in mine, please?'

'I know how you like it, babe, even though you're sweet enough already,' I say, which makes Harley stick his fingers in his throat, keeping the group of girls giggling.

'What about me, *babe*? Am I sweet enough already?' says Harley, in his highest voice possible, before licking my face, covering me in slobber. The girls start squealing, Mandara comes crashing through the front doors with his CD hold-all over his shoulder and Barney emerges from the back door with a cheer, Charis following behind him.

Who needs Dick when you have fannies like these?

*

The bar is busier than I was expecting. There must be a good seventy people in here and Big G has arrived to lend us a hand. Barney has taken responsibility for the club because he knows there won't be any EHO officers on duty on New Year's Eve. With the Noise Abatement Order, this has to be the very last one. It's a shame that Mr Morrissey and his surly wife don't enjoy a good 'skank' (which is what the liberal mud-slingers upstairs call dancing) – then we could all skank the New Year in together.

Harley and I have sold £400 worth of drinks each and it isn't even midnight yet. Mandara has the music turned right up to distract people from the ravers upstairs. Apart from Big G carting one of them away for peeing on someone in the smoking section, we've kept things under control. Lisa pulled the short straw and has been sent upstairs (much to her disgust), but I couldn't be happier, and for the most part, sane.

Gemma is dancing away with her friends and Mandara has been calling their names out over the mic every few minutes, which they can't get enough of. I think I may have under-estimated our very own DJ Man-Dem, as he's always been the supporting act to Dick. I knew he was capable on the decks and passionate about what he does, but he has really found his form lately and a serious contender in the DJ stakes.

I ask Big G to keep pouring a pint I'm holding (and to watch out for Harley making a reach for his tap) and head over to my fiancée, as we're coming up to the countdown. Gemma sees me edging my way across the dance floor and her face lights up. *She* is my DMX controller. My mental state is completely dictated by her and her ordinance alone would see me happy. Mandara does a huge shout out for 'the boss and his boss' and Gemma's friends even cheer for us, which is a remarkable turnaround from their slapped-arse faces just a few hours ago. Maybe Barney was right, maybe it is this simple.

I pull Gemma in close to me and her glassy emerald eyes are trying to tell me so much, over the blaring music from Mandara's speakers below us and Martin's Void LabSubs above us. They are telling me that she's sorry for being so hard on me. That she is glad that we're together, and that no amount of tree hugging could ever come between us. They are telling me that they love me. They are saying happy birthday and happy New Year and they are saying kiss me. Five, Four, Three, Two and we are One. I have won. Dick can have his club, he can have the night and he can have the town. I have Gemma and that's good enough for me. I let go even though neither of us wants to. We could stand on this dance floor in one another's embrace until Barney is switching the lights off and Dylan is pretending to lock up.

I head back to the bar because Big G and Harley will need all hands on deck to serve the four groups of lads that have walked in. I give Gemma another quick kiss and she wishes me a happy New Year, even though her eyes already went to the trouble. I dash through the contented sea of people and there isn't a Fish in sight.

*

As we approach 1am, people start to leave. I send Big G over to Mandara with a drink promo I'd like him to announce, but after a few vigorous attempts at getting our message across, both of them just look at me and shrug. They have a much better view of the dance floor than I do and it would seem that their view is getting better and better as people disperse. I am reminded that they aren't *our* customers at all. We simply borrow them for a time – on loan.

Within ten minutes there is only a scatter of pissheads left. Everyone else has disbanded, dissolved even. This bothers me at the best of times, but tonight Barney has paid for a Temporary Events Notice that allows us to trade until 4am – which is the same number of people we must have left, apart from Gemma and her friends. They've left quicker today than they did when the fire alarm was going off, which, to be fair, sounded better than the music being played upstairs.

Gemma, Kelly and Stacey stagger over to the bar, spilling more than drinking. They pull up some stools and ask me where everyone has gone. Before I get the chance to say 'Where do you think?' Gemma violates me with the most unexpected question. I wasn't even braced with a 'We need to talk' first.

'Would you be mad if we went to The Havana Club?' she mumbles, her eyes lighting up again. I begin to doubt what those eyes of hers have actually been saying.

'Would I mind if you left me on New Year's Eve, on my birthday, to go to *The Havana*?' I clarify, in case someone had interrupted her when she was trying to say something else; something far less offensive and far less cruel. It's like a poorly dubbed martial arts film from the seventies, where the words said don't match the sound heard. 'What the fuck do you mean, would I be mad?'

Harley decides that now is a good time to start sweeping the dance floor. The chance to chat to Stacey isn't worth getting caught in the middle of this.

'Well, everyone has gone and loads of my friends are up there,' she replies. I am starting to realise that nothing in life is simple. Everything is in fact a complex type of lukewarm. 'There's no one here anymore.'

'*I* am, Gemma! Can't you see me stood right here?' I shout, but she is too drunk to reason with. I told Barney this wouldn't work. If it was actual champagne she was drinking instead of a weak cava, she'd already be at The Havana now. 'You would actually leave me to go there? Of all places?'

'No, if you want me to stay, I will.' She turns to her friends, pulling a cheerless face. 'You lot go on ahead.' Gemma slumps her drunken head into her drunken hands and the guilt trip is the longest trek yet.

'You have to come,' says Kelly, driving the wedge that I felt I had only just removed right back in. 'You have to.'

'I can't, I have to stay here,' she replies, talking to her hands, one of which is wearing a ring that means you don't leave your fiancé's bar to visit his arch rival on his birthday.

'You don't *have* to do anything,' I say, and she doesn't. She can do whatever she wants. I just thought that what she wanted was to be with me, through thick and thin, through busy or quiet, through Cranium or Crusher. 'If you want to go, then go.'

'Really?' Her head jolts upright as if she's been struck with a cattle prod.

'Let's stay here,' attempts Stacey, but she isn't strong enough to swim against The Havana current. No one is.

'I'll see you at home. I'm tired,' I mutter, trounced by my fiancée and her even guiltier pleasure. My very own missus wants to go and part with her hard-earned cash, having not spent a penny in here.

This is how the system works. The manual is too complicated to read, but I will be trying to decipher it all night long, instead of reading Gemma's good books, as I had hoped.

And just like all the other sheep, off she goes, baa'ing all the way.

15

'I know we're called The Bomb Bar, Harry, but we need to start stocking something cheaper,' says Barney. 'Stagmeister, maybe? Ice cold and stained, they'll never know the difference. It's only £9 plus vat. With 28 shots to the bottle, that's under 40p a shot! And they don't even get a full shot do they?' he asks rhetorically, which is just as well as I haven't brought my abacus.

'*He* knows, Barney. He knows we stain them. He will have told Sammy to spread the word and it's probably all over the net,' I say, visualising the devastation.

'Snoopy has made his decision,' he says, trying to be realistic. Barney has so much on the line, so much to lose.

'Dick. His name is Dick. Dick by name, Dick by nature,' I reply. 'Snoopy is gone and I'm not going to sit around like his Charlie Brown.'

'Let's get things back to the way they used to be. You and me, mate. I want to see some of that old Harry magic.'

'How about a free shooter with every drink? I'll use that out of date fruit juice and call it Candy Slammer. Then I can get Dylan to kick off up at The Havana and cause a huge scrap, which will clear them out, think that'll work?' I declare, convinced that revenge should be on the specials board all weekend.

'You have to let it go,' urges Barney, as he takes off his glasses to clean.

'I'll fill their club with cockroaches and report Dick for drink driving,' I rant.

'Enough! We get Stevie Mac back for Saturday nights, move Mandara across to Fridays in the bar, find something to replace Funk'd Up Fridays in the club and we're sorted. I need you fully focussed,' he says, with urgency. A key player has left without even handing in his notice, so Barney requires me to be on top form.

'He's an administrator on all our websites. We'll need to change the passwords pronto,' I say: more potential cyber sabotage to worry about. Dick's like a bad password, too short and too weak.

'We'll use his wages to buy some cheap liqueur to decanter into the Sourz bottles.' You can't teach an old dog new tricks when he happens to know them all. If Barney isn't part Chinese, he's Albanian. 'When sales plummet Dick jumps ship,' Barney continues, opening my Cantonese eyes even wider.

'He was too concerned with pulling girls and taking advantage of the free drinks. At least we won't have to buy a new bottle of brandy every other day.' I try to turn these sour grapes into a palatable plonk.

'I have some good news,' he says, and I could do with some. 'Make sure you keep Valentine's Day free. We have a big Live Performance Act lined up.' He is dying to tell me who it is but wants me to ask anyway.

'Who is it, Barney? You should've run it past me first. I'm the one that has to be out there flyering to all the colleges. I'll have to do it on my own now,' I say, sounding impatient even though I am building up my own suspense.

'Only the rap-trio Pyre! Remember when we hosted that girl Asha? She does the warm up for Pyre when they go on tour. I've booked her too, which allows us to call the event The Pyre Showcase,' he says, looking mighty pleased with himself.

'I love it. That Indian chick Asha that I tried to convince Harley to have an arranged marriage with! The Havana won't see this coming. The last person they booked was that munter from a dating show. Famous because no bachelor wants her!' I wonder if I can arrange her marriage to Big G.

'Our events are showstoppers,' Barney says, suitably impressed by our résumé. 'They blow that Fish out the water,' finally joining the We Hate Havana parade.

'We still have four weeks to promote it. Tenner a ticket for the kids, with the over eighteen show to follow, yeah?'

'This time it's free entry to the over eighteen show. If that's what Snoopy wanted, then that's what he'll get,' he says, now leading the parade, trombone in hand.

For the first time since Dick has left, I rate our chances.

*

The last month has been a constant struggle: relentless flyering, endless amounts of driving, hours of internet promotion and the occasional dodgy takeaway in between. Dylan volunteered to stand outside college gates with me, forcing flyers into the hands of as many students as possible. He was reluctant to help me in his spare time, until I explained to him that college girls go to college and a flyer is a reason to talk to them. He never missed a session after that.

Most of the colleges aren't too bad to flyer. You aren't allowed on the actual campus, but if you stand to the side of the gates acting reasonably discreetly, and assure the teaching staff that you'll pick up all the flyers the little shits throw on the floor, then you usually get left to it. It helps to pretend it's a Council event and spin them a line about giving kids something to do in a safe setting.

The difficult part of flyering, apart from timing and a confident pitch, is the ungratefulness of the students. Anyone would think they were spoilt for performers to see. Acts like the ones we book wouldn't normally come to Bury St bloody Albans. The monstrous brats that scrunch them up and throw them back will soon be crying out for events to go to, they just don't realise it yet.

During our flyering run, I only lost my cool with two students, which is pretty good going. One lad said 'Pyre is shit and so is your club'. He almost got a fist full of flyers to the temple. What annoyed me the most is that it's a discernment he'd only be able to make if he has a) attended a Pyre concert, watched them on telly or listened to their albums, b) visited my venue, the hypocrite, and c) been born as a wanker.

The second incident was worse. We were outside a college in Haverhill and a guy not much younger than Dylan walked past him and, completely unprovoked, smacked all the flyers out of his hands.

Two hundred pieces of overpriced card started to float away in the wind as dozens of students laughed at us. More importantly still, there were dozens of pairs of hands quickly leaving the building without flyers in them. Not only did that cost me time and money, it nearly cost me Dylan's assistance. To stand our ground, I grabbed the guy by the scruff of the neck and pulled him down on to his knees. The flyer Nazi crumbled under my unexpected reprisal and picked up all the fallen flyers just as he was told. He didn't find the second part nearly as funny as the first, and Dylan thanked me profusely on the way back to the club.

Yes, I assaulted a school kid.

d) I am also a wanker.

Isolated confrontations aside, the promotion has gone well. Every kebab shop, billboard and phone box in the area has been plastered in our posters. Gemma has been remarkably understanding and even took a thousand flyers to help distribute. She reassured me that any promotion I was doing was a bonus and that the event will sell itself. Everything was going well, until Sammy Fish launched his attack.

You name it, they were saying it. It started off with rumours that the showcase would only be for fifteen minutes instead of the two hours as promised, and then claims that the drink prices would be quadrupled. Soon enough, reports began to surface that Pyre wasn't actually contracted to perform and would only be there to introduce Asha. The list goes on. I wouldn't put much past Sammy Fish, until I read what they were promoting that same evening: 'MYSTERY SPECIAL GUEST.'

Dick used to bring that one out every six months or so when he worked for us and it's near enough his calling card. He knows that this town is so small-minded that if he offers a mystery prize in a question marked box, people's curiosity to find out what's in it will supersede their desire to come to our event. They would rather pass up on the chance to see an A-List music artist at ours to see a reality-tv reject, again. Saying I was more than a little disappointed would be an understatement. I was well beyond a lot. With Sammy's cavalier and bullying approach towards the competition and Dick's guile and astuteness when it comes to tempting the town, they have created a Pied Piper that not only gets the township following them in the conga, but takes the rats from Funk'd Up Fridays too.

What shocked me the most was that when I told Barney, he saw the bad press as something positive! He said that the more attention they place upon us, the more exposure we get. According to him, their vicious hate campaign shows they're threatened. With the event just a day away, we'll find out soon enough if there's no such thing as bad publicity.

Tell that to Gary Glitter.

*

The Showcase night is finally here and Dylan and I have done all we can. With the doors now open, the bar and club is good to go. We stand outside the front for a cigarette, waiting for Harley to arrive. Everyone knows about his health issues now, but no one can quite bring themselves to call it what it is. Cancer isn't something that any of us have had to deal with before, which is quite remarkable, considering there were five key members to our team. I don't know the actual figures, but affecting one in five would sound about right, and yet all of us up to this point have been untouched by it. The last thing I want to do is become a statistic, especially considering forty-four per cent of them are made up on the spot. I've let the Cancer Research people in to do a whip-round with a collection bucket, but that is the extent of my experience (and support). Either way, none of us know what to say, or how to act.

Half an hour before he's due to start, Harley emerges from around the corner. The first thing we notice, and it would be hard to notice anything else, is that his hair is completely gone. Bald as a bowling ball. His hair, or lack of it, is the most visible change yet.

'I'm your new doorman. Does that mean I get a tenner an hour now?' Harley jokes, as he strokes his head, smiling. 'Think of the money I'll save on haircuts. Kristina is loving the lack of pubes. Makes the ole todger look bigger!'

'Namaste, Mahatma! It looks good, really good. The head that is, not the bare ball sack. It suits you,' I say. He's paler than when I last saw him, but he looks nice. Even if he didn't look good, I would have told him so, but luckily I haven't had to lie. He is fortunate to have such a round-shaped head, if 'fortunate' is even a word you can use in such an instance.

'Even if you didn't have cancer, you should have your hair like that,' Dylan says, his face clearly struggling to say the c-word, which is normally 'cunt.' Though none of us have any difficulty saying that. Alarming how the word for a recognised and widespread affliction is taboo around here and no one can bring themselves to say it without great difficulty, but a word many would consider the most offensive they know slips from the tongue like Sigmund. Dylan realises that he is still smoking and turns his head from Harley and exhales sharply, flicking his fag as far away as he can. 'Sorry man, I should have realised.'

'You're a bit late now, Dildo. I already have *le cancér*. I might as well take up smoking myself!' Dylan offers Harley a cigarette as we head into the bar, business as usual.

'At least I don't have to do my hair anymore.' This is going to take some getting used to. He'll have to dig his turban out.

'No need for hair gel, bro,' Dylan says, light-heartedly.

'Or shampoo! A little spit and shine and you're good to go,' I add.

'I might have to borrow some furniture polish! Alopecia, the doc's called it. I call it a free trim. Do you mind if I sit down for a sec?' Harley asks, much to my surprise.

This is a perfectly understandable request, what with the chemotherapy and God knows what else they've done to him. What has stunned me is that he has been *weakened*. Harley has never been weak. He's never once phoned in sick or asked to leave early. He has never had a cough or the flu or been anything less than a pillar of strength for the entire time I have known him. I don't think he has ever asked me for a five-minute break.

'Sit down as long as you want, Tandoori. Have a pint of IPA,' I offer. 'Indian Pale Ale is your favourite, right?'

'No thanks, Chow Mein. Gotta watch my figure, you know.' Harley is aware that he looks thinner and that we needn't mention it.

'You've lost weight,' says Dylan, blindingly oblivious to reality, while he pours himself what looks like a triple brandy, only standing to remind me of Dick.

'I haven't been able to work, have I? Usually I'm lugging building materials around and carrying heavy tools all day. Now I can barely take the dog for a walk. I only drag myself here because you're so crap!' He sounds morbidly jolly, but from that, some of my own cells have been killed.

The ones that live in the part of the heart that feels love and the bit of the belly that suffers from gut wrench. How can someone so strong, capable and independent be reduced to sitting on sofas with the arms still ripped, with the strength for little else?

'And I'm self-employed in my day job, which means I'm not even getting sick pay. They said I have enough in the bank, so I don't get a carer or qualify for incapacity benefits. Tight fuckers.'

The soul. If there are cells in the soul, they have been killed too.

'That's terrible,' I say, paying no attention to the first group of lads that have come in.

'Serves me right, all those cancer jokes I texted you,' he replies, although this time, not entirely jokingly. It is fair to say he must now have a new-found perspective. I suppose it's easy to joke about things until they personally affect you. All Harley needs to do now is experience a landslide in Romania and an earthquake in North Korea and he'll give up on owning a phone altogether.

'You didn't do anything to deserve this. But stick to sending me the Chinese jokes,' I say, jokingly serious rather than my usual approach of seriously joking.

'I've got a good one for you. A bald Indian bartender and a soppy Chinese manager walk into a bar. The Indian one has cancer so the Chinese one turns into a namby-pamby, bumbling idiot,' Harley says, cheekily.

'Very funny. Now if you don't mind, some of us have things to do around here. We can't all sit back with our flip-flops up. I bet you've shaved your head to get out of doing work and there's nothing wrong with you! Should we order pizza?' I have to shout the last bit, as Dylan is pouring a round of shots for our rowdy early arrivals.

'Sorry mate, I'm trying to quit,' replies Dylan, who is going through a phase of saying 'I'm trying to quit' to just about anything you suggest or offer him. Sometimes it produces comical results; this one fell a bit flat. It's not as bad as his 'Like A Boss' phase, which he would say after every sentence. Eating pizza 'like a boss' or missing deliveries 'like a boss'.

'All I can taste is metal, so I'm afraid you're on your own,' Harley replies.

'You can't quit if you get fired first!' I start, but we are sharply interrupted by Mandara, who comes racing through the door leading from the club.

'HK, I need to tell you something A-SAP. Can we go in the back, somewhere private?' asks Man-Dem, who looks frantic as he throws an alphabet of initials at me.

'We already know. We're cool with it. The closet is truly open,' Harley teases, but I am too concerned with what urgent news he needs to impart to make gay innuendo of my own.

'He wants you somewhere private to see his privates! Queer!' squeals Dylan, with so much delight even the four lads he's serving look round and laugh. 'What a mincer!'

'Fuck you guys and no, that doesn't mean I want to fuck you guys. The ladies don't even want you. Harry, please,' says Mandara, having a lot more patience than I would with this lot.

'Let's go to the ice machine room. Harley, don't get up. Please, allow me, Mr Gupta,' I say, getting one last wind-up in before I have to put my manager's hat on.

Mandara and I head into the back room and I agree with Barney, the ice machine is unnecessarily large. Forget the drinks; we should start selling ice.

'Any more ticket sales?' I query.

'Yo, forget that shit, nigga! We got bad news. They ain't coming! Pyre's in Los Angeles signing to a music label or some shit. You need to do something to fix this real quick, otherwise peeps gonna be demanding their money back and shit,' shouts Man-Dem, so loud that everyone queuing up probably already knows. He is saying 'shit' a lot. I'm the one being used as the paddle.

'*Fix this?* The under eighteens are already lining up! The Havana is going to go fucking crazy. What the fuck do we do now? Fuck. Dick will be all over this.' Mandara looks even more flustered. He was hoping I would offer him a solution, rather than a foray of F-words and a broken mop bucket I've just kicked.

'I *need* you to do something, kinfolk. I have to introduce the act to these bambinos. They're gonna take it out on me when they see he ain't here. B-man is on the phone to the agency that was meant to be hooking this up.'

'When it rains, it pours.' My manager's hat should be a waterproof hood on a windbreaker.

'B is screwing, demanding a refund or some shit. That don't help us now though, does it? You need to come up with something and it gotta be good. People will associate me with the No Show. I ain't going down for this shit,' says Mandara, who is just telling it like it is, but I can't help feel that everyone is in it for themselves, looking to cover their own ass. Especially Mandara, who you'd think would be looking to expose it. Still no time for gay jokes.

'Keep it all about you and the music. As soon as Asha rolls up in her shades, these tykes will eat it up and we just keep her set going. Can you do that?' I ask, fairly content with my fire-fighting efforts, even though it's quite clear I'm making it up as I go along. I just hope that two hundred under eighteens don't piss all over my hydrant.

'Thanks man, I can work with that,' says Mandara, clearly not convinced, but we're seriously strapped for options. If my half-baked plan doesn't work, we are forever removed from the local party scene. Mandara gives me a reassuring pat on the back as he darts out of the room, as if I have given an inspirational pep talk. He could have at least carried some ice up with him.

I head back to join the lads and find that the place is starting to fill out. Harley has joined Dylan behind the bar and they are serving at least forty people between them. Harley could be connected to a drip in a hospital gown and he'd still have hopped behind the bar to help his fellow man. I am just about to find Barney up in the club when Natalie – Dependable. Sweet. Nervous – beckons me over. She is our part-time receptionist and panic is written all across her face.

'Harry, they know. Everyone knows,' says Natalie, who looks disconcertingly unnerved as she sits in her booth, surrounded by what seems like hundreds upon hundreds of bags and coats. 'And this clothes rail is about to break.'

'They know what? What's the matter?' I ask, hurriedly.

'These little shits are saying that Pyre isn't coming. They're all going to The Havana instead.' Impossible. There is no way they could have found out before I have.

'No, no way. Tell them it's a hateful rumour spread by a jealous club. Tell them Elvis is going to be here, I don't care, just get them in,' I say mirthlessly, taking the last ten minutes of bullshit out on our poor, minimum-wage earning cloakroom receptionist. They can't be heading to The Havana anyway, they're all under eighteen. I wouldn't put it past Sammy to let them in though. Clinton Cards have run out of badges. I wouldn't put anything past him. It wouldn't surprise me if he paid our act not to show up or even booked their flight to California himself.

I race upstairs, passing a contingent of irritated youths on the way. I hear an assortment of disparaging claptrap such as, 'We knew Pyre wasn't going to be here,' and 'What a rip-off.' The only remark that I consider turning around for is 'Swindling charlatan.'

'Barney, what the fuck? There's going to be a riot down there. If the over eighteens at the bar catch wind of what the staircase is saying, we're in deep shit,' I dispel, showing warranted malcontent.

'They know already? Damn, that was fast,' screeches Mandara from behind his DJ console. He is furiously flicking through one of his many album cases, his task overwhelming enough without my front of house issues.

'Okay, thank you, chat to you tomorrow,' says Barney, finishing up his phone call. His suit jacket is off and scrunched up on the floor, shirt un-tucked and tie loosened. Indication that his call has lasted some time and was less than pleasant.

'What's the verdict? Who was that? What are we going to do?' I ask, slightly more tentatively, not knowing what I want the answer to first. I should have booked the night off.

'That was the talent agent. They're only going to charge us £100 for our act tonight, instead of the original £4,000. They've also told Asha to mention on her fan page that she's appearing at our venue. We've saved ourselves a fortune, not bad hey?' If Barney had taken that phone call from inside the reception booth, I doubt he would have formed the same opinion.

'I don't think the people arguing at the box office care about how much money you've saved. We're fucked and that's all you can say?' I question, wishing I could retract my last comment, considering Barney is doing the best he can with the hand he's been dealt.

'The Havana got lucky. They called a bluff and it came true. Even if Pyre were coming, they'd have spread the rumour and we'd be in the same position,' he explains, equitably.

'Want me to start the music? They're gonna be up here any second,' shouts Mandara.

'Just fucking start,' I say, defeated before we've even begun.

16

'Try to enjoy the night, Harry. Play gracious host to the over eighteens downstairs and get as much money out of them as you can. Downplay Pyre and up-sell Asha,' says Barney, which is pretty much the plan I had. Thinking about it, the idea is ludicrous, considering I've told half the county how lucky they are to get to see Pyre, but I appreciate being relieved of under eighteen duty and leave them to it.

I enter the bar below from the opposite side of the club, so that I can avoid the fracas on the front staircase. Usually I'd be helping Natalie hang up coats or check people in, but not tonight. She will be earning her wage right down to the grubby penny, that's for sure. Natalie will be cursing my name, as I am cursing Dick's, who must be behind the rumour (the rumour which happens to be true). But she doesn't want me in the reception booth with her, she just thinks she does. She can continue to take their money at full price, because she is 'just doing her job.' Or so I tell myself.

I walk through to the bar and it's heaving. There must be a good eighty people here and there's bound to be more spread throughout the smoking section, dance floor and toilets. Behind the bar, Dylan and Harley have taken a section each and they look relieved to see me.

'You alright for glasses, want me to run the washer?' I shout over the ruckus.

'Big G's on the case. Serve this guy here in the middle, he's been waiting ages,' says Dylan, pointing at a Chinese guy with his elbow, his arms all tied up pouring someone a shot.

The bar is busier than our Drop The Bomb debut and New Year's Eve. I can't remember the last time I've seen it like this. Before I allow myself to feel the slightest bit excited, I remind myself that they only tend to stay for an hour before they leave in mass migration, with or without a Pyre-less Showcase.

'What can I get you, buddy?' I ask, and the guy points at the cider font. 'Where you from my man? Hong Kong?' I continue, despite his silence, trying to build rapport with my country cousin, to encourage repeat custom.

'I'm from Bury,' says Chinese-looking guy, with a distinctive English accent. I look over at Harley and he has overheard the exchange and is laughing himself better.

'If I'd said that you'd have called me racist,' says Harley. 'Someone comes in here with a sun tan and he's Indian!'

'Just pour your fucking drinks, Samosa,' I say, chuckling to myself, enjoying the fact that he's on form and showing Dylan how it's done.

'That's £1 please,' I say, as I place his pint down. The guy grins at us, having heard more of our conversation than I had thought, which Harley has a simper at too.

'Wonton, look!' Harley points at a girl stood behind the guy I've just served. 'That gal next to your brother over there is the one Gemma hit.' I glance over the shoulder of my new sibling and there is a short girl in a floral dress. Petite. Snooty. Tidy. I don't recognise her.

'You sure?' I ask, as a few other customers try to get my attention.

'I never forget the back of a lassie's head,' Harley says, while he checks someone's bank note under a light.

'Oi!' I shout, with more force than was necessary. 'Hey, excuse me!'

The girl looks over at me, as do her four friends. They are all drinking cocktails, which should push our average spend for the night. This pleases me, even though she doesn't look particularly pleased that I've shouted at her.

'Yeah, what?' she sneers, which I find slightly rude, as for all she knew I was offering her a round of Candy Slammers on the house.

'Boxing Day. You got in a fight with my partner.' I try to sound neutral, but come across as somewhat aggressive.

'What you on about?' she replies, with a face like a welder's workbench. I look over at Harley to see if he's stitched me up, but he is serving a round of gas chambers so his attention is elsewhere. 'It's none of your business.'

'I just want to hear what happened.' I try to sound professional, as our altercation has caught the interest of several people around us, who continue to wait.

'Harry, serve some drinks man, leave it,' says Dylan, who would normally revel in this kind of tedious natter. The girl ignores me and turns back to her friends, who are looking at her inquisitively.

'One minute you fancy me and now you're ignoring me?' I proclaim, narcissistically.

'*Fancy you*? I don't think so!' she snaps. 'Ask your girlfriend.'

'So something did happen?' I persist. Harley has joined Dylan's standpoint on letting this one go, to serve the occasional customer instead.

'Tell me, or you can leave,' I assert, pulling rank. People have stepped aside, forming a small circle around her and her friends. A few customers have only caught the tail end of this stand-off, which accounts for the random chanting of 'Ooooo' from equally random people. I don't know why I've pressed to get a response out of her; perhaps I'm just venting the frustration that has built up over the evening.

'Kicked out of The *Bum* Bar? Fine, fuck you then.' She slams her drink down, causing her ice and straw to fall to the ground, before leaning in towards me. 'You *really* want to know what happened? That psycho attacked me cause I caught her all over my Dickie and that greedy slag wants *two* blokes. I'll have her done for assault.'

I am frozen to the spot. A new round of 'Ooooos' have surfaced, louder than the last, but this time they are directed at me. At this precise moment, I'd rather be stood on the front staircase, swindling like a charlatan. I open my mouth to speak, but no words come out. I didn't know that our Mystery Special Guest would be shouting at me, defiling life as I know it. I can feel Harley and Dylan staring at me as they continue to serve. I can feel a lot of people staring. I am trapped behind the bar with no escape. There *is* no escaping information like this. I want to kick her out; I want to kick them all out.

'I've been seeing him for weeks, then that tramp comes along and ruins it. This place is a joke,' snorts this harbinger of devastation. Her friends laugh.

'Just fuck off! You're not welcome here, so do one!' shouts Dylan, and I've never been so thankful for him. She has knocked all the flyers out of my hand, in front of everyone, and Dylan has grabbed her and told her to pick them up. His way of returning the favour. There is a momentary lapse in people's gaze. Harley has stopped serving drinks and is following the girls out. I turn to Dylan, who is red in the face, looking bemused.

'Take five, Harry. We can handle it from here.' I push a few people out of the way that are blocking the hatch and stagger towards the ice machine room, which has seen its fair share of tension tonight. Behind the door to the club, there is teenage angst and anarchy. Behind the arching door to the bar, there is humiliation and hearsay. I'd really like to know what's behind door number three.

This can't be right. There must be some kind of mistake. Gemma wouldn't do that. This is all a misunderstanding and a drunken case of mistaken identity. It has to be. I need to phone her. I reach into my pocket but I can't feel my hands. My phone isn't even on me; it must be in my coat. I slump down on a box of Christmas decorations and can hear that I've broken a bauble or two. They aren't the only balls that have been crushed.

I don't have any proof but I don't need any. We may have had some unpleasant conversations as of late and I haven't been around as much as I should have this past month, but that's what couples do. They occasionally don't pull their weight and give in to other commitments. They don't cop off with their partner's best friend, then slap someone, then forget it ever happened, or at least Gemma and I don't. The whole thing is preposterous. I know it is. But I'm still perched on a box of squashed ornaments, in the ice machine Hall of Horrors, on what should be one of the most successful and defining nights of my career to date. I know that much too. I'm sat on the uncomfortable, jaggy box a little while longer before Barney walks in.

'What's going on, mate? I heard all this commotion over the radio. Some girl is kicking off outside, giving the doormen a right earful. Says you groped her?' Barney doesn't look like he believes her, but then he probably didn't believe he'd find me hunched over a box of balls.

'No,' I whisper, so quietly Barney stands closer.

'What's up? Make it quick. I've got a hundred kids upstairs, so we're not doing too badly,' he says, taking consolation from his small, but appreciated triumph.

'That girl was the one Gemma hit,' I explain, slightly louder than my previous whisper.

'Her *again*?' I'm not sure if I can bring myself to tell him what I've been told. He will dismiss it immediately, which is exactly what I want him to do.

'She saw Gemma and Dick kissing, or shagging, I don't know.' I wince at the words as I say them. If they really were in the toilets together, somehow I don't think he was installing a hair straightening machine for her to use. 'How long was Gemma down here after our fight?' I ask lamely.

'Not long,' he answers. 'This is silly, Harry. Don't let it spoil our night. Asha phoned to say she was nearly here.'

Gemma took ages getting home. There are lots of obvious explanations though: kebab queues, taxi queues, a zigzagged attempt at walking when pissed, visiting your fiancé's best friend for a romp. Was she late because her legs were telling the time four-forty? I need to talk to Mandara. I tell Barney that I'll meet him upstairs in the club and that he should wait for the acts to arrive. I run through the bar, which is looking a lot thinner on the ground than when I had been serving (which should be singular, as I only served the one pint) and head up the front staircase. Natalie looks absolutely shattered. She is usually reading a romantic novel at this point in the evening or begging to go up and watch the act. Instead, she is simmering on the boil, ready to froth up, her anger about to spill all over my cooker.

'Where have you been? Did you not see the shit I had to put up with?' growls Natalie, pulling an angry face. I think the wind may have changed direction because it doesn't seem to be easing off. 'You dropped me from New Year's Eve, but let me show up for this?'

'I'm sorry Nat, I got preoccupied,' I say, gloomily.

'You always help me in here! You know how stressful it gets. That's before everyone starts swearing and accusing me of lying!' shouts Natalie. Dependable. Sweet*ish*. Livid.

'Gemma is cheating on me with Dick,' I say, even though I don't know or necessarily think that to be true. It was a quick way to get me out of a bind. My very own cancer card, as it were. Harley will applaud me for its effective use when we chat about this later.

'Oh. Crap. Sorry, Harry.'

'Is it busy up there?' I ask, running up the stairs, considering myself lucky to have gotten off lightly and not waiting for any kind of answer.

For the first time, I don't care how much money we make. Or don't make. I care about being reassured. I want someone to shake me, or slap me even, like in the movies. I want to be told how much Gemma loves me and that I'm being as silly as Barney said I was. Warm embrace, big kiss, roll credits.

I push through the crowd and no one moves aside. Some of the girls up here look older than the ones downstairs, what with the hair extensions, heels and the entire contents of the makeup counter on their faces, but this is no time to criticise questionable parenting skills. I finally make my way through to the front barriers by the DJ booth.

'Harry, the audio cable, it came loose. I need you to tack it back up. And can I get a drink?' Mandara shouts over the music and the sound coming out of one half of his headphones. I'm starting to feel that this isn't the best time to raise the concerns that have followed me from downstairs.

'Is there something going on between Dick and Gemma?' I shout, whilst a hundred students crush me against the barricade. I try to shake a few of them off me, but this kind of erratic arm movement only ever leads to a dance-off.

'What?' He is bopping his head vigorously to the next song he's about to bring through.

'Are they getting it on? I know you're still friends with Dick, but you'd tell me if they were, right?' I ask, just as someone smacks me in the shoulder. I turn around and it is some dickhead flailing his arms about. I remember my first time out of the house too.

'You got in a fight?' He is totally immersed in the character of DJ Man-Dem, who isn't the person I ran upstairs to speak to. I desperately need to chat to Timo Mandara.

'No. Well, sort of, yes.' I inch over a few rungs of the barrier, then try and hop the fencing. Mandara shoots me an irritated look. I am neither fastening a cable nor fetching him his sought after refreshment. 'I need to talk to you about Gemma and Dick,' and I am instantly back at secondary school. I have more in common with these children than with the adults downstairs.

'What are you doing? I'm busy! You should be too.' A reasonable observation, but not one that I'm interested in. I fall on to the raised stage area and clamber to my feet. Everyone is too engrossed in jumping around like idiots and pulling cables off the ceiling to have noticed my epic fail of a barrier climb. I pull the headphones away from Mandara's head and ask him to put a mix-tape on so that I can talk to him. He very reluctantly agrees.

'Right, this mix is only four minutes long. What's so urgent that it can't wait? If you tell me Ash ain't coming, I'm going home. It's too hot to be dealing with this shit and it's just me on the decks.' I have completely forgotten that any second now I need to be in the VIP room. 'I ain't getting paid enough for this shit, bro.'

'I know it isn't true, but I need you to tell me that it isn't true.'

'Are you for real? I don't wanna get involved H, this ain't got nuttin to do with me,' he says, clearly frustrated by my line of questioning. I can see him counting down the seconds until his mix-tape runs out.

'So you're not denying it then?'

'Did I get with Gemma? No, I did not. You're fucking up my set. Took me ages to get these guys into it,' he says, confirming his pissed off-ness. It is hard to fully understand what he's saying over the screaming twats, making it all the more maddening.

'If it wasn't true, you would have said no, but you didn't,' I say, getting to the bottom of a problem that I could very well be imagining.

'First I get stuck playing this gig on my own. Then I have to tell everyone that Pyre ain't coming. Now you're climbing over my booth to accuse me of keeping secrets from you. What's next, a lynching?' he cries, showing a real odium of his own towards the way tonight has panned out. Some of the partygoers have started to peer our way. The cracks in our concert amplify louder than the speakers.

'You told him, didn't you? That's how they knew so quickly. You two are in this together?' I presume, really excelling myself this time. Whether there is truth to this or not, I am barking up the wrong tree. He is the only tree in the entire building that knows how to use any of this equipment and co-ordinate a Live Performance Act. Beyond the immediate selfish reason of technical ability, he is also my dear friend and colleague and those are in seemingly short supply.

'Fix the wire and get Lisa to bring me a drink,' he says, before putting his headphones back on and doing a big shout out to the crowd. At least someone in this building is sensible.

I climb back over the fencing and make my way to the VIP room, pushing people aside, totally disregarding Mandara's need for a drink and a secure cable. When I get there, a cameraman, a tour manager and our act are sat on the sofas. Barney comes over and asks quietly if I've got everything sorted. Considering we are surrounded by celebrated company, he is unsettled by my general lack of positivity.

'Dick looked at me funny in the meeting the other week, didn't he? When I came down to the bar after my argument with her, he was surprised to see me.'

'It was your day off, Harry,' says Barney, trying to soothe the situation. 'You work too much, you're a *professional*.' Barney articulates the final word strongly.

'Is that why he wanted to know if I was staying down the club or if I was leaving?' I ask, to myself more than to Barney, the tour manager or the cameraman.

'Have you met Asha? You said you really liked her song. Which one was it again?' Barney is desperate to get me off my train of thought, which is running late, missed its station and barely sticking to the rails.

'It's Over Now.' The irony hits me like a hot iron to the face. Gemma is a huge Asha fan, but didn't want to come tonight, despite it being Valentine's Day, because she has work tomorrow and might be tempted to drink. She asked me to get her a signed autograph instead. That's why God invented soft drinks, bitch. I'm angry, I can feel it.

'That's safe man, respect,' says Asha, with genuine gratitude. She seems like a nice gal, they all seem nice, which is why I ought to do some work. I take the CD that she's brought for us to play, push my way back through to Mandara, get her on stage and set the lounge up for the meet and greet.

I send Lisa to get my coat and decide to text Gemma. I stand in the corner next to Barney, but he knows better than to try to get a sensible dialogue going, leaving me to sulk quietly behind him. I have spent the entire evening building something up in my head and it's not only wearisome, but highly unproductive. I could have made Barney an extra £500 behind the bar, but instead embarrassed him in front of guests.

'Gemz, event is going well. The girl u slapped was in 2nite and said u were getting with Dick. Ur thoughts?' This is my text to her, in all its glory.

Asha performs 'Heat of Love,' Gemma's favourite song from the album, when my phone beeps. I usually smile every time I get a text from her: this one, not so much. I take a deep breath before opening the message:

'That was a messed up night. Glad it's going well 4 u, I'm listening to their CD! Don't 4get my autograph :) x'

Your *autograph*? I can't see that being top of my list of priorities. She isn't denying it. Is there more to it than this? Was Gemma with her dad? She wasn't out getting a saveloy or a battered sausage – she was out getting some Dick, in every sense of the word.

There is enough here. Not beyond a reasonable doubt and not enough to convict, but the penny has dropped. Except it isn't a penny at all. It's a massive lump of copper ore.

17

I don't stay until the end of the night. Barney tells me it's pointless being at the club in my current state of mind. I can hardly blame him. I don't want to be around me either. I also don't want to get home to find Gemma asleep, as this can't wait until morning. This is something we need to talk about now. Barney has enough staff on to see him through. Lisa has been joined by some new bloke that I was meant to train, but Dylan can bring him up to speed. I head downstairs and Harley sorts me a stiff drink. He just pours it, no questions asked. Harley and I are great at mucking around and cracking jokes, but we aren't so good at the serious stuff, like cancer and infidelity. I thank him for coming in, which by his own admission was no easy task. I call him a 'Buut-buut Ding-ding,' but there is no pleasure to be had from the jousting.

I let myself out by the fire exit, slamming it shut behind me with an unnecessary amount of force. On the drive home, my mind begins to wander again. Just before Christmas I was chatting to the lady that Gemma works for, at Millie's fourth birthday party. She is from Australia and told me that down under you're more likely to be killed by a falling coconut (I didn't even know they had coconuts in Oz) than from being eaten by a shark. Fourteen times more likely, in fact. It sounded like some gimmick the tourism board had spun to win back frightened holidaymakers, but if there is any truth in it, it looks like it's the unexpected, silent killers that get you.

I take the long route, detouring past The Havana. Dick could very well be on the front door smoking, if he isn't DJing or stealing fiancées. I occasionally drive this way to scope out the competition, as they have a later licence than us. Four out of five times I wish I hadn't, today being no exception. The street is packed. Numerous gormless drones make their ascent, as they do, week in, week out. I usually try to count each drone as I drive past, but the sums just stand to torment me. I recognise a few groups that had been in our bar only an hour ago and it would appear that the 'critical mass' Barney often refers to has left even earlier tonight. What makes matters worse is that the front of the club is orange.

It looks utterly ridiculous, but this lot love it. The Bomb Bar looks ten times better.

As I pass the doors of The Havana, one of the doormen gives me a wave of recognition and I give him the slightest of nods back. No Dick. The doorman is bound to mention that I've been cruising past, at drive-by speed. There are half a dozen police vans parked up, ready to deal with the inevitable drugs, thugs and mugs that will come spilling out at closing time. What a waste of taxpayers' money. Not that Dick or Sammy even pay tax. I may slate them, but I would love to have pigs sat outside my venue. That would mean we're packed and those drones would be mine. I acrimoniously brand everyone in this town a sheep, but only because I've failed as a sheepdog.

I meander round the police vans carefully, as if sitting a practical driving test. There would be nothing more humiliating than scraping one in front of twenty coppers and two hundred pissheads. The only thing that would be more humiliating would be trying to talk my way out of it by saying that Gemma is cheating on me with Dick, Cloakroom Style. As soon as I pass the panda cars, I think about how Gemma always calls me her Panda and I put my foot down. I should be getting home as quickly as possible to see my girl, instead of roaming the streets like a lecherous man in search of sex to solicit. I'm getting fucked over either way.

As I pull onto our estate, the lights are still on in the house. I park the car, slam the door and storm towards the front entrance. I find myself enraged even though I haven't had the conversation yet. Perhaps Harley's stiff drink is starting to kick in. Perhaps the best defence is a strong offence. Perhaps I already know what the outcome will be.

There is a song by Doris Day called 'Perhaps, Perhaps, Perhaps,' which Mandara played to me when he was in one of his gay icon moods. The only lyrics to the song that I can remember are 'If you really love me, say yes, but if you don't dear, confess.'

Perhaps that's the only answer I need. *Que sera, sera.*

I open the front door and don't bother to shout my customary 'Honey, I'm home.' I carefully untie my shoelaces before slowly hanging up my coat. I creep upstairs to the living room. I'd rather draw things out down here than have Gemma spell things out up there.

I drag my feet up the last few steps and when I get to the top, Gemma is in the front room, wearing her dressing gown, the TV on mute. She looks guilty as sin. Some Valentine's Day. The house is so silent, so tacit, that nothing needs to be said. I have my answer. Gemma doesn't acknowledge me. She is looking at the photos of us that line the windowsill.

'*Why*, Gemma?' I mumble. There is a long, long pause. She is expressionless, in no kind of thought. At least if I could see the cogs in her head turning, trying to get her story straight, we might have something left to talk about, but nothing.

Blank. Cold. Panda-less.

'Why what?' she murmurs. She looks frozen stiff.

'Why now? Why him?' I mutter, a grimace rapidly gorging on my face. My eyes burn, not with hot tears, but with rage. Her silence is deafening and I want the racket to stop.

'Why what?' she repeats, conceding the battle. In between the mumbles and murmurs and mutters, I can't help but feel I'd rather be playing the bush game.

'Answer me!' I growl, pulling her to face me. She isn't frozen anymore. Her frosty exterior has begun to thaw, her cheeks flushed with embarrassment. She pulls her knees towards her chest and lowers her head, forcing my hand away from her. She can't get her story straight because her story is crooked.

'What do you want from me?' she shouts. I am taken aback by her question. It has truly thrown me. I stare at the wall, trying to absorb its meaning. I know a lot of people stay together for the wrong reasons, but she is *breaking up* with me for the wrong reasons.

'I want you to look at me when I'm talking to you.' I sound just like my father. I don't know what I want. I want to go back to the beginning, before all of this, back to when things were good. I don't want anything from her and at the same time, I want everything.

'It happened, okay? I'm sorry, but it's not my fault,' she says, sniffling. Of course it's not. It takes two to tango, right? Well, I'm not familiar with that dance and I don't know the steps. The only time I've ever seen it was on *True Lies*. Gemma is named after a different type of dance, a skank.

'Not your fault? Dick pinned you down, did he? He forced his tongue down your throat and his cock in your mouth? Is that where you were when I was waiting for you at The Spitfire? With him?!' I scream, so loud that it hurt.

I want our neighbour to wake up and to bang on our door. I want her baby to be woken and to never get back to sleep. I want the whole street smashing at our door like a mob of battering rams, so I can explain to them all how wretched the girl at number forty-four really is. How it is impossible to honour and love thy neighbour.

'No, he didn't. He didn't have to. This is your fault.' My fault? I may not have been the perfect boyfriend or the model fiancé, but this *cannot* be my fault.

My blood has gone beyond boiling point; it has started to haemorrhage and coagulate. The Gemma I am looking at isn't my Gemma: this isn't her. This is an impostor – an evil, identical twin. I have walked into the wrong house. This is someone else's world and someone else's life. The Gemma I know isn't a falling coconut.

'I did this? Are you listening to yourself? I'll tell you who fucking did this, seeing as none of this is your fault, and I'm about to call him right now. Let's see if it's still my fault,' I bawl.

I reach for my phone and hunt for Dick's number. As soon as I find the number I'm pressing dial and it's going on loudspeaker. Then we will see if it's still my fault. Hot tears start to fill the corners of my eyes; the body's attempt to cool down my fury. My blood has expanded as a result of the soaring heat and is escaping from the most painful holes it can find. Dick is the shark.

'Do *not* call him! Don't! I mean it!' she bellows, her face glowing red, glaring up at me with a wickedness that I have never seen before.

'Too late,' I shout, directly in her face, the spit from my words spattering on her as she makes a grab for the phone. No one would ever guess that this was the young woman I wanted to dedicate my life to, the girl I defied my father for. The lady I love.

'Give it to me!' she screeches, like a feral child or a banshee as she frantically stretches for the phone, my elbow keeping her at bay while the call struggles to connect. The phone reception in this house has always been awful, but I think the reception I have received tonight has topped even that. 'Give it to me!'

'Is that what you said to him? Give it to me? Fucking slut!' I roar, sounding like an equally foul apparition. Gemma begins to scratch me, digging her nails into my wrist. She then clings at my shirt with one arm and claws at my face with the other. It was calling her a slut that did it, just as I thought it might. She makes another desperate reach for the phone before piercing her nails into my neck, which is when it happens.

When my entire life changes.

The flash-bulb, stop-the-clock, pin-drop, photo-finish moment.

I slap her across the face, as hard as I can.

*

It's romantic when people say things like 'It was love at first sight,' or 'I knew you were the one,' isn't it? But these things don't really happen, at least not in real life, or at least not to us. There is no script or cues: things either happen or they don't.

In our case, things did happen (lots of drinks, sex, picnics, moving in together, engagement) and then they didn't (the minute I slapped her). I am still in the room. She is still on the sofa. The back of my hand is still stinging from the blistering contact it has made to the side of her beautiful, weeping face. But we are frozen again. I have dropped the phone on the floor and the house has fallen silent once more. The neighbour never came, no rams were battered and no baby was awoken. I was only trying to get her off me and I didn't mean to hit her. I close my eyes, to take my mind away from this room and away from the truth.

In between the things that did happen and up to the point we're at now, where they didn't, there were a lot of heart-to-hearts, dreaming, reverie and planning for the future. The biggest plan set in motion being the day I asked her to marry me. For this brief moment, post-face slap and pre-eye opening, I desperately cling to that memory: that better time and that better place.

*

The time was about 8pm in the evening and the place was Holkham Bay, on the coast of Norfolk. I remember feeling a combination of both excitement and nervousness, but also a deep, fulfilling sense that there was nothing to worry about for the rest of my life, if I was able to pull it off. That everything I did from then on would have purpose and meaning, with Gemma by my side: a captivated audience member to The Harry Chen Show. She was to be the backdrop and the safety net to everything I may or may not accomplish.

I remember texting to tell her that despite being completely swamped with work and stuck in meetings all day, I would still be taking her out for a meal that evening, as I'd been promising all week. By leaving her with the impression that I was trapped in the club, with the possibility of running late, everything else I managed to achieve would seem all the more unexpected.

I went to pick up the ring: a 14ct, white gold halo quarter-carat diamond solitaire in size N, to be precise. I was happy with it and I remember thinking that she had better be too, as it set me back near enough £800. I could have bought a car with that, or four hundred bottles of beer, as Barney put it. A Haribo ring or a Hula Hoop crisp would have been a cheaper option, as Dylan suggested.

I then went to a tattoo parlour called Ink Treats on Westgate Street. I asked the tattooist for her initial on my ring finger. The *G* looked beautiful, in a classic Edwardian font, symbolising that this finger was to be hers and hers alone, forever and always. This same artist recently completed the 'Harley' tat on my wrist for only a tenner when I explained to him why I was getting it: like sympathy pussy, except painful.

I then went to pick out a suit: a smart, silvery-grey one, blagging a student discount with an expired card. My next stop was the florist on the market, where I complained that all the roses looked limp and lifeless and that I wasn't prepared to pay more than a fiver for a big bouquet. I pretended to walk off, then got called back and was given them for £4. Nothing was too good for my girl. The lucky lady had landed on her feet!

After sticking the flowers in the ice well, I changed into my ensemble. I went into the ice machine room, dug out some red spray paint that I had used for the stencils and sprayed some of it on to a dishcloth. I drove back to the house, flowers on my lap, engagement ring in my pocket, red rag covering my tattoo. When I pulled up outside the house, I slammed the car door as hard as I could and let out the most dramatic of cries. When Gemma asked me what all the fuss was about I told her that I had trapped my hand in the car door. I distracted her with the flowers and after putting them in water, she took another forty minutes to finish getting ready. Harley once texted me a joke saying that a girl's 'ready in five minutes' and a guy's 'be home in five minutes' is the same length of time.

When Gemma was good to go, she looked beautiful. The drive to Holkham Bay is easy enough, basically a straight line up the Isles. We sang along to the radio the entire time. She loves singing along, but hates it when the artist gets the words wrong.

When we arrived, we parked up and took a picturesque walk down the wooden embankment. From here we looked out at four miles of shimmering white-gold sand, which had a couple of horseboxes on it. I told her we should take a stroll before our meal. Hidden away behind pine trees and across the dunes there was a row of shabby-chic, brightly painted beach huts that made her smile when she saw them.

The air was cold and wintry, but I held her close and neither of us seemed to mind. Gemma ran her fingers along some purple flowers and picked one before beaming up at me, showing off her pretty pluck. She held it up and sang *'Here's a tree in summer,'* before pulling the petals off, *'Here's a tree in winter,'* and chanted, *'Here's a bunch of flowers,'* before throwing the purple petals over me, *'Here's the April showers!'* Gemma had a song for every occasion. She was my song for all occasions.

When we got to my favourite part of the beach I told her that we needed to stop because my hand was hurting too much and that we may have to cut our evening short. With a compassionate face that I will never forget, she asked to see my injury. Once Gemma peeled away the dishcloth (revealing a tattoo of the letter 'G' instead of a gaping flesh wound) she stared at it for ages before making any kind of connection, which made me love her even more. She looked up at me and burst into tears. Close to casting the engagement ring into the sea and telling her it was a removable temporary tattoo, she threw her arms around me, signifying happiness instead of horror. In her embrace, I recited one of her favourite poems, which she had planned to get tattooed herself. I whispered to her slowly and carefully:

*'Dance like no one is watching, Sing like no one is listening,
Love like you've never been hurt, Live like it is Heaven on Earth.*

*A dream that is dreamed by two
Will always come true.'*

I got down on one knee, reached into my pocket and showed her the ring. She had thankfully taken my bait and it was time to reel her in. She was the only fish I ever wanted to catch. I felt the waves had stopped lapping, the wind had stopped swishing and the world had stopped turning, to allow me to recite her poem to her in stillness. I told her that she meant the absolute world to me. Nothing around us moved. The perfect standstill.

It's also romantic when people say things like 'it was the happiest day of my life,' and 'I remember it like it was yesterday.' Those things *did* happen to us, or at least to me, and that was it, that was the day. I told her that I would protect her with my life, which only had any meaning because she was in it, and that I would never let any harm come to her. I explained that I was prepared to dedicate my entire being to her happiness. That I would love her no matter what. And I meant it.

She said yes.

Then I opened my eyes.

I could have kept my eyes shut forever.

I look down at my battered fiancée and it would seem her eyes have been opened too. She has seen the type of person I really am, beneath all the layers of the things that did happen. I am the type of person who strikes a woman, the type of person who hits his fiancée in the face. I try to speak but there is nothing I can say, and no words pass my trembling lips. I have gone beyond stooping to her level, committing a far greater crime altogether. I want to apologise. I want to hold her. She pushes past me. I desperately want to chase after her but I don't, just like the last time she left.

Instead I just stand here, my hand still searing from pain, long after the sting from the slap has subsided. I brace myself for the sound of the door being slammed shut, but it doesn't come. She closes it gently, too shocked to slam doors.

I fall to my knees and quietly ask God why. He is speechless too.

18

The doorbell wakes me up. I can't believe I fell asleep on the floor. It takes me a while to realise where I am, curled up at the top of the stairs. Gemma. A prickle of panic hits me: there could quite easily be a passel of police officers stood behind our front door, or worse, her father. I carefully open it, as gently as she closed it, bracing myself for the cuntstabulary.

'Took you long enough,' says Barney, who never does house calls. He must be collecting door-to-door for the club now, selling event tickets and canvassing Coronas through letterboxes.

'Alright, mate. What you doing here?' I ask, surprise not masking disappointment.

'You haven't been answering your phone. We need to talk.' He looks very concerned. At least I know I haven't gotten him pregnant.

'Gemma hasn't been to see you, has she? It just happened. I can't even explain why –'

'The club is closing,' he says. 'Effective immediately.'

'What? But we did all right last night, didn't we?' I utter, mind racing and heart pounding. 'Didn't we, Barney?'

'The shareholders have had enough. We made a couple grand, not a couple *hundred* grand,' he says in a humourless monotone. 'I'm sorry. I was dreading coming over here. I had to practise on Dylan and Harley first.' An uncharacteristic sadness pours out of him.

'We could have done things differently,' I start, but my thoughts trail off. There is nothing we could have done differently. We could have pushed a 'Closing Down Sale,' but even then, it's hard to push 'Everything Must Go' when most of the drinks are already priced at £1 a pop.

'This *was* my exit strategy. I wanted us to go out with a bang: a huge Live Performance Act and a packed club. A night for everyone in this miserable town to remember us by, but mainly you – an event for *you* to be proud of.' He doesn't sound like he's even convinced himself, let alone me. If that really was his intention last night, I feel rotten for ruining it, but it wasn't by choice. 'As soon as we had to stop hosting Funk'd Up Fridays, that was it for us.'

'What the fuck are we going to do? This can't get any worse,' I say, with fate being the last thing I need to tempt. If I went for another hat trick in the bad luck stakes, I'd be on for greatest goal scorer of all time, or at least the season.

'The club has run its course, but you kept it going longer than anyone else could have,' he says, trying his hardest to soften the blow. I thought we were on the precipice of something great. That the ends would justify the means. I was determined to regain our stolen title, robbed from us by an undeserving recipient.

'We can take on somewhere smaller Barney, somewhere more manageable,' I plead, not wanting it to be over, at least not yet and most certainly not now. I still want to be a manager, to give myself importance. I think they call me the manager because I barely manage. My boss looks weary, worn and clearly not in the mood for plans of action. This is the one time he won't want to sit down for a meeting. He is also no longer my boss.

'I'm done. I haven't got the energy for it anymore. If I could go back and do it all again, I wouldn't change a thing. We aren't at fault. It's the mentality of the town. They all want The Havana and there's no logic behind it. I wish you'd moved over there too,' he says selflessly.

'They can suck a nut.' No amount of money would entice me to associate myself with them. Barney has come here to make me feel better, when it is I that should be consoling him.

'We've had some laughs along the way, haven't we? It was fun while it lasted.' A reflective, wistful beam finds its way through the fog of squander. 'I have an inventory list here for the accountants. It's all the stuff that needs selling.'

Barney produces a crumpled sheet of paper, covered in hastily scrawled handwriting that can only be described as Dylan's. He passes me the list and asks if I can hawk any of the assorted assets.

'Not really. I'll take some booze off your hands if it needs a good home,' I say, not looking at the list and in full knowledge that my home is no longer good.

'We can have another look at that later.' He takes the sheet back and shoves it into his pocket. 'Harley and Dylan are at the club now. They're stripping everything out as we speak. Fancy taking a drive down to see if there's anything you want?' he proposes, even though I know that means spending the rest of the day (and night) helping them pack.

'Let's do it,' I say, unsure as to whether or not I should leave the house in case Gemma returns. She said if it weren't for her I'd live at the club.

'Cool. We'll go see the lads,' he says, reminding me that I have friends out there that I haven't got round to slapping in the face yet. I join Barney out on the front step and close the door. 'You know Mandara is working for The Havana Club now. I'm glad he's got something sorted, but talk about not wasting any time.' There are definitely friends I haven't got round to slapping. 'My car's full of energy drink, so take yours and I'll meet you there.'

During the drive to the club, for what is going to be the last time, I realise that running a venue and running a relationship aren't so different. It takes years of work to build and only a moment to break.

*

'Spring roll, my man!' shouts Harley, who is using a crowbar to remove some steel panelling. He looks like he has been at it for a few hours, because the place is an absolute state and his t-shirt is showing the signs of a good sweat.

'Gandhi. How are you? I've really fucked things up.'

'Shit, how'd it go?' asks Dylan, who is wrestling with the other plasma telly this time, probably still looking for that model number.

'So bad, I don't want to talk about it.' This must seem like a first. Usually I will chat about anything, especially the domestic dramas of Gemma and I. These guys are my communion, or confession or whatever.

'What have I told you, Hoisin? If you can enjoy the hamburger, don't buy the cow,' says Harley, who has never told me that. It's also a bit rich, coming from someone with a live-in girlfriend.

'Why buy books when there's libraries, innit,' adds Dylan, relishing the fact that my relationship is over, as he always predicted.

'Dylan, you can't even read, otherwise you'd have found that model number by now,' says Barney, trying to get the conversation away from Gemma. He's only set the number hunting task to keep Dylan distracted until some heavy lifting is required.

'I want my own book. Not one that every Tom, Dick and Harry has taken out on loan.'

'Who's Tom? He smashed Gemma as well?' jests Harley. If Dylan said that I'd have swung the crowbar at him.

'Tom – that new guy that started yesterday? He worked one shift and the club closes. What a faggot!' shouts Dylan. There is no way Barney would have taken on new staff if he knew the club was closing. 'Remember, there are fish in the sea ready for the sticking!'

'Once you've had caviar, how can you settle for catfish? And there is only one Fish I want to fuck over,' I say, menacingly.

'Forget Sammy. Onwards and upwards, mate,' replies Barney, the only sensible one here. 'All you can do in life is hope for the best, but plan for the worst.'

'You're right.' He gives me a look that suggests his work here is done. 'It's *Dick* that is going to fucking pay for this.' Barney's look of accomplishment fades.

'Will I get a pay rise for helping out?' asks Dylan, not grasping that this is it, the end.

'A rise? Choose a box to stand on, there's loads here!' says Harley.

'Will you give me a hand with the sofas?' Barney seems happy that I've agreed to tag along. 'We should have taken them out ages ago. No one wants to come to a bar and see people slouching. They want motion and movement. The sofas look too eighties,' he says, as if some great depression from the 'eighties' is to blame for all of his financial shortcomings. 'People drink up to four times quicker stood up.'

Even though it's all over, Barney is still thinking about ways he could have made more money, or lost less. I have to hand it to the guy; he really did give this place his best shot. 'And those straws, they should have gone too. People get drunk more quickly when they drink through a straw and they're 49p per box,' he bewails.

I agree to help with the sofas and the rest of the moving, packing and dismantling, only because it might keep my mind from darker thoughts of what I did to Gemma and what she has done to me. Despite my unspeakable night, it's nice to be working with Harley and Dylan on a project again, with Barney 'supervising' (which is what he calls pointing and making the odd joke), even if it's the wrong way round. Normally we are building something to better the club, to change and improve it. Now we are gutting it out.

This edifice was Harley's legacy and his own unique stamp on the town: not for the unappreciative township, but for very appreciative friends. This was his mark, built off the back of sausage McMuffins, KFC family buckets, hundreds of texts, thousands of jokes – not to forget an amazing friendship – but just like his stolen tools, now gone. Thinking about all that we've achieved together, I begin to realise that I may never get to see Harley again. We saw each other every Friday and Saturday night, so had no reason to meet up outside of work. Harley always said that when it came to employees (and he used Dylan as a case study) that I should see them as staff first and friends as a very distant second. So if he feels like an employee and not a friend, would he even want to meet with me? He would only call me a 'poof' if I were to ask him.

After helping Barney shift some sofas from the 1980s, I take a wander round the building looking at all the stencils I had painstakingly cut and sprayed. I notice a particularly intricate stencil that I haven't seen in a while from the French writer Hilaire Belloc: 'When you have lost your inns, drown your empty selves, for you will have lost the last of England.' Cheers Hilbo, fucking frog. The number of times we have painted this place, each layer promising the new look that was bound to take our troubles away. The countless tins Barney had to drop to get a discount at Homebase. Everything we attempted to do here was met with a set-back. We were constantly being knocked and I think there comes a time in everyone's life when they take one knock too many. I think Gemma would now agree.

I go downstairs and ask Barney if I can pour a drink to drown my empty self with. He tells us that we can help ourselves to anything we want, which is met with a cheer all round. He is grateful that we have stuck by him. Even if we had left, he wouldn't have held it against us.

When we've done all that we can, we take a perch on boxes scattered across the room. Barney has borrowed a van from his friend to remove the remaining stock, but not before I take some vodka and a case of beer. I grab a bottle from the fridge and Dylan gives me a funny look.

'Where's my drink, huh?' he asks in mock outrage, too lazy to fetch one himself.

'Always put on your own oxygen mask before helping others,' I joke. He chuckles, before taking a few Estonian beers and some hazelnut liqueur, both of which he suggested we stock and neither of which ever sold. Dylan and I ceremoniously down our final bombs. Harley asks for a case of bottled water, despite Barney's insistence that he takes more.

'You can have anything you want,' offers Barney, one last time, just to be sure.

'I'm a mess as it is. Imagine if I drank like these two? I'd already be dead,' says Harley. 'Might take some Malibu for Kristina though.' I never even considered taking anything for Gemma.

'Thought you'd choose some Mother's Ruin,' I suggest.

'Gin?' he asks.

'*Bombay* Sapphire!'

'Did I tell you my energy drink plan?' asks Barney. 'I've told The Spitfire we're closing and pretended that I have cases left over. I then told our Badwell Ash supplier to do me a deal on the cheap – fifty cases for £200. The Spitfire's buying them at £5.44 plus VAT per case. Basically, we're making over £100 out of it,' says Barney, to our utter disbelief. 'Twat Tax!'

Del Boy right to the very end.

19

Leaving the bar for the last time is hard. Harder than I thought it would be. Everything ended so abruptly. One minute I'm being introduced to an award-winning music artist and the next I'm moving sofas and taking what drink I can carry. Saying goodbye to Dylan and Barney isn't an issue: they live locally and I've met them outside of work lots of times. Harley, on the other hand, is a different story. There is nothing that he won't joke about, but I grab him for a big hug regardless, and thank him for everything. I thank him for his hard work, for his reliability and for his companionship.

Camaraderie and loyalty are not for sale. You can't buy friendship. I hope that in time, Sammy Fish will figure this out for himself. Harley always said that this would be his last venue. I never thought for a second that it would be ended by cancer and closure. Do all good things have to come to an end? I give Harley, Barney and Dylan one final wave. I drive home slowly, trying to grasp everything that has happened. It's getting late, but I'm not sure if I want Gemma to be at home when I arrive.

I bring the booze inside the house and have a look for any signs of life. I head upstairs to find that the majority of her things are still as she left them, minus a few essentials. Her beloved Nibbles is no longer on her pillow and her travel bag is gone. She should have been able to trust me – I promised to protect her. That could very well have been the first time she has ever been hit. I have a pressing need to ring her. I wait and wait for the call to go through.

Voicemail. This 'sucker' has fallen for it again.

The house should feel bigger now that I am standing here on my own, but it doesn't. I am not an aggressive person. I have never been in a proper fight. I don't even play contact sports. Yet I have struck the girl I love. Maybe this *is* my fault. I've been neglectful. Perhaps Gemma has been trying to reach out to me, ignored like the health warnings on a fag packet.

I've only been here for a minute, and it's been one minute too long. Needing to get out of the house, I search through my phone for someone to call. Before I've even gotten halfway down the list, it rings. It is Big G. He asks if I fancy a game of pool at The Fox & Hound. I never bother calling Big G. I am always half-expecting him to be on his way to another delivery.

I look for a reasonably clean jumper from the washing basket, but they are all beyond wearing. Gemma used to affectionately call me a 'smelly ole thing' as a term of endearment. Now it would seem a reasonably accurate description. I head into the bedroom and rummage around for something warm and washed. After pulling out boxes of summer clothes containing brightly coloured floral shorts that I will never wear and sleeveless tank tops I will never have the upper arms for, I find an unfamiliar carrier bag under the bed. It is heavy, jagged and full to the brim of Showcase flyers. Gemma hadn't handed out a single one. The stockpile here looks even larger than the one I gave her. She's been lying to me, to help Dick and The Havana. That bread and circus bitch.

I put on an unwashed and not very warm jumper and head to the door to await my chauffeur. With Gemma and I beyond any kind of swift reconciliation and with Dick now my greatest adversary, there is nowhere else to turn but the pub. The number of times I've 'gone to see a man about a dog,' I'd own my own kennel.

When we get to the Fox & Hound there is no one I recognise, but more importantly, no one that recognises me, for which I am incredibly thankful. Dick will have broadcast to the town that the club has shut and I am the manager that saw it driven into the ground. The Fox & Hound is likely to see a lot of me from now on, if it can maintain this clientele of anonymous, opinion-free strangers. It's getting late, so Big G quickly gets the drinks in before they stop serving. I stick a quid in the pool table and Big G makes a joke about my balls dropping. The girl put way too much post-mix in my drink. I think it was Belinda, the ignorant cow. You know you're in a bad mood when cola gets you upset.

I slump on the nearest stool as Big G racks up the balls with the broken plastic triangle, and I reach for a well-worn cue. If Dick were to walk through the door right now, I'd gladly wrap this pool cue round his head. As Big G searches for a missing red, I scan the room for promotional posters to see whether their offers and deals compete with the club. Old habits die hard. Barney told me to achieve a 'work-life balance.' Now I'd just settle for work, because this life bit isn't all it's cracked up to be.

Big G's smash sees two yellows go down in the one shot. The white English ball is going out of its way to knock the yellow Chinese balls off the map. 'I think I've snookered myself,' he mutters, looking at the table as if it's the brunette from Boxing Day, wondering which bits go where. He thinks *he's* snookered himself? I'm the one without any options.

'Just take your shot, Bug-Jug!' He pots another two, with the flukiest Hail Mary I have ever seen, his game more pinball than pool. With Big G pondering his next go, drawing on his vast life experience of four games, I find myself in a reflective mood of my own.

My career moves haven't been dissimilar to the way I play (or attempt to play) pool. I always take the tricky shots, often intentionally overlooking the much simpler and obvious choices. The easy shot, like my old job at The Officer's Club (a clothes shop, not another nightclub), required little imagination. Folding jeans and stacking shoe bays would impress no one. The more taxing shot however, requiring a certain degree of top spin, would garner much more kudos. The Bomb Bar was my tricky shot and I had whacked the ball completely off the table. But this is where my pool table analogy comes to an end because Big G has potted the black, winning the game, and because the shabby pool table is making money, and I am not. My game was over before it even began. What a waste of a quid. I've never been seven-balled off the break. Maybe this cue should be used for hitting people after all. He must have been cheating. Like Gemma.

An old codger who was sat at the bar walks over towards us. I thought he was going to hurl an insightful insult of his own to add to my 'schooling' in the realm of pub pool, but he was only politely waiting for us to finish our game before sticking a fifty pence piece in the jukebox, tucked away in our corner.

We would pay two resident DJs and our guest DJ Stevie Mac, forking out almost £800 a week, to press a green triangle. That equates to selling two hundred and forty bombs a week just to break even. The Fox & Hound, however, is being *paid* to play music. Poor Barney had it all wrong. I bet this jukebox isn't going to abandon the venue and run off with the manager's missus. Harley once told me that the reason the 50p piece is shaped the way it is, is that you'll need a spanner to prise it out of the hands of Barney. While I sit and wait to see what song this portly pensioner decides to stick on, Big G contemplates whether or not to answer his phone, which has started to ring.

The old-timer picks a Michael Bublé song and I took him for a bit of a crooner. It was the side parting and smoking jacket that did it. I think for 50p he gets three songs. If he paid what Barney did, he would get to choose 4,800 tracks. Barney got stitched up. Big G's phone has started to ring once again and his ringtone is the Jay-Z track '99 Problems.' We bop our heads for a bit before he eventually answers. Big G turns to the tiny smoking area, evidently struggling to hear with the jukebox speaker blaring above us, unnecessarily loud for a pub this small. I'm just glad to be out of the house. I'd only be pacing around the front room waiting for Gemma to return, driving myself insane. Add drinking to the waiting game and I'd turn into a right head case.

I look over at Big G nattering away, smoking on his fag and he looks back at me and smiles. This goofy, cumbersome ginga ninja is a true friend (not duty-bound or work-affiliated). Everybody only really needs one good, honest, decent person to believe in them to make things okay, right? Some say 'the more the merrier,' but I say too many cocktail barmen spoil the Bellini. It is a sad realisation when you discover that nearly all your friends happen to be colleagues. Except for Big G.

With Bublé's song coming to an end, the next record is one I know all too well. I wish I'd gone over so that I could have told the coffin dodger not to choose this one. Almost every night when she's in the shower and I'm brushing my teeth at the sink, she is sure to play 'Against All Odds' by Phil Collins. I need to hear lyrics about feeling good, not songs about ex-lovers failing to reconcile their condemned relationships. She chose the power ballad intentionally. The heartless siren was setting me up for the fall all along.

When Big G returns he can tell that I'm down in the dumps. 'What's wrong?'

'Nothing, never mind,' I reply, fed up.

'You look depressed man – smile! It might never happen. Could be worse, could be cancer!' He is trying to lighten my spirits. This works as effectively as a Phil Collins 1984 original sound track.

'If you're depressed you are *void* of emotion. You are numb and can't feel anything. I can feel everything.'

'Not depressed then, just depressing!' he quips.

'You're actually making cancer jokes?' His wise-crack is as funny as missing the call for last orders. I thought that I'd gotten it all out, but there's more. 'Don't tell me that it might never happen. It *has* happened!' I blab, even though I know his comment was one to be thrown away.

'What the fuck? I'm mates with Harley too, but it's okay for you to joke about it?' He's absolutely right. It is far from funny that we joke about it, it's the last thing I want to do, but it's all I'm allowed to do.

'Bring me a drink, this round's on me. Get yourself another juice,' I say, trying to apologise by way of drink purchase. I could do with wetting my whistle after that fiery exchange; I want my whistle drenched.

'I'll pay for the drinks, seeing as you're jobless and all. Stick another quid in the pool table.' I am thankful that my friend isn't a complete and utter waste of space like me. I bet with this next game of pool, I pot the black on the break.

When we bid Belinda farewell, she replies with a sad smile. I feel sorry for her, what with Dylan messing her around and the way I spoke to her for wasting my once precious time. Belinda wouldn't be out banging any of Dylan's friends, but he couldn't give the slightest of shits. I think I'll find it in my heart to forgive her for the cola thing.

We make our way over to the car and the air is cold. Big G fires up his Golf and we are blasted with a droning DubStep beat; the subwoofer trembles the entire frame of his car.

'Sorry for having a go at you earlier. It's Gemma –' I begin, still longing for depression.

'If she was a car you would've gotten rid of her ages ago,' he says. 'Even Rick Astley would have given her up.'

'If you say so,' I remark, disinterested.

'We should have some fun; take your mind off things. The weekend forecast is mostly wasted with a slight chance of getting laid! No rush to get back is there?'

'A fun weekend for you is filling your blow-up doll with helium so *he* plays hard to get!'

'Let's drive around for a bit. Home is the last place you should be,' and he's right. 'You'll get some looks in this pimp mobile, son. I had a couple of young cuties in the back this afternoon.' We all know they only wanted the transit without having to pay the fare and most certainly didn't put out. Other than perhaps their hand – after one of his fags that is, not a job.

'You're a glorified cabbie.'

'I may as well have a meter running.'

'What is it with you and young girls? You love em.' I'm sure Big G has picked up a number of sexy women in his car this week. Sadly, that number is zero.

'Especially on non-uniform day, bloody tart convention!' he retorts.

'You won't get any honeys hitch-hiking a lift with this shite playing. I thought your normal DubStep was bad enough!' I can't distinguish one song from the next.

'This is exclusive. No one has this tune,' he says, proud of his avant-garde illegal download.

'No one *wants* this tune. It sounds like an octopus and a crab having a fight to the death.' Captain Nemo decides to turn up the volume in protest. Gemma finally has a use for her pointless dolphin impression.

'I'll throw *you* in the ocean if you carry on like that!'

Before I can tell Big G that I'd use his size fourteen shoes as canoes, my phone bleeps. I pull out my under-performing HTC Desire and it's a text from Gemma. The butterflies in my stomach have turned into angry black moths and I can barely bring myself to read it. I ask Big G to do it for me, but he opts for looking away and not because I suggested that his music belongs with the seaweed and barnacles. I begin to read the text out loud, but silence myself:

'Harry, I need to tell u that it's over. It's the right thing to do. All the best, Gemma. TB.'

That's it?! After everything we've been through? After our four years together, engagement and sharing a house, that's all I get? No explanation, no apology. I know I raised my hand to her, but ending it like *this*? This is the first time I've ever received a text from her where she has written her name out properly. No 'Gemz' or 'G-Star.' I'm surprised she hasn't gone all out and written 'Miss G.A. Goodman,' for fuck's sake. Her initials are 'GAG.' Where to begin with that one? Not even a goodbye kiss. Gemma places great importance on the 'x.'

TB? I presume that means 'text back' to confirm receipt of her heinous message, rather than wishing tuberculosis upon me. Somehow

I don't think I'll be dignifying this with a response, until I get drunk and text her repetitively. Gemma thinks that 'it's the right thing to do,' does she? A moral obligation? How very decent of her. The right thing to do would have been to stop copping off with my promo manager. *All the best?* She cannot be serious. Gemma has taken all that is best in me and left me wordless in Big G's car, driving nowhere, listening to the mating calls of the sperm whale. You do not say 'all the best' to someone whose heart you have broken. I bet she's more sincere with little Millie when she calls to say goodnight. If that's even Millie that she's been speaking to each evening. Oh God.

I never thought she'd be the one to break up with me. I would have put money on me doing the breaking. I'd prefer to be the pain that she'd remember rather than the love that she forgot. I feel as unwanted as the ends of a loaf. The evidence of our entire time together covered like her gammy toe, hidden under a sock and a shoe, never to be seen again.

20

This isn't how things were supposed to pan out.

I had good intentions: a grand design for us. For the first time, I had a plan. I never had a plan before Gemma, not for anything. My romanticised idea of how things were going to turn out didn't involve anything like this. Everything that has happened seems so surreal, so bizarre. It's all so out of sequence. No sense of continuity, like a Tarantino movie – back to front and upside down.

Quentin Tarantino wrote a screenplay called *True Romance*, starring an enigmatic Christian Slater and the beautiful Patricia Arquette as his love interest. Tarantino's finest work to date. Arquette plays Emma, a call girl, paid to 'cheer up' Clarence (played by Slater) on his birthday, as a secret gift from his boss. Emma's job is to show up at the same cinema as Clarence, as if by chance. Emma drops her popcorn all over him, making it seem accidental and tries to clear the kernels off his lap.

After the movie she asks him if he'd like to go and get some pie and before you know it they are back at his flat making sweet sensual popcorn of their own. Clarence wakes up to find her sat out on his rooftop, crying. She has unwittingly fallen for her client, in a trendier and edgier version of *Pretty Woman*. Emma wants Clarence to know that she isn't 'damaged goods' and not 'what they call Florida White Trash.' That when it comes to relationships, she is 'one hundred per cent.'

'If I'm with you, I'm with you, nobody else.'

Emma is only four days into her career as a call girl and Clarence is only her third customer. The scene is so remarkably believable that it makes me shiver just thinking about it. Richard Gere would have kicked Julia Roberts out into the hotel hallway if their 'transaction' actually happened beyond the silver screen; but there is something genuine about *True Romance*. It doesn't have to be fairy tale and perfect to be real.

Their True Romance isn't too dissimilar from our own tale of imprudent love. Gemma and I had a whirlwind of an introduction. Our first proper encounter was on my birthday at a New Year's Eve event at the club: both realising that the time was winding down to the Midnight Kiss. After an hour (okay, ten minutes) in the VIP room, through a magnum of champagne, Gemma and I said those three dangerous words, 'I. Love. You.'

This was how we met and this was our True Romance. Much like in the movie, our relationship developed so quickly that it was often hard to keep up. If Dylan was to ask me again, I wish life happened at half the speed. In declaring her love, Emma says, 'Clarence, I feel really goofy saying this, what with only knowing you the one night and me being a call girl and all, but I think I love you.' My notion of romance was false and as fake as a film. They say romance is dead. Well, it is. Gemma killed it.

'Want to talk about it?' asks Big G, before turning off his stereo. I know he is only trying to help but, it's pointless. As pointless as non-alcoholic beer and indeed, this whole situation tastes horrible. 'Let's get you back, buddy,' he continues, not wanting to look at me, instead deciding to stare at the perfidious phone that lies in my limp hand.

'Back? Back to where? 1996? I didn't know this was the DeLorean. She said it's over. How can she do this to me.' I don't expect him to know the answer to a relationship problem, so I leave the question mark out of my voice. The poor bastard is still a virgin, despite his every effort to try and lose his VW V-Plates.

'It's done now. Forget about her,' making it all sound so uncomplicated.

'Will you stay there with me for a while?' I sound as pitiful as I must look. The thought of being alone is unbearable. I've always needed at least a few drinks to enjoy the pleasure of my *own* company.

'I can't, I'll have to drop you off and go.' He knows that coming round will be as dismal as getting dumped by way of text message.

'You're right. I should go home and try to forget.' Not that I am inundated with offers to do much else. 'I've got some vodka in the freezer.'

'It'll be all frozen.'

'Spirits above a certain percentage don't freeze. It's eighty proof and that vodka won't even touch the sides,' I say, emptily.

'Eighty per cent? Don't drink that man, beer is only like four per cent, right?' I can't decide if he is playing ignorant to change the subject, or if he is just plain ill-informed.

'Proof is double the percentage. Vodka is forty per cent. Gemma said she loved me a hundred per cent, but that was a lie.' From now on everything anyone ever says to me will be related back to my failed relationship with Gemma.

'I don't get it,' he says. Just plain ill-informed.

'I don't get it either, buddy,' I say. Just plain ignorant.

Big G looks at me blankly, and I decide not to add anything further to our sullen conversation. I delete the text message, not wanting to read it ever again. He turns the stereo on and drives me to my estate in Formula One fashion. We travel in silence, the noise of his voluble music and raucous dump-valve attempting to fill the space our lack of chatter has left, but I don't hear either. All I can hear is the hum of my phone, even though I've turned it off.

Big G parks under the archway to my maisonette and allows me the customary moment's pause to shuffle about to find my keys. I drag myself out of the car and close the door behind me. I wait for Big G to reverse out and give him an indolent wave, before lugging myself towards the house. I open the front door and make a beeline for the toilet. Without pulling up the toilet seat, I lower my zip and start to pee with no regard for my aim. Getting more piss on the floor than into the bowl, I let out an irritated sigh at how little respect I have for my home and everything in it, especially myself. I tried my surname against her forename countless times. Gemma Chen. Mrs Chen. The Chen Residence. She said she loved the sound of it. So did I.

I head up the stairs and notice that the house feels a lot colder than when I left it. I totter over to the sofa, slump down and realise what has happened.

All of Gemma's stuff is gone.

She has been here, to the house, to take her things. The text that she sent me, only moments ago, was erased in a matter of seconds. I received it, I read it, I felt a deep sense of desertion and then I deleted it. It didn't quite sink in and didn't quite feel real – a feeling I fear is about to change.

I have been surrounded by her worldly possessions for so long: I didn't expect them to ever be *gone*. If it weren't for the fact that my large flat screen television was still on its stand, I would think I'd been robbed. I never realised how much stuff in this room belonged to her. It has now become clear what she truly placed value on. Insincere items that I am unable to inventory. All vanished. The few remaining bits and pieces that belong to me are a drab reminder as to how untaken my life is without her. The tattoo on my ring finger being the largest reminder of them all, one that I take with me everywhere I go. The pain of the tattooist's needle is nothing compared to this.

I look along the windowsill and there are pictures missing. I would have thought she'd either take all of them or none of them. She has taken every picture that doesn't have me in it. You get so used to being with someone that you can't picture life without them. And then, before you know it, before you even got to the really good stuff, they are taking your picture out to put someone else's in.

This was no in and out, supermarket sweep, bank job. There is no way she could have cleared out all her stuff on her own. How did she know I wasn't at home? Have Dick and Gemma been spying on the place? Have they been sitting in a car together, watching and waiting for me to leave?

Do you know what other creature happens to mate for life? Black vultures. They've destroyed the swan and devoured the golden eagle. I pull myself up from the sofa and head into the bedroom, wondering what might be missing from our once cherished queen size.

Gemma hasn't taken our animals. They would have seen her clear out her wardrobe, makeup drawers and jewellery stand, before leaving without them. I can't bear to look at our bears for a moment longer and head for the kitchen. She has even remembered to take her magnets from the fridge, but she chose to leave Pandi. Her magazines are gone, but she decided that there wasn't any room for Cottontail. Our relationship had issues and now she's cancelled her subscription. I know what it feels like to be left behind. The only animal she has taken is Nibbles.

Termites. They mate for life too. How I wish I was an exterminator.

21

'I Love You.'

The Great British public's most commonly spoken untruth.

Gemma was my validation. I would look at her and know that there had to be something about me, to hold down a girl like her. A gorgeous gal that could have her pick of blokes picked me. She's a head turner. She has left me turning my head in this very moment, as I scan my ransacked house. My validation is gone. I already miss the constant reassurance. I miss being told how great I am, even if it was just to humour me. I need it. I *crave* it. There is no one to contradict my self-effacing remarks. I had what Barney referred to as 'a comfortable life.' Every time I doze off, I can feel the absence of her arm around me. I wish I could fold myself into her, wrap myself around her once more, even if only her little finger. I can't stand the thought of waking up alone.

I look through what's left of her belongings. The things she didn't care to take with her. I find a big brown box, full of random bank statements, useless paperwork, and every Christmas, birthday and anniversary card I wrote her. She told me she would treasure them forever. She takes her DVDs, yet leaves the record of our love. When I throw the box back on top of the wardrobe, a pair of her frilly purple knickers fall to the floor. This only reminds me of all the lingerie that she had once worn to excite me. Over the last year of our relationship, I don't think she even bothered to wear a matching set, but now she will be carefully selecting the most seductive items to adorn. For Dick. I much prefer Victoria's Secret to Gemma's Secret.

With jolts of jealousy coursing through me, my fist tightens around the lacy panties and I slump back on to the bed, staring at them through murderous eyes. I don't know what brings me to do it, but I press her knickers to my face and breathe in deeply. There is the faintest smell of her scent and I find it so painfully arousing that it makes me sick, right down to my core. It has been so long since we last made love that the aroma turns me hard as a rock. I cover my throbbing erection with the underwear and slowly begin to masturbate into them, ignoring the shocking glimpse of myself in the mirror, which is urging me to stop.

What has become of me? I am abusing her underwear like some sort of pervert with a sex toy, in spite of everything that she has done to me. This level of erotic masochism is on par with being a gypsy caravan slave. Perverseness. That is what has become of me. I need to burn them. I head into the kitchen and grab the matches from the counter. I throw the cards and her now sticky panties into the metal bin and try to torch them. It doesn't have the dramatic, satisfying effect I had hoped for, seeing as it takes a good fourteen matches to get the bin going. When it finally catches light, the smell of the black fumes soon replace the musk of her soiled g-string.

Gemma used to be: Fiancée. Compassionate. Mine.

Now she is: Ex. Traitorous. His.

I still can't work it out. Dick may be the talk of the town, running the most desired establishment in the area, but if it's stability Gemma is after, then she could do so much better than him. I wish I'd subjected her to a real-life *Indecent Proposal* and we could have been rich together. The Disney film that Gemma has seen the most is *Beauty and the Beast*. If it has taught us anything, it's that looks don't matter, provided you're a billionaire prince who lives in a fucking castle. Gemma told me that I was the epitome of her 'type' – another lie.

Her new relationship must feel forbidden and dangerous, heading back to her mum's the following morning in the same clothes as the night before. The night she has spent with him. She called it the 'stride of pride' when we were first getting together. This is bound to make her feel youthful and reckless again, after the doldrums of would-be married life. It is the 'walk of shame'.

The real reason for her being with Dick is because that *used* to be me, as self-regarding as that must sound. When Gemma and I first met, *I* was *exciting*. She told me some months later that she was initially 'intimidated' by me and that was part of the attraction. There was an element of danger to everything we did because I'm not someone her mother would have approved of. I had the 'treat em mean to keep em keen' thing going, and it worked – the very same strategy that Dick employs. I should have been as arrogant as Dick is as well, and told her not to slam the door on her way back *in*.

Once her mother and I started sharing a peapod, and I stopped working as many hours, and I stopped drinking and partying as much, and I set up shop with a million plush soft toys, what has she done? She's gone looking for who I *had* been, who I was at the start. This assumes the universe revolves around me.

It's always been clear that Dick has the gift of the gab, the confidence and what he refers to as 'the lyrics,' but he's no oil painting, or at least not on a high quality canvas. He may be half-Spanish with a Spanish permatan (and speaks Spanish and his step-dad has a villa in Spain – other possible damning advantages over me which I may have forgotten to mention), but under that infallible skin tone, actual appearance has to account for something, right? Perhaps she chose him for nothing more than the melanin in his skin. I don't know if that should make me feel better or worse.

I am 6ft1, whereas Dick can only be 5ft4, after Harley gives him a box to stand on. Gemma herself stands at an impressive 5ft10 and that's before she puts the high heels on, truly earning her nickname 'Giraffe.'

I'm sure his Body Mass Index works in his favour, being so short, but he is endomorphic, the fattest along Sheldon's chart. I on the other hand am skinny, although I prefer the term 'streamlined.' I may have a bit of a beer belly, but Dick has a beer body. Then there is endowment. Dick's dick does not do what it says on the tin. He may only have two inches, but he has forty stone to push it in with.

Dick can't buy somatotype, height, length or girth (at least not easily and most certainly not on the NHS), yet he has taken her from me. I don't have natural selection to blame it on. I cling to the hope that she simply didn't want to be with *me* anymore, and that he was just a convenient rebound. I doubt he would even care if she broke up with him. He is forever enjoying hamburgers. Of course, she could just be a cold-blooded ice wraith. I can belittle him all I want and I can label her conceited, but either way, she has left. My rosé-tinted glasses have been drunk from and trodden on.

Gemma knows how to get a reaction out of me. When she wanted me to love her, she wanted to consume my heart right down to the last deoxygenated cell. She was the donor to my rare blood type and made sure she was the only one that could provide the transfusion. When she wanted me to hate her, she wanted to engulf my mind until the very last neuron fired itself against my skull. It only proves how much I actually cared. How much she would make me *feel*. When my blood would boil and we slammed doors and shouted until we were blue in the face, it was *passion* and *feeling*, too much to contain. Perhaps if my mother and father screamed more and smashed the odd plate, they'd have still been together.

This plonk is far from palatable; sour grapes must be in season.

I call Dylan.

He must feel like I do: forced to question what went so horribly wrong, so quickly.

'Harry the Hong Kong Hooligan!' says Dylan, sounding hyper.

'You sound... chirpy!' I reply, realising that he doesn't need me at all, and I'm the one looking for some purpose. Or someone just as lost. Misery likes company.

'Chillin out, havin a chong. You?' Everything we had worked so hard for has ended and there he is, 'chillin,' smoking marijuana. He didn't work all that hard, I guess. Maybe the club didn't mean as much to everyone as I had thought.

'Gemma and I are done. Fuck that bitch,' I declare, which sums things up in a nutshell. A Nutshell I wish I had rammed my car into after all. I was lucky to be alive when I came out unscathed. I should have totalled myself and been done with it.

'You two are great together,' he says, coming from the guy that told me to enjoy the single life and to be a 'ledge'.

'It's over now,' I rasp, even though I know he's only trying to help.

'Go get laid, pay for it if you have to! Bell me up if you fancy coming round for a zoot,' he replies, in his own thoughtful way. 'Hey, what animal would you have sex with and what would the room smell like?'

'A kitten and candyfloss, or a sheep and petrol. You've asked me that one before.'

I don't fancy a 'zoot.' I don't fancy anything, apart from finding someone as tangled as I am. Or someone who can show me that it doesn't have to be like this.

'Mine's a gorilla in a room smelling of cheesy chips. You could cuddle it afterwards and have something to munch on,' he says, the strange child.

'Gorilla and cheesy chips?' I clarify. You'd have to have serious munchies to crave mozzarilla.

'Hey, Belinda's pregnant. Trust me to win the Irish lottery! That's why she doesn't drink. Tried to tell you before, but you were pretty mad about the missed delivery. I'll kick her down some stairs, innit? Just kidding! I'd go to jail. I gotta dip man, in a bit,' he says before hanging up, casual as you like.

Here I am at the brink of collapse following everything that has happened and Dylan can treat life-altering news with nonchalance. It beggars belief. Dylan really is something else. I don't know what that something is – slapdash, cavalier blasé? I think they call it 'youth.'

A baby? One crisis at a time.

7. A few months after my mother moved back to London, my father started taking me to the old village he grew up in. He wanted me to spend more time with my Chinese relatives – perhaps his way of allowing me to get to know him better. I kept complaining that it was too hot, too impoverished and that everyone kept gawking at me; generally making him regret the decision altogether. It was during one of these trips that he told me never to smoke. I couldn't bear to tell him that I had cigarettes in my pocket, but he had a nose like a bloodhound, so I'm pretty sure this was another 'clock' situation and he just wanted me to admit it.

When I asked him why he was so dead against smoking, he pointed to an area of open marshland. He explained that it used to be a rice paddy field, and that when he was fourteen years old he was paid peanuts, along with a handful of other children from the village, to dig up the ground for a local landowner. After an exhausting and scorching day, all he wanted was the few promised dollars so that he could buy himself some food. When the owner of the land eventually showed up, hours after the agreed time, the guy paid him with a twenty deck of Marlboro and a lighter.

My father said that he was utterly distraught, but sat and chain-smoked the entire pack, hoping that he could stave off his hunger, and wishing that he'd been paid in actual peanuts. I should have realised how truly privileged I was, and how he had dragged himself up from the irrigated muck. All I could think was how great it must have been to not have someone to answer to for smoking.

6. My father would occasionally have friends round to the house playing Mahjong late into the night. Mahjong is a noisy, exciting game of skill and chance that fascinated me. I would endlessly hassle my father to teach me and, every once in a while, when he finally gave in, we would gamble with silver dollar coins. He would demonstrate how to read body language and mislead the opposition. I was useless at it. I struggled to remember what all the different tiles meant, and which Cantonese phrases to say and when, as he rinsed me of my pocket money. He said that even a doomed hand that was sure to lose could still 'blossom into flower.' I have nothing left of my father beyond a few keepsakes, and some disjointed memories, but this seemed a lesson worth remembering.

People have turned their luck around before, so why can't I? Rap sensation 50 Cent was shot nine times, once through the face. The bullet that entered his mouth changed his voice. It led to the sound that created platinum albums. His bullet blossomed. Legendary music mogul Kanye West recorded his first hit from a hospital bed following a car accident. His debut song was named 'Through the Wire,' because a metal brace was holding his jaw together. Mandara said that Kanye West did for car crashes what 50 Cent did for gunshot wounds. It's going to cost more than four quid at a market to make my flowers blossom.

5. When I was in primary school, my mother used to give me a packed lunch in a green Ninja Turtle lunchbox. Every day, she would pack these chocolate Bourbon biscuits, starting me on the alcohol-related products from a young age. I absolutely hated them. In fact, I would have preferred the whiskey.

I would always give the biscuits to a girl on my school bus, so that my father wouldn't get mad that I didn't eat them. One afternoon, I invited an older boy from the bus to come over to our house to play. I forget the kid's name now, but when he came over he grassed me up by telling my father that I'd been giving my snacks away, the little snitch. His name was probably Bebop or Rock Steady, true Ninja Turtle villains. My father challenged me on this, asking why I didn't just say that I disliked them. He wanted to know how I could fritter something away so easily.

4. When I was fourteen, my father took me to see the horseracing at the Hong Kong Derby. I had been looking forward to it for weeks. I have vivid memories of watching the horses get ready, and my father told me to look out for the one that pees before the race, because it is bound to win. I had picked my favourite from the second we arrived. There was this one horse called Super Fit and I had a premonition that it was going to win. I begged my father to put some money on it because everyone in there was talking about betting. He reminded me what my Mahjong was like, and that soon put an end to my argument.

Super Fit won the race. I told my father that had he listened to me, we would have ended up with some winnings: not said quite like that of course, but in the words of a spoiled fourteen-year-old brat. He told me that the horse wouldn't have won, had we actually placed the bet.

This isn't the only time something like this has happened. Some years later, my friend Midas invited me to watch Arsenal play at The Emirates Stadium because he had a spare ticket going. It was against Bolton Wanderers and I had a feeling that Rosický would score all three goals. After getting stoned all morning, we rushed to the bookies and despite the massive queue, I decided to stick it out. I was on to a winner, despite knowing nothing about football, Arsenal FC or its players. When I eventually got to the counter, they refused to take my £4 and told me to fill out a betting slip and queue up again.

When we entered the stadium, kick-off had already taken place and I had missed my chance. I didn't know any songs or chants and didn't have the appropriate scarf to shake about, but even if I did, I wouldn't have enjoyed the game, because it played out exactly as I had envisioned. This is rather unremarkable, considering the number of other punters undoubtedly predicting that same bet. For all I know it was an expected forecast, but it now signifies so much more. My father was right. I didn't win Gemma because I placed the bet.

Treat em mean to keep em keen.

*

I decide to call Barney to see how he's getting on. Maybe he's eyeing up another opportunity, like a small pub I could live above. I could do that, sharing war stories with the ole boys perched on their stools, bar towel slung over my shoulder, name above the door. That would be ideal. I know it's a long shot, but if Barney is in a position to help me, I know he will.

I've always seen myself as some kind of entrepreneur. I don't know why. Truth be told, I'm just another out of work *employee*. Barney takes ages to pick up, as he always does.

'Mister Chen! How's you?'

'Not too bad. Still alive. Any boozers going?' I sound more desperate than I would have liked. I called Barney, not Barnardo's.

'Haven't spared work a second's thought,' he says. 'Charis and I are painting the nursery, so I can't chat for long. She's eight months heavy and we're only just getting round to it.'

I can make out the sound of Charis rollering and nattering away. Only Barney, in true slave-driver fashion, would make his pregnant girlfriend paint a nursery. I bet he's only 'supervising,' pointing and making the odd joke. Hearing Charis laughing in the background makes me miss having the love of a good woman, if I ever had it. Maybe I merely had the lust of an unscrupulous girl.

'Oh right,' I say, after an uncomfortable silence. 'You must miss it a bit, right?' I chuckle to myself, which sounds lifeless even to me. Barney doesn't say anything, and I change the subject. 'Need help?' I ask, sounding as low as his skirting boards. Not that I mind helping Barney and Charis paint. From dented, discounted tins.

'Under control here, mate. I can't tell you how great it is to not be burdened with the club. Once I get this debt out the way, I don't think I'll ever be happier.' I wish I could share that view.

I miss being part of something. Having a sense of purpose and belonging. I miss the taste of omelette. There was always the uncertainty of whether or not we were going to have a decent night, or a completely abysmal one. However, that is still preferable. Now I am guaranteed an abysmal one, for certain. I am shocked that he wants out; he even has the word 'Bar' in his name.

'Anything comes up, let me know, yeah?' I wonder if Barney likes gherkins on his burger.

'I doubt I'll be speaking with anyone. Looking back, I can't believe I wasted so much time and money. I should have been saving for the baby,' he says, affably.

'Wasted' – that's all we were to him. A *waste* of time. I don't recognise the person on the other end of the phone. I might as well be talking to a large purple dinosaur.

Tight git, I'm surprised he even gave away the sperm.

There is no place for me now, an impostor in my own home – a foreigner and a fraud. Gemma was my local knowledge, my local connection. I should exile myself to a soulless, lifeless place where I belong. Like the Sahara Desert, or Hull. I should chance it in the big lonely city of London, where my mum lives: a place where you're lucky to find someone in the street that speaks English. A place where everyone belongs, because no one belongs.

I can picture Gemma and Dick laughing together. At me. At my expense. I may have had it coming professionally, but surely not this. Not her. He had already taken everything I worked for, and now he has taken everything I lived for. I am left surrounded by the remnants of Gemma: her unwanted belongings, her white elephant stall of dead weight, which I feel obliged to keep, like an old passport with the corner cut off.

I stagger to the fridge to pour myself some orange juice. The urge to sex it up with vodka is strong. This is my new circle of life: a drunken, adult version of *The Lion King*. One filled with profane obscenity, where Simba throws up and Scar punches a prostitute. Today I need to pull it together, by creating a cocktail of positive change. The humourist Robert Benchley said: 'A real hangover is nothing to try out family remedies on. The only cure for a real hangover is death.' I wonder what my stencil would say, if I was to be remembered for one quote above all others, for someone to spray on a dodgy nightclub wall.

I need to take it easy with the firewater if I'm going to get through this, or at least until I can feel the blood in my alcohol stream again. A million questions rattle around in my head, like Rafiki's shaman stick. Will she keep the same side in her new bed? Will they be banging away at the head board? Will they be biting and scratching and licking instead of politely pecking and smooching like we were? Will she remember what my love making was like before I had it down to a science, when we were still the exciting mix of bumping elbows and knees? Was she thinking of him when we were making love? Will he be able to make her come? Harley tells me the only reason women orgasm is because it's another excuse to moan.

Will she cheat on him too, or was that an indulgence saved up only for me? The one person that I would have taken a bullet for has pulled the trigger. I wish I could do a 50 Cent and shoot her straight in the face.

I put the Bitter in Angostura.

23

Gemma and I had talked about having children together. She believes she was put on this Earth to create life. As unprepared as I was for the thought of fatherhood, and despite my plan to buy her a puppy (real, not stuffed) to keep the sleepless nights and dirty nappies at bay, I knew that my most dedicated swimmers were at the ready, whenever the time was right. Our imagined progeny would no longer happen. The bridal suite in the Maldives, in a few years' time, would no longer be the setting for conception. Instead, our dream is to be replaced by a toilet cubicle or store room, in The Havana, with *him* – a glorified sperm donor. Unplanned. Unexpected. Unwanted.

I turn on the laptop and my worst fear is confirmed.

'Richard Priory is in a Relationship with Gemma Goodman.'

That whore. Fourteen people have 'Liked' it and there are a couple of comments, but I can't bring myself to find out what they've said. Only a moment has passed and she has eradicated me from her social network. Gemma is a banana peel.

Dick *wants* me to see this. He wants me to know. I was expecting him to go all out and have a photo of them together as his profile picture to really rub salt and lemon into my wound, but instead I am met with something far worse. He has a black and white cartoon picture of a father and son, reminiscent of a pre-war era newspaper, with the following caption:

'Son, someday you will make a girl very happy, for a short while. Then she'll leave you and be with new men who are ten times better than you could ever hope to be. These men are called DJs.'

The 'DJs' bit has been doctored in a cut and paste job and probably originally said 'Footballers,' or 'Frat Boys,' but its meaning, directed entirely at me, is perfectly clear. Gemma belonged to him now.

Dick has used an obscene set of Mahjong tiles and his tactics could never have been anticipated. I want to confront him, but I can't. He has already humiliated me and the thought of him debasing me over the phone is too much to bear. It would only be feeding an ego that doesn't need to be fed.

I thought Gemma loved me because I was different and unique.

I am unique, just like everybody else.

I have to get out of the house. No keys. This is all too much. I start swearing and cursing and hating life for robbing my collection of metal shapes meaningless to anyone else.

When I was in secondary school, we had an assembly to welcome a representative from The Samaritans Hotline. They did this talk every year to tell the student body that there was always someone to talk to. The bloke said that people call up for all sorts of reasons, and he named most of the usual suspects: abandonment, loss of a loved one, financial failure. Then he mentioned that someone once called up because they had misplaced their keys, much to the amusement of everyone listening, including myself.

The speaker said that if you're at the very end of your tether, the slightest thing can set you off in a spiral of despair. I am no longer laughing and if I had the number, maybe I would have someone to call after all. Unless they can undo the violence I have caused, bring back Gemma, ruin my nemesis and drive a thousand more people through my now closed club each week, I think I'll save the credit. If anyone could do that, I'd happily concede the keys. Fortunately, my dilapidated 316c comes with a spare. A flimsy piece of plastic that looks like it should be used to check a meter reading rather than start an automobile, but it will do. I leave the house unlocked, as the only thing I ever aimed to protect has already gone.

The jaunt to the off-license doesn't take long. Quicker still when you have no care for speed limits, traffic police or right of way – I now lack any sense of self-preservation. Stopping in the disabled space closest to the entrance, I park my shit car with no regard for space markings.

Four quid for four Fosters, or six quid for eight? Despite all the disarray surrounding my tumultuous life, this is currently the most important decision in it. I contemplate the cheap Special Brew, but even I need to maintain some scrap of dignity. The wine we used to get for the club was only £1 each at cost; a price that will take some beating. Value Australian red wine is the cheapest. The Ribena Gemma pours herself looks thicker than this. I head to the till with amber nectar and poorly located grapes, my hands full of the land down under. Bloody convicts.

'Anything else for you, sir?' clerk number four cordially enquires.

'EuroMillions ticket, Lucky Dip,' I request. If a forty-nine million pound jackpot doesn't win her back, nothing will. Then I remember that the worst things in life are free.

As the sloth fills my bag, I think about my peach-coloured lottery docket. Barney once told me that I had a better chance at dialling a random, eleven-digit number and getting through to the Queen – not that Liz and I would have much to talk about. I'd ask her if she's been shagging Dick too.

On the drive back I pull the Australian shit from the carrier bag – the red shit, not the yellow shit. I take a swig, spilling some on the steering wheel. It tastes like wine and that's good enough for me. I try to screw the cap back on, a difficult task with gnawed fingernails, chewed right down to the cuticles.

I pull up to the house and park the car sideways, blocking the archway. I enter my unlocked door and slump on the bottom step. I don't even bother walking up the stairs before cracking open a can of lager. I look at my liquid lunch and realise that it isn't going to be enough. My edge is too large for this small bag to take off. I need something harder. I need something illegal.

It's been a long, long time since I last used drugs. I had a go at Dylan for it, but now I want to be a slug too. They don't keep cannabis in the fruit and veg section in Tesco and you can't purchase ecstasy and MDMA by the pint or loaf. I've never seen cocaine in amongst the colas, and I think I would be swiftly seen out by security if I asked the lady at the pharmacy counter for a big bag of speed. For this purchase I need to make a phone call, which, in my experience, usually ends up in several phone calls and varying degrees of disappointment. I scroll through my contact list for anyone that might be able to aid my search.

I look for keywords that I may have used to loosely disguise dealers. I look for the surname 'Green' and the first name 'Charlie,' but it would seem that I haven't dabbled in the time I've had this phone. I no longer travel in circles that can readily acquire drugs and the only person that comes to mind is Dylan. But he is only an additional middleman in a supply chain that is mostly middle as it is, and we know how I feel about middlemen. For every additional person sat between me and my contraband, there is usually an added unwanted ingredient, to account for what they have helped themselves to. Even though I trust Dylan, 'trust' is a word I have begun to lose faith in. I do tend to like at least a little Class-A with my bicarbonate of soda, flour and teething powder. Someone even sold me salt once: nothing else, just salt.

Mandara was forever playing songs by rapper Lil Wayne at the club, and there was one song in particular that referred to something called 'purple drank.' The recipe consists of strong cough syrup, codeine and promethazine (whatever that is), mixed with Sprite and Jolly Rancher sweets. Obscure as it sounds, I can imagine 'purple drank' tasting quite nice. Someone tries it in that film *No Strings Attached*, and ends up having their stomach pumped. That means it must be good. Gemma loved that film, I thought it was rubbish. I should have read into that more, because our strings couldn't be more detached.

I take a swig of beer and call Dylan, hoping that he will answer his phone. It rings ten times, my impatience growing with each passing tone. Just as I am expecting the voicemail to kick in, he answers.

'Yup, what is it?' says Dylan, who has realised that he doesn't need to be nice to me anymore.

'Dylan, you numpty.' I try to make light.

'Oh shit, hey man! We've hot-boxed my bedroom. My mum's in Cambridge so we're smoking out my room! Wanna join us? Weed is bad, let's burn it!' he says, excitedly. If weed is ever legalised, I can't wait to see the commercials.

'Sounds cool man, but I need something a little *harder*.' I hope not to sound ungrateful, even though being sat in a confined space with the windows shut, and a draught excluder forced under the door to the point of suffocation, does sound quite enjoyable.

'Harder? Seriously! Harry the Hatchet is looking to get mash-up!' he says, before coughing up a lung into the receiver. I have no idea where the 'Hatchet' bit came from, considering the only thing I have ever cut is his wages. Hopefully he has called me that because I will soon be cutting up lots and lots of lines.

'Can you help me or not?' I want less interrogation and more insufflations (or snorting, to you and me).

'Chill. I've got my dealer right here. Hold up.' It then sounds like he has dropped the phone trying to pass it. I wish I had my lines (spoken ones) ready.

'Thanks buddy, that's handy,' I say, to his shoes and a knocked over ashtray.

'Wha'gwan! You my brair's boy, innit?' asks Dylan's dealer, or something equally ciphered. Intensive weed-smoking aside, he can't honestly sound like this. For the sake of the remainder of our conversation, I hope that this isn't his actual voice, and is just a peculiar form of introduction. His accent is from the roughest part of Brixton, even though he's from a picturesque Suffolk country home in the placid village of Flixton.

'Hi, I'm Dylan's friend Harry.' Not sounding nearly as 'street' as I should.

'Safe blud, you my boy's brethren. Now what you sayin?' Never mind what I'm saying, what on earth are *you* saying? At least we've finally reached the part where I place my order: he tells me I'm getting the deal of the century and the best stuff in Britain, before I realise that I am a hundred quid down and could have made it myself from household ingredients in my cupboards.

'Whatever I can get the most of for my money, and quickly. I want to do more lines than a bar code,' I say, opening myself up to an even worse quality of powder than had I just been specific. 'I'm not fussed: whizz, crack, schrooms, m-cat – anything.'

'You a fucking clown, yea? This ain't no circus round ere Bozo, fuck you. I oughta give you a straightener fam, wind ya neck in yea.' I am back on the floor again following what sounded like the dropping of the handset.

There is muffled shouting in the background, but I can barely make out even the occasional word, which is pretty much all I could understand when he spoke directly into the phone. I can now hear Dylan's Labrador puppy (which he named 'Harley' after word got out about *le cancér*) barking loudly in the room. What was otherwise a relaxing smoke for them has been transformed into chaotic, hostile smog. I seem to have that effect on people. I take another swig of my beer and wait for someone to speak to me.

'What the hell?' squawks Dylan, who should really be directing that comment to the dealer who threw his phone on the floor, and who should also come with subtitles.

'I've hardly said two words to the guy.' I'm glad I didn't accept the offer to pop round, because then I'd be in the same room as him.

'You said too much,' replies Dylan, as cryptic as his friend.

'I couldn't have made it easier for him. He's a dealer with morals, is he? He doesn't deal rock, is that it? It's not like I asked for a bundle of smack or a stud farm of ketamine,' I snarl, really starting to wish that Tesco reassessed what they keep in stock. 'If I wanted sheets of acid, then fair enough.'

'You've done it again. Stop saying things over the phone,' he whispers, genuinely convinced that Scotland Yard are listening in on their calls.

'For Heaven's sake, Dildo! Should we check to see this line is secure before scanning your mum's house for taps and bugs?' The hope of scoring anything other than a headache has diminished. 'Put him back on the phone. I can meet him in an undisclosed location and pay him in used bills. No names, no faces. The swallows fly at midnight.'

'Hold on,' says Dylan, who starts up another dialogue with the Artful Dodger. He eventually puts his dealer back on the phone.

'Yea, okay. Cause it's you yea, I'm gonna do dis one ting yea, ya get me? One ting then I ghost, vamos!' He is about as clandestine as Dylan's puppy applying for a job as a sniffer dog at Terminal 4 after a hot-box.

'Thank you. Sorry. So what did you have in mind?' I try to keep the chat as middle of the road as possible, seeing as my Morse Code isn't quite what it used to be.

'I'll do you a Henry of meow for a ton, cash.' A 'Henry' is an eighth of an ounce, or three and a half grams, and 'meow' is that plant food stuff called Mephedrone, which is now classified, and no longer readily available off the internet. A hundred quid for that doesn't sound too bad, considering my lack of options and the time wasted on this phone call. The only slight issue is the cash. I hadn't really thought that far ahead and I doubt he will accept a cheque guarantee card as proof of payment.

'Any chance I can tick it til next week?' I compel, really starting to push my luck.

'Nah, I don't do dat. Why should I part wiff me ting if you ain't got the reddies for me ready? Ha, a ton is some change blud.' I can't decide what I want to be more: an exterminator or a cryptographer.

I'd prefer to be Pablo Escobar if I had a choice, though – get it straight from the source, munching on a coca leaf. Escobar wouldn't worry about Gemma leaving for a more successful rival or deal with small-time pedlars like this. He allegedly used to spend $4,000 a month just on the rubber bands used to wrap his stacks of cash, the Columbian coffee bean bastard.

'You know I'm good for it, mate. I'm a friend of Dylan's, aren't I?' giving it one last fleeting effort.

'Dylan's brethren. I dunno, bruv. Yea, aiight. Fuck it. Be here in thirty then, peace!' There was nothing peaceful about it. I've managed to delay my payment by a week though. Who would have thought knowing Dylan would have its benefits? Good lad.

Proof once again that even a broken clock is right two times a day. Unless it's a digital one like me: then it's just broken.

24

I take a final swig from the can of beer, despite hating that last bit at the bottom. Stepping over the bag of booze, which suddenly seems a lot less appealing now that I have something stiffer waiting for me, I throw the door open and head to the car. Not only have I given up on locking doors, now I don't even bother to close them behind me. It is opportunity that is meant to knock, but it seems to be temptation that is leaning on the doorbell. I get in the car, pausing for a moment as I try to remember how to get to Dylan's house.

I reverse out on to the street, knocking over my neighbour's blue wheelie bin, scattering a mass of dry recyclables all over the pavement and on to the road. I consider getting out, but conclude that anyone who deems it important to separate their waste the first time round would be thrilled at the chance to do it again. The Inconsiderate Thought of the Day award goes to Harry Chen. Take a bow.

Dylan's dealer said to be there in half an hour and I intend to be waiting outside the front door counting down the seconds. Firing on full cylinders, the car is pushed to the limit and I am driving like Big G on a promise. I am on my way to purchase some new medicine, stronger medicine. I too will soon be high, on a tall building, on stilts, flying a kite. The IFC in Hong Kong perhaps, a building so tall you can't see the top of it through the clouds. I think about what I'm going to say once I meet the dealer, and how things are likely to go down. It's hard to know what to expect. There is always the likelihood that he doesn't have anything on him. The number of times I have been 'guaranteed' a delivery or collection, only to find out that it has already been sold, consumed, delayed, or didn't even exist in the first place.

Drug dealers, by their very nature, are unpredictable. They set the terms and conditions and you have no choice but to work within them. There is no 0800 number you can call to put in a formal complaint, no Head Office to write to and no regulatory body. Also, unless you happen to carry your own set of digital scales, the dealer also sets the quantity. There is always that awkward moment when you size up your purchase and question its amount and authenticity, usually to a pusher who seems genuinely insulted.

I try not to think about it too much. My preoccupied mind is leading to increasingly erratic driving. I do not need to get flagged by the Ole Bill, at least not until I am too high to give a shit. As I drive past the Fox & Hound, I think about the last time we were in there and how much of a state Dylan was in. If that was him after a few pints, I can't begin to imagine what I'm about to walk in on. I hope he has some spag bol for me. I'm starving.

As soon as I get plant food up my snout, that will take the hunger away. Whether or not my pale powder can stifle the other groans and grumblings that I am haunted by is yet to be seen.

I have found myself driving past a cemetery. I've taken a wrong turn. I look through the tarnished black spiked fence and across the grounds. I can make out a lone magpie perched on a fence spear in the distance: one for sorrow indeed. She flew off after something shiny, once and for all.

There are some grand marble headstones surrounded by flowers and wreaths, with gold details that catch the last rays of sun and glint through my jammed window at me. There are also some untended gravestones, which look ignored and hang at crooked angles. I can make out some eggshell coloured blobs on some of the older stones, which look like a form of rust. Rust not caused by air or by water, but by neglect. The shiny headstones must belong to people who have only passed away recently: either that, or the people that they left behind cared about them enough to ensure they were maintained.

I can't help but wonder what my father's place of rest must look like. I have been too weak and too self-seeking to pay my respects and visit it. I couldn't bring myself to attend the funeral. Disgraceful. Reprehensible. Dishonourable. If my father were to look down upon me now, on my way to buy drugs, he would be turning in his overgrown, worm-infested grave. I pull a U-turn at the end of the road, trying not to look at the cemetery and all that it represents. I came off the roundabout one turning too soon. I can't miss my appointment, as I really need this prescription filled.

I come to a house that I decide is Dylan's. House number fifty-one. I've always thought Dylan was one card short of a full deck. All of the blinds are drawn and I catch a subtle whiff of cannabis. For a dealer that was so concerned about being caught out by my unencrypted terminology, having a stench of marijuana linger several feet from the terraced house in which you are smoking it (and no doubt selling it) seems a bit careless, if you ask me.

My crusade for tranquiliser begins. After a moment's hesitation, I ring the doorbell. I don't expect an answer any time soon. Smoking cannabis makes even the simplest of tasks an absolute chore. They will be dreading the sound of this bell like it was the walk down the *Green Mile*; the journey from the sofa or beanbag, feeling like Hillary's ascent up Everest.

I am likely to be asked for the secret password while they perform a retina scan through the peephole. I find myself nervous at the thought of meeting someone who was quite willing to show unprovoked aggression towards me over the phone, despite having never met me. For all he knew, I could be some brute of a beast, ripped and ravaged by bulging muscles and steroids, with tattoos on my face and jagged piercings through my eyelids. I once had a doorman work for me who looked like an underground, bare-knuckle boxer. Big G told me that the cage fighter used to get his jollies from having women taser him in the bollocks. I could have been having my bollocks tasered by a dominatrix.

The only problem is I'm nothing like that. A stun gun to my nut sack would reduce me to a babbling, infertile mess, and I am most definitely someone you could call a bozo without any worry of repercussion. It wouldn't be such a bad thing to have. I could taser this dealer guy and take his stash, taser Dylan for having a go at me, and then taser the dog for barking into my ear earlier. Failing that, I could zap myself (only not in the crown jewels). People that subject parts of their body to serious doses of voltage experience something called 'Excited Delirium.' It is a term for the combination of psychomotor agitation, hallucinations, speech disturbances and an elevated body temperature. That sums up my standard night out, so is worth a try.

Just as I'm wondering how you'd ask a girl to taser you in the testicles, I hear someone clambering about behind the door.

'Who is it? Are you there? Are you here?' witters a doped up Dylan. I'd have it resting on a tasselled ornate pillow.

'It's me, you wank stain. Hurry up,' I patiently request.

'Mum?' he asks, and he doesn't even sound like he's joking. He actually thinks I'm his mother. What a thought that is.

'Yes, it's your mum. I'm here to buy some drugs and to break it to you that you're adopted,' I say, slightly amused, but I'd enjoy it a lot more from the other side of the fifty-one.

'This is Harry, isn't it? One sec.' Nothing escapes this man.

Dylan pulls across a dead-bolt lock and slides the metal chain from its runner. I then hear him turn the key to his Alcatraz and what sounds like the moving of furniture. The front door is gently opened and I can see Dylan stood on his tiptoes, peering through the gap, not at me, but over my shoulder.

'If I was your Mum I dropped you on your head as a baby. Let me in, you bellend.' I was just as bad when I used to smoke a quarter a day too.

'I have to keep an eye out, man. He said he ain't never going back to jail.' Dylan is completely hoodwinked by his dealer's imagined importance.

'Want to frisk me to check if I'm wearing a wire?'

'Dude, you don't look so good.' If Dylan, who looks white in the face, unshaven and recently dragged out of bed is saying that *I* look sketched out, that really doesn't bode well.

'It's been forty minutes, has he got my shit or not?'

I have a soft spot for Dylan because I know he means well (hence keeping vigil for all the undercover investigators running surveillance on his cartel headquarters), but fondness aside, he is starting to do my head in.

'Just you, yeah?' he prattles, even though I am clearly the only person stood out here.

'Okay, just me.' I humour his felonious alter ego for the day.

I side step into Fort Knox through the small space afforded to me. Sure enough there is a rattan side-cabinet pressed up against the handle. I have barely got myself through the door before he scrambles to the bolt and chain, as if he's dealing in some kind of hostage negotiation.

I've never been inside Dylan's house, but it has a homely feel to it. Then again, I have just left a demolished morass of a maisonette, so anything would seem homely to me. There are family portraits along both sides of the wall and corridor. I stop to look at some of the pictures. Dylan used to be such an innocent-looking boy. Where did it all go wrong? Bless him. To be fair, I don't suppose there are any childhood photos of me visiting drug dealers in smoke-filled houses.

His home looks a lot nicer than I thought it would. The Dylan I know, who occasionally showed up to work, doesn't live in a house like this. The carefully chosen furniture definitely didn't come flat-packed like mine. I peer into his front room and everything has its place. I miss that sense of order. In his kitchen the back door is wide open. The fence that surrounds the garden is low enough to both see and climb over.

'You've gone to all this trouble to keep the feds out, yet I can see your neighbour trimming his hedge?'

'I was only told to guard the front. He said that you can't trust anyone, not even your reflection. Normally he comes strapped, but today he doesn't have his piece with him.' Dylan has lapped up this guy's every word. 'I had to leave the back door open for the dog. I'm training him to shit in the garden and not in my bed.'

'You're telling me this guy has a gun? But not today. Because he was coming round to your mum's house to hot-box your bedroom.' Just making sure that I've got everything straight, before he gives me that 'straightener.'

'Once you meet, you'll get on great. We can chill and smoke together. There is method to my madness,' he says, wanting us to all be friends. Maybe we can hold hands and sing 'Kumbaya' around the bong, then pretend to fire our imaginary guns into the air.

'Your room is upstairs, yeah? I want to get my stash and go.' I hope Dylan doesn't try to get me to commit to anything more. I refuse to learn their new handshake or contribute any more hot to their box.

'That's all I ask. Be nice.' If it means I can get more, leave less and depart sooner, I will be Mary fucking Poppins up there, don't you worry, mate.

'Did he have it on him, or did he need to go and get it?'

'He carries it on him, loads of it. He has some shit called DMT – stands for Dead Man's Trip, the same chemical that's released in your brain when you die. Proper dark!' he says, excitedly. 'There's one more thing.' Knowing my luck, it's going to be something that I really should have been warned about sooner; at the foot of the stairs perhaps, or at the front door maybe.

'What's that then?' I whisper, considering we are only a few steps from the top.

'Have a listen to his freestyle gangsta rapping.'

Home. I really should have been told about this before I left home. Another drug-dealing, wannabe rapper. You have got to be kidding me. I think I've met the lot now.

25

Dylan shoots me a final apprehensive look before knocking on his blue bedroom door. It has the words 'Police Box' written above it. No wonder he rips the arms of sofas at the club, rather than bring girls back here. He's a closet *Doctor Who* fan! I thought the baby photos lining the hallway were embarrassing enough, but this is priceless. I stare at Dylan in disbelief, incredulous that we are waiting for this guy to respond to our *open sesame*. I push past and press into the door to force it open. Before I can get any welly behind it, Dylan raises his hand towards my face, urging me to hold tight.

'Please bro, please. Wait. For me,' he whimpers.

'This is your house and you want us to wait? Next thing you know he'll be charging you rent and bedding your mother,' I say to Dylan, utterly baffled.

'He isn't to be fucked with. Hush your noise,' he says forcefully. I am taken aback by his tone. For just a moment he seemed to have snapped out of his stoned state.

Dylan raps his knuckles on the rapper's door and doesn't look at me to witness my disparagement. You wouldn't see David Tennant or John Pertwee knocking on the ole Tardis door hoping Rose Tyler or Amy Pond would let him in off the landing.

'*Okay*!' says the dealer, in an aggravated tone, higher pitched than I was expecting. God forbid we should be intruding on his studio session. He bellows as if we've been summoned. What a cock.

Dylan nods at me before opening the door slowly, struggling to get any movement from the hinge. On the floor there is a wet towel shoved under the gap to confine the cannabis cloud. The smell is thick and harsh. It soaks into my bronchioles, the THC in the weed about as useful as the HTC in my pocket. The lights are off in Dylan's room, but as far as I know, this could be the usual level of light: this may even be bright. It also turns out that the Tardis actually is bigger on the inside. Dylan is blocking my view of his Don, but I can hear an instrumental version of The Wu Tang Clan's song 'Gravel Pit' playing. The clever, original words soon to be replaced by ghastly ad-lib lyrics.

'That was nang, bruv. I laid down the sickest verse Dino,' says the dealer, who has probably spent the last hour nattering away to himself into a microphone; a time I would have preferred spent on sorting my flipping stash out.

'We should stick it on YouTube, bruv,' replies Dylan, who seems to have adopted his friend's ridiculous accent and hand gestures. I have a suitable hand gesture for each of them too, waiting to unfold on each fist.

'They would bite my rhymes, blud. Peeps dissin under vids.' His lyrics are undoubtedly a common source of plagiarism.

'Only read the top half of the internet,' I add, over Dylan's shoulder to a poster of Holly Valance, rather than to any one in particular.

Dylan turns around sharply and stabs me with disapproval. He looks at me as if I have spoken out of turn in the presence of a God and shat on the floor in his company. Or at least farted in church.

'Straight dramas out here, blud! Haters fuel my fire and give me more to spit about!' says Dylan's dealer, who has finally acknowledged me, even though he still can't see me.

Dylan gapes at me forgivingly, bashful and apologetic, happy that what I've said has led to an agreeable response from his owner. He steps aside and parks himself on his bed, allowing me to take a step forward, as if his new boss is a mezuzah.

'This is Ronald Benjamin,' says Dylan, pointing to his superior, the personification of chav. He is everything that is wrong with Britain: ambassador for the *Jeremy Kyle* show. I wish he was a Dalek so I could peg it down the stairs, with him unable to follow. Unfortunately, I need his contraband to exterminate me.

'Nah, that's my slave name fam. I'm Benio, innit. No one calls me Ronald in my ends but wastemans, unless dey want beef. What you sayin rude-boy? You da badmans is after me ting,' says Ronald Benjamin. There is no way I'm calling this dickhead Benio.

I was expecting a big yardie the size of Mr T, the way Dylan was carrying on – not a pasty Ali G reprobate. His accent sounds so rehearsed that it can't be his true voice. 'Wasteman' seems to sum me up pretty accurately though, whatever that means, so 'Ronald' it is. He is trying to sound like a Cockney/Rapper cross, but is coming across as a knee-high cock.

He is wearing a black and red striped top, making him look like Dennis the Menace, with Dylan being his Gnasher lapdog. Over his *Beano* top, he is wearing a big Puffa with an ostentatious fur trim on the hood. He has a silver chain around his neck with an oversized cannabis leaf emblem hanging from it. A big, bright, dangling ganja leaf – how very inconspicuous. I bet this guy used to visit Club Verity.

Ronald's hair is short and spiked up, as his thin bristles didn't take to dreadlocks or cornrows. He has shaved far too many lines into his eyebrows: it looks like he did it with a cheese grater. His face bears the scars of childhood acne, but he has convinced Dylan that his uneven skin is the result of a gunshot wound. I inch further into the room, tripping over more wet rags.

'Screw the haters,' I say, trying to have this eejit warm to me. I hate the fakery, but the way I see it, this entire person is a hack, so I'm simply playing my part in the charade.

'Laters haters! Fuck dem wiseman! You like Hip Hop? You gots to hear this verse I'm working on, it's gonna be peng!' My catalyst for a quick transaction fails dismally.

'I love Hip Hop. I'm in a rush though, maybe some other time?' I propose, trying to sound both hurried and polite, through watery eyes and tender lungs.

'Don't disrespect me, you here now, so chill.' He switches from something out of *Lock, Stock* to a Rastafarian gangbanger straight out of Kingston. I'm not sure if he's being serious or joking. I find his whole caricature laughable. However, I need him and he doesn't need me, despite his insistence that I stay.

'I can stay for a bit,' I concede, mortified by my sperm-less balls. He can easily give me what I have come for and let me be on my way, but he is hell-bent on ruining this for me. I bet as a child he used to circle Wally in the *Where's Wally?* books in the library.

'Don't disrespect him. Stay and chill for a bit, in my manor,' says Dylan, acting like Ronald's Mini-Me and sounding like a brown-nosing, green-smoking echo. If anyone deserves getting tasered, it is Dylan, for saying '*manor.*'

I begin to question whether or not this entire exchange is even worth it, but I've committed. To leave empty handed would be a greater crime altogether.

'I gots a wicked instrumental right here. Wu Tang Clan, what a touch,' says Ronald, pointing at the screen with his fingers shaped like a gun. He sounds like he has just got his hands on something brand new, even though it came out decades ago. He reads the name 'Wu. Tang. Clan.' carefully, as if he is learning it for the first time.

'Are they Chinese, like you, Harry?' says Dylan, his ignorance proving why this Ronald guy has managed to infiltrate his entire life. Dylan is so greatly under Ronald's control, he may as well come with a fucking remote. He begins to cough and choke, the hours of hot-box finally catching up with him, although he might be choking on his ridiculous words.

'They are Americans, but African, you knobber. Trust.' Ronald, just as stupid.

'They come from Staten Island in New York City, which they refer to as Shaolin.' I am amazed that I have allowed myself to be drawn into this conversation. I just want to do my deal with the dealer, whose very suggestive title is beginning to sound misleading.

'Nah man, it's cause they rap about Kung Fu and shit,' insists Ronald.

'Really? I didn't know that, sorry.' I decide that biting my tongue must be the way forward. As if the big blaring word 'Shaolin' is flashing on a big screen behind us in all its faux-pas glory during an episode of *QI*, with Ronald Benjamin sitting in for Stephen Fry as tonight's quiz master.

'Shit, close the door, man. Close the door, quick, please! My mum's gonna smell it when she gets back, quick!' shouts Dylan, even though the door has been open for over five minutes and the house already stinks. Paranoia rears its ugly head.

'Fuck that hoe, she's butters,' says Ronald, to my absolute astonishment. It's one thing to treat us like subordinates (duly earned, considering I need him for his stash and because Dylan needs that hug) but to cuss Dylan's mum? Referring to her as a lady of the night – that's a bit much, even for this guy. Burberry. Lambrini. Phony.

'Yea, I suppose,' Dylan replies, making me feel better about my lack of guts. I have a twinge of sympathy for him, but it's his own damn fault. My pang of pity is replaced with a growing impatience. I don't know much about Dylan's Time Lords, but lord, this is taking a long time.

Ronald seems to accept Dylan's agreement that his mother is a whore that should be fucked, and turns back round to the monitor. He scrolls through a long playlist of music, his large sovereign rings tapping against the mouse as he searches for the next instrumental he intends to ruin for me forever. I look down at Dylan, sat on his bed, hands in his lap, feet crossed. He looks so harmless and I have forgotten just how young he is. When we were back at the club I expected so much from this guy, constantly telling him to grow up and to be professional, but he was only acting his age. Perhaps it actually wasn't that long ago that he was watching *Doctor Who*. They probably weren't even on chunky cassette tapes either, but on DVD. I must have had fake idols like Ronald of my own when I was his age. As unsuitable as I may find my replacement, I am bowing down to him too, in pursuit of drugs. At twenty-seven I should really know better and have no excuse for pussy footing around this guy. They say you live and you learn. I am doing neither.

'Snap! I gots the heaviest beat! Y'all ready for me to spit sum flow?' I don't think I will ever be ready to hear his spit flow. He double-clicks a song on the list but through the dark fog I can't see the screen, and I have no desire to move any closer. If anything, I should be slinking back towards the door.

Dylan doesn't look up from his lap, but begins to bop his head to the music, which hasn't even started to play yet. I think he has soaked up enough marijuana to last a shortened lifetime. Ronald has chosen to play the instrumental for 'Dead Wrong' by Notorious B.I.G. I really hope he doesn't intend on passing an imaginary microphone over to me halfway through.

'*Yo... Yo... You feel me yeah? You feel me?*' Ronald begins to chant, shaking his face from side to side like he is possessed by the devil of rap, speaking in tongues or in some bewitched, entranced incantation. He begins to swing his head up and down and looks like he might be suffering from a seizure.

Some of his bops bring his head inches from the desk. Hopefully he gets so into his rap song that he knocks himself out on the table. Then I can rifle through his pockets, jack his shit and go. An act Biggie Smalls would be proud of and adequate revenge for what this guy is about to do to a legendary song.

'*Yo… This is for my gangstas, my face so angry, I love to rhyme, all my fam try stay out the bully van!*' screeches Lil' Ron, his out of synch rendition of 'Dead Wrong' making the song quite appropriately named. He swivels on the chair towards us, looking for a reaction – one I really hope isn't applause. Ronald definitely doesn't have a bullet in his tooth.

'That was ill!' mumbles Dylan, looking rather ill himself.

'That was *unique*,' I add, drawing the line how far I humour this guy.

'I was propa feelin dat cuz!' Ronald looks incredibly proud of himself. I can't begin to imagine what a bad take must sound like.

'Sounds even better with a few lines in you! Got my ting, yeah?' I try to reiterate the reason why I'm here, hoping not to sound patronising, but unfortunately sounding as much of a tool as he does. Using the word 'ting' doesn't sound right when I say it, or when he does for that matter.

'How much is you afta again? You ain't neva tried me ting before, av you?' says Ronald. No, no I have not and for a minute there, I didn't think I ever would.

He reaches into his ridiculous jacket and produces a huge zip-lock sack containing an assortment of packages. This Mr Bassett with his bag of Allsorts is only moments away from sorting me out and it's about to seem worth the wait. He may have a lot of gear, but he's no Howard Marks. There is nothing Nice about him.

I look at his stash longingly, wishing that I had enough money to purchase the lot. There would be no space for thoughts of Gemma after consuming all of his wares. His bulge of overdose, which would indisputably hospitalise me, would be considerably more enjoyable than drinking bleach. He holds up a few baggies to examine, prolonging my wait. He comes to a folded paper wrap, smaller than I had hoped. He offers me his gold-knuckled fist in a handshake as if he was bribing a maître d' for a table at a posh restaurant, not that he'd get seated dressed like that.

I extend my palm with too much enthusiasm. I seem like a crack addict in need of an immediate fix, rather than a casual guy looking for a little rebellious entertainment. Ronald firmly traps the origami package between our grasp.

'Three days, homeboy,' says Ronald unexpectedly.

'I doubt this will last three hours mate, but thank you.'

'Nah bruv, I want my money in three days, ya get me?' he imperils.

'Oh right, three days. Of course, that won't be a problem,' I lie.

'It betta not be a problem. You don't want the agi.' He stares at me menacingly, with a face not even a mother could love. I nod submissively, even though I can't take him seriously, especially now that I have what I came for. What exactly will happen in three days? He'll tell my unsuspecting partner, causing her to leave me? He'll trash my gaff? He'll cost me my job? Beat you to it, buddy.

Ronald releases my clammy hand and I nearly drop the wrap, which has been torn and folded from a Cineworld magazine. *Paranormal Activity 4* is on at 8.40pm. I hope that the activity within this package will make me para. Whenever I've unfolded a wrap of drugs, it's always torn from either a Chinese takeout menu or cinema listings. Nothing ever worth reading. One day, I'd like to purchase my goods from a more perspicacious dealer who wraps his product in a page from a Tolstoy novel.

I carefully unfold the tiny envelope with the most delicate of movements, as if I was untying the lacy knot to honeymoon negligee. I'll sniff this instead. I pull back the triangular corners, revealing some sparkling plant dust. The creases in the paper suggest that this wrap has been opened and refolded a few times before, so it is likely these two have been chipping away at it. My lungs swell at the sight of the shiny granules and I breathe in more smoke than I can handle. I let out a sharp cough, nearly dropping what I have waited so long for.

'Steady on,' says Dylan, who looked ready to try and catch it, although I doubt his hand-eye coordination would provide the necessary reflex. I am glad that he has rejoined us in the land of the somewhat living, as I don't want to be left alone with this guy.

'I didn't drop any, I'm fine.' I feel far from fine. There is a hunger in the depth of my belly, numbness deep within my abdomen. What can only be described as a sense of longing, for what, I don't know. More than for Mephedrone I fear.

'Rack sum up and spread da love yea,' says Ronald, as more of an order than a question. He is in possession of a substantial drug haul and he wants dibs on my paltry movie listing. I wonder what time *Gone with the Wind* is on, because that's what's about to happen to my stash.

I shift myself over to the nearest surface, which is Dylan's wooden chest of drawers. I jostle a fat, Mr Creosote figurine to one side, which apparently doubles as a vomiting sauce dispenser. I have never seen Monty Python's *The Meaning of Life*, but I hope theirs means more than mine. I wipe the dust off the cabinet and carefully lower my wrap on to what is now my operating table. I turn to ask Dylan if he has a card, which is to be my scalpel but, before I speak, Ronald is stood right behind me. He managed to creep up on me so silently, I wonder if he was trying to catch me unaware. He hands me an ominous-looking razor blade, making me all the more uneasy. I have never cut lines using a blade, but taking a sharp weapon away from Ronald seems like a good idea.

I surgically cut about a quarter of it on to the work top. I take extreme care not to ping any crystals away, using all the concentration I can rally. The powder seems hard and jagged and nearly translucent, almost like fibreglass fragments. The smell of the drug is strong, even in this smoke, and I can't place what it reminds me of, something industrial or pharmaceutical perhaps. Or an arsehole, which is probably how it got here.

Ronald hasn't sat back down. He is stood watching, checking that I don't hold out on him, which seems as greedy as the tuxedo-sporting Mr Creosote glutton next to me. Under the scrutiny of his gaze, I cut more from the packet than I had intended, parting with about a third of what's there in total. All I wanted to do was drive back to my house and consume the stash at my leisure and welter in my own filth, not someone else's.

Hoping that Ronald is content with my offering, I centre the remaining powder into the middle of the wrap and slowly fold it back up. I slide the wrap into my pocket, and hope that I don't need to open it again whilst in this house. I partition the pile of off-white goodness into three separate lines, hoping that my one is the slightly larger of the three, without being too obvious. I'll have to make sure that I go first. Ronald takes the razor and shakes his head with a contorted look. He makes the most irritating of 'tsk' sounds as if I've done it completely wrong.

'You're long man,' he says, before he scrapes the lines back into one pile and continues to chop away at the powder with more vigour than I had done. He reaches into his jacket and produces a stack of £20 notes. There must be at least three or four hundred quid there at a glance, compounding my hatred towards him. He pulls a note from the wedge and lays it out flat over the pile like a purple blanket. He runs the blade up and down the note flattening out the powder making it as thin as possible. The scraping noise is shrill, accompanied only by the sound of Tupac.

Ronald repeatedly runs the razor against a small sample of his wealth, before carefully peeling it away. The powder looks much more appealing. Instead of handing me back the blade, he begins to separate the powder into two lines. He better be leaving out Dylan and not me, or this would be the ultimate taunt, and that razor is destined for his throat. He makes one line considerably bigger than the other, and, without saying anything, points at my pocket. He makes a two-fingered 'give it to me' gesture, like Bruce Lee used to do when he beckoned someone to fight. Without the strength to argue, I rummage inside my pocket and reluctantly flick the wrap on to the counter. Without the faintest sign of gratitude he unfolds it and adds more, leaving me with less than half to take home. I am hoping for him to say 'the big one is yours' or 'me na wan big one, blud,' getting his lingo more accurate, but it's unlikely.

He repeats the refinement process on the extra stash, adds it to the already larger line, then flattens the note and rolls it up, turning it into a cone. This guy is well-versed in all things snort-related. I'm surprised he doesn't produce a metal pipe with a funnelled end to complete his paraphernalia. He clears his throat and presses his thumb against his nostril, breathing in deeply. The smoke doesn't affect him and he doesn't splutter like I did. He does the big line. I say nothing. His throat won't be seeing any razor blade tonight as I am too small to voice any kind of objection. Coming here was a bad idea.

'Safe geeze, you hav dat,' says Ronald. I reach out my hand to take the note from him but he places it to his mouth, inhales, and sucks up any powder that found itself stuck inside. He then unrolls the note in front of me, smoothing it out flat, Queen's head up, and tucks it back into his jacket pocket. He sits back down, relights a joint and returns to his playlist. He's more of an Indian giver than Harley.

I ask Dylan if he has anything I can use, but he's nodded off. I can't blame Dylan for being knackered, I've been with this Ronald guy for ten minutes and I'm exhausted. Even if I did have the courage to voice my discontent, I don't think I'd have the energy. I open the top drawer to the cabinet and in amongst the useless shite Dylan has accumulated throughout his time in the Tardis, I find a used train ticket which, once upon a time, took a child to Burntisland, wherever the fuck that is. Dylan undoubtedly dodged a full fare: I'd do the same. I roll it into a cylinder, giving the stylish cone method a miss. I look at the line and feel overwhelmed with that sensation you get before the big drop on a rollercoaster, after a slow ascent, when your belly floats and you don't know what to expect.

I take a long breath and force the meow up into my brain. I get halfway up the line before I have to stop – the sensation is excruciating. I try to compose myself by quickly swapping the ticket to the other nostril and hoofing the remainder. I pinch my nose, trapping any crumbs trying to escape from my cilia. As uncomfortable as the hit is, I deserve the pain. My jaw has become tense, my teeth involuntarily tighten into a clench and Ronald and Dylan are about to see me chunder. I retch but manage to hold back my empty stomach and a tear wells up in each of my eyes.

People have died from doing this stuff, but the plant food has worked. It has managed to turn a little weed in my viscera into Jack's beanstalk that wants to force itself from my mouth, up into a cloud well past nine. The plant that this food is meant to feed must be stinging nettles or brambles. I want to throw up like the fat statue guy. I doubt that Dylan will hold my hair back, stroke my neck and whisper shush noises. I am disorientated and finally it is a disorientation of my choosing. Tonight I have pushed the boat out big time. Gemma was my anchor.

Despite the agitation to my sinuses, I frantically run the rolled up ticket across the worktop to snatch at every particle of my synthetic stimulant. My teeth start to grind and my hands and feet become sweaty. I didn't think I would get a reaction so quickly. I turn to Ronald, and, as if by magic, I no longer feel anywhere near the same level of detestation towards him. In spite of the searing pain, the only thing I really want to do is another line, even bigger and more painful than the last.

As soon as I have finished snorting the remaining specks, I let out a gasp, as if I have managed to grab a lung full of air after being held under water. A shiver runs down my spine and the hackles on the back of my neck stand to attention. I take satisfaction in the knowledge that Gemma would find it highly offensive. Even though the thought of her witnessing this would be demeaning, part of me wants her to see what she has made me resort to.

My headstone will not be made of black glossy marble.

'You don't know how badly I needed that,' I say, to Holly Valance, with genuine gratitude towards this Ronald character, in the face of his stinginess.

'Yeah, you know dat,' he replies, without looking away from the computer screen.

'Know what?' I can just about say through the sandy bitter taste on my tongue as I lick the edges of the train ticket I have unrolled.

'Two and a half days.' Douche.

'I'll ring Dylan when my money comes through. Should be tomorrow,' I fib, in full knowledge that no call or payment will be made. Ronald will probably find a way into my bank account and take half of what is left of my overdraft, just like he did with the stash.

No one says anything, suggesting that what I have said is a given and there are no two ways about it. I mutter some form of farewell, thanking both Ronald and Dylan for their gracious hospitality, before exiting the Tardis. I try to close the door behind me with the wet towel roughly in its original position and dart down the staircase, gripping the handrail to try and keep my balance. I move the side cabinet, slide the bolt and chain and step out into the cold. It is dark – I was in there for far longer than I had hoped. I look up and down the street to see if anyone has seen me leave and the coast is clear, not an MI5 operative in sight.

I walk towards my Beemer with my hand pressed firmly against my pocket, protecting the wrap. I pull my hand away for just long enough to find the emergency key and then lower myself into the cold, damp car. I look into the rear view mirror and can't believe how noticeably dilated my eyes appear. This is the reflection that Dylan warned me not to trust. My hand is shaking uncontrollably, from nerves and narcotics, as I try to turn the flimsy key to start the engine. My palms are so wet I may as well be driving a jet ski.

This journey is going to be one of *Fear and Loathing in Las Vegas* proportions, except instead of an expansive stretch of desert to roam through, I have backed up, one-way streets. The other difference between my expedition and that of the Hunter S. Thompson novel (apart from their considerably nicer car) is that they had two bags of grass, seventy-five pellets of mescaline, five sheets of high-powered blotter acid, a salt shaker half full of cocaine, a whole galaxy of multi-coloured uppers, downers, screamers, laughers and a quart of tequila, a quart of rum, a case of beer, a pint of raw ether and two dozen amyls. I have a near-empty folded cinema listing.

My chemical romance is not dissimilar to my actual romance. Horribly pointless, leaving a bad aftertaste. When I reach my cul-de-sac, I let out a sigh of relief. I need to find a dealer that delivers. I park up and head into the house, grateful that I have managed to arrive back to my forsaken bachelor pad, which I desperately wish was my marital home. The measly contents of my pocket aren't what I wanted to be carrying over the threshold, but it's all I have left. I climb the stairs and a glass of government-issue council pop is the first port of call. I'd prefer a shot of port, but there you go. Any port in a storm and my storm has driven me ashore, on to the hard white rocks.

26

Now that I have my wrap opened out in front of me, it doesn't bring me the satisfaction I had hoped for. It was more about fulfilling a craving, than the actual drug itself. Back in Hong Kong, my mum used to have a poster behind the door of our toilet, which read 'Everything I need to know about life I learnt from *Star Trek*.' There were a few gems on there that I would peruse while taking a shit, often testing myself to see how many I could remember.

Some of them were twists on existing sayings, such as 'Don't put all your commanding officers in one shuttlecraft,' and others were weird Trekkie things about Klingons and Vulcans, but one quote in particular has always stuck with me. 'Having is not as great a thing as wanting, it is not logical but it is often true,' or something like that anyway. Captain Kirk or Spock or Bones didn't go where no man has gone before, throughout the galaxies in search of plant food to snort, but he might be right about my pursuit of drugs, maybe even about my life in general.

I had Gemma and for a time, she was all mine. I used to firmly believe that no matter what happened in my life, I would have her. That my birthday would never again be forgotten to the occasion of New Year's Eve. I had a mate for life. Now that she's gone, I *want* her and the desire to have her back is far greater than anything felt during the entire time I actually had her. I think perhaps it is in our very nature, on a basic human level, to never be satisfied or appreciate what we have.

I stare at the DVDs under the television and at the box sets scattered across the floor, looking for a suitable case on which to do my remaining lines. I scan the pile, hoping to find one of Gemma's that she may have forgotten, as it would be more insulting to her if I could find the one disc she didn't remember to pilfer. I see a film the wrong way round and it is *Moulin Rouge*. Bingo. I open it, but the DVD is gone. She couldn't even leave the movie that I spent an hour and a half of my life pretending to enjoy.

Gemma was always a romantic and has watched *Moulin Rouge* countless times, knowing every word to every song. This is why she had such strong ambitions to be looked after, like the Shining Diamond

Satine. 'The greatest thing you'll ever learn is just to love and be loved in return.' That is the greatest thing I will ever *regret*, but the show must go on.

I try to draw the process out for as long as possible, to postpone the inevitability of running out of stash. I tip it all out on to the DVD case and rack up another line. As soon as I do it, I am already thinking about the next one, dopamine receptors flying about in my head like the Starship Enterprise. I take far more care in the preparation of my last two lines and split it into three, then four. I wish I'd asked Ronald for more, or done a runner once I got my package. I should have put up some kind of resistance when he decided to take his lion's share back. I wish for a lot of things.

When the very last of the fibreglass is gone, I wish I could start over. I should have used it sparingly, savouring it when I had the chance. I call Dylan again. I can drive back. Anything will do. The phone rings a few times before Dylan answers.

'I need more.' I cut to the chase, as I no longer have any stash to cut or chase.

'What? Let me ask him,' he replies. I'm in luck, he's still there.

'Ask him, ask him.' This is a process that needs to be speeded up. There is no way I'm going through that fiasco again.

'He won't until you pay.' There is little I can say in response to that.

'He's a fucking arsehole.' There is always that.

'No he's not. He's just misunderstood,' he says, too stoned to see the bad in anything.

'You're right. I didn't understand a fucking thing he said all night! Fuck you lot.' With that, I hang up on the capitalist dogs.

I head into the kitchen and over to the sink. I fill my cupped hands with water and inhale it sharply into my nose to get one last hit. With my gear gone and drink drunk, and with no chance of obtaining any more, there is no reason for me to be awake. I close my eyes before standing up and the entire room slides to one side, from seismic tectonic drug movement. I am now an alcoholic *and* a drug abuser. Gemma called me an alcoholic once and I nearly choked on my pint. I am no longer available in sober.

*

The faint sunlight manages to creep its way through the curtains. Another joint possession I'm surprised Gemma didn't take with her. The curtains that is, not the sun. She's welcome to the sun: it might defrost that frozen heart of hers.

Despite shrouding myself in duvet, the sun is relentless in its attack. The light signifies a new day and I was only just beginning to forget the last one. I have no idea what time it is, but I know I've slept for far too long. There is only so much sleep you can have before it does more harm than good.

I have fourteen missed calls from Big G and eight from Barney. I gather that the reason for the excessive dialling is down to the seventeen hours of sleep I've had, borderline hibernation. Definitely more harm than good. Not wanting to speak to either of them, I toss the covers off and stagger through to the kitchen. My entire body is drenched in lactic acid. I need some hair of the dog that bites you in the arse. Get the shears out; make that bitch bald. Perhaps not as stiff as my white nightcap though. How can I be so thirsty, when I drank so much last night?

There is no call or text from Gemma, again.

Seventeen hours of sleep. This is a definite WTF moment. I scored a headache after all. Wearing only a pair of dank trackie bottoms, the last thing I am expecting is the doorbell to ring. I cannot allow Gemma to see me like this. I have to open the door though, just in case. Maybe she misses everything we once shared and life isn't all it's cracked up to be with DJ Dickface? If she's here for her box of cards, some of which were from her parents and friends, she will soon realise that I've set them all on fire.

I look for something to wear, a shirt that Gemma gave me perhaps, but with no other option, I am going to have to greet her semi-naked. I poise myself for what could be one enormous confrontation. I swing the door open. Like ripping off a plaster, I want the suspense to be over as quickly as possible. In an instant, I can decide if the wound is healing or infected.

'About fucking time,' says Big G, blowing into his clenched hands.

'Bugz, I wasn't expecting you. I thought you might've been someone else,' I reply. Big G has no illusions as to whom I am referring.

'I brought your favourite dish from The Golden Dragon. Mr Ho said he can prepare the food just the way you like it, Hong Kong style, but it's gonna cost ya,' he says flatly. Of course it's going to cost me, typical Chinaman. I take the plastic bag from Big G, which contains the first solid food I will have eaten in days. There is a God after all: he is big and ginger.

'Come inside, there's no chance I'm listening to your blether in the cold,' I reply, as my moobs turn into ice moobs.

'There's something I need to tell you.' He looks more like 'Little G' with his dwindling eye contact.

'What is it? Has Gemma asked after me?' I begin, stopping before I embarrass myself. She won't have asked after me. That's when you know it's over: when you have the opportunity to get information on someone and don't even feel the urge to.

'No, it's nothing like that,' he says, as I knew he would.

'I hate them. Well, hate's a strong word. I mean I *fucking* hate them. You're gonna tell me she's engaged to Dick, aren't you? I can tell by the look on your face. I bet he bought her a bigger engagement ring than I did.' I'm infuriated that they could get engaged so soon, just to spite me. If we were in a different era, he'd be a Viking, raping and pillaging.

'Did she give you back the ring? Looks like you could do with the money. No offence. It's about Snoopy.'

'Dick, huh? Scum. I bet they're celebrating our closure,' I say, enraged that Dick has slandered me, all over the internet. 'What has he written about us?'

'Harry, please. There's a bottle of Tropicana in the bag to sober you up. Let's dish you up some food and have a chat, okay.' I am starting to think that 'G' is short for 'Guesswork.'

'Sure, let's talk. I'm famished. Dick's bought her a car, hasn't he?' I bleat, bitterly.

Big G stares at the floor and says nothing.

'Fuck him. Whatever it is, let him get on with it. He's won. I get it. I was foolish to think that Gemma was going to show up. He's come out on top. He's probably on top of her as we speak. What's left for him to do now? Frame me for murder?' I entreat, never realising until now that hitting rock bottom meant that it can't get any worse.

'I work for him now.' I spoke too soon. His words slice through me: this food, my home, like *The House of Daggers*. My entire body is struck with the sensation of pins and needles, deep disloyal lacerations under my skin. 'At The Havana Club.'

Big G's face is a mask of shame, and I no longer recognise my friend. My legs start to judder, as if they're about to buckle under the weight of this new knowledge.

'This better be a sick joke. After all he's done to me. To *us*! Since when? How long, G? How long has this been going on for?' I stutter, dropping the bag of bribery sent to soften me up, to fatten me up, like in Hansel and Gretel before the cannibalistic wicked witch makes her move. How did I fail to notice the breadcrumbs that led to this crooked twist of the knife?

'I need the money, mate. The hours he's given me will make up a big part of my income. Snoopy called me when we were playing pool, when Gemma was getting her stuff. He told me there would be an assistant manager's job waiting for me once all of this was sorted.' I feel the blood leave my body, all sensation from my person vanishing. I am a cadaver stood upright, stiff and skeletal.

'You *knew* Gemma was getting her stuff?' I spatter. I am by now accustomed to betrayal, but this revelation is the final nail in my coffin. The camel's back was already broken and Big G is covering it up with straw to set alight. 'Have I not been through enough?'

'I'm sorry Harry, but you need to look out for number one. Lisa did, and she loves it there.'

'Lisa works at The Havana?' I wasn't especially nice to her, but that doesn't mean she had to go and set the fire alarm off in an act of sabotage. She was only meant to be back in Bury for the holidays, but if Dick can convince Gemma to leave me, I bet he didn't have any trouble getting Lisa to drop out of university. I bet she was texting Dick on our tree hugger night. She probably left us to go work up there that same evening.

'It's also my chance to find a woman. This isn't personal. Stevie Mac is starting this weekend. They do Drop The Bomb there now too.' I wish he'd just stop talking. 'I could try get you a job there? Glass collecting maybe?' he offers. This is why he is called 'Big' – the 'G' stands for 'Grievance.'

'Collecting glasses for Dick? Are you fucking *serious*?! You had me sit there, singing along to your bloody ringtone, knowing exactly what they were up to,' I say, truly horrified. 'I will never forgive you for this.' Now I have 100 Problems.

'It doesn't have to end like thi–' he says, before I cut him off, like an amputation.

'It's ended. That was why you suggested taking a cruise around town? To buy them more time. The text I received from her – that was the signal for the all clear, was it?' I cross-examine, these accusations unsubstantiated, but I'm throwing them around regardless. 'The sheep wants its clothing back, because you are a fucking wolf.'

'Harry, stop –' he starts and I can see he's had enough of this, but he can wait.

'I'm sure you three will be perfect for each other. The deceptive wolf, the greedy pig and his bitch dog: quite the trio. Wolf, pig and dog! Probably the Chinese dinner in this bag here.' I won't be able to bring myself to eat this now. 'Do you know what they say about us Chinese? The only thing with four legs we don't eat is the table, you big ginger cunt!' I grunt, bark and howl, much louder than my usual oink, woof and pant. This is the first time I have ever threatened Big G and every ounce of me means every word of it. I wish The Bomb Bar was an abattoir after all.

'Don't be stup–' he starts as he rolls his eyes, aggravating me further.

'*Don't* say another word. Get the fuck out!' I fume.

I throw the food against the door to the house, signalling how badly I want him to exit from it. The food makes more of a mess than I had intended, with the paper lids coming away from their foil containers. Red glazed meat and boiled rice smear down the door and ricochet onto the wall and carpet.

'You're a mug. I came here to try and help you.'

'*Diu lei lo mo hai! Pok ai jai! Homm gah chaan!*' I yell vehemently. The seldom used Cantonese swear words make an appearance. I suggest that something highly offensive will happen to his mother, and that he and all his family will die. Not only has he brought me nefarious food, but he's also brought me Tourette's.

'I don't need this shit. Sort your life out and get a fucking job,' he says, suitably insulted by my barrage of canto-expletives.

His size fourteen shoe forces the cap off of the orange juice, spraying OJ all along the floor. Whether this was intentional or not, it doesn't matter now. I was only going to stomp on it myself, creating an even greater mess than the char-siu pork and white rice has already caused. Built like a brick shithouse, he would have taken my house of shit bricks down with it. If you were going to knock over someone's pint in the pub, you'd rather it was mine than his. He could quite easily OJ me, of the Simpson variety.

I slam the door behind him, so hard that the catch doesn't hold and it flings back at me with the same force, ramming itself deep into my wrist. I cry in a shrill of muffled pain, falling backwards into the bathroom and on to the washing basket, breaking its wicker lid. I struggle to my feet, pulling myself up with the towel rail. Gemma took her favourite pink towel (the same one she threw in when things turned sour) and mine does just fine on the floor, so I rip the rail off the wall with both hands, blinded with hate. The four small screws and wall plugs are powerless to stop me.

Big G: Deserter. Malicious. Poisonous.

Towel rail in hand, I begin to wreak havoc on my cold, rented bathroom, swinging wildly, not allowing a moments silence between deafening smashes of tile and glass. I thrust the railing into the set of speakers on the windowsill. Phil Collins' music shall be heard here no longer. Next to go is her scented candle, which she never used once. It is now a piñata. I swing my improvised weapon like a drunken brawler who has been backed into a corner. I deftly hail my fury on the cabinet mirror. I can't even handle seven *days* of bad luck, forget seven years.

I catch a glimpse of myself in what is left of the broken shards. I thought I no longer recognised Big G standing in front of me. The image of myself in the shattered glass seems more of an impostor still. This cannot be me. The damage I have caused this time cannot be undone. My skin is ragged and blotchy, like a ghost with eczema. Here I am, aged and unfamiliar, decimating my water closet. My face looks gaunt, skin as white as a Funk'd Up raving lunatic. I wouldn't look out of place jumping around a sweaty nightclub, full of ketamine, with the out-casted country bumpkins, drinking perspiration from a passing bucket.

I continue to hack away at the hanging cabinet, vanquishing the remaining mirror from sight, subjugating the stranger hidden within it. If Big G is a wolf, I am a werewolf. I can still hear Big G, muttering to himself as he fires up his car, a car I would never be entitled to, or desire, a lift from again. He reverses out and speeds off, taking not only his VW Golf and his friendship, but my worth. As I turn to swing the bent towel rail towards the shower curtain, I step on a scatter of glass but can barely feel it. Nothing can hurt me now. I didn't realise that beneath rock bottom was another chasm of hopelessness in which to wallow.

I try to break the toilet bowl with the towel rail, which is about to snap. The porcelain proves too much for the flimsy aluminium and I try to kick it instead. The Armitage Shanks is too solid for rail and foot, so I punch at the cistern until my knuckles fracture. I grab the toilet lid with bloodied hands, which I have cut to shreds, and rip it from its metal hinges. It takes a fair few attempts to break, but once I free it from its restraints, I fall backwards. I land on the floor, cracking the base of my back into the side of the bath, taking both toilet lid and seat with me.

As I lie on the freezing cold floor, covered in glass, toiletries and bog roll, my heart pounds through my chest. It has been ripped apart and trodden on, beaten by a metal rail itself, yet there it is, trying to force its way out of my breastbone. How am I going to explain this to A&E? I am in dire need of a doctor, but even he would tell me I am beyond help. Doing shots of Calpol with my GP is all I'd be good for.

I can feel the stillness of the house. As quiet as the moment I slapped her. The landlord will be round to ask me why this month's rent hasn't come, only to find his bathroom and house trashed, but I don't care. I don't care about anything now, or perhaps I care too much? This is what's left of me, bloodied and dispirited and numb. A peculiar, unfamiliar burning trickle passes down the side of my face and onto my ear. Unless we bleed or sweat or squeeze OJ from our eyes, I think it might be tears. I can't remember the last time I cried. I mean *proper* cried. I didn't even cry when I heard the news about my father. Not because I wasn't sad, because I was, I was truly distraught. But it was a billion miles away, and I was in disbelief.

I immersed myself in the club and had Gemma to occupy my mind. Unremitting work and caring fiancée managed to anaesthetise me from the entire ordeal. When you distract yourself with everything you can, and work late into the night, I suppose mourning never comes. I never allowed myself to truly feel it. But I feel it now. I feel it all now, everything. Here, laid out on my busted back, on the debris of a bathroom floor. The tears refuse to stop and the floodgates have opened. My eyes sting from the sensation and I let them fall. I am weak.

Gemma was the eye of the storm, which ruined my house. Big G was the epicentre of the quake that has ravaged my home.

27

I wake up freezing and shaking. As my vision starts to focus, I try to sit up but I'm near enough paralysed from the chest down. Every inch of me aches and digging into the side of my hip is the pine duckboard from my washroom.

Look at the fucking state of it.

I have obliterated my bathroom and everything breakable in it. It looks like the love-child of Hiroshima and Normandy, on a dirty weekend away at Pearl Harbour. There is something strangely satisfying about being able to create carnage. Putting it all back together again is a different story.

A chilling gust of wind catches my face and my cheeks are bitter cold. I rub the side of my head and wipe my eyes. I hold the palm of my hand under my chin and push, hoping to click my neck, a manoeuvre I've never quite managed to master. As my failed neck click turns into an uppercut to the face, I notice that the front door is wide open and I can see a pair of boots, with someone standing in them. I shuffle backwards along the carpet, curious to see who it is. I am surprised to find that the postman is staring down at me, puzzled by the half-naked oddball before him.

'Jesus man, have you been robbed? Do you need me to call the police?' says a concerned Royal Mail representative. How long he's been there I don't know, but better him than the landlord, a debt collector or my ex-fiancée.

'No! Don't call the police.' I feel slightly embarrassed that a member of civilised society has stumbled across my ludicrous alternate reality. 'I think I did this.'

'*You* did this? You don't look so good, pal. I think you need medical attention. Is all that blood yours?'

'Damn,' I say, looking at my feet. They are disgusting. 'Of course this is my blood. What kinda party do you think this is? No Ipswich prossies here. Got any mail for me or what, I'm kind of busy,' I continue, trying to convince the guy who just saw me wake up that I am preoccupied.

'Some junk mail and a bunch of bills, but here you go. Mind if I come in?' he asks, taking 'kind of busy' as a cue to invite himself inside.

'Watch the food! Don't step on my rice.' This situation couldn't possibly get any weirder.

'So why did you trash your bathroom, Mr Chen?' says Royal Mail Guy, who is really starting to impose himself on my life, which should be kept behind closed doors and not wide open ones.

'How do you know my name? What the fuck you want from me?' This spying operative in disguise knows my name and shows up at this exact moment.

'Your name is on your letters,' he replies. My paranoia subsides.

'That, my friend, is a fair one. You gonna help me up or what?' I appeal, extending my arm in his general direction. If this guy wants to be part of my pantomime of a life, he can at least help me off the floor.

'Sure. I do recognise you though. I've seen you flyering outside the club on Church Street. Right then, ready? On the count of three.' He drops his bag of swag and steadies himself for a cumbersome lift of self-inflicted casualty.

'Fuck three. Lift me, man.' I want to get vertical and clothed as soon as possible. He doesn't cringe or pull away when his shins are spattered with my blood.

Royal Mail Guy: Tall. Dark. Handsome. Gemma would love him. Just as well I don't have a milkman.

'So tell me again why you beat yourself up?' He now has every right to pry, considering he has helped me up, delivered my post and allowed me to bleed all over his shoes.

'Some prick told me I needed to get a job. Royal Mail aren't hiring, are they?' I joke.

'Ha! You don't want a job with the Mail. You get roped into all sorts of things. You're going to need a decent wage to pay for all this,' he remarks. The towel rail alone is going to set me back a tenner.

'I'll do Church Street for a tenner.' Still not quite five million a job.

'Have you tried getting some work through an agency? That's your best bet,' he says, opening up a whole realm of possibility never previously considered.

'Agency, huh?' I ask, 'I'll look into that. Deffo. Fancy some of this Chinese food?'

*

Agency work? Quick, easy cash without responsibility or commitment, which only ever results in broken bathrooms and the abrupt ending of relationships.

Dylan's dealer is going to want that money soon and even though I had planned to dodge the debt, I don't want to drop my friend in the shit and make him fork out over my bill. Ronald would end up having Dylan chipped and neutered. This bathroom is also going to need a lot of work. I wonder if Barney still has the number for the owner of Taps!

I have managed to make it up the staircase, moaning each and every step of the way, after closing the door on Royal Mail Guy, who rejected my offer of soiled barbecue pork and contaminated rice. Posh ponce. My right foot feels swollen, so I have wrapped it in a towel and don't dare look at it. At least if Ronald sends the boys round to break my legs, I've beaten him to that too.

I will never speak to Big G again, not in a *year* of Sundays, but he did get a couple of things right. I do need to sort my life out. I do need a fucking job. I reach for my phone, trying not to disturb my disturbing foot. Agency work: definitely worth a Google. I am astonished that the battery is still going as it often requires two charges a day, but you don't use much juice when you have no one calling you and even fewer people to call. What is fewer than no one? Having enemies rather than friends.

I type 'agency work' into the search bar. The phone asks me if it can use my location and I ask it why it would want to use anyone else's. An address and number appear for an agency called Phoenix Placements. If there is one thing that I need to do, it is to rise from the ashes. Without giving it too much thought, I click on the phone number and it starts to dial. What have I got to lose? After only one ring, a professional voice answers and confirms that I am indeed calling an office full of burning birds. I know one bird that I want to burn, that's for sure.

'Good morning, Phoenix Placements. Steve speaking, how can I help?' says Steve from Phoenix Placements on 14 Eastgate Street, Bury

St Albans, IP34 4AD. *Save Number* or *Get Directions?* This phone isn't that bad, I suppose.

'Yes. Hello, my name is Harry and I'm looking for some work, preferably local and paid weekly.' I list my priorities as not requiring petrol and the need for quick cash.

'We pay weekly, but you work a week in hand. Our clients are based here in Bury and the surrounding areas. I just have a few questions for you first,' he says, hitting two for two on my wish list. I like this guy already.

'Ask away.' I want to get to the bit where I give him bank details, so that he can pay in my urgently required wages.

'Can you handle a fork lift?' First hurdle.

'No, I have a valid driving licence though. No points or anything.' I know that has no relevance whatsoever, but want to show that I am not what is referred to by *The Inbetweeners* as a 'bus wanker.'

'So, no shunting experience then? Okay,' he says. What the fuck is a shunt?

'No, I haven't been shunting,' I reply, although I am definitely looking that up next.

'Can you drive a heavy goods vehicle?' he asks, making me look as small as I feel, which isn't even a *light* goods vehicle.

'No, no HGV licence,' I say, my virtue fleeing, taking with it my chances at a job.

'Can you operate any machinery?' he asks, patiently.

'No, sorry Steve. I can work a till though,' I say, looking to redeem myself any way possible.

'We aren't retail or customer-based. How about specialist equipment?' Come on, man, give me something, anything I can work with Steve-o.

'No, I can't. How useless am I, huh?' I tell Steve. He doesn't know the half of it.

'Stop me at any point as I list the following, okay?' Agreeing that I am useless.

'Let's have it then,' I say, on the brink of hanging up.

'Carpentry, joinery, plumbing, electrics, metal works, laser cutti–' he says, leaving a second's pause between each trade, not expecting me to stop him at any point, but I interrupt him anyway, cutting him off while he says the word 'cutting.'

'No, none of those, Steve, nothing.' I never realised how little I could do. I invested everything in my job and left myself with no other options outwith the bar trade. Looking at what it has done to me, I don't think working at another venue is a good idea, even if I have had an amazing offer to collect glasses from Big G, the newest addition to the Havana hyenas.

'Then you can do plugging,' he says, revealing the lowest common denominator on his list of available vacancies. My fraction is getting more vulgar by the minute.

'What's plugging? Whatever it is, I'll do it. What's the pay?' I ask, getting to the point.

'Plugging is down at the brewery. Knocking bungs into barrels. I don't know much about it, but I have four lads down there at the minute and they've requested a further two. The pay is minimum wage but one of the spots is yours if you have a National Insurance card and the right to work in the UK. You would also need to sign a Health and Safety waiver,' he replies.

'I have no regard for my health or safety. Knocking bungs, I can do that. Knocking bums at the knocking shop, sounds good. I can bring my stuff in to you tomorrow if you like?' I offer. Probably not the right time to be making jokes about brothels.

'The waiver confirms that you are willing to work outside the maximum number of hours. Bring your documents down tomorrow at 5.30 and I'll make photocopies. That should give us enough time.'

'You're still open at 5.30? I don't have a job, so I can come during the day.' Impressed that a recruiter on the high street would be open so late.

'You start work at 6*am* tomorrow, so come see me at 5.30. That's 5.30 in the *morning*.'

'Oh. I see. Shit. What else do I need to bring?' I ask, knocked for six.

'As well as your documents, you will need steel-toed boots and a high visibility top. If you do well, I'll upgrade you to shrink wrapping.'

'No problem. See you on the other side,' I say confidently.

'See you tomorrow,' he says, assured that I am qualified for 'bung plugging' if nothing else. Sounds too much like 'butt plug.'

'Upgrade me to shrink wrapping? You're all heart, Stevie. Thanks a bunch, you dopey daft bastard,' I say. But only after I say my goodbyes and hang up.

Fuck. How am I supposed to find my passport and National Insurance card, undergo a foot transplant and acquire both steel-capped boots and a high-vis top before 5.30? It has just gone noon. Maybe there is enough time to beg, borrow or steal my boots and yellow vest. I should have robbed the postman of his boots, although I'm pretty sure he knows where I live. I roll off the sofa and drag myself across the floor to the bedroom to search for my required identification.

A large bruise has formed down the instep of my foot, particularly purple on the ball bit. I remember from my A-Level Biology that the foot has twenty-six bones, thirty-three joints and over a hundred muscles. Surely I don't need all of them. Apart from some superficial cuts and a bruise that makes my dorsal look like an aubergine, it isn't as bad as I thought.

I plough through the piles of crap that hide my bed and spill from my cabinet and drawers. I just hope that in my drunken state I didn't burn my passport when I was torching Gemma's cards. Barney once told me that a British passport fetches up to £4,000 on the black market! Think how many butt plugs you could buy with that. I eventually find an old passport that expired a number of years ago, but still proves that I'm not an illegal immigrant fresh off the boat. The corner is cut off, but I'm glad I felt obliged to keep it after all.

My next mission is getting hold of some boots and a neon jacket and for that I need someone mature, adult and stable: not words that tend to describe my peers. The only person in Bury I can think of that might have the stuff I need is Fred Coleman. 'Freddie' is a friend of Barney's who lent the van that helped empty the club. He is also the only person who won't ask a million questions because Barney would have kept him updated throughout our entire ordeal. He also only lives four streets down from me. With text sent, I need to sort out the rest of my ensemble. I dig deep into the depths of my cheap polyester and cotton and find an array of damp and dirty.

There is a reply from Freddie. He has agreed to lend me both high-vis and work boots and is even going to bring them round. I think this is a good opportunity to practise social interaction again, in the form of a congenial conversation. Not a postie walking in on me battered on the bathroom floor and not throwing tainted takeaway at a ginger nut. I used to interact with hundreds of people over a weekend, building rapport, entertaining them and playing the gracious host. Now, I fear seeing my own friend in what should be the safe haven of my very home.

The sound of the doorbell wakes me from my unconstructive power nap. I hop down the stairs, clinging on to the banister for support. Stepping over mounds of festering food, I open the door to Freddie, who is dressed in his overalls and looks like he hasn't stopped all day.

It is great to see my ally Fred. Mature. Adult. Stable.

'You okay, Harry? Got a five o'clock shadow on the go there!' he remarks, noticing my designer stubble, if the designer happens to be somewhere shit and Made In China. 'Here are your boots and a high-vis.'

'You're an absolute life-saver.' I take the items from Freddie and can't believe I have everything Steve has asked for, minus the National Insurance card, but even then, I know the number for it.

'You heard from Barney lately? I'm sorry you had to lose the club.' In spite of his reassurance, I am still a fake, a sham, the Milli Vanilli of the clubbing world.

'These boots look brand new! You sure this is the pair you meant to lend me?'

'They're all yours. Size twelve, but if that's too big you can tighten the laces,' he says, before looking down at my feet. 'Your foot is swollen.'

'Wait until you catch a load of this!' I open the front door wider, beckoning him in to see the pig-sty of a bathroom, showing it off as if it were the talented child of a proud parent.

'Holy shit!' It must not occur to him, or to any other ordinary person, that it's perfectly natural to destroy your bathroom like a psychotic Tasmanian devil.

'Some people turn to God, I turn to vodka. Still guided by a spirit.'

'Don't let it get to you. Clubs open and close all the time. You've still got your sense of humour, that's the main thing. I just don't understand Gemma and Snoopy moving in together. She's just a kid, no disrespect, but Snoopy should know better. I never trusted him. So smarmy.' Out of everything he said, I only heard one thing and one thing alone.

'They *what*? They fucking live together? How do you know that? I thought she was staying with her mum,' I tell Frederick, who is regretting spilling the beans all over this bag-less cat he's let out.

'It's on Twitter, everyone knows. Anyway, I hope tomorrow goes well and that you enjoy yourself. Where did you say it was?' He is clearly trying to change the subject, and who can blame him. You could cut the tension with a bar blade.

'Cheers for everything. I'm sorry. I really – please, sorry. I gotta go.' I try not to sound rude, but didn't expect Fred of all people to be privy to such information, even if the entire World Wide Web happens to know. Neither of us had Twitter accounts when we lived together, so the last thing I expected to be hashtagged with was this.

'You're very welcome, buddy. In a bit,' he says, warmly.

'Thanks again, Freddie, you're a star. Take it sleazy.'

I let the door close slowly in front of me, just as paralysed as when I woke up on the cold floor. I wish I had another toilet to destroy. Anger rises in me, like Bruce Banner metamorphosing into the Incredible Hulk, although I'm more of an 'Intoxicated Bulk.' The temptation to smash my working foot into the toilet is strong, but it's bad enough hobbling around on one leg and I doubt plugging is a sit down job. There is something tasteless about them moving in together. It's one painful step too far. They had to make it public knowledge, for everyone to see, apart from me. I am in mental anguish, beyond comprehension, beyond explanation. They are rubbing it in my face like a dog in training, being shamed, shoved face first into his own shit.

I place the shoe box next to my unopened mail, and drape the bright vest across the scraps of fallen food, which will start to attract pests and vermin. I have enough of those in my life as it is. After picking at the odd bit of meat, I head into the bathroom, careful not to step on any glass. The bathroom resembles a shipwreck out of *Swiss Family Robinson*, but unlike their exploits, nothing is salvageable here. I pick up the wooden duckboard and try to scrape away the shards. With my other hand, I grab the set of scales and manage to shift most of the flotsam and jetsam aside, creating a walkway to the shower.

I turn the taps on, more red tap than blue, and let the water run warm before stripping off and shambling in. It is soothing. I forgot how much better a good hot shower can make you feel. I wash my face and rub my eyes as vigorously as I can without actually removing them from their sockets. They have seen too much of late. There is one remaining bottle of shampoo that hasn't been battered and I pick it up to find enough for this shower, possibly two. I work the shampoo into my greasy hair and I glide my hands up and down it, in an attempt to hear it 'squeak.' This reminds me of my friend Midas. Dreamer. Insecure. Gone. He would often tell me the most infuriating superstitions (half of which I'm sure he made up) and the hidden meanings behind them. He once told me that your hair isn't clean until it squeaks.

He had another absurd idea that you must never walk over the third manhole cover on the pavement if it's in a chain of three. I was forever bumping into people following this outrageous practice. He also told me that if you check the time and it's a number in sequence or in repetition such as 1.23 or 4.44, then your life is 'in sync,' or some pish like that.

I remember explaining to Midas that the number four (*sai*) is a mark of death in Cantonese custom, as it sounds like the word for 'die,' and fourteen (*sup-sai*) sounds like 'die for sure,' which is why there is no fourteenth floor in many Chinese buildings. He thought I was having him on, despite being the one trying to connect astrology to the time on his Casio. Midas died of a heroin overdose in a tower block above Yau Ma Tei station nearly four years ago, probably at 23.45, so it just goes to show how much good his drain walking and time syncing did him. As preposterous as his beliefs were, the hair thing has stuck with me.

I finish reminiscing about my late, zany friend and his humorous (albeit inconvenient) foibles, and turn the shower off. I wish I still had my friend Midas with me. He would be here now (preferably not in the shower, but certainly contactable), keeping me company, listening to my problems aplenty. He wouldn't offer any advice, but would tell me about his own toils, which provided some form of perspective. He'd tell me that I should be thankful because I could be picking up smack down a back street in Sham Shui Po, from a shadowy figure that he refers to as Mars Attack because he looks like an alien, injecting into his foot because none of his surface veins work. Somebody always has it worse off. But Midas is gone too. I will never hear about Mars Attack or squeaky hair again.

I step out of the shower, pick up my jogging bottoms and use them to dry myself off. Through the steam I catch a glimpse of myself on a shard of glass and a couple of serious looking bags have formed underneath my eyes. At least now with my ruined foot, I have the shoes to match. I wish the mirror didn't have to be so honest. Anyone walking into my unlocked house would think that I had dragged Gemma back here and inflicted serious harm on her, based on the blood and the glaring signs of a struggle. I'd love to abduct, torture and maim her, all in front of her lover boy Dick.

I have nine hours before I am due to meet stuffy old Steve down at the Phoenix. I head upstairs naked, with no regard for neighbours peering into my fishbowl of a home. Too exhausted to sort anything out, I roll the mass of clothes off the edge of the bare mattress and plump up a frayed pillow that has evaded its case. I miss fresh and ironed sheets. I miss having her in this vacant space next to me. I miss the little scar on the side of her knee and I miss the tiny mole on the inside of her thigh. I miss feeling warm.

I set six alarms, all five minutes apart, to give myself every chance at making it to the Phoenix on time. I turn off the light and slump down for another lonely night in my empty, desolate house.

I miss her smile, but I miss mine more.

28

Please let this be a dream. Please tell me that this deafening disturbance isn't my alarm going off. If I don't wake up properly to silence this unyielding siren, there are a further six billion to follow. I haven't heard a noise this unpleasant since the 18k Martin Audio Void LabSubs.

How Steve wakes up this early every day I don't know. He should be given a medal or something, a laminated certificate at the very least. He probably has a loving wife who gets him up, finds his valid passport and doesn't flee with his friend. The temptation for 'just five more minutes' is strong, but not as strong as the prospect of earning some much-needed money.

After allowing myself to drift in and out of sleep for far longer than I should, I get a call from Steve telling me he is running fifteen minutes late. Perhaps his wife isn't so perfect after all, and his magnificent marriage is coming apart at the seams. Next thing he knows he'll be selling the Phoenix to another HR firm who will be recruiting his missus, leaving a big gap in his résumé. Or he needs diesel.

Begrudgingly, I force myself up and I am pleased to find that my foot doesn't hurt nearly as much. Still fucking hurts though. I've dragged my sorry self out of bed. The bar for success isn't set too high now that I am bar-less. I pocket my passport and head to the kitchen to fill a glass with water. It tastes as bland as I had imagined. On pay day I am confident that I will never spend money so fast in all my life. I put my high-vis and boots on before heading to the car, which unlocks without too much protest. The driver's seat is wet because the broken window has started to slip. I allow the engine to purr for a moment and feel quite masculine in my new work gear: all I need is a dirty white van, a copy of *The Daily Sport* and the ability to wolf whistle with two fingers.

I reach Eastgate Street, parking on a frustrating pair of double yellows and head into Phoenix Placements. I am greeted by who I'm guessing is Steve, and he's only just arrived himself, as most of the lights are off and he's still wearing his overcoat. The office is miniscule: three desks and a photocopier. It's straight out of an episode of *Murphy's Law*, everything lacklustre and grey.

'Morning, Harry. Hope I haven't made you wait. I hate being late,' says Steve, fully aware that his phone call woke me up. He is smartly dressed: his tie even has a clip on it. All he needs is a handkerchief in his breast pocket and I'd be speaking to Mr Belvedere. I like Steve instantly. Courteous. Gentle. Money.

'Wife not have the breakfast ready on time then?' I ask, rashly. Why? I just can't help myself. It isn't that I don't think before I speak. I thought it, I decided that I shouldn't say it, and then found myself having said it anyway. I don't even know this poor man.

'No, no wife, not anymore,' he replies, with an uncomfortable smile. He chuckles nervously, wondering why he should grant a job to someone giving him a hard time at quarter to six in the morning. Steve has a charming honesty about him and I can see why he's in the recruitment business.

He seems an approachable and jovial guy, which is no doubt what led me to believe it was okay to discuss his wife in my opening sentence. The main question now is: 'Dead or divorced?' Whatever I do, I mustn't mention it.

'Unfaithful bitches. I'm going through the same thing. She left me for my colleague,' I say, astonished that those words escaped from my fat gob. What a way to impress your employer, I should write that on my cover letter. I sincerely hope his wife hasn't passed away. Please let her have run off with the pool boy. What is wrong with me? However patient Steve is, I'm pretty sure I'm not getting this job now. I'm not used to being up this early and I'm not thinking straight.

'Yes, quite. Everything happens for a reason though, I suppose. Sorry to hear about your partner, that is most unfortunate. People can be false-hearted,' he says, genuinely concerned about my negative outlook on love and undoubtedly surprised to witness someone speaking so candidly.

'Adulterous whores. I thought she was the one, you know. I really did,' I say, cursing to a complete stranger. I don't really know what has come over me. I have jumped at my first chance to open up and speak to someone. Steve is also obliged to listen. We made an appointment and I have shown up to said appointment, so he is compelled to hear me out. If everything happens for a reason, it better be a bloody good one.

'Some things just aren't meant to be. That's the way life goes. My wife and I were married for twenty-eight years and we've recently finalised a fairly messy divorce. Consider yourself lucky that you've spared yourself the trouble. Now, did you bring me your passport and NI card? I can see you've got your high-vis on, which is good.' Twenty-eight years. Phil Collins would have a field day with this guy.

Steve seems sombre and thoughtful, as if his marriage was the most important and cherished thing in his life, and now it is over. There's a real sadness to him, as he talks from experience. He didn't raise his voice or speak out of turn about her. He remained respectful. There is a conservative, reflective wisdom behind what he is trying to tell me, as if he has deliberated over this very matter for a long, painful time. Steve has still come to work, opened up his business for the day and dressed himself immaculately. He is cut from a stronger, more durable cloth than I am. Yet the existence he was leading with his wife, for as long as I've been alive, has ceased, and the only visible change to an outsider like me, is fifteen minutes in arrival time. I bet his bathroom isn't smashed to bits and his foot isn't bruised and bloodied from kickboxing a toilet bowl. Or maybe it is? I'll have to ask the Royal Mail Guy next time I see him.

Steve's marriage lasted seven times longer than my entire relationship with Gemma, yet here he is, looking healthy, professional and in one piece. He stands before me in a finely pressed suit from Marks & Spencer or the likes, his hair combed back and his wrists and pits sprayed and splashed with Old Spice and Brut. I am wearing sodden rags, sporting a malodorous head of hair and my fragrances are victims of domestic violence, littered across my bathroom floor. I think my undies might be from Marks & Sparks, but that's where the similarities between Steve and me end. I have felt so sorry for myself, so defeated, but Steve. That could've been his final shot – the risk you take when you base your entire being around *the one*.

I know there are plenty of people that can move on and start afresh, get themselves back out there in the dating world and try it with someone new. I can't picture myself ever being in that realm again. I will never be single and ready to mingle. Not even with Paul McCartney. Steve doesn't look like he will ever be ready either. Maybe Stevie and I have more in common than an M&S purchase after all. I notice he is still wearing his wedding band, which he has turned on his finger twice now since I've been here. I'm still wearing mine too.

'I had the high-vis and boots already. I have a passport but it's only just expired and I didn't want to bring my National Insurance card in case I lose it, but I know the number off by heart,' I tell Steve, lying to him, like our women lied to us.

'That's enough to get us started then, let me get the Health and Safety form for you to fill out while I make a photocopy of your identification,' replies Steve.

'I borrowed the high-vis and boots. My passport expired ages ago and I've lost the card,' I tell Steve. Where that came from, and why, I'll never know, but I didn't want to bullshit someone who has been dicked about enough as it is.

'Thank you. I really appreciate that,' says Steve, who turns back round, genuine in his gratitude. I feel he is thanking me for more than my admission of falsehood, but for talking about our sensitive situation in general. Maybe Steve doesn't have anyone to talk to either and I'm sure he would never make brash, satiating remarks like 'unfaithful, adulterous bitches.' Perhaps my comments were even refreshing for him to hear; voicing an opinion that his well-mannered sensibility would never have allowed him to express.

Either way, Steve seems like a decent guy who is helping me out, not just financially, but emotionally. He has given me a reason to get out of the house and shown me that sometimes cupid gets it wrong. That bad things can happen to good people too, and not just the scummy ones like me. Just because your world has been turned upside down, your life doesn't come to an end. You still need to have your suit dry-cleaned, your hair slicked and your tie clipped.

He still hasn't asked for my bank details though.

*

I park my car on Rancor Road, which is only a few minutes from the Phoenix. It takes me less time to get to the brewery than it did to get to the club so, if I can make a go of this, at least I'll save on fuel. I'm pretty sure my car is running on fumes as it is.

I've managed to follow Steve's directions to the letter and arrive only ten minutes late, which isn't too bad. Steve even told me to blame my unpunctuality on him, which was nice. I wonder what the lads that work here will make of me? If I can get in with a couple of people early on, it would make the graft here a whole lot easier. The site is vast, with parking spaces for at least 100 cars. Thankfully only a dozen or so are parked here now. I have chosen the space that requires the least amount of walking and have carefully positioned my Beemer under a tree so that if it rains again, not all of it will end up on my driver's seat.

I make my way down a long, steep set of steps, as cautiously as I can. There are at least four paths that lead to buildings from this car park, but I decide to walk towards the most dilapidated one, as that is where the butt plugging takes place. There are two forklifts whizzing around the yard, quite possibly shunting.

As I walk down the steps there are hundreds, if not thousands, of kegs, stacked several pallets high. The amount of stock that fills the yard is enough to last several lifetimes, even for the most hardened of drinkers. You would die of liver failure before you even scratched the surface, but I'd still give it a good go. There are barrels in all kinds of shapes and sizes. In the distance I can see pallets of firkins, which hold nine gallons of ale. Next to those are the gigantic barrels called Kils, appropriately named, because you wouldn't want one of those to fall on you. We used to stock Kils until The Havana opened, then we no longer had a need for so much. We started buying Pins; tiny squashed barrels that only hold thirty pints.

I let myself into the entrance marked 'Transport Depot,' the first door I come to. The reception window has the shutters pulled down, so there isn't anyone obvious to sign in with. There are several men walking around carrying rucksacks and clipboards. I get a few stares as they walk by, but most take no notice. I am in disbelief at the amount of people up at this time of day. I step into a room marked 'Transport Office' hoping that someone can transport me someplace else, without all this hustle and bustle. There is a guy sat behind a large, well-organised desk and he looks important. He definitely knows where the plugging takes place. Managerial. Experienced. Efficient. He is in the middle of a conversation, and I hover by the doorway.

'You're on bay seven, Luke. There's a non-ullage to collect from the social club in Royston and it needs to be back by today. What do you want?'

'I'm here for plugging. Am I in the right place?' I reply, sheepishly, surprised that my presence has been acknowledged considering no one has even looked my way.

'Plugging? You've come here for *plugging*? Does this look like Drongo Island to you? How about you walk to the next warehouse and play Donkey Kong with the spacko's over there for the day,' says the Immense Cunt. Condescending. Noxious. Fascist.

'I'll show him where to go, Paul. Bay seven, barrel from social club, got it,' says Luke, who seems to know how to handle this damnable drill sergeant.

'That's all,' says *Paul*, the artist formerly known as Immense Cunt.

Luke ushers me out and we walk to the end of the corridor, away from the fiery gates to the Transport Office. He kindly opens the door and waits for me to walk through before speaking.

'Harry. It's been a long time.' Luke is starting to look strangely familiar. I don't want to concede the fact that I can't recall my only friend here at the Destroy Your Spirit Institute for Wayward Boys.

'Hey, Luke. He really gave it to me in there,' I reply. 'It's my first day. I haven't even had the chance to screw it up yet.' My initial reaction to Luke is a good one. Friendly. Welcoming. Saviour.

'Don't worry about him, mate. He used to be in the Army. Now he takes complaints on the phone all day and his only battle is with a spreadsheet.'

'His eyes were glowing red. If Genghis Khan and the Grim Reaper had a son, it would be Lieutenant Paul!' I am stalling for time, not getting any closer to how I know Luke.

'We can't all have bosses like Barney. I heard about the club. Wouldn't have happened if I was still doing the doors down there!' says *Luke*, the doorman, circa some time ago, when I had only just started. He looks older than I remember, which is probably because he is.

'Yeah, that's right. Was good having you on the doors, I was wondering what you'd been doing since,' I reply, having not wondered what he'd been up to in the slightest.

'Bit of this and a bit of that. You should come out with me and the lads after work. Bring the missus, Jenny, is it?' he asks, fortunately not as fully in the loop as he thinks he is.

'Gemma. No, we split up. But I'm skint either way, hence why I'm off to Drongo Island.' I hope that my declaration of poverty will result in Luke offering to get the drinks in.

'She's fair game then?' he asks jokingly, and I try not to take it to heart. 'I'm only messing. Shame you can't come out, maybe next week.' Drink offer denied.

'Sure,' I say as I look around the warehouse, lost.

'They call it Drongo Island because everyone down there is a little bit special. Anyone that didn't cut it at the dray work gets stuck down at Donkey Kong. You'll be given a big hammer to bash into barrels all day.'

'Well, I need the money, so I don't have much choice. Where do I go? I'm running late.'

'Over the small bridge, turn right, through the metal door. Don't worry about being late, Drongos can't tell the time. You're going to need a hard hat and some gloves. I have a spare set on the lorry you can have. They say once someone enters Drongo Island, they're never the same again.' Good.

'Thanks. When I get some coin we should definitely go out on the piss.'

'Do well today and you might bag yourself a jolly box,' says Luke. It sounds far more appealing than Dylan's hot-box. 'If a case gets smashed, sometimes we get to take it home. Here's the gloves and hat. Don't let the drongos steal these from you. If you come into contact with one, be careful. They are beyond dead. They are *undead*.' The next seven hours of work sounds like a stage on *Resident Evil*.

'We'll get legless. Lean like the tower of Pisa,' I say, as I head off, half an hour late.

'Sounds good to me. I have a VIP card for The Havana Club we can use.'

Sounded too good to be true, more like. No wonder I haven't seen him. He's been down there: filling their tills, filling their dance floor, and filling me with false hope.

Friendly. Welcoming. Disappointing. There is nothing even remotely jolly about that.

29

As I get to the bridge, still incensed that my newfound long-lost friend is one of *them*, a Havana-lover, I take a look into the pallet that must be used to build up the jolly boxes. It is just as Luke described. This Shangri-la of succulent ciders, ales, and beers, is an amazing marvel. Ripe for the picking and crossed off the system. I am wrought with envy at the bastard that gets to enjoy a slice of this eighth wonder of the modern world.

If ever there was a time for driving a forklift, this would be it. I should hijack one of the spiky vehicles, pinch this pallet, and take it straight to my house. If anyone tries to stop me I will tell them to shunt the fuck up, and then kick them in the shunt. As enticing as that sounds, I turn my back on the Elysium Xanadu of aqua vitae, and feeling far from jolly, head into Drongo Island for my six quid an hour before taxes.

The inside of the warehouse looks like an aircraft hangar, large and industrialised. The sound coming from the echoing metal beast is unlike anything I have ever heard. The crashing and banging of barrels must be the monotonous noise of Donkeys being Konged.

There are countless conveyor belts moving in every direction, some travelling in ways that don't even seem possible, a combination of horizontal, vertical and diagonal. Everything looks so highly mechanised I wonder what possible need they would even have for me. If they have machines that can wash, transport, spin, fill and label these barrels, then surely they don't need me. However, what with unpaid rent, outstanding drug debt, mounting hunger, and a debilitating thirst for something with a percentage, there is no way I'm going to suggest being replaced by a robot.

I wander around the noisy monstrosity looking for signs of life. I stroll past a window, behind which there is a woman wearing a white lab coat and safety goggles, like a scene from *Outbreak*. She is surrounded by pipettes, microscopes and a full on chemistry set, for what purpose I can't begin to imagine. This is my first glimpse of a drongo and she seems moderately human in appearance. I knock on the glass to get her attention but she doesn't turn around. She must not be able to hear me. Are the drongos really that bad that this young female needs to be confined behind reinforced glass?

I understand that I am new and that it must be frustrating for people like Paul to have rookies like me stumble in on their busy schedules and Transport Offices, but surely everybody has to have a first day at some point. Steve has done his part and told me the time and the address. Luke has even done his part, in saving me from the corrupt grasp of the war criminal Paul. And I am here ready to do my bit, to wilfully smack bananas into barrels like a massive ape, but where is the guy to show me to my barrels?

I continue to walk around the hazardous arena. I am a miner from the movie *Armageddon*, about to fly into outer space to destroy a lump of comet. I have never before had to wear a hard hat, fluorescent top, big clumpy boots and big gloves. I have entered somewhere radioactive: about to experience weightlessness as the gravity is sucked from the room. As I practise my slow-motion moon-walk, I feel a tap on my shoulder. Someone has managed to creep up on me under the deafening noise of steam and whistles. The warehouse resembles a cartoon railway station, stuck on fast forward, with the volume up. Thomas the Tank Engine is throwing a temper tantrum and the Fat Controller is shouting and swearing, having smoked some crack that Ringo Starr has sold him. As I turn around to see which web-fingered, fuse-footed, half-man, half-beast drongo has infected my shoulder, I am surprised to see a homosapien figure before me. He points towards a hut, positioned directly above a steel ladder. The drongo reputation is probably derived from their lack of speech, what with the background noise being so loud. They must resort to sign language to communicate.

'Drongo' seems like an offensive and un-politically correct name to be calling people. I'm going to look the word up on my lunch break, if I haven't forfeited my right to one, turning up forty minutes late. If the term is as rude as it sounds, I'm going to the union, or starting one up. Dressed like a construction worker for less than an hour and I'm already thinking about going on strike. I nod to the man-compass that has helped me in my orienteering. Our brief but successful interaction is reminiscent of how I imagine the early form of man had to converse, when they were explaining where to get the best bananas for bashing.

I climb the steps two at a time, in the hope of saving valuable seconds, even though I am already two thousand four hundred seconds late and sporting an inflamed foot. I knock on the door and I think I am told to enter, but with the incessant noise it is impossible to distinguish what he has said. He may have shouted 'Placenta,' but I take my chances with the former.

'Alreet matey. Shut the door. Shut the door! Loud in't it. You after an autograph then?' says the most peculiar of individuals. He is at a desk in this porta-cabin on stilts, perching on a swivel chair that looks really out of place.

His desk isn't anything like Paul's and from the mountains of mess I can tell that this guy has been here for a very long time. He is middle-aged with a shaved head and is eating beans out of tin-foil. No plate, just beans out of tin-foil, with a plastic fork. Please tell me this isn't my new boss. Unusual. Common. Drongo.

'I'm from the agency. My name's Harry – Steve sent me.' This strange, quirky and possibly rabid character resembles an illustration from a Roald Dahl book. 'What autograph?'

'Thought you was after a signature see, deliveries and them lot. You agency? I've got all the agency I need for today. Sure you for me and not for Pauly?' says clueless drongo.

'No, I'm definitely down here. Any chance you could call the Phoenix for me? I'm keen to get started.' Code for 'Get me out of this office immediately.'

'Let me call Stephen. I'll just call Stephen,' says serial killing weirdo. This is too much. All these crazy sounds have driven him insane. I'm surprised he can even operate a telephone, let alone run a warehouse. I can't believe the agency have allowed me to be left in a room with this guy. No wonder I had to sign a Health and Safety waiver.

'Ello? Ello, matey. It's George. I've got Barry ere. That isn't right, is it? Ya sure? For me?' George the Foreman. A bit like the boxer, I think he's been hit in the head one too many times.

'It's Harry,' I say, but he's probably forgotten I'm even here, and that he's on the phone to Steve, and that he's the foreman who has requested me to work today. I certainly hope that this guy isn't the one who will be submitting my timesheets, because I have little confidence in anyone who eats beans from a lump of foil. This guy couldn't organise a piss up in a brewery.

I can hear Steve on the other end of the phone and George's head-shaking soon turns to head-nodding. He puts the phone down and claps his hands together loudly, which I find disturbing.

'Silly George, my fault. One of the shunt boys is off sick. Follow me matey and let's get ya started.' Even this guy knows what a shunt is.

He suddenly seems in a rush to get me into position. I try not to lose him but he knows his way round like the back of his hairy, six-fingered hand. We eventually come to a standstill and I am beckoned over to what must be my very own stretch of conveyor belt. There is already someone there and this town ain't big enough for the two of us. George asks him if he can work a forklift. The tall chap, who is pushing 7ft, looks bored stiff and is clearly another agency worker. Lanky. Pale. Lurch. He squints at me with pity. Freedom by way of forklift, which even drongos know how to drive, and I do not.

'Larry, ave you been ere before?' George shouts, as if he's ordering a drink at Funk'd Up Fridays. The last thing this deranged man needs is more Grappa. I reckon he's done his fair share of sweet air, too. Not only has he got my name wrong again, but he's shown just how faceless and abundant us drongo recruits must be.

'No, first time,' I say, the thunderous noise too loud for me to make smart alec comments. My humorous remark would only fall on deaf ears.

'Okie dokes. You're PN2 Line Feed in. We're firkins today. You're checkin em. On sheet are two lines, one keystones, one for shives. If firkin goes past ya faulty, hit button, take firkin off, hit with mallet, mark down sheet, ya got that?' he asks, quickly, with every other word muffled out by the hissing of steam behind us. I have no idea what a 'keystone' or a 'shive' is, and looking at the sheet he is showing me, it says 'shires,' which confuses matters further. I am out of my depth here. Maybe this George Foreman isn't as stupid as I thought, as I've been KO'd with a right hook of information.

'I think so, yes,' I say, with no intention of doing any kind of meaningful work. If plugging is the lowest of the low when it comes to Phoenix employment, then what's to be said for the guy that doesn't even plug, but admires the work of someone else who has plugged? That guy is now me. Harry Chen, who studied at expensive international schools, now watches kegs go by and pushes a big red emergency stop button.

Where was my emergency stop button when everything was going so wrong? When Gemma was out canoodling with my promotions manager, or when Big G was fraternising with the enemy, or back when my father was deciding to hop on a minibus? Where was my button then?

'Martin over there'll take care of ya. I'll send someone to cover ya for a break at 9am.' Martin: Retiring. Jaded. Unimpressed.

'Hi Martin,' I say. Martin doesn't say hi back. He shares his name with a speaker stack used by ravers and skanks, and judging by the sound of this warehouse, they could very well be named after this bloke. Martin is responsible for the Audio Void LabSubs, which means I have to hate him.

George wanders off, to assign a forklift or to get back to his beans. Either way, I'm glad I've been left to my own devices, though I don't quite know what any of these devices are for. I look over at Martin, who must be at least sixty years of age, to see if he can offer any insight into what I'm meant to be doing. He is spraying down kegs, weighing things, and carrying out tests using hooks and bellows. Seeing Martin hard at work, masterful at what he does, multi-tasking to the max, only makes me feel more useless. It is impossible for me to take any pride from this work.

With my head starting to itch under the hard hat, I wonder why I'm even obliged to wear it. There is nothing here to fall on top of me, apart from maybe Martin, whose funny looks might be his way of giving me the eye. This job wouldn't be so bad if I had a hip flask. I'd give all the firkins in the world for a Champagne Supernova, which I've always wanted to try. Cocaine sprinkled into champers – bit better than a Costa Bomb. I'd kill Martin here for the chance to neck one. George said he'd send someone to take over at 9am. Lying bastard. Maybe Luke was right and they can't tell the time?

Behind our work station, there are numerous arms and claws. They resemble a series of contraptions The Penguin would bind Batman to, in an old Adam West original. There is a big counter-clock above us which says we've had a thousand firkins pass through the system and I didn't get to drink from a single one of them. The production line powers down and Martin glances over, making a 'T' signal with his hands. I take this to mean 'Time Out' and hopefully not a gesture of what he intends to do to me, ramming his outstretched hand up into my batty.

I head out of the side entrance, which involves jumping over a conveyer belt, and enjoy a moment's respite away from the constant clamour of the warehouse. There are two drongos sat in a make-shift smoking area, consisting of an empty keg used as a table and four worn plastic chairs rescued from a skip. I sit down in the fourth seat along, leaving a space between myself and the other two guys. 'Alright?' I ask. Neither of them even look at me and I feel stupid for trying to exchange pleasantries. My chances of scrounging a cigarette are nil, so I don't even bother. For no particular reason other than to detract from the awkward silence, I pull out my phone and for the first time I am happy to see my HTC.

I open up a web browser and type in the word 'drongo.' I am half-expecting to see a photograph of the plebs sat next to me. I really hope that it isn't a word used to describe someone with a mental handicap, because then Luke really is a disappointment, and Paul is getting a serious letter of complaint to an ombudsman, or his commander-in-chief, or his mother.

'Drongo: Australian slang for a no-hoper or fool; derives from a racehorse of that name in the 1920s that never won a race out of forty starts.'

With the research I had been planning all morning over in less than a minute, I open my inbox and read through some old text messages, anything to keep me from making eye contact with these two. The main people I used to text were Gemma, Dick and Big G, but with them deleted from my life there aren't many texts left. I should have read what the messages said between Gemma and Dick when I had the chance.

I find a funny one from Harley: 'What do you call a fat Chinaman? A Chunk.'

This cheers me up no end. My friend Harley is worth every drongo in Oz. I walk back into the warehouse and make my way to George's office, ascending the steel ladder once more. I knock on his door and this time he definitely says 'Placenta.'

'Close it. Quick!' George is desperate to keep the hissing piston and valve demons at bay.

'Hi George, I was wondering if I can work through my lunch break and finish early today?' I don't want to be here any longer than I have to, as fulfilling as it was socialising with my fellow employees.

'I'm fraid not Garry, but listen ere. I spoke with Stephen and he agrees that you should be shrink wrapping. It's away from the noise, it's easy and it don't start til 9am. It also pays 50p more an hour: an extra score a week. Look after them pennies and you'll ave more pennies,' he counsels, telling me the best news I've heard in ages. You know you've had a shit week when the best news is about shrink wrapping, but it'll do.

'Sounds great, George, thank you. An extra £80 a month will do nicely and the noise is getting a bit much.' I am already mentally spending my extra money, which is an income far from disposable.

'What? Can't hear ya! Just kidding! You're a top man Garry, d'ya mind if I call you Gaz? It's about time we had someone ere that takes his work seriously and you're a smart guy.' For £80 a month he can call me whatever he likes.

'Course you can.' I am chuffed with my promotion after less than one day of doing absolutely nothing and I prefer the name 'Gaz' anyway.

'You can clock off at ten to two, matey. Need ya ere till the next shift change, otherwise there's no one to watch those firkins,' he chuckles, convinced that I am actually checking them.

I say my thanks and goodbyes and close the door behind me as quickly as possible. I head down the ladder having hoped to finish early, but instead leave with an extra £4 a day and three hours longer in bed. Lurch can keep his forklifting and Martin can keep his Time Outs. I put my gloves back on and continue with the last keystoning I will ever have to do.

The final hours fly by as I take a genuine interest in the humdrum task, knowing I will never have to do it again. No one comes to take over from me until 2.40pm, but it doesn't matter. From now on I am an official shrink wrapper and although it won't stimulate me quite like operating a sizable venue did, at least I only have to work a forty-hour week.

I will also never have to clean up another vomit, sweep up another broken glass or put up with another drunken pisshead, other than 'Gaz.' £260 a week isn't too bad, over a grand a month. I am no longer a drongo. A friendly-looking guy approaches, seemingly ready for his eight-hour stint of quality control. I look down at him with the same degree of pity that was bestowed upon me and head for the exit, a new man. I can't wait to tell Luke that they have found something better for me to do: a small milestone that shows I am still redeemable, however slight.

It feels good to be out in the open, away from the hectic factory. If only I was off to the pub for that 'first pint refreshment' the cider adverts are always on about. Their target market is labourers just like me – the brickies, scaffolders, plumbers, shrink wrappers. As I approach the bridge, the jolly box pallet is even taller than it was this morning. Added to the pile of cases is a box of Raspberry Kopparberg, a flavour that I've never tried, a case of Crabbies alcoholic ginger beer and some bottles of Sam's Island Chardonnay. The temptation to take a couple of each is strong, especially considering that most of this will be destroyed, if not given away to the draymen that broke it in the first place. I look around the yard and apart from a forklift driver with his back to me, there is no one in sight. I have also been in both Paul and George's respective offices and there were no CCTV monitors to be seen, so it's unlikely that there is someone watching the cameras dotted around the yard in real time.

My pulse starts to race and my legs begin to shake, but I make my decision and roll with it. I grab a bottle of the Sam's Island, hoping that it's better than Drongo's Island, and tuck it into my hard hat, covering it with the high-vis top. I reach for a bottle of Kopparberg, careful not to cut myself on the glass sticking out the side of the mushy box. I slide the heavy bottle into my trouser pocket and I wish I'd worn a belt. I pull away at the cardboard that holds the Crabbie's ginger beer together and wriggle the bottle in the middle of the case. I slip it into my other pocket. Job's a good'un. I shuffle about on the spot until the bottles fall into place, nestled away and hidden.

Without drawing attention, I slowly walk towards the car park, trying not to look suspicious. A surge of panic courses through me. I consider back-tracking on what I've done. I do not have the stones to walk past Paul's office. As much as I want the drink, so much so that I felt the compulsion to steal it, I can't follow through with this. I turn around to head back to the pallet to cut my losses.

Shit.

Storming over towards me is a drongo from the island. Crap. Why did I have to be greedy? Why did I have to compromise everything for the sake of three bottles of booze?

'Gaz! Wait right there! Come back ere,' screams George, who has caught me red and white and beige handed.

'George, hello! I'm really late and I need to go, now.' My words move even more awkwardly than my fidgeting hands.

'I caught ya. I'm gettin on a bit, but I can still move if I have to!' George hands me a brand new maroon shirt still in its wrapper. 'I wanted to give ya a uniform for tomorrow, seein how you're in charge of the shrink wrapping now. Paul left me a couple spare last time he came by and I want yas to look the part. Good work today. Here ya go, matey.'

'A spanking new one! Who shrink wrapped this? Decent job!' I have never felt so relieved in all my life. I thought I was done for.

'Very welcome, Gaz. I see the same ole faces every day. It's nice to get some new blood round ere, with a bit of piazza.' I think he meant to say 'pizzazz' as in 'vava-voom' rather than 'piazza' – 'an open square for gathering.' His kind words are well received nonetheless, and if I wasn't holding stolen wine with two more bottles down my skyrockets, I would go in for the man hug, or at least an emphatic handshake. Right now though, all I want to do is get home and stick these beauties in the fridge.

'Nice one, thanks for the shirt. I'll see you tomorrow.' I have escaped by the skin of my teeth. Our conversation could have easily waited until the morning, as it doesn't take long to whip a shirt off and put on a new one. Maybe a drongo would need all night to fight through the packaging.

'Great stuff, see ya on the morrow me good man, nice n early, but not *too* early!' he says, before giving me a big hard slap on my shoulder.

The left shoulder, which is supporting the weight of the hard hat.

The hard hat, which is hiding the bottle of Chardonnay. Fuck.

Slipping from my grip, the wine slides straight through the gap and on to the kerb. I try to intercept it with my foot but my reflexes aren't fast enough. The bottle smashes and my jaw drops with it. Even though it won't make the slightest difference, I fall to my knees, covering the glass with the new t-shirt George has only just given me.

I can't bear to look up at George's face, but he doesn't say anything. My cheeks scald with embarrassment and my stomach sinks into my gonads, which shrivel up, like my job here. The humiliation is mortifying, and I can feel George's gaze scorch through the back of my head like two smouldering, red hot pokers, making me wish I had the hard hat on to deflect the heat. I can't believe this has happened, it almost doesn't seem real. It feels like I am looking down on this happening to someone else and I pray to God I was.

'Gaz? What were yous doing with that? Look at this mess. You could ave asked me for that and I would ave given it to ya. Didn't take yous for a crook, Garry.' His disappointment is comparable to my own sense of shame. The fact that asking him has been made to sound so simple only makes the blow that much worse. It's like my packed lunch, only in reverse. 'I've a good mind to go down Pentax and let Stephen give ya what for.'

I don't know about the Garry that works for Pentax, but the Harry that works for Phoenix is screwed. Screwed like a screw-cap bottle of shattered white wine. If I'm going down for the crime, at least let me enjoy the booty. Somehow I don't think it would be appropriate to ask George for a replacement bottle. George has grounds to call the police on this one.

'I'm sorry George. I thought they were to be destroyed,' I say, in a fleeting hope that pleading such ignorance might make him see the situation differently.

'Save it Gaz, it's too late. I'll be aving that shirt back now.' It doesn't.

'It just takes one bad apple to spoil the barrel, after all,' I mutter, defeated.

Sacked on my first day. I couldn't organise a piss up in a brewery either.

I can't even keep a job at Drongo Island.

30

The walk back to the car park is a long one. The two remaining bottles jammed tightly into my pockets begin to dig their way into my thighs. I really hope George doesn't tell Steve. If I was to stencil the entrance to the club now, I'd spray 'People who drink to drown their sorrow should be told that sorrow knows how to swim – Ann Landers.'

I struggle to find my Beemer because I've come out from a different exit and there are a lot more cars than there were this morning. I look to see if there's anyone around and when I'm sure that I'm on my own I tap the cap of the Crabbies against the edge of a nearby wall until it opens. I wipe some brick dust from the lip of the bottle and give it a guzzle. Fancy calling the brand Crabbies. I hope Dick has given Gemma crabs.

When I eventually find my car, I slump down into the damp seat and finish my drink, which was hardly worth the trouble. Disgraced, I rest my forehead on the steering wheel for a brief respite. This sets the horn off and startles me. My phone begins to ring and I fear the worst, but it's only Dylan.

'Harry! I got great news, bro.' I desperately hope he is about to tell me that I'm on a hidden camera show and this was all a hilarious set up. 'That Belinda chick got rid of the baby! Can you believe it?' He is delighted, as if there has never been greater cause to celebrate. His 'great' news isn't great at all. Belinda will have made one of the toughest, most heart-wrenching decisions anyone could ever be expected to make, and he is elated. 'If they're old enough to bleed, they're old enough to breed, right?' he jibes, laughing down the phone. Laughing at Belinda, laughing at her terminated child, and laughing at me for not sharing his amusement.

How can he be so gleeful about the destruction of life? I never took him for someone so callous. Can we extinguish life so quickly?

All Gemma wanted was a baby and I couldn't give her one, or at least not soon enough. I'm not the first person to think that a child would solve their problems but, in our case, it certainly would have kept us both at home more, together, away from the nightclub scene and all the scheming, underhanded people that come with it. The connection would have transcended everything else, a bond above all. She would have loved our child more than life itself and I would have been the person that gave her that child. But our time hadn't arrived. We never got our turn, and Dylan here had turns to spare. A strong hatred intensifies in me that I can't contain.

'You prick.' Dylan's laughing soon stops. I feel a loathing towards him. 'Calling me up to chat about this shit? I fucking hate you!' I continue, before hanging up and throwing my phone to the floor. I wish I could kick *him* down some stairs. As angered as I am, I know that my outburst wasn't solely intended for Dylan. He is too young to even know what he wants, let alone what is right and wrong. He acted irresponsibly, didn't know what to do, longed for it to all be over and when his wish came true, he was relieved. I hate many things, his situation, my situation, but I don't hate him.

I have started to realise that the behaviour I've been exhibiting of late has always been there, deep-seated. The fury that swelled up, as silly as it sounds, is *within* me. It may be hidden beneath a joking and sardonic surface, sure, but it's there. Gemma subdued it, keeping it at bay with her presence, her frowns, her scowls and her scolds. Having her in my life made me behave like the person I thought deserved to be with her, the part of me she wanted to see.

I debate whether or not to stop into the Phoenix to spin my version of events before Steve takes the call, if he hasn't done so already. Just as I decide to pull out of the car park and head to the recruitment office, my phone rings from below the seat. It is no doubt Dylan, having decided on a suitably insulting response. I pat my hand along the floor, frantically trying to find the handset, as it's only a couple more rings away from going to voicemail.

'Dylan, I'm sorry. I didn't mean that.' I try to get my apology in before his torrent of retaliatory abuse.

'It isn't Dylan you should be apologising to,' says an unmistakable Steve. My HTC Desire leaves a lot to be desired. It is getting me back for all the nasty things I've said about it.

'Shit. I thought you were someone else.' I really wish it was Dylan.

'Someone that can be walked over, perhaps? I had a good feeling about you when you left my office. I thought this was a turning point.'

It should have been. 'I am an understanding person, but what you did this afternoon was unforgivable.'

'It's not how it sounds, Steve. There was a misunderstanding–' I say, before he interrupts.

'*Don't* lie to me. You may have tested my patience, but please don't question my intelligence. I am sick and tired of being lied to.' There you have it. I knew it then and I know it for certain now. 'The brewery is my biggest client. What does it say about me when I send them a thief?' I wonder if he listens to Coolio.

Even the most reserved of individuals will snap when pushed too far. I snapped at my bathroom because it all got too much, and then I snapped at Dylan because he struck a nerve and now Steve has snapped at me for lying to him.

'You trusted me and gave me a chance and I've messed up. I'm sorry, genuinely.' My cheeks start to burn again. 'It would never happen again. I promise you that,' I continue. 'There isn't any chance I can collect my money for today is there?'

'No, there is not. Goodbye, Harry,' he says, before hanging up.

When I look up from my lap, I realise that I am still in the car park, and likely to be seen by George if I hang about here much longer. I straighten my back to pull out the Kopparberg bottle that is digging into my pelvis. I give up. I just fucking give up. I know I should drive home, but I can't be bothered. I'm done. What is the point in driving home? What is the point in staying here? What is the point in doing anything? My phone rings again. When I thought it was Steve calling, it was Dylan. When I thought it was Dylan calling back, it was Steve. Who is this going to be? Steve is probably Belinda's dad and he is calling me thinking I'm Dylan.

'*What?*' I demand, without even checking who it is.

'I didn't mean to piss you off. I don't wanna fall out with you, innit,' says Dylan, and I much prefer getting an apology from him than getting a bollocking from Steve.

'I owe *you* the apology. I'm sorry. I've had a bad day. It's one thing after another. First the whole Gemma thing, then the club thing. I'm just a general mess,' I reply, attempting to get some of the thorax-crushing weight off my chest.

'I'm not surprised, buddy. I would get that bitch back, him and all.'

'I know, fuck those guys, right?'

'No, I'm being serious. I would get them back, Harry. They ruined your life, so why aren't you ruining theirs?' he quizzes, avidly. I don't quite know what to make of what he's saying, but it all seems very adolescent.

'What are you proposing? Revenge?'

'I'm not suggesting anything. I won't be around for much longer. My mum has enrolled me at uni. She said that I either go and study, or move out, so I may as well have a crack at it. *You* need to get them back, whatever it takes,' he says, as ambiguous as always.

'You're leaving town? Education – where's that going to get you, huh?' He has found a way out. A place to go that is new and fresh and away from here. I can't picture Dylan attending lectures and writing a dissertation. He farts loudly when he has his headphones on, thinking no one can hear it.

'Yeah, end of the month I'll be out this shithole. I'm gonna get a job before the term starts. I don't know much about it, my dad's sorting it.' I am envious of him, having his father around to sort out all the details.

'Can you take Gemma and Dick with you?' I plea.

'They're bang out of order. It's beyond wrong. It's evil. Fight fire with fire,' he continues, as if narrating an advert for a blockbuster that will go straight to DVD.

'I wish I could get them back, I really do,' I say, powerlessly.

'You *can* get them back, both of them, and you will,' he says compellingly.

'I *will* get them back,' I say, convinced, even if for only a moment, a split second. Fight fire with fire. If I am to be remembered for one quote above all others, for someone to spray on a dodgy nightclub wall, let it be this one: 'I will get them back.'

'Before I go: if you had to choose between a pint full of maggots fed through your penis or a pint full of leeches shoved up your arse, which would it be?'

I'd choose either of those over the week I've had.

31

If it had just been her, or if it had just been him, I don't think I would be feeling the way that I do now: destitute from a double betrayal.

Gemma Goodman. Her name seemed quite fitting, because she brought out the best in me. Ironic, that a name like Goodman is now attracted to a 'Bad Boy.' Dylan was right: fight fire with fire. I need to get her out of my system. She is the last person I have slept with and I am not the last person she has slept with – a score that needs to be evened. In fact, she is the only sexual partner I've had in four long years. Apart from her underwear.

I want something meaningless. Something insincere and inconsequential. Something empty. Big G used to talk about a website where he would drool over the women he could be sleeping with if he didn't spend all his money on fuel, carting about girls who will never sleep with him. He said that it was like an online supermarket, except instead of browsing for groceries, you were walking down virtual aisles of Eastern European immigrants. I have a little look on the website, just for inspiration, and within the Suffolk area there isn't an awful lot going on. I expand the parameters of my driving distance and everything seems to lead me to Cambridge (well, the fit ones anyway). I never would have thought that the heart of education and culture would be home to strumpet and streetwalkers.

I find that the problem with buying things over the internet is you never get to inspect the goods before they turn up at your door. You can't get a real feel for what you're purchasing like you can in a shop, so I decide there is no choice but to drive to Cambridge. It's still light outside, which means by the time I get there I can cruise about, looking for the shady parts, maybe even stop in a pub and ask around. I can imagine that the shadiest looking part of Cambridge looks like the nicest area of Bury St Albans. I head for petrol and cash. I have no idea how much it's going to cost, but I withdraw £50 for the floozy, and then stick less than a tenner in the car. Needs must. I don't know what overdraft that leaves me with, but this has to be done and it has to be done right now. This is my revenge.

Before I know it, I am completely lost. I am soon taking right turns on roads marked 'No Right Turn' and it would seem that the Tour de France is taking place in Cambridge this year because there are bloody bikes everywhere. I pass a Waitrose and a couple of Sainsbury's, but it is only once I find an Iceland and an Aldi that I know I'm in the right place. The supermarkets are closed so I park the car and hope that some of the stock from their Eastern European aisle has found its way outside. I take a wander down the road and if I was a down and out, drug-abusing, alcoholic, looking to have sex with strangers, this is the street I'd choose.

I hang about under a nearby bridge for half an hour or so, as it looks like the sort of place *they* would stand, but not a single kerb crawler in sight. Part of me wants to back out, but you can't trust your better judgement: the devil on your shoulder used to be an angel once. I continue walking, trying to keep my bearings. There is a recreational ground down a small path, but there isn't even one leather-clad, working girl to be seen. I need to head further out of the city.

On my walk back to the car park there is a woman outside the Co-op having an argument with someone and her choice of words is fairly unmannerly. She looks like she's in her mid-thirties, although she's wearing a lot of makeup so it's hard to tell. From here, her eye shadow could very well be a pair of black eyes and judging from her colourful language it wouldn't surprise me. Vulgar. Loud. Smutty. The bloke she is shouting at has jumped back into his car and is about to drive off, so she isn't in any apparent danger, not that I was going to leap to anyone's defence. The spectacle is over and I missed most of it anyway, but the woman has caught me staring. The Chinese in me wants to ignore her, keep my head down and leave, but the self-destructive, curious heathen in me wants to see where this might be heading.

'Ey, got a spare fag?' she bellows, 'spare' suggesting one that I would otherwise rip into pieces and discard for the sake of it. Her accent is an interesting dialect, somewhere between chav and townie, from the county of *Trisha*.

'Sorry love, I don't, no,' I reply, and she looks at me with utter contempt. I think one of them might actually be a black eye. She turns to walk away, but this is the first glimpse I've had at a potential purchasable moll, so I urge her back. 'Hey, I'm wondering if you can help me?'

'Wassat then, hun?' she replies suggestively, turning to face me. I think I've found my lead. She isn't what I had in mind. She's definitely not Patricia Arquette, but I've already established that romance is false, so casual coition is likely to be equally fake. I can't believe that I used to get to sleep with Gemma for free and now I'm about to *pay* for this.

'Do you know where I can find a lady?' Judging by who I'm speaking to, I'm about five miles too far for a 'lady.' I've also noticed that she has a couple of teeth missing. If Belinda is a four and a half, this woman is a zero. The vanilla has melted and it's sticky and gross.

'Course I do, what's ya name?' she replies, and at no point do I want her knowing my name.

'My *name*? My name is, it's, um, Dick.' I wasn't expecting to pull that one out of the hat. The hat that never laid a golden egg, but laid a rotten turd instead.

'I *love* dick! I have a place we can go, you got money on ya?' Why is it that every girl I ever speak to seems to love Dick? And money. She appears very nervous and twitchy.

'Is there anyone else on tonight?' I know that must come across as incredibly rude, but considering she's a slapper, I couldn't give a toss.

'We don't need anyone else. You a copper? Cause I'm not breaking any laws,' she replies, and it looks like I've found my own tango partner to tell *True Lies* to.

'No, I'm not a copper. Where you from then?' I ask, although I really don't care much for her origins either.

'Born in Arbury Court,' she says, even though I didn't need her life story. 'Nuff bout me. What ya after?' I hadn't thought that far ahead, although head wouldn't be a bad place to start.

'What am I after?' I reply, buying myself some time to think, before I actually commit to buying. The question she's asked me has always been followed by the name of a drug, rather than a sexual act of preference.

'Sweetie, I'll suck you off for a score, £50 for a shag, and a ton for anything else,' she replies. I thought that the shag was the highest level there was. A hundred quid for 'anything else'? That's an expensive pair of knickers.

'£50, okay, fine.' It will be money well spent.

'You ave it on ya, yeah?' She gives her wrists a good scratch. '£50, yeah?'

'I have it,' I assure her, and with that we start walking.

I saunter a couple of paces behind, as I don't want anyone to think we're together. This makes me feel better about myself, reaffirming that rock bottom isn't the last floor on the way down. We carry on along the road, cut through the recreation ground and head over to the other end. She leads us through a hidden alleyway and into a shady-looking tenement. You'd never know this place was here, unless you did your weekly shop between Aldi and Iceland, comparing which one gives you the most frozen shite for a quid. I wasn't far off though, past a set of broken swings and a mucky sand-pit and I was pretty much there. I follow her up to the second floor and she suddenly becomes very cautious. Never a good sign. If we have to stand outside a blue *Doctor Who* door and whisper before entering, I'm leaving.

The building looks like something that should have been ripped down years ago, the Cambridge version of the Kowloon Walled City. The lights flicker above us and I can't imagine what her squat is going to look like. Chung-King Mansions maybe, which, contrary to the name is not a mansion, but a rat-infested nerve centre of squalor.

'You ave that money?' she craves, as we stop at a door, which thankfully isn't a Tardis. Her constant questioning must say something about the company she keeps. I thought my lot were bad. I hand her the cash and follow her through the door, which she hasn't even bothered to lock. She mustn't have anything worth protecting either. See how simple that was. She doesn't need to lie to me for four years to bleed me of my money.

Once we're in, she quickly closes the door behind us and I see now why she doesn't secure it. The lock has been damaged and the doorframe is split. I hope this is because someone has forced their way in and not tried to break their way out. The bimbo doesn't seem to own very much – not that I was expecting a home cinema with surround sound and a Jacuzzi, but this woman is taking minimalism to the extreme. There is an electric fan in the corner, a mattress on the floor, a couple of chairs, a few bin liners full of crap in the middle of the room and not a lot else.

Her flat is freezing and it smells of damp and mould, with a slight hint of semen. The Feng Shui of this place is all wrong.

If I feel as unwanted as the ends of the loaf, then she is the first slice as you open the bag - everybody touches it, but nobody wants it. Considering Gemma and Dick have moved in together, maybe I should move in with this bitch. An *incredibly* Indecent Proposal. She points at one of the chairs and tells me to take a seat. I'd really rather not, but I perch myself on the edge of it to humour her as she heads into the bathroom, closing the door behind her. I stand up and have a little look around, not that there is much to look at.

Opposite her bathroom is a disgusting kitchen that smells of piss. She probably doesn't even bother with the tin-foil and eats her cold beans out of the toilet bowl. I can hear an angry couple arguing in one of the flats next door, the walls here even thinner than mine. Although it startled me when someone slammed a door, I am secretly revelling at the sound of them fighting, knowing that someone else is suffering from a familiar affliction. I wonder if he has slapped her yet, because I know how that one ends.

She is taking her time in there. I could still leave if I wanted to. I could sneak away without her even knowing. I don't have to go through with this sordid exchange, but something compels me to stay. Not just the fact that I've already paid, but because staying here is the *wrong* thing to do. The devil on my shoulder is Gemma, after she fell and broke her halo, and she weighs a tonne. This is how I intend to exact revenge. I should have hit the gym, stopped drinking, found a new job, booked a stylish, overpriced hair-cut, quit smoking, covered up my tattoo and bought an entirely new wardrobe. Whenever two people meet after a break-up, however long it's been, someone always wins. Contracting syphilis does not bring me closer to winning. On the day I asked Gemma to marry me, as far as she was concerned, I had slammed my hand in a car door and was in need of stitches before we had even set off. She was distracted by a bunch of flowers and a few songs on the radio. That should have been a sign that she had no care for my well-being. You can't cover that up.

It sounds as though my evasive escort is shooting up, as I can hear the flicking of things: needle and lighter. I wonder if she knows Mars Attack.

This woman can clearly handle herself, allowing her mind and body to be compromised in my presence, a complete stranger who solicited her own services for me. I must not seem intimidating – something else that Gemma lied about. This strange creature, pumping her arm with skag, is a *survivor* of sorts, making her a stronger person than I am, but I still intend to look down on her, if and when she surfaces. I return to the chair and wait for another ten minutes or so, before she emerges. The scrubber heads straight into the kitchen and begins rummaging around, making a great deal of noise. To remind her that I am still here and waiting for my own injection of illicit entertainment, I ask whether she has anything for me to partake in.

She steps back into the room and drearily points to the floor by the fan, before returning to whatever it is she's doing. She tells me that there's a wrap of speed in the shoebox that I can have for a tenner, because she doesn't touch the stuff. I'm sure heroin is much safer. I open the shoebox and pull out the wrap. It isn't made from a page of a Tolstoy novel. Once spiked, Dylan said I should take it as a compliment. There are a few loose cigarette papers scattered about inside the box, along with a burnt spoon, gauze and some drinking straws. I tip most of the speed into a Rizla. There is nowhere near a tenner's worth in here, but I can't be arsed complaining. I don't even have the money for it. I wrap the paper up tightly, encasing the little crystals and place it right at the back of my tongue, before swallowing it sharply. I bomb it. The taste is bitter but if I'm going to push the boat out again, without an anchor, I may as well capsize.

She returns for what I hope is the last time and her face is all wet. She must have been sorting herself out, which is all well and good, but I'm the one that's here to be sorted out. She takes her dress off and she isn't wearing a bra, which goes to show how often she must do this. She dries her face with her dress and mumbles some shit to herself, but I am too distracted by the sense of urgency rising inside me to listen. The speed is kicking in and, like Keanu Reeves, I won't be able to get off the bus. I look across at my naked friend and realise that I don't even know her name. It definitely isn't Sandra Bullock.

She falls to her knees, creeps towards me, and pulls down my trousers and boxers. She is trying to be sexy, but is so out of it and so unattractive that I'd rather she didn't. She puts my lifeless cock in her mouth and looks up at me. I don't want to look at her, so I stare up at the cracked, nicotine-stained ceiling instead. I shouldn't be here. She begins to run her tongue up and down my balls, which is a new experience for me, but I can't take any pleasure from it. I guess my heart's just not in it, which was the whole point to begin with. Meaningless. Insincere. Inconsequential. She won't be empty for long though. As I look at her, all I can picture is Gemma going down on Dick. The real Dick.

My doped up vice girl is jerking away at my knob, clearly wanting me over and done with, so she can get back out there to make more money. I didn't travel all this way for her to have an easy and painless ride. I glance at her breasts and reach for one, causing her to murmur something and gag. I put my other hand on the back of her head. Her hair is like Pandi's: matted and dry. I pull her in deeper, until my cock hits the back of her throat, really giving her something to gag about.

It doesn't feel as good as I thought it would. You'd think that someone who did this for a living would be better at it. I think she might be Katy Perry's mum with a yeast infection. She rips open a jonny with her teeth and slides it over my penis, carefully unrolling it. I suppose you need a cautious hand when preparing and injecting drugs intravenously, so her steady dexterity is put to good use. It seems like a pointless exercise, as there is nothing her clunge has that her mouth doesn't. Whatever she may have certainly isn't 'cooties.' If I got her pregnant, I'd blame Dylan.

She throws herself onto the mattress and puts her arms behind her head, revealing hairy armpits. Combined with her large burger-bap nipples and her skinny, scarred white body, there is something grossly gratifying about the degeneracy of her, and the depraved situation I have placed myself in. She is so delightfully disgusting that I can't help but smirk. The clock is about to be reset. Single and ready to mingle. She beckons me to lie next to her by patting the stained mattress. She pulls her panties to one side, revealing a reasonably shaven and fairly tight-looking pink pussy. The girl means business if she doesn't even take them off. As I turn to lie on my back she clambers on top of me, nearly falls off, and laughs, in a blurred state of heroin-induced euphoria. At least someone's having fun.

She pushes herself down hard, thrusting me inside her, right to the base of my shaft. Her shoulder is angled towards my mouth and she arches her back to get in a better position. The motions are awkward and definitely *not* science. I place my lips against her shoulder blade and sink my teeth in, to stop my jaw gurning from the speed, more than anything. She tastes of salami swathed in sweat. She lets out a slow groan, unfazed by my bite. I want to maul on her again, hard, until I draw blood, until I cause her pain. This must be where the other £50 comes in.

She pulls away from me and sits upright, stretching back, my member still inside her. She bobs up and down, releasing vigorous sexual noises, which I know to be over-exaggerated. Her moans get louder and more frequent and I wish she'd stop. She is trying to patronise me, con me. I am being tricked by a trick. I grab her by the neck firmly, but again, she seems untroubled, numbed by the smack. This must be common-place; her typical Friday night in. This frustrates me further and I squeeze her throat, choking her.

'You think this is funny?' I screech, pulling her face right up against mine. I have never spoken to anyone like this before, never in this way.

'*Let go –*'

'Why? Look what you've done!'

'*Fuck you!*'

'Why?'

'*Stop –*'

'Why?'

I can feel her struggling to breathe as she attempts to lift herself off me, my cock pinning her in place like a tent post peg. I raise my pelvis so she can't move and with my firm grasp she is completely under my control. She is desperate for me to stop, her face turning even paler than before. The pressure from my handprint is spreading across her neck. She places her hand across my face and tries to scratch me, but she is too hazy and I am too alert.

'This isn't my fault.'

'*I'm sorry –*'

'This isn't my fault, Gemma! This is your fault. Say it!'

'*I'm sorry –*'

'Don't lie to me, say it! Say his name, SAY IT!'

'*I can't –*'

'Call out his fucking name, I DARE you!'

'*Dick, please –*'

I can see Gemma's green eyes staring at me through hers, and I know that everything they are trying to tell me is a lie. I remember how they lied to me on New Year's Eve, each lie more painful than the one before it. I want the green eyes to stop, to fade, to mist over. I need to make them stop.

'*Please, I have daughter –*'

'Say my name you fucking whore!'

'*Stacey –*'

And with that I let go.

Part of me wanted to bereave the life from her, wanted to *kill* her. My heart is pounding; I can hear it smashing against my chest. I feel the skin that covers my face and it feels tight, my palms sweaty, and my arms cold from dread. I am fucking high, despite being stuck in the lowest of low. This gratuitous ballet of violence is worse than a K-hole. I can't bear to imagine what my guardian angel must be thinking at this precise moment, or hers, for that matter. My angel pushed a big red emergency stop button, so that it could watch over someone else. It abandoned me, out of sheer disapproval. My guardian angel is probably pissed up.

I don't need to be wearing a hard hat or a fluorescent top to experience weightlessness. The gravity has finally been sucked from the room. I was expecting her to cough and splutter, but she doesn't move. I don't even know if she's still breathing and I can't bring myself to check. Scar was only meant to punch a prostitute, not strangle her to within an inch of her life.

I pull the condom off and it is heavy. I have managed to ejaculate without even realising and I don't know what that makes me, but 'monster' comes to mind. What have I done? My shades of grey are in the millions. I shove the wet, full condom into my pocket and pace the room. I begin to search for something but I don't know what. I need to get out of here.

It's just a matter of time before someone shows up – one of her regulars maybe, or her daughter. I look down at her body and maybe she's just sleeping. I'm sure she's fine. The drugs have taken their toll. *The drugs.*

I turn towards the shoe box and pick up what is left of the speed. Tolstoy wrote a play called *The Living Corpse*. I hope for my sake he's right. I try to open the wrap, but my hands won't stop shaking. I scatter the rest of the powder over her face. That'll have to do, fuck, I gotta go. *Now.* I open the door carefully, making sure I block the entrance with my body, obscuring the view. I try to look back, but I can't. I slip through the small gap and quickly close the door behind me, wedging it into the splintered frame. I head back down the way we came and even though it's only the second floor, it feels as though we're on the fourteenth.

I run across the green, which is just as deserted as before. Darkness has descended on Cambridge and although it provides me with cover, I am scared and wish to be back in the light. I don't mean a well-lit room with high wattage bulbs. I mean somewhere that isn't blackened by voluntary manslaughter. As I near the main road, I slow right down and try to compose myself. I need to act calm. I'm not calm, I am far from calm, but it is imperative that I *appear* calm. Come on, you can do this. I turn the corner sharply and find myself in front of a Domino's Pizza that I didn't notice earlier. It has a large glass front and there must be ten people waiting to be served. None of them look my way and I am grateful that it's busy. The customers serve as a line-up of potential suspects. I need to get away from here. I need to get home.

Across the road is a large boarded-up pub called The Ranch and to the side, I notice a dark, narrow passageway, looking as though it might lead to a private car park. I stall for a break in traffic before sprinting across the road. I keep going, right down to the end, by the back gate of the beer garden. I wait quietly in the corner, having truly lost the plot. I need to call someone. I can't go back out there. I just can't. I need someone to save me. A delivery guy sees me skulking as he approaches his motor. He realises that he doesn't get paid enough to challenge a shifty person crouched in a poorly-lit car park who is breathing heavily, so he leaves me be.

I need to remind myself that she is overlooked by society. She lives by herself, in a shady block of flats and no one will miss her, apart from her daughter maybe, whatever her name is. The toxicology report, if she'll even get one of those, will be full of hard drugs. I'll be fine. She'll be fine. She's probably woken up by now. She'll be washing her face in her kitchen, or doing another hit in the toilet, about to settle in for a night in front of the fan.

Dylan. I need Dylan to come and save me. I try to hold it together, although my infuriating phone doesn't make it easy. I can't figure out this phone sober, let alone when I am mashed up on speed. Please answer, please.

'I need you to come get me,' I say, in a strained and nervy voice. I chant the words 'Okay, okay,' desperately willing him to say 'okay' back.

'What do you mean *come and get you*? Why?' Both reasonable questions. Neither of them a solution.

'Help me. Take your mum's car. I can't talk, please, I'm begging you,' I continue, and it's as if we're back at the club again, with me pleading for him to do something, except this time he has no obligation and isn't even going to be paid.

'Where are you? What's the matter?' The less he knows the better. If someone called me up in the middle of the night, begging for a lift because they have taken amphetamines and may or may not have killed a hooker, I don't think I'd be making a grab for the keys and doing ninety down the motorway.

'The Ranch, Cambridge. Please Dylan, come quickly.'

'Fuck man, fuck, opposite Domino's, yeah?' he replies, and I am as astonished that he knows where I am as I was looking over the body of a comatose call girl.

'Yes, how'd you know that? Yes, opposite Domino's. Yes. I'm in a car park.' I lower my voice, which the Class-B has caused to be louder than usual.

'My Nan lives in Chesterton, innit. Where's *your* car?' he asks, as if I have forgotten how I got here. Like I'm some sort of deranged psychopath that doesn't know what he's just done or what he's going to do next.

'I'm trapped. Please Dylan. There's no one else I can call,' I implore.

'Okay, okay, I'll leave now. Mum's out and they took Dad's car, so you're in luck. Sit tight. I'll be there in twenty minutes.' I have never been so eternally grateful. If he gets me out of this car park and away from this place, I will pick up every flyer he should ever drop for the rest of our lives.

'Thank you, hurry, thank you,' I babble, incoherently.

And I wait.

It takes Dylan half an hour to get to me, but he is here.

'What did you do, steal a pizza?' asks Dylan, leaning out of his mum's car window.

'Keep it down,' I say, before creeping into the back seat of the silver Audi A6, quietly closing the door behind me.

'And you didn't even save me some? Was it pepperoni?' he jokes, but I'm not paying any attention. I need to get back to Bury in a fraction of the time it took him to get here. 'When you suggested pizza with Harley, this wasn't what I had in mind.'

'I'm trying to quit.' Very soon he is going to want some answers that don't involve a pizza. 'My car is that way, take a left, left.'

'Your car? I thought you didn't have a way home,' he says, glaring at me in his rear view mirror. 'What are you doing out here? You look fucked. What happened to your clothes?' he asks and asks and asks, incessantly.

'You told me to get laid, even if I had to pay for it, but –', I try to explain, before Dylan turns round sharply and raises his hand towards me, making me flinch, until I realise it's only for a high five. I need him to pay attention to the road. I need him to drive carefully.

'My man! Histon Road is famous for that shit,' he declares. 'You don't pay a hooker to come, you pay her to go away, right? Did you wear a condom? I never know why they wear condoms in pornos? Guys can't get other guys pregnant!'

Famous? Infamous.

'You can't tell anyone, okay, I'm serious Dylan, promise me, *promise*,' I demand, and he looks at me hesitantly, as I am now sounding as unhinged as I appear.

'Dude, you smashed a prossie, relax. Hope you didn't pay too much. Which way do I turn here?' He doesn't know just how hard I smashed it. I should have taken the £50 back. It'll make the foul play look even fouler, and she won't be needing it.

I point him in the direction of my car and then notice the blood on my top. The Royal Mail Guy would be right to ask this time. My fingerprints will be everywhere. I pray that the Hong Kong police force don't have me on an international database. Every person we drive past is staring at us; every car we pass is searching for me. *What have I done?*

'This is us, stop, stop! Here will do.' My car with the broken headlight and the inverted bumper has never looked so good. 'Thank you so much, thank you bro, I love you.'

'Two minutes. I drove all the way here to take you to your car, which is less than *two minutes* away! Are you fucking serious?' He doesn't look impressed. 'You're a dick!'

'I know I am,' I reply dolefully, and nothing good ever comes from being a Dick.

I run to my car, frantically unlock it, climb inside, and exit the car park as quickly as possible, thankful that I have Dylan to follow. He is my knight in shining Audi. Saving my ass Like a Boss.

On the drive back I try to make sense of it all. I thought I saw Gemma. I saw her eyes, and I wanted her dead. I tried to kill that woman and could very well have succeeded. I now know what I need to do. Tonight was supposed to be about revenge. I failed. Next time, I won't. As devastating as my act of revenge will be, I don't want it to be swift for her, *for them*. Not quick, not painless. Let her life flicker before her eyes. Let her see what she has driven me to do. If revenge is a dish best served cold, then we might have had a use for Barney's million ice cubes yet. I loved you Gemma, and you said you loved me too.

When I get home I park the car right round the back, a few spaces down from the house. I run inside, lock and bolt the door and welcome the darkness. Treading the remaining rice into the carpet, I flush the soggy jonny down the toilet, hide my clothing in the cupboard under the stairs, and vigorously scrub my hands in the sink, before crashing on the couch with no one to strangle.

And I wait.

32

I've never been particularly close to my family, which probably comes as no surprise. We all love, or loved, one another in our own unique way, but it was in the most dysfunctional of manners. I don't know if it's my newfound isolation or lack of a female figure in my life, but I have a longing to contact my mother. I have had this urge several times over the last ten years without her, but now more so than ever. I have no job, no partner, nothing.

I need to get out of Bury. If they link me to what happened in Cambridge last night, this will be the first place they'll look. I can't stay here. I depress myself enough as it is, should I really let the venom spread? I don't have a choice. I Skype my aunt, asking after my Mum's number. She doesn't question why I want it or what I intend to achieve. I wouldn't have an answer for her. She sends me the number and after some deliberation, I opt for the text message, rather than the phone call.

London. It's crazy to think that I could be with her in a matter of hours, if she has any desire to see me. After writing and re-writing my text, I decide to keep it short and sweet:

'Mum, its Harry. I know its been years but I need to see you. Is it ok if I come down? Might need train fare wired across, unless I dodge the conductor? x'

If that doesn't fill her with the confidence that I am at an adult place in my life, nothing will. Not only am I imposing myself on her, I am asking her to pay for the privilege. My mother and I are complete strangers and I know more about the customers that used to come into the club than I do about her. I instantly regret my text, but it's too late. It's out in the ether of limbo now. I throw my phone down next to me with little hope of a reply. I should try to appreciate what could very well be my last few days of shelter, as my landlord isn't the most patient of types. I have already decided that when he asks for the next instalment of rent, I will offer the hefty deposit we laid down for an extension of my stay. I'll even throw in a free fridge freezer and washing machine.

Just as I doze off, my phone hums. It's a text from my mum. I've never received a message from her before. My heart sinks as I open it, as I have no idea how she will react to my impulsive request to rendezvous.

'Don't jump train, send me bank details. £40 should cover it, depending on where you're travelling from,' replies mother. I text her my bank details and she replies with an address and time. I put three kisses, she puts none.

'The Hand & Racquet, Wimbledon Hill Road, London, SW19 7NE, 4.30pm, tomorrow.'

This is either a pub or a sporting goods store. I am hoping for the former. I have never been to a pub with my mum (she left before I was old enough) or a sporting goods store for that matter, but whichever it is, we are meeting somewhere informal, and that's fine by me. Tomorrow is sooner than I had expected, but at least I won't be able to fritter away the money in the meantime, which I certainly wouldn't put past me.

I look up the train times and there is one at 12:54, pulling in to Wimbledon at 15:31, with a glorious three changes. It comes in at just under £24 return, leaving enough for a bottle of vodka and a couple of beers. No wonder she hasn't made any effort to reach me. I should at least save a little to get the round in when I arrive.

I let an hour pass before checking my online banking to see whether or not the money has gone through. No joy. Clever woman. Accepting defeat, I stick the telly on and try to picture what it will be like seeing my mum again and what I intend to say. I'm not looking forward to the journey, but it's but a small drop in what is to be a huge ocean of things not to look forward to. Eviction and possible arrest are the nearest tides approaching my tiny rubber dinghy.

*

I wake up to some stupid infomercial. Bring back teletext, at least that was silent. Even if it did make Barney's 1980s sofas look decidedly futuristic. Being greeted by adverts each morning is a constant reminder that I pass out on the sofa every night, having no reason to make it to the sheet-less bed. I feel absolutely ghastly and cannot believe I took that speed. One of the side effects is psychosis, so maybe I simply hallucinated the whole thing yesterday. I don't know why I throttled her. Why couldn't I have tasered her, like a normal person. Is this Excited Delirium?

I still have hours before the train is due, but I don't want to stay here, and I decide to walk. The long march will air out the smell of stale smoke from my clothing. Hopefully I can avoid bumping into anyone I know. The walk is unpleasant and cold. Even though I have the street to myself, I feel I'm being followed. Probably all the things I've tried to put behind me. I take the long way round to the train station so that I avoid the front of The Havana Club.

When I get there, I withdraw my mum's money, but the hole in the wall only wants to give me £30 of the £40 sent. Stingy bastard. I purchase my fare at the window and as I hand over the money, I contemplate the long arse trip ahead. I really hope an inspector comes to stamp or hole-punch my ticket, because if I get from here to Wimbledon without having it checked, I will be furious. Last time I held one of these tickets, it was to snort meow. I'm the cat that curiosity should have killed. It would seem that I still have a couple of my nine lives remaining.

As I wait for my train, I think about how Gemma and my mother have never met. I really wish they had, beyond the obvious reasons for doing so. Everyone knows it is customary to meet the future in-laws before marriage, but more than that. I wanted to *show off*. To show her that I am capable of getting a girl like Gemma, and that I must have some worth for her to deem me suitable 'in sickness and in health' and 'for richer or poorer.' Gemma would have pulled the short straw with that one. I wanted her to like Gemma, to love her even. To make jokes about sending me back on the train and keeping her to adopt. I wanted them to find common ground in my general uselessness and compare notes. I wanted them to share and revel in embarrassing stories about me. I sought to show my mother that what should have been her place as the main woman in my life had been taken by someone far more deserving. Not that any of this matters now of course.

The train journey seems endless, but in all fairness, there is little else I'd be doing. The bloke next to me is rifling through a mound of paperwork, shuffling and rearranging his documents. I hope he gets a paper cut. The couple across the aisle from me are holding hands and talking about some restaurant. I hope they get food poisoning. There is a couple somewhere behind me nattering away in Cantonese. Hearing them chat reminds me of Hong Kong. The home that I can no longer call home. Everyone around me has something going on, something to keep them occupied on our journey. Well, their journey. I have no journey, only a series of stops. There is a first-class section at the rear of the train that I could retreat to, but I am most definitely part of the common rabble. In fact, I am below this lot. It is unlikely that anyone else here has caused a harlot to asphyxiate. At least they haven't made me sit outside on the roof, like one of Harley's slum dog cousins.

When I finally get off the train and head out of Wimbledon station, it feels strange being somewhere different. It is disconcerting not knowing what is round the corner or even which direction to head in, although I should be used to that by now, in the metaphorical sense. Wimbledon is nothing like what I was expecting. Everything seems to be on a slant, like we're in a cold version of San Francisco, and there isn't a tennis court in sight. It looks more like Brighton than London, but it is somewhere new and I take solace in the fact that no one will recognise me. I could be anyone or anything I wanted to be.

I eventually find the pub and dash across the road, passing another venue called The Beehive, which is heaving, buzzing even. I enter The Hand & Racquet and it is completely empty. These guys have been stung. I wonder if this is a painful juxtaposition that happens all too often in the bar trade and that perhaps I had been a tad self-centred in believing I was the only one.

'You waiting for someone, mate?' says lone barman, in my lonely direction.

'Yeah, my mother was supposed to meet me here,' I reply, sounding like a young kid who has lost his mum, despite dragging myself up the last ten years without her.

'Smoking section down the back there,' he says, in an attempt to keep me in his pub that little while longer. I used to pull the same trick all the time, so I tut and slump myself down on one of the sofas. 'I'm telling you chum, there's someone out there that said she was waiting for her son. This isn't some social club.' My venue definitely wasn't the only one with problems.

'Where's this smoking section then?' I offer. He points towards a doorway in the back and I walk over in vain, knowing that my mother doesn't smoke. Through the door is the tiniest smoking section I have ever seen – even smaller than the one at the Fox & Hound, where Big G takes his corrupt, secret phone calls. Stood in the centre is my mother. Elderly. Spindly. Elapsed. And she is smoking. Seeing her smoke her Silk Cuts, or whatever they are, is quite possibly the last thing I expected when I arrived here. But life is full of surprises, which I can say with the utmost certainty.

'You alright, Harry?' she asks, minimally. She looks at me as if I'm the glass collector coming out to clear the ashtrays, rather than greeting her long-lost son.

'Never been better,' I chuckle, as lifelessly as I did when I called Barney. Maybe we should all meet up and paint this smoking patch, that'll get them in. I struggle to think of anything else to say. This is how most chats go with strangers in a smoking area, which is all this really is.

'Take it the money went through?' I still can't believe she's smoking. She must have been in her forties when she left Hong Kong and she had never smoked then. It isn't my place to comment and there are probably a lot of things that have changed that come above nicotine fixes, so I decide not to bring it up.

'When did you start smoking? It's bad for you, ya know.' That last bit just came out, and I have no idea why. I hate it when people tell me that I shouldn't smoke, as if I've been under the misapprehension that it was healthy for me. When people enter the 'everything in moderation' debate I always promise that I'll only smoke them one at a time.

'Don't teach your grandmother how to suck eggs, Harry.' She will never be a grandmother herself. Why would anyone want to suck eggs? Gemma is sucking Dick's eggs this very second.

I take a step towards my mother and move in to hug her, to fill the uncomfortable silence more than anything. She looks away for the briefest of moments and then obliges, extending her frail arms out beside her. It is awkward as I kiss her cheek. She then turns her head for me to kiss the other one, continental style, but caught me unawares making it all the more discomforting.

'You look *different*,' she says, putting on a face of weary concern as I take a step back. Given the time that has passed, it is highly likely that I look different, even though I know that this is her polite way of saying that I look dreadful. The last time she saw me was the afternoon she left us, after I got home from school. She should have gone when I wasn't there. She shouldn't have waited until I got back.

'I know I do. You look the same, although you seem smaller.' We have reached a dead end in our conversation already. Maybe that was the common ground that Gemma and my mother could have shared – a mutual consensus that I am generally a dead end. When I last saw my mother she wore nice clothes and had jet-black hair. Now she looks like a dinner lady – prominent grey roots overpowering her once dark locks.

'Would you like a drink? I think I'm going to need one,' she says, chuckling uncomfortably herself, which makes me feel better about my own feeble chuckle-to-returned-laugh ratio.

'I could murder a stiff gin and tonic.' I hope she makes it a double.

'Mother's ruin they call that, you know,' she says, passing me her egg to suck.

'I know they do. Am I not mother's ruin? You couldn't wait to get away.' I sound more cross than I had intended. I should have at least waited until my drink was poured before turning her against me. I have always felt that my mother considered me a burden, but I never thought I'd find myself talking to her about it, and certainly not two minutes into arriving today.

'You should write Mother's Day cards. You don't know what it's like, Harry,' she says, shaking her head as if she has had to spend much of her life trying to impart wisdom on to me. 'Before you judge me, put all your faith in someone else's choices, Harry. When it doesn't work out the way you assumed it would, what do you do? You don't put up with it. I'm not my mother, Harry. I had no choice.' She keeps saying my name, as if she is meeting someone for the first time and repeating it so that she doesn't forget it. Anyone listening in on our conversation would be fooled into thinking she was a concerned parent. I barely know this woman. 'It was no life for me over there, Harry, but it would have been okay for you,' she persists, in a tone that is meant to sound reassuring.

'Is that how you justified it? Deluding yourself that everything would be *okay* for me?' I ask, very un-reassured. There is so much I want to say. So many things that I told myself, promised myself I would say if I ever saw her again, but I can't find my voice. There must be guilt locked away inside her, even if she has found a way to rationalise it.

'Listen, I know about shit not working out. More than you think, Mum.' It feels weird calling her that. 'Mum' is familial and close-knit. We are not.

'You're too young. Talk to me in thirty years.' She hasn't spoken to me in ten and now she wants me to wait another thirty.

'I know about stuff,' I say, quickly and unintelligibly. I want to mention the hooker, but it isn't the wisest argument to make in my defence. 'My friend has been diagnosed with cancer.'

'Oh, I'm sorry to hear that. How old is your friend?' She finally accepts that there may actually be other planets and moons that rotate around the centre of her universe.

'He's my age. His name is Harley,' I say, cautiously. 'He's an amazing guy. A real grafter. Doesn't drink or smoke or any of that. He made my job bearable, knowing I could banter with him each weekend. Anyway, it's all over now. My venue has closed. Other people have problems too you know,' I continue, exhausted.

'It's time for that drink,' she says, looking sombre, to which I nod in agreement. I lead the way back inside, the barman smug in his I Told You So.

We walk towards him and I am tempted to say 'I can't make my way through the crowds of people,' knowing how much he will hate it. Whenever someone said that to me, they got under-poured and over-charged, so I settle for a clumsy wave instead.

As my mother gets the drinks in, a couple enter the bar, followed by a family of four. I notice that there is a big bar caddy on the worktop, full of straws, branded serviettes and stirrers. She pays for the drinks (doesn't leave a tip) and we head over to the nearest sofa. Straws, napkins, cocktail sticks and sofas. They can't have it that bad. Maybe I should see if he wants to buy some tellies.

'Cheers for the drink. My mate said he wanted everything to go on as normal. He wouldn't take anything seriously. He encouraged me to joke about it,' I prattle. 'What do you suggest I do? His chemo's already started.' I didn't speak to my mother when we lived together and now I have opened my heart and soul. I have lost my keys and she is my Samaritans Hotline.

'I'm very sorry about your friend, Harry. The only secret to surviving cancer is to attack it as aggressively as possible.' She pauses to look at me, to make sure I am paying attention, 'Masses of radiation, as much chemo as he can stand and demanding to go on every experimental drug available is his only hope. If he asks for your opinion, tell him that. If he doesn't, then just act the way he wants you to,' she says, carefully. I don't know how someone displaying such a sincere compassion for others can be the same type of person that walks out on her son and husband. She might not be a good mother, but I bet she makes for a good friend.

'You're right,' I reply, grateful that the ball has been taken out of my court. Maybe we're in Wimbledon after all, except this conversation is more clay than grass. 'I don't know if I'll get to see him again now that the club's shut. I don't even have Gemma anymore.'

'I hope that wasn't because of your father. Ignore everything he said. He resented me and put all our problems down to the fact that we were worlds apart. If I was a docile Stepford wife, or Sai Kung wife, he could have had his traditional, perfect family. If I didn't leave when I did, I'd have bound feet too,' she says, slowly swirling the ice around in her drink, trying to sound clever. The right to speak ill of him should have ended when she left.

'I got dumped.' If only Gemma's heels were designed for binding feet after all.

'I'm sure you'll find someone else,' she replies, half-heartedly.

'What? Like *you* did?' I wail angrily, and for all I know, she has remarried countless times.

'At least you didn't have children. At least she didn't make you move abroad with her,' she says, as if this is some kind of competition to see who has it worse. That's one game I don't mind losing at, although we've reached a deuce. Gemma and I had started to plan our wedding invitation list. Dick had agreed to DJ the event. If they ended up shagging on our wedding day, I think I'd win the game, set and match.

'Meh,' I say, under my breath.

'There's something you need to know.' I am half-expecting her to tell me that she has started working at The Havana Club too. 'Yes, your father and I had problems, and yes, he disapproved of your relationship, just as he did with your choice in friends, clothing, music and near enough everything else you put up as a barrier between you, but that's in the past now.' She is doing nothing but reiterating how disappointing an offspring I truly was.

'I don't need you to tell me how shit I was in the son department.' I feel myself becoming agitated. If we were in a sporting goods shop I'd be reaching for the ear defenders.

'The day after he died, I got a call from his sister in the middle of the night,' she begins, shamefacedly, as the call should have come to me instead; that I better qualify at being 'immediate.'

'She emailed me,' I interrupt, proud that I'm still in some form of loop, even if an earth-shattering one.

'If you would let me finish,' she says, slamming her hand down on the table making the glasses shake. 'She was given his personal effects.'

'You wanted them, did you?' I stab, quite hurtfully. 'One last pay-out?' I don't know where this mean streak has come from, although she is being deliberately vague.

'Is that what you think? That I married your father for money? Fat chance. He didn't have any. He was too busy telling me how I should be spending my money that he forgot to keep any control over his,' she says, making me feel foolish for having a go at her. 'They found a ticket on him. He was coming to see you.'

'He didn't want anything to do with me, if I went through with my plans to wed a white woman.' It sounds as ludicrous to say as it was to hear. Race had nothing to do with it. My father had given up on love because of this woman, my mother. She made him as bitter as I am today. It didn't matter what colour Gemma was, he'd have thought the same. I get it now.

'He booked a flight to come and spend time with you, *both* of you.' A ridiculous twist in our unfortunate soap opera. The occasional murder or fire and this could be the Queen Vic.

'When I lived with him he was never there. We were passing sampans in the night.'

'Well, he wanted to make amends. Gemma sounds good for you, the way you speak about her,' she says. 'When I left, I bet your father didn't have anything good to say about me.'

'Maybe cause you manipulate people and make up stories like this one.' I know my father (or *knew* my father) and this isn't like him, or wasn't like him, whatever.

My mother may have known the original family man who was full of dreams and ambition that I was too young to remember, but that guy left even before she did. The father I remember was cynical, melancholic and distant. He wasn't soul searching or going back on his word, which he argued and defended until the very end. What is my mother trying to achieve? Is she hoping to give me closure? Because all she is doing is burdening me with more guilt.

'The bus was on its way back from the travel agents. He was going to surprise you.' The final turn of the corkscrew perforates my remaining fortitude. This is contemptible. I want to get up and leave; throwing my drink at the cock of a barman on my way out before boarding the first train back to Bury. Back to a place where glimmers of hope don't make any kind of appearance, especially where they don't belong. I want to walk out on *her* this time.

'Come off it. Even I'm not this naïve.' I am not going to be fleeced by her story.

'Call your auntie if you don't believe me. Ask her yourself.' She leans back, raising her hands up as if she is pushing the matter in my direction. She stands up and heads to the bar. The ball is back in my court and I don't know whether I should do a drop shot and agree, or smash it to the baseline and declare myself out.

My mother returns with more drinks, and she has already made a start on hers. It looks like she's a keen drinker – must be hereditary.

'There you go,' she says, placing my ruin in front of me. Why didn't anyone tell me sooner? Why would a change of heart come so late? I suppose Gemma's did. I wanted to come here today with questions and leave with answers, not leave with more questions and no answers. Advantage – Harry.

'I nearly went back to Hong Kong. I even packed a bag, but I didn't want history to repeat itself. A few years ago, I was going to buy one of those tablet things to see if I could send him a message on the interweb, but I didn't, in the end. I didn't want to get ripped off by buying a lid without a computer,' she says, smiling to herself ever so slightly again. Most people would want to see their mother smile, but I don't. I want her to be irate and gnashing her teeth like I am.

'What changed?'

'It all happened so soon, there was so much more I wanted to do. As soon as we had you, that was it. When you have a child unexpectedly, you're no longer only responsible for yourself,' she says, revealing another home truth that could have waited until we meet again in thirty years.

'So I wasn't planned then? Anything else? Get it all out now. Were you hoping for a girl? Am I an abortion survivor?' I ask, a little too loudly. The woman at the table next to us has started looking over. My birth certificate is nothing more than an apology letter from Durex.

'I loved your father and I loved you, so stop being daft. I've told you what I know. It's up to you what you do with it.' I don't know which part I should be offended by first. Not only did she say that she 'loved' me, past tense, but it's up to me what I do with the information I have recently come into, as if it's an inheritance that I can save or spend. My assets have been frozen. Next she'll be telling me that he's left everything in his will to the grandchild that he was so desperate for!

'Everything you've told me makes me feel like there was something salvageable, if only I'd known. Another huge let down to add to my list,' I say, beaten. My ball hits the net on the serve.

'I was training as a paediatrician, but I was whisked off to Hong Kong. Before we emigrated I wanted to use the money my dad left me to purchase a house in Clapham, but he talked me out of that too. Either of those things would have given me a solid footing, certainly more than I have now.'

'This isn't about you. You make *everything* about you,' I say, even though it isn't about me either, and I have a tendency to make everything about me. Like mother, like son. It seems as though resentment must run in the family too. 'Be a paediatrician now. Help everyone else's kids, since you clearly did such a great job with your own.'

'Don't be a prat,' she says, unimpressed with my career advice. 'I wanted to let you know more about what went wrong between your father and me, now that you're older. I didn't want to argue with you. When you reached out, I thought that's what you wanted too.' Some sincerity finds its way through almost four thousand days of silence between us.

'I'm sorry. Thanks for putting that money in. It could've been completely eaten up by overdraft limit.' I'm glad that the tone of the conversation has changed, now that we've moved on from late father wanting to reconcile differences before his untimely death, and on to my fast approaching state of bankruptcy.

'Is it money you need? I don't have an awful lot, but I can give you a little to tide you over,' she says, with a warm smile that only radiates kindness this time.

'I'm about to be kicked out of my house. I need somewhere to stay as soon as possible. I couldn't stay with you for a while, could I?'

'I'm sure you'll sort something out soon.' The egg we were sucking on is now all over my face. 'It wouldn't work, you moving here. It just isn't feasible. Plus, what would you do with your return ticket?'

I am as unwanted now as I was back then. No one wants to share a house with me. Not Gemma, not even my own mother. The journey home is going to be a lot longer than the one here.

33

I left the pub too soon. My mother wasn't keen on putting me up, but as much as I want to, I can hardly blame her. She seemed willing to stay a while longer, but I didn't want her company. I wanted her to make my problems go away. I wanted her to tell me that I was finally home and when she didn't, I spat my dummy out.

Part of me has always thought that my parents' breakup didn't involve me. That someday, things would be good and that when they moved on, I would have *two* fathers and *two* mothers and *two* homes. Instead, I have nothing.

I wait an eternity for the train. When it arrives I dart inside and find myself a seat. My mother had more to say, but I didn't want to hear it. I just needed to get out of there, taking my sense of rejection with me. She is a cardboard cut-out of a character in my life and isn't even worth naming. My attempt at sleeping is useless. I can't get comfortable. No one comes to punch my ticket on the way back: the *return* journey – even though I am more single than I have ever been.

When I get to Bury I head to my house. I want someone to recognise me. Anybody will do. A wave from a neighbour whose name I've never cared to know, or a smile from a girl who used to like the way I made her Woo Woos. I don't want to be faceless. I don't want to be forgotten. Back on my street, I look to see if Gemma's car is there: force of habit. It is not. I walk under the archway and there is a note taped to the front door. A feeling of dread travels through me, considerably quicker than my recent travels. The scribbled note reads:

'Mr Chen + Miss Goodman,
Disappointed to find that rent hasn't gone through, call me immediately. Regards.'

Bastard, I thought as much. You'd think that with the number of drinks I've given to people on the house, someone would help me with my own. What the fuck do I do now? I have no dependents (that I know about), no disability (at least not officially), and I am deemed capable for work (despite distinct lack of options), so there's no way I'll get a council house. There might be a YMCA, but I don't know the first thing about that. Mandara might. I should've taken that money from Barney on New Year's Eve.

I let myself into the house, head upstairs and collapse on the sofa. Dylan's room will be going spare once he moves out, although Benio probably has his name on the title deeds. I am out of alternatives. I don't know how long it takes to evict someone, but I don't want it to come to that. Impulsively, I decide to call Harley. He will think Barney has asked me to rope him into more work, like so many times before. I really hope he picks up.

'Egg Fried Rice! How are we?' It is good to hear his voice. I've missed his cuisine-related jibes.

'I've been better, Mr Bicycle Seat,' I reply, which sounded better than 'Naan Bread' in my head.

'How's the single life treating you then? Enjoying some time off?' His assumption as far from the truth as Bangor from Bangalore.

'I went to see my mum for the first time in, well, ever. She didn't want to know. She told me some shit about my old man.' I want to return my fortune cookie and open another.

'So who is it?' I don't quite follow.

'So who's who?'

'Who's your real dad if it wasn't Mr Soya Sauce?' he asks, laughing to himself.

'Very funny! How is the cancer?' I ask, with instant regret, as if it can be marvellous and the highlight of his week.

'Still there last time I checked, still killing me,' he replies frankly. 'The fuckers gave me the wrong chemo, can you believe that?' I am expecting a punch-line.

'What do you mean the *wrong* chemo?' I probe, making it sound like all they had to do was reach for the bottle labelled 'chemo' and follow the instructions on the back.

'The hospital found a new lump. They're all scratching their heads about it. I'll have the biopsy results in two weeks, as if I have all the time in the world.' My phone reception starts to falter and I shuffle along the sofa towards the window, praying it doesn't disconnect.

'Which chemo were you meant to have?' I ask, even though I wouldn't know one from the other. I don't even know what form it's meant to come in or how it's administered. Is it a liquid? A pill? A jab? A massive radiation machine? There is so much I don't know.

'They first diagnosed it as Hodgkin's Lymphoma and gave me ABVD. When my condition worsened, they found it was non-Hodgkin's and gave me something called R-CHOP.' I am struggling to keep up.

The drugs I have taken had innocent nicknames to disguise their true intent. I don't think you can call chemo words like 'meow,' 'snow' or 'nose candy.'

'Have you felt any better since they changed it?' I detest that my friend has been harmed.

'Better? Fucking hell, man. In between the mouth ulcers and the weight gain, I'm left with waiting, followed by more waiting. That's the worst part about it, the uncertainty. I've stopped making plans. I've stopped looking forward to things. Sad, right?' he beseeches, making out that it is sad, as in pitiful, when really it is just downright heart-rending.

'Weight gain? You were looking streamlined, last time I saw you.'

'The second chemo contained a steroid which made me constantly hungry. I never felt full, no matter how much I put away. I could eat forever. I've gone from twelve stone three to fourteen stone four.' He sounds far from streamlined.

'Oh, fuck, man.' Not the most constructive of offerings.

'Everything still tastes of metal. I bet you don't know what metal even tastes like, right? Neither did I. Why couldn't it be buffalo wings?' he muses, sniggering to himself. 'The craziest thing is my heightened sense of smell. It's as if everywhere has just been cleaned, and is now *too* clean. I've stopped washing as much so I can feel the dirt on me.'

'Even at the club? You know what Dylan's cleaning was like.' I look around at my filthy, soon-to-be ex-abode.

He certainly wouldn't have found that hooker's house too clean; that's the last place you'd want a heightened sense of smell. I'm not sure if I should mention what happened. It sounds like the kind of thing we'd joke about, but it's no laughing matter. This is the most honest conversation I've ever had with Harley, and I'm ruining it by worrying about what I did to that woman.

'How's Kristina and your folks?' I ask, hoping to hear that at least there are girlfriends and mothers out there that aren't absconders.

'Mum's not interested. I've seen her once in the last year. She feels that she's done her job in raising me, and anything else is my problem. As for Kristina, she moved out. I thought she was going to leave before the cancer anyway, but then, I've been saying that for years!' he replies, with more merriment than those words should normally evoke. Likewise, my mother didn't want to know and my partner left me. My life has been turned upside down and inside out. Harley has had a similar experience, and even with his life-threatening, soul-destroying cancer, which trumps the lot, he is still sounding more upbeat and optimistic than I am.

Harley is about to continue, so I heave a deep sigh to let him know I'm listening. 'As for my dad, well, he left when I was four, then became part of my life again when I was twenty-six. I got cancer at twenty-eight. I bet he wished he had stayed away, right? It's weird, cause now he plays the caring father, like he's been there all my life. If I had more energy I'd tell him to do one, but I prefer to keep the peace. He texts me more than anyone else in my family, but it's out of guilt,' he explains. 'Guilt and Boredom.'

Beijing. That is how far *my* assumption was from the truth.

'What was his reason for getting in touch again, after all this time?' I try to highlight the positive: that his father returned and is still very much alive.

'Mainly boredom! He's in his sixties now, he's not married, no other kids apart from me and my brother and now that we're adults, he just seems interested,' he says, squarely. 'I swear on my life, whatever's left of it, that if Kris or my mum had cancer, I'd be there for *them*. Hey, how spooky is this? My dad texted me, right after you asked about him! Hold the line; let me see what he wants.' It's as if he's talking about someone's life on *Coronation Street* rather than his own.

Harley is opening up to me about the happenings in his life, both past and present, but he isn't talking about how he *feels*. He is describing things in some detail, telling me about his outer struggle, but it is the inner one that I want him to share with me, for me to help him through. I want him to tell me that he had a strict father. That his old man hit him for crying when he was growing up and it was drilled into him that men don't talk about their feelings. That he was told to have a stiff upper lip. Failing that, I want him to tell me that his troubles are too difficult to mention. I want there to be a reason why he won't pour his heart out to me, because I damn sure want to pour mine out to him, until there isn't a drop of bloody burden left. My stiff upper lip is more of a cleft palate.

'He texted me saying that *Law Abiding Citizen* is on at 10pm tonight on Channel Four. What a result, definitely watching that. He asked if I've seen it.' Our serious cancer conversation is brushed aside to discuss a film he has already seen, that I loaned him, and which he has failed to return.

'We're pretty much *in* the film. We're in the jury when Clyde Shelton tells the judge she takes it up the arse! Emancipate yourself from him for questioning you!' If he wants to talk about things, he will. I know Mum, I know. 'I swear you stick the films I lend you on Amazon when you're done with them. It's the Chinaman that's meant to sell DVDs!' I jest.

'If I emancipated him, he'd hang about until my brother gets diabetes,' he says, with a slight undertone of spite finding its way into his voice.

'Kris left?' I ask, after a long and thoughtful pause.

I've never met Kristina, but Harley would talk about her often. Never anything good. He showed me a picture of her once. She looks like Gemma. Even though he would bitch and grouse, she was a long-term and constant factor in his life. Now she is gone.

'She's always been a nagger, but she was moaning about how much I was sleeping and that I wasn't at work. Things weren't about her anymore, once I had my own shit to deal with. At least now I can watch *Road Wars* and make a mess about the house. It's only me and Pippen now, so the dog's allowed up on the bed. Her blowjobs aren't as good, but that's the only difference,' he jokes, but he must miss her. He must do. I miss my partner terribly, and no number of cute dogs, real or plush, can replace her gap in the bed, regardless of how good they are at giving head.

'She left you when you needed her the most. How are you so cool about it?' I question. He put her picture in his wallet and you don't do that unless you want that person close to you, even if it is just glossy paper. I bet it's still in there.

'The best thing about the worst time of your life is that you get to see the true colours of everyone in it.' If that's the *best* thing about the worst time of my life thus far, which is without a shadow of a doubt my present, then that is the most depressing thing I've ever heard.

'I've seen some new colours myself. Kristina isn't friends with Gemma, is she? They would get on like a house on fire. Should we set their houses on fire?' I suggest, pigeonholing our ex-partners, whom I'd love to shoot like clay ones. 'Gemma isn't the only one that's left me. Did you hear about Big G, Lisa and Stevie moving to The Havana as well?'

'I heard about Stevie. He texted to say they were getting busier and that they needed me down there. Don't worry though, Buddha. I think you know what my answer was.' I have never been so grateful to call Harley a friend. I know for a fact that he will refuse any offer they might make. Many facts in my life have now turned out to be fictions, but this one, above any other, could be set in stone, or tattooed, like his name is on my wrist.

'You don't know how much that means to me.' If only it was possible to hug people over the phone. 'Gemma is living with Dick now. She cleared out all her stuff. Just as well really, because I'm getting evicted.'

'Damn, Yin-Yang. I wish Kris would come and collect all her shit. When I renovated my house a few years back she made me buy the most expensive tat. Fancy curtains from shops I'd never have gone in, ornaments and appliances I never would have bothered with. Now I'm stuck with all of it,' he says and I realise that he was in a lot deeper than I was. They might not have been engaged, but when I think how intertwined my life was with Gemma, she managed to separate them in a matter of hours. Harley is stuck, unable to walk away.

'You don't reckon she'll come back?'

'No, it's over. Why are you getting kicked out?'

'Couldn't pay the rent, bro,' I say, which must come as a surprise to Harley. He has been off full-time work a lot longer and has been able to maintain shelter.

'Gone and spent the kids' trust fund already, hey? Listen, why don't you come and stay with me? I've got a spare room.'

'I couldn't possibly,' I say, even though there is nothing I want (or need) more.

'You're totally right. You enjoy life out on the street while I enjoy the warmth of my big empty house. Don't be a dosser. Get yourself over here. I could do with the company. There's only one condition though.'

If there is a catch, I'll catch it. Whatever the condition is, the answer is 'Yes.'

'Anything, mate,' I reply.

'You need to take the dog for a walk every day,' he says, chuckling to himself. I have just seen Harley's true colours and they are better and brighter than any colours I have ever seen.

'I think I can manage that. In fact, I'd love to,' I respond, gratefully.

Dick can keep Mandara, I have Harley.

I'd choose Pippen the dog over Snoopy the dog any day.

34

I don't waste any time. Finally, I have something worth looking forward to and I intend to seize the moment. I grab the same sort of things I reached for the last time I planned my great escape (a suitcase full of photos and chopsticks) and relish the prospect of being anywhere but here. The landlord can keep his shoddy house with its poor internet connection. I didn't fancy the job they did of the bathroom anyway: hopefully he'll appreciate my renovation. I can't believe I'm about to leave the house in this state. Every property I have ever vacated in the past has been cleaned meticulously for the next tenant (but mainly for my deposit), painting over scuffs to the walls, filling in picture hook holes, dusting, mopping and all that other shit.

Why didn't I think of this before? I will embrace the nomadic lifestyle of the gypsy, the itinerant and the parasite. Fuck em. I call Harley back to ask him for his postcode and tell him that I am driving over tonight. He calls me an 'eager beaver' before providing an overly detailed description on how to get there, knowing how useless I am. I can't remember any of it, but it doesn't matter. I have somewhere to go. Once I'm content that my paltry possessions are packed, I kick my suitcase down the stairs. I look over at the television stand and wonder what to do with the console and flat screen. I no longer care about the menial things once cherished. My telly is probably shagging the DVD player behind my back.

Harley is my salvation. He *is* my escape. I take one last look at everything that used to make this house a home, and realise that it is neither. I was only home when Gemma was here, and this was only a house when it was tended and cared for. I used to treasure my few moments away from work in this place, with my gorgeous fiancée, and now I can't wait to leave. It is an affliction – a beacon of blight. A weekend colleague will put me up and my own mother won't. I try to think of anything I may have forgotten. If I am able to turn my back on almost everything I own, I can't see what could be so important that I haven't already packed. Considering I'm a hoarder by nature, this goes to show how bad things have become. This is a tad bit worse than having to cut some bombs from a menu.

Our stuffed toy animals are scattered about the bedroom. Our children. A painful reminder of what has happened between their mother and me. I unexpectedly feel sympathetic towards my own mum, though I know it isn't the same. Taking LambLamb or Kiwi-Bear with me would be too difficult. They will still smell of Gemma, and I think Harley might reconsider his invitation if I show up with a deer and a koala. Nibbles would have made a perfect chew toy for Pippen.

I kiss my children farewell, but they can't bring themselves to say anything. I head downstairs and scan the bathroom, but the hazards are too plenty to enter. I look at my watch and calculate that if I have a decent run to Harley's and don't get too lost, I'll be just in time to watch that film with him, providing a good hour and a half of silence before having to worry about our new living arrangement. I think we could both do without the immediate 'let me show you to your room' business and it would give us the chance to lose ourselves in someone else's struggle, before confronting our own. It will be a dark drive out of Bury, which is fine by me. This is the last time I'll ever have to be in this town and I'd rather not see it. Bury St Albans is what Barney would call 'too eighties' and I need to bring myself up to date.

For a moment I think my car has been stolen, until I remember that I've parked a few doors down and that it isn't worth stealing. I pop open the boot and empty all the crap I have accumulated out on to the street; a parting gift to numbers forty-two and forty-six. They will have to fight over the anti-freeze and my old car seat covers. I dump my suitcase in the back and look up at the house. I've left the front room lights on and the beacon of bleakness shines bright. Farewell number forty-four and good riddance to you. Old tower blocks in Hong Kong don't have a number forty-four either, and now I know why.

When I join the motorway, I realise that I am running on unleaded vapour. I wish Gemma had left the 'Boob Job Fund' for me to raid again. The petrol light was already on when I left the house, so I will be cutting it fine. I try to keep a steady speed, as Barney once told me that fifty-six miles per hour is the most fuel efficient. Having said that, Barney would also tell me to work hard, trust my friends and not to slap my partner in the face, so what the fuck does he know?

Vacating your house with no intention to pay your outstanding rent and utilities is one thing, but driving off without paying for petrol is in a league of its own. That shit is on CCTV. I can't double back now. I have made the right decision. After a long line of poor decisions, leaving Bury is finally a choice I take pleasure in. In answer to Dylan's question, I'd rather be really, really happy, but considered mentally unfit, than to never be happy again *and* mentally unfit, which is where I'm at now.

The motorway seems endless and I pray that I can reach the petrol station in time. I can sort everything out when I get there. I should beg and borrow before I decide to steal though. Eventually, I see the glow of a BP in the distance and pull in towards it. There is a queue to get on to the pumps, despite there being next to no cars on the motorway. I cut the engine and begin to search the coin tray, glove box, floor, side door and down the back of seats for loose change. I will need at least a fiver, which is the minimum fuel spend.

I have found £1 and 74p. I should have become a treasure hunter. I'd already have more to show than my non-existent savings from working bars and clubs. I had a treasure in Gemma and it was stolen from me. I can't stop thinking about Gemma and Dick, even though I have broken free from the grasp of Bury. I realise what Barney was talking about now when he would say 'Out of sight, but never out of mind.'

Before I can find any more silver, which is bound to be copper, a car behind me starts to beep. I look out of the grubby rear view and give an apologetic wave before starting the car up again. I squeeze between the unnecessarily large Land and Range Rovers and mumble to myself about the pointless need for Chelsea Tractors. We're in Norfolk, use a real one. They are filling their large tanks with fuel that would last me a month. I bet these bastards don't have to stick their hands under their seats to forage for pennies.

My parking is atrocious, diagonally positioned as if there was an archway that needed blocking. I head over to the multi-coloured guns and opt for the cheapest. They should start selling bargain petrol for half price, which you can take a chance on, as you may run the risk of your windows malfunctioning and your bumpers hitting bollards. I flip the fuel flap open and stick the green nozzle in the car's rib cage. I try to squeeze the trigger as gently as possible but as the numbers creep up, I realise that I've committed. I've started filling a car with fuel that I have no means to pay for. I wish I had Midas here so that he could touch some of this bronze and silver and turn it into gold.

I don't know what other choice I had but to push the car the rest of the way. I begin to panic and look around at the other people filling their cars. It's late and they all want to be on their way. What can I possibly say? Spare a pound for the poor beggar in his BMW? *Big Issue*, mate? Magical magazine that makes you turn invisible? I am fucked. I climb in the back and check the pockets behind the seats but they aren't even pockets, just nets, full of flyers we never handed out. I start checking places I know I've already checked and become frantic. Anyone would think I was searching for a winning lottery ticket, rather than a fiver in forgotten coins. I don't even know where I put that EuroMillions ticket. Dick stole it and cashed in the top prize.

There is a short plump lady at the kiosk looking straight at me. She can see on her screen that I have taken my required petrol. I have a decision to make. I can go to the counter and explain that I have forgotten my wallet and see what she says, or I can drive off. It's hardly robbing a bank. Driving off would be a serious gamble and I know from experience that I have no luck when it comes to gambling, or stealing for that matter.

Harley has been gracious enough to put me up. The last thing he needs is the police showing up at his door and I owe him more than that, more than £6. I head over to the garage. There must be at least four people in there and I really don't want to cause a scene. I could just about handle a one-on-one with the woman at the till, but in front of all this lot? Shit.

It's a push rather than a pull door, which causes everybody to stop choosing their magazines and their sandwiches and to look over at me after the noise I've made. The store is far too bright and I feel exposed and vulnerable. I glance over and the woman is still staring at me. No smile, nothing. She looks a bit like Penguin from *Batman* and I'm back at the brewery, on a conveyer belt, slowly being drawn towards her. I can't even buy myself some time by having a gander at the chocolates and car accessories, because my opening argument will be lack of necessary funds. Her name badge says Helen, but she looks more like a Hagrid or a Helga. Intimidating. Moody. Dreaded.

'Pump four. £6.08. Do you need a VAT receipt?' asks Hograd, morosely.

'Hi Helen, you may have seen me searching my car?' I submit, waiting for some kind of response. I get a slight grunt. 'Well, I can't seem to find my wallet.' Suddenly sandwich-buyers and magazine-flickers have lost interest in Ham & Cheese Weekly as they leer over at me, the nosey Ploughmen.

'I need £6.08 for pump four,' she says, my genitals firmly gripped between her Emperor Penguin flippers.

'I know. I know you do. I'd be happy to pay it, but I've left my wallet at home. I can send a cheque or bring it by tomorrow?'

'You have the petrol. Now you need to *pay*,' she says blankly, like this is a conversation she has often, even though I thought it was fairly original.

'Okay. Can I speak to a manager?' I demand, turning things up a notch.

'He's not in till tomorrow.' Helen of Troy was the face that launched a thousand ships. I need Helen of Trumpington's fat face to launch the one.

'What are my options? Please help me,' I beg, even though the only person she has ever helped is herself, to another pork pie.

'You can get someone to come and pay the balance. Failing that, you have to leave your car in the bay by the jet wash, hand over your keys and arrange alternative transport.' It is less than seven quid. I'd have been better off buying a scratch card.

'That can't be right?' We're on a motorway. 'I have £1.74.'

'It's not a car boot sale. You can't change the price.' I'm not trying to change the price; I'm trying to get out of paying altogether.

'I just want to get home. I've apologised for my mistake and we all make mistakes, right?' I continue, except it is *away* from home that I am trying to get and I have used up all my mistakes. I am halfway through Helen's quota too.

'If you don't pay, I'll call the police. I'm sorry.' She doesn't sound the least bit sorry. I find it hard to concentrate on what she's saying as all I can think about is how long it takes to choose a bloody sandwich. The guy won't need to buy the magazine – he's had time to read the whole thing cover to cover. I am a freak show and these people are lapping up the spectacle. They probably cover thousands of miles of motorway and this is finally something to talk about over their CB radios or whatever it is they use. I will forever be the guy who couldn't pay for six quid's worth of petrol.

'How about my phone? You can have this, not even as a deposit, just keep it. Pay for my petrol and it's all yours,' I offer, trying to show my desperation more than making a genuine proposal. As much as I hate my phone, it is my only means of navigation.

'I can't accept that as payment,' she replies, unconcerned that I was prepared to part with my contacts, emails, photos, music etc. She should leave this joint and get a job at The Havana.

'What phone is it?' asks random sandwich selector from the chilled section. I turn round to face the guy and his beady little opportunist eyes.

'HTC Desire. Good phone, great phone actually. It's the newest one,' I say, trying to pimp out my handset. If I can part with my large plasma and my console then what's a slow, difficult phone. Harley is the only person I have left that I'd ever need to call and I'm going to be staying with him, if I ever manage to leave the A11. I should have filled the tank though. I think it's too late to pour some more.

'This isn't the new one, it's covered in dents,' he says, truly testing my nerve considering the meal deal at a service station isn't far off the £6 I need.

'It might not be the newest, but twenty quid for a smart phone, come on man, be serious.' I try to bring some sense of reality back into this warped petrol provider.

'*Twenty*? You only owe her six summat?' He points at The Penguin. He must be The Riddler, because he is chatting some right shit. This is taking the Twat Tax way too far.

'Cheers for listening in on our private discussion,' I say, aligning myself with her.

'Didn't sound very private to me. You were raisin yer voice at the young lady. You alright there Helen, me darlin?' asks beady bastard, who clearly knows her, making my kinship efforts fail dismally. Helen nods. I shake my head in defeat.

'I've already offered you my phone. Please,' I say, lacking pizzazz.

'How's about that watch?' Bog-eyed Bob: Greedy. Ravenous. Half-empty.

'*What*? No. My father gave me it. This isn't for sale.' I am puzzled that someone could even fathom moving in on something that has such sentimental status. When I left the house I only wanted to keep my photos and my chopsticks, which my father had given to me. So much of my life I have resented him, or been angered by him, yet in my burning-house-fire moment, the only things I made a grab for were from him.

'Tenner, take it or leave it,' he says, gratifying himself at exploiting my situation. I should have floored it. I can't see the police pursuing a nationwide arrest for bilking £6 of petrol. Strangling and leaving a prostitute for dead is another matter. This watch is water resistant to a depth of four hundred metres. Ann Landers was right: sorrow truly knows how to swim.

'I can't. I just can't.' All I want to do is get out of this fiercely lit auction house. I'd rather give him the car than the watch. I want to tell him that if he heads over to number forty-four he can help himself to anything he wants, but I don't. Who leaves their front door unlocked for anyone to enter? Someone on the run.

'I'll give the money straight to Helen and you be on yer way. My son would love that, he would. His birthday's in a few weeks.' He pulls £20 from his wallet. There must be a good hundred quid in there and he is about to walk off with what was originally a £400 watch. I say nothing in protest: if fortune favours the brave, it's no wonder I'm skint.

My father went out of his way to select, purchase and surprise me with this watch and this cretin before me is prising it from my arm, to purchase for his own son, quite literally second-hand. My old man would never have dreamt of doing something like that. Despite what I may have said about him over the years, he had morals and was a decent human being. He would never take advantage of someone, not like this. I remove the silver Hamilton from my wrist, my hand shaking, eyes welling and Helen smirking. I feel like breaking down and crying, but I don't want to give them the satisfaction. I am at the end of my wick. I'm like the mum in *Home Alone*, selling her jewellery to pay for a flight home. She got a plane ticket. I get four and a half litres of unleaded petrol.

Bob, or whatever he's called, snatches my watch from me and turns it over, inspecting the glass and the kinetic mechanisms underneath, visible though the crystal casing. I take a final look at what should have been an heirloom. I am as hollow as my petrol tank. I turn to walk away, not wanting her filthy change.

As I leave, Bob utters a grumble. I think it's going to be the start of another complaint, about the marks on the links maybe, but instead he moans, '*You're welcome!*' in the most sarcastic of tones. As if his grand act of kindness warrants a thank you. As if I am being ungrateful. He stands and stares at me, wanting an apology for my lack of appreciation, but I glower at him frostily, trying to hold back the tears. I don't think I even thanked my father when he bought it for me. I can see now that this timely gesture was his token of love, his way of apologising to me for my mother leaving, for which he must have felt deeply responsible.

I do owe an apology and I do owe a thank you, but it isn't to you, Bully Bob.

35

I drag myself back to the car, feeling the nakedness of my wrist. There is a black band of dirt where my watch has been, as I never took it off. A million things are going through my head, none of them making any logical sense and none of them a bullet, which would be preferable: a single shell to put me out of my misery.

I want to turn around and head back in there, grabbing my watch before killing the pair of them in cold blood. They must be cold-blooded creatures to take a watch from someone who has nothing left of value. If I was a treasure hunter, they most certainly would have been grave robbers.

I look over at the pump and try to read the numbers that have cost me so much, but they all seem a blur. Stunned, I open my car door, slump down in the seat and glare across at the shop. Bob is leaning over the till, showing Helen his new prize, no doubt complaining about how badly he got ripped off. He has no idea of the importance of what he's handling and I will never get to wear it or even see it again. The watch didn't remind me of the time gone by without my mother; it reminded me of how much time I had until I would see my father. An American watch, assembled in Switzerland, bought in Hong Kong, and now given to a repulsive wretch off a motorway in Norfolk.

I want to drive the car straight into them, through the glass and across the counter in a fury of flames, but it's done now. I have been allowed to leave and should be on my way. Sitting here and watching them isn't going to achieve anything. The longer I stare, the more I imagine what they must be saying: gloating triumphantly, scoffing at the feeble half-caste kid they've just done over.

I send Harley a text telling him that I am nearly there and that I'll need a strong drink. I need to hear from someone who cares about me, to wash away this lot that hate me. I don't tell him about what happened, as it's too raw to serve. I don't want Harley making a joke about it just yet, at least not for a good few days. As I'm waiting for a reply, Helen's voice booms across the forecourt over the tannoy. She tells all drivers that the use of mobile phones are not permitted. Something tells me she is referring to me.

I pull out sharply onto the motorway and the phone slides down the side of the passenger seat. If only I had put my change on the seat more often, then maybe I could have found enough to pay for this petrol. The engine screeches as I put my foot down, both of us desperate to get to Harley's as soon as possible. It's a straight road to his, unless Bob runs me off the dual carriageway, demanding the grime from my wrist too.

The road ahead is clear and I am the only car heading towards Norwich. I can't wait until Gemma has found out that I'm gone. When I was cooped up in that horrid house, I was right where she left me, back at square one. Whereas now, she has no clue what I'm up to, who I'm with and what amazing, outlandish and successful things I might be doing. I may only be sleeping in a spare room watching late night Channel Four films in exchange for dog walking, but she doesn't know that.

If only he had accepted the handset instead. A phone can be replaced, but that watch. That watch was priceless to me. You don't sell something priceless for £6. I should have pleaded my case. I should have sat in the car and refused to move until I was too much of an inconvenience to entertain. I should have driven off. I shouldn't have given them my father's watch.

According to my phone, I have arrived. The journey here was a long one (significantly so, considering my disastrous detour), but the distance just goes to show how dedicated Harley truly was, having made this same trip every weekend. I call Harley to tell him that I must be close by and I don't know which will go first, the battery or the signal. He asks if I've been doing a spot of dogging in a lay-by and moans at me for not waiting until the adverts to ring. It is a great film – I'd have done the same. He tells me to drive down the same stretch of road until I reach a gate and that he'll buzz me in, before swiftly hanging up.

Gate? Buzz me in? Forget becoming a treasure hunter, grave robber or DJ. The money is clearly in building work. I continue along with my one working light on full beam, craning my neck left and right, searching for *The Kumars at No 42*.

I eventually manage to find Harley's pickup parked outside what looks like my dream house. It is something from *MTV Cribs*, only the

East Anglian version. I honk my horn at the gate and they begin to swing open. I think about Mr Morrissey and his ugly wife. If our club was somewhere out here we could have played the music as loud as we liked, and there would have been actual trees for our customers to hug.

If only Gemma could see my new house. She would love a place as impressive as this. If this were the lifestyle I had afforded her, she would have hung about. Or maybe she'd be shagging Dick in a nicer, more expensive, four-poster bed. I drive the car in slowly, surprised that the petrol I bartered has held out, and Harley comes to greet me. He is in his dressing gown and with his shiny bald head he looks like a monk.

He moves his hand in a circular motion, signalling for me to roll down the window and I wish my car did have wind down windows, because then they might actually work. I open the door, explaining that my windows are broken and he laughs, as if that is typical Harry behaviour. He heads back inside, presumably to push another button as his garage door folds open automatically. Incredible. I drive in and it's enormous.

There is a wall of power tools, along with a vast array of building materials, all carefully organised and laid out. It's a good thing none of these were pinched – there's no way I could replace any of this. I am thankful that my car is tucked away: it makes me feel that I am here for more than just the night. Harley walks over to me and looks so different in his dressing gown and slippers, rather than his suit trousers and long-sleeved bar shirt. His face looks gaunt, but the rest of him seems to be wider. His complexion is ashy and he doesn't look well at all, which makes me all the more glad I'm here. I hope he likes cheese on toast. If he does, he will be waited on hand and foot, and treated like the king that he is. Finally, I have arrived at the castle.

'Crouching Tiger! Only you could manage to park at a funny angle in a space this big!' I step out of the car and my legs nearly give way, acting out the will of my tired brain. Harley leans in to give me a handshake which turns into a half hug and it is so good to be here, away from all things Bury.

'It's huge in here, Peshwari! It's bigger than my whole house, or what was my house. I can't believe I left all my stuff there.' It still hasn't quite sunk in. 'I should have brought them for you, sorry.'

'You've always been tight with the lai see, you Terracotta bastard,' he says, in his Buddhist robes. 'I built this garage myself you know,' and it truly is magnificent. I couldn't put the racks together that hold his gardening equipment, let alone a free standing concrete out-house.

'You aren't going to believe this, but I had to use my father's watch to buy petrol just now,' I say, dejectedly. 'I can't fucking believe it.'

'What?' He is struggling to picture a scenario where fuel isn't paid for in approved currency. 'Well at least your old man won't find out about it.' A good few *months* – that's how long I wish would pass before the watch jokes come out.

'I didn't realise how much it meant to me until I was handing it over to some troll.' Bob took my wit as well as my watch. 'My arm is sore without it, as if someone has twisted it, like an Indian burn.'

'Did you say an *Indian burn*?' he replies, looking at me dumbstruck. 'It's a Chinese burn you idiot, don't try turn this one on me!' It hasn't taken Harley long to cheer me up. 'Only Peking Duck would trade his watch for some petrol. You should have called me and I'd have picked you up. I'm missing the film anyway, might as well have gone for a cruise. Which services was it? Not the first one off with the dumpy thing?' Helen's foul reputation as wide-spread as her full-fat butter.

'Too right it was. She said she was going to call the police and I panicked. I thought time was meant to fly when you're having fun, not when you're fucking miserable.' It will be some time before I can let this one go, regrettably not as easily as I let go of the watch.

'Every weekend when I left the club, I'd pull in there at five in the morning to get some food and it would always be her. Vile woman,' he says, making me feel better that she didn't single me out, but is thorny with other mongrels too.

'She's evil. She wouldn't accept my phone as payment for six quid's worth of petrol.' I am relieved that someone shares my pain.

'You offered your phone? You only put in £6?! My truck wouldn't get me out the drive for that. She doesn't give a shit, Tai-Chi. Neither should you. Let's go inside, it's freezing. Grab some firewood,' he says, pointing at a large pile of lumber in the corner of the garage.

'The judge in the movie is probably being killed by that exploding mobile phone right now,' I reply, as I grasp two handfuls of wood.

'Shame you didn't have one of those to give her. That would have learned her!'

'Can you make an exploding telephone?'

'I don't think you could afford that many phones with the number of people you'd want to blow up!' He's not wrong. This garage would have to become a Carphone Warehouse.

36

Harley leads me into his Hindi hotel, and it is amazing. He didn't lock his door, for a start. When you have a colossal gate protecting your property, you really do feel important and this isn't even my house. We should build a moat and a trebuchet, but I'll get my feet under the table before I start suggesting modifications to his property. His house looks like a bloody show-room: truly stunning. He has LED mood lighting running along the base of his breakfast bar, centred within a stylish, open plan kitchen. He has a large feature wall displaying a collection of chic artwork with a striking gold and grey motif. You can tell Kristina influenced the décor, because it's feminine and looks like something out of a magazine.

'It's the Taj Mahal in here, Harley.' I carefully place the wood down next to the fire. He failed to mention that he's a Bollywood superstar. He has a black leather chaise longue that matches his three-piece suite and I'm keeping an eye out for the grand piano. Further inside, there are opaque sliding doors leading on to a large, decked patio.

'Cheers, Lychee. It might not be The Ritz, but at least it's not the pits,' he replies, 'the pits' accurately describing the shithole I have just left. My pagoda was barely a motel. If we were living in India, I would be several castes below this guy. 'It's really good to have you here.' This puts me at ease. Someone that is strictly a hired hand doesn't open his electric doors for his co-worker and allow him to make himself at home.

'Where's Pip?' I ask, getting stuck into my role as godfather.

'Sleeping upstairs. She's getting old and only wakes up when she hears the tin opener going. I sleep for a lot of the day now too, I always feel so drained. She's awesome though. Won't nag me for being in bed all day and doesn't make me do the dishes. The perfect girlfriend,' he says, making the most of his new domestic arrangement. Gemma used to do everything for me and I never appreciated it.

Harley sticks the kettle on and reaches for the remote. Turning the volume up, he calls time on our casual canine conversation to watch the rest of this film I've made him miss.

'Got anything stronger than a cuppa? I was thinking more Special Brew than a brew.' I left all dignity in the off-license when I went wine shopping.

'I can barely keep down the tea, so the only white spirit around here is turps. Thankfully it comes with a safety cap: you'd do them in bombs!' He never was much of a drinker. Seeing as I'm a guest and I'm broke, I should be content with my Darjeeling or Chai. The poor guy has the urge to gorge himself on food, yet struggles with a cup of tea. It's strange seeing Harley in his home. I feel that I know him so well, yet at the same time know next to nothing.

'A cup of tea would do lovely. Milk and two, please. Want a mobile phone for it?'

'Cheers for the offer, but I don't have anyone to call. My dad asks me to review the occasional film, Kris doesn't talk to me, and you're here, so I don't even need the ancient Nokia I have now.' We might be kindred spirits: Harley and I against the world, with no one to text or call but each another.

I laugh, Harley brings me some tea, and I make myself comfortable on the armchair, which feels amazing. Maybe it's because it doesn't have a rip in it, like those at the club, which Harley said I should have gotten one of my Chinese sweatshops to fix. We settle down to watch Clyde in solitary confinement, and I'm grateful that I am no longer in the same creaky boat. Harley makes a few comments about the film, but my thoughts are elsewhere. I mutter the occasional reply, but I can't get into the movie. I am thinking about my father and about Gemma and about the hooker and wondering what the fuck I'm supposed to do next. I have a boot full of clothing and some Cantonese dining utensils to my name, and not a lot else.

I look over at his DVD rack and several of the films are ones I've lent him. I can't help but laugh. I look over at Harley to say something about it, but he has nodded off, with his cup of tea still in his hands. I reach over, taking it from him as carefully as I can and place it on the table. I can't believe he is letting me stay here. I simply can't imagine what this world would be like without Harley. I don't know what would happen if the cancer got the better of him (even though he would say it's already taken a lot of what was best in him). I felt like a lost child when Midas died, but his death was completely self-inflicted. Harley has done nothing to deserve this. I hope if I can offer him anything, it is what Midas offered me. Proof that it doesn't matter what you do or which way you turn, your life will still end in shit.

I look down at the glass-topped, ornate coffee table, which would have taken up my entire front room, and there is a litter of tablet boxes scattered across it. I scour through the cartons nosily, eyeing what's on offer. I am surprised by the sheer number of pills Harley has been prescribed. I never considered just how much medication was involved in battling cancer, and this isn't a scratch on what must happen at the hospital. When he was misdiagnosed, so many of the pills he was trusting would make him better were doing nothing of the sort. I wonder which of these might work as an ambient or high.

Ondemet Ondansetron tablets 8mg? Domperidone 10mg? How does he even keep up with what's what? Maybe some of these are from his old medicine regime and no longer needed. I can't bring myself to wake him up, but when he comes out of his slumber I will ask him if I can pop a Ciprofloxacin 500mg. The Aprepitant 80mg must be good because the box is empty. Morphine 100mg. Jackpot. I bet Ronald Benjamin doesn't have this in his bag of tricks.

'What you got there, Taipei?' Harley looks at me through a half-opened, weary eye.

'Can I take one of these?' I ask, embarrassed that he's caught me being nosy.

'Fill your boots, mate,' he says, before wheezing from a tender windpipe. 'You won't feel very well after one of those.'

'I haven't felt well in a long while.' I take one of the pills and place it on my tongue, followed by a sip of tea. I hope this can erase the week I've had. I put the tablets back down, and there is a book buried under the pile of boxes. It is open face down, and I brush the packets aside to have a better look. *The Scarlet Letter* by Nathaniel Hawthorne. 'What's this?' He just shrugs and looks at me sheepishly. The title sounds familiar. It was mentioned in the film *Crazy, Stupid Love*, which features a hilarious scene where Cal's colleagues think he's dying of cancer when someone hears him crying in the toilet, only to find that he's actually getting a divorce. They all rejoice, delighted to hear that he is only ending his twenty-five year marriage rather than suffering from cancer. I wouldn't find that quite as funny if I was to watch it now, given that they're both rather sore subjects in this household.

Harley doesn't seem like the type to read anything beyond the back of a cereal box. He's the kind of guy who will wait for the book to come out on DVD. If he was to read, it would have been *Men's Health* – collecting dust now, considering he doesn't have the energy to walk his dog, let alone work on his biceps and quads. I pick the book up to examine it further. Harley squirms on the sofa, looking uncomfortable. I think he'd prefer if it was written in Sanskrit. I flick through the book and it lands on a page that has been earmarked.

> 'None, nothing but despair. What else could I look for, being what I am, and leading such a life as mine? Were I an atheist, a man devoid of conscience, a wretch with coarse and brutal instincts, I might have found peace long ere now. Nay, I never should have lost it. But, as matters stand with my soul, whatever of good capacity there originally was in me, all of God's gifts that were the choicest have become the ministers of spiritual torment. Hester, I am most miserable.'

I don't know who Hester is, but I want to ask Harley why this page has been dog-eared. I never realised words could so strongly encapsulate how I feel, even if I don't entirely understand them. I don't think I need to for me to relate to his pain. I think Phil Collins must be Nathaniel's great-great-grandson. Before I get the chance to question him, Harley tells me that it's Kristina's. He had started to read it to pass the time and the passage summed up how he felt when he went through the first bout of chemo that didn't show any improvement. I am about to ask him if I can read it, but what he says next commands my full and undivided attention.

'There are so many people putting up the good fight on the ward.' I reach for the remote and turn the volume down. 'But me? I feel *cheated*.' These are the 'feelings' I have been waiting for, but I never considered what I might hear and what I'd do with it. I don't know what to say to him. I don't think my comments will bring him any comfort, so I remain silent. 'I don't want to live forever. I don't even want to live any longer, if it means feeling like this. I know some people can do it. I've met them.' I can almost sense them in the room with us as he stares up at the chandelier, as if there is a bulb for each of them. 'But they have family. If I put Pippen in a kennel and never went to pick her up, that would be my responsibility over. No one relies on me.' I want to tell him that I rely on him, more than he'll ever know, but as before, what comfort would that provide him? It would probably distress him further. 'The treatments are too intensive. The quality of life they're offering doesn't seem to justify the battle to get there. Not for me. The doctors have made no promises and no guarantees,' he says, stopping to catch his breath.

Harley has built his entire life on just that, guarantees. Wensum Maintenance Limited is based upon the promise and assurance that certain conditions will be fulfilled. When Barney once said that Harley's wages were to be pushed back for the second month on the trot, he responded with some hostility, explaining that he didn't care if he was paid fortnightly, monthly or even annually, but if someone says they are going to pay on a specific date, then they pay on that date. We went to weekly wages with him after that, but again, guarantees.

Harley lets out a long, heavy sigh as though he has been waiting to get that off his chest for some time. I admire his honesty and I am thankful that he has confided in me, even if I can't offer anything that may help him. I close the book in front of us and arrange his medication neatly in a row on the table, covering the book up like before. Harley turns the volume back up on the telly and takes a sip from his tea. We watch Clyde's prosecutor trying to talk him out of detonating the bomb, which he is determined to set off, killing all the bureaucrats in City Hall, or some equally important building.

The morphine makes me feel strange, but it wasn't without warning. Clyde decides to set the bomb off regardless, taking no heed of the lawyer's warning. I wish life were as simple. I wish we could press a button and blow up all of our problems, fire with fire.

I wake up to Pippen licking my hand and she startles me. There is a large throw covering me on the armchair, and it takes me a moment to figure out where I am. Harley isn't on the sofa so he must have made his way to bed, whichever way that is. The room looks different in the daytime, still really nice, just not in the same way. He has cleared the book and tablets from the table and I feel a shooting pain of guilt, as I remember picking up his paperback last night.

'Sleep well there, Wasabi? You're not used to sleeping in a chair. Usually the back of the restaurant on a bed of prawn crackers for you lot, right?' Harley is stood at the foot of his staircase, with an orange juice in one hand and a newspaper in the other. I bet he doesn't sex up his OJ.

'Dumplings for a pillow and a rice sack for a blanket! Cheers for letting me stay here.' The thought of hot, shrimp dumplings and white boiled rice is good.

That has to be one of the saddest things about no longer having my father in my life. If I could go back to Hong Kong now I could do the tourist thing, sure, but gone are the days of the back-street restaurants, off the beaten track, and ordering alongside the locals.

My father loved his food and always made sure I was well fed – one of the few things we could agree on. When we were sat in a Dai Pai Dong or a dessert house and he was filling my bowl with countless treats I'll never know the name of, we were content in one another's company.

'Sleep in the guest room tonight. I didn't want to wake you,' he says, looking away from me, as if he has just remembered all that was said last night.

'About yesterday – ' I start, wanting him know that if he needs to talk, I am here to listen.

'Yeah, sorry. Got a bit deep there. I've been in a bad way,' he replies, apologetically, as if I'll be performing lip stiffness checks all morning. He waves his paper at me dismissively, and he must get it delivered because there is no way he left the house dressed like that.

'Deep is good. Better than being shallow. We know a few of them and you aren't anything like that,' I say, trying to put him at ease. 'Everyone needs someone to talk to and you understandably have a lot on your mind.' We covered some serious ground last night. 'You're a great guy, and you should know that you can let it all out.'

'You want to talk to me or bed me? Jesus, man.' His macho drive needs to overcompensate for last night's heart to heart.

'You know what I mean. I *can* make a promise and a guarantee. If you need me, I'm here,' I say, with what I hope sounds like the drawing of a line under it.

'I've given up. I don't know what that actually means, but I want out. I was in agony last night. I feel like death.' He rubs his face with the back of his hand, spilling some juice, which Pippen appreciates. 'I'm not even exaggerating. I felt like my guts were burning and my sides tightened. They wouldn't loosen up. I was even punching them, it was horrible.' He looks as dreadful as he describes. His eyes are blood-shot and there are two dark rings perched angrily above each of his cheeks, which have dug their nails in so they don't fall off. I thought I had it bad, itching from the morphine.

'I know what you mean. Not the physical pain, which sounds awful, but the other stuff. I've given up too, on everything and nothing. It's hard to put into words. It all seems so pointless. All of it,' I say, making this the most cheerless and downright depressing conversation I have ever had, even worse than the true colours thing. I wish I could take some of his pain away. We could decide it was my turn tonight so that he would rest easy.

'So what are you saying?' he asks, as if I have some kind of solution I'd like to propose: a plan of sorts, even though we have both put planning in our lives on hold indefinitely. Harley kneels down on the floor to stroke Pippen, who has slumped on the rug, and we both stare at his gorgeous staffie in silence.

'I don't know what I'm saying,' I eventually admit.

'I thought you were going to suggest a pillow over my face.' He doesn't laugh or smile about it. I think considering the night he just experienced, which doesn't sound like a one-off, he would take me up on the offer.

'I could never bring myself to pull your plug, Biryani.' He doesn't look at me, but seems disappointed, as if I have broken my promise of guarantees already, having only just promised it.

'Something has to give,' he says, bluntly.

'There are other ways. There must be.' He looks up at me as if I am patronising him. That if there was another option, I think him too stupid to have considered it. He's already using enough drugs to take down an

Indian elephant and he's in and out of hospital as frequently as Dick is in and out of Gemma.

'You have a way to get me through the night without being curled up in pain, do you?' he asks, in an acrid tone. Harley is the most easy going person I have ever met, so for him to talk in this manner he really must be at his wits' end. He seems offended, like I'm holding out on him, and that if I was a decent and caring friend I would suffocate him in his sleep.

'I don't, Harley. I don't have an answer for that, but we will get through this, together,' I say, making it sound so straightforward. As if I too have been misdiagnosed and endured the wrong type of chemo. As if I too await biopsy results and find myself unable to sleep without wanting to die.

'Together? How are we going to get through it together? You've got cancer as well?'

'We *will* do it together. I'll go with you,' I reply, as if it's a trip down to the store for the weekly shop.

'Go where?' he asks, even though he knows exactly what I'm insinuating. He wants me to say it out loud. 'Where do you plan on going with me, *Harry*?'

'There, anywhere, the end. If you're going, you're taking me with you.' We pause for a moment to absorb the weight of what has been said, except we're both fully saturated and can't soak it up between us. 'I have an idea, but I need your help –'

'I'm the one that needs the bloody help, Dim Sum,' he says, cutting me off sharply.

'I know. I have nothing to offer you, man. Nothing at all, but at least we can die with some kind of purpose.' I put a name to the faceless answer.

'I have a perfectly reasonable purpose already. I know I may laugh and joke, but I've never been more serious about anything.' I hadn't realised how much Harley was going through behind his closed, mahogany doors and large, automatic gates.

'I'm not holding a dumpling over your face while you sleep. If you want to do it, really truly do it, then we take a trip together,' I say, and I am on to something. A man that is professing his own desire to die should be open to some degree of suggestion, however wild.

'Go on.' He looks at me apathetically, as if he has already decided that my suggestion is senseless and of no benefit to him.

'One final project together,' I declare, and I almost want to cover Pip's ears so she doesn't have to hear what I'm about to say. Harley knows what my 'projects' are like – he does all the work and I pop out to buy the cheeseburgers. 'We take them down with us. Gemma. Dick. Even Sammy fucking Fish.'

'Fine, good, I don't care, but I want it to be soon. I've witnessed first-hand what they did to you,' he says, as he rubs the side of his ribs. They are distracting him from thinking this through properly.

The Harley I know wouldn't hurt a fly. If I caught one with my chopsticks, he'd try to rescue it. He would never intend to harm someone, let alone *kill* them. He's the type of person that would write a will, leaving everything to Pip and check himself into a Swiss clinic. It's either some form of mind-altering brain cancer that he's suffering from or these pains are more severe than anything I could possibly imagine. Worse than pouring ten pints only to realise that the gas has gone, and they're all flat.

I am about to let him know how surprised I am by his willingness, but he points at me, and says, 'You aren't doing it though.'

'What do you mean, I'm not doing it?' I ask, as if he is going to a party that I haven't been invited to. 'Course I'm fucking doing it.'

'I honestly thought you were going to suggest a lad's holiday to Ibiza, or some of that Chinese acupuncture stuff, not a murder mission.' He ignores my protest at being denied entry. I want to be on the guest list, not turned away for wearing trainers. 'One final project. When you called me with nowhere to live, I jumped at the chance to have you here. Maybe this is the reason why?'

I assumed he wanted my company and someone to hold the pooper scooper – not an agent of death.

'Maybe you wanted someone close to you when you *did it*. You want to know why *I'm* here?' I reply, and he doesn't look like he wants to know, but I'm going to tell him anyway. 'Because this is it, mate. This is all that's left for me, sleeping in an armchair at someone else's house. This isn't the morphine talking. The partner, who I was prepared to spend my entire life with, left me. She fucking *left me*, for Dick, along with everyone else. I have no job. I have no siblings, as if I was a mistake my parents didn't want to repeat. My mother has rejected me, for the second time, and my old man, well –' and I can't continue. I shouldn't need to convince him how shit my life has become. Harley is my closest friend and ironically, he is the only one who can't see how awful it truly is, as he has a larger dipstick with which to test. I have nothing to live for, but he has cancer, drastically reducing his chance at a life.

'These things are bad, but some of them can be fixed.'

'I don't want them to be fixed. You've spent your whole life fixing things, but this isn't a leaky pipe or dodgy electrics. I *want* them to be broken. I want to cut their power and for it to never come back on. I want to be vilified. They will feel the same pain that I experience every day, so much of it that they can taste it, like metal,' I declare, and he stands up suddenly, making Pip jump. I shouldn't have mentioned tasting metal, as if I know what it's like. I think he is about to walk off, but instead he sits opposite me.

'I always thought I was going to be young forever, Sushi. Looks like I was right about something after all.' He is warming to the idea of letting me in on it, as he isn't saying no anymore.

'Only the good die young. Looks like I have my chance to cheat too,' I reply, looking back at him and trying to read what he's thinking.

Harley reaches over and places his hand on my shoulder. 'So, when do we start?'

37

We don't waste any time. I can see the thought of another restless and agonising night etched across Harley's face. He instructs me to fetch his laptop from the desk in the study and says he'll be back downstairs in ten minutes. I feel an unforgiving churning in my stomach, which I put down to the morphine rather than the decision to start work on killing ourselves, and other people, in the process.

I head into his office and it is as equally well designed as the rest of his house. I unplug his laptop (probably bought from Currys) and pull the cable out from a tangle of wires. As I leave the study, I notice a large picture frame on the wall (one of those fancy ones that are made up of loads of little pictures that surround a clock). Each of the photos is of Harley and Kristina and she is as beautiful as the glossy paper in his wallet said she was. There is a snap of them on a beach somewhere hot, and another picture of them holding a monkey somewhere tropical. There is a larger photo of them in front of a Christmas tree with Pippen (who is only small) surrounded by neatly wrapped presents. In each picture they look happy, healthy and in love.

He can say what he likes about her, but a picture tells a thousand words and these ones are telling me how much she meant to him. These prints look like the pictures that come in a frame when you first buy it: attractive models posing in idyllic settings that will always look better than the photos you'll end up putting in them. Unlike Gemma, Kristina left the frame just as it was and I don't know which is worse. I don't accept her leaving him, but part of me understands it, even if I don't want to. People handle things in different ways, and it must have been hard for her to see a life she had built with someone (or allowed him to build around her, quite literally) come to a halt.

Harley is on the beach with his top off and is tanned and strong and your archetypal man's man. She looks like a footballer's wife, sporting immaculate makeup and clearly taking serious pride in her fashion and frippery – the type of girl that wants to be looked after and provided for – and he is now unable to do either. She walked out on Pip too. If she really was the ball to his chain, she's left the chain for him to hang himself with, mounted here on his study wall. I head back into the front room, still unsure as to why we need the laptop, and Harley is leaning into his kitchen sink.

He has changed into his work clothes and is donning a well-worn pair of dungarees: a stylish fireman kind rather than a childish *Oor Wullie* kind. If I tried to wear that get up I'd look like a Hillbilly. Apart from staring down into a plug hole, he looks ready and means business.

'Harley, you okay?' I ask. Another stupid question.

'You know these morphine pills are slow releasing,' he says, spitting a watery dribble into his sink. 'They break down over time and can't just do their job quickly. They drag it out. I'm sure that's the point, but I'm still not getting it.' Harley has clearly been upstairs losing the jackpot.

'They're fucking strong. How many do you have to take?' I ask, unable to imagine taking another, considering how abnormal I feel from just one. 'I keep getting rushes, waves.'

'More than I'd like to,' he says, spluttering what seems like the last of it for now. 'Let's go. It's too comfy in here.'

I let Harley lead the way and follow him across to his garage. We head out into the cold and I understand what he means about being comfortable. It would be hard to plot and scheme something so monstrous from the comfort of a warm armchair, sipping on Horlicks or Ovaltine with daytime telly on in the background. We need to be cold, damp and miserable.

When we get inside, Harley takes the laptop from me and pulls down a work surface from the wall. He turns on his computer, before scanning the shelves and racks, as if he is making a mental checklist. I have come to the right place, which is just as well, seeing as it was the only place left for me to go.

'We're going to need a lot more stuff,' he says, in a desperate hurry. He is working against the clock, the same clock surrounded by pictures of Kristina.

'Tell me what we need and I'll write it down,' I reply, even though I have no idea what he has in mind and what stuff this list might comprise of.

'No need. That's what the laptop is for. We order everything online and it will arrive tomorrow before 4pm,' says Harley, who has played this game before.

'What's the plan?' I ask, knowing that Harley doesn't do anything half-heartedly, and has already thought the entire thing through from start to finish. I can't help but feel unnecessary in all of this. I'm only slowing him down. 'Fill me in, Jalfrezi.'

Harley kicks the rear bumper of my car with his steel-toed boot. The sound resonates throughout the whole garage and I am put in my place for encumbering him with pointless questions.

'Sorry, tell me what website to go to,' I say, embarrassed, even though I would only slow him down with that too.

'Your car,' he replies, simply. 'My car is too sturdy. Yours on the other hand, yours is perfect.' My car has never been described as 'perfect' and I am glad that Harley wasn't kicking my car as a way to shut me up. I suppose it's better than Del Boy Barney's Reliant Regal.

'My car's a piece of shit, bro. I wish I'd given them my wheels instead of my watch.' I'm off the wagon indefinitely, so at least my actual wagon is being put to use.

Harley carefully inspects my vehicle, opening and closing the doors and looking under the bonnet. 'With a few modifications, this is what we're going to use.' He pushes the front of the car into the floor, presumably testing the suspension.

'To do what though?' I quiz, hoping that this is the last question I need to ask before I am set to work, even if that work involves taking Pip around the garden.

'Fish and Dick. They want to drive people through their club doors, right? Well, be careful what you wish for.'

'Drive the car into The Havana?' I reply, wanting to see what the words taste like.

'Yes, full of explosives.' These words must taste even sweeter.

'My car is perfect,' I say, and so is Harley and so is his plan. 'This is our Nuke Bomb.'

We will be the final drive of their wretched lives.

Barney was right about something after all: hope for the best, but plan for the worst.

It is strangely fulfilling to have something to apply myself to, working alongside Harley again. We've taken on two hundred revellers all pushing for our service at the bar, Harley and me, two against two hundred. We are used to being up against it. No matter how stressful it got, I would look across at Harley, knocking the drinks out and towing the line, without a moan or a murmur and knew I wasn't alone. This is to be our new challenge and there is no way I would, or could, do this without him.

He decided that he was going to end his life all on his own. I didn't put the idea there, I didn't need to. He managed to voice what I was secretly thinking this entire time, and I didn't even know it. Doctors might not be able to make him any guarantees, but I can. I guarantee that I will let him get his way, and that I will be there until the fast-approaching end.

I used to think that people who killed themselves were being selfish, and that they hadn't considered the knock-on effects their death would have on everyone who knew them. When Midas died, his family told everyone that he 'took his own life' (which somehow seemed less sinister than a heroin overdose) and made it more of a conscious choice on his part, as if death was something he decided he wanted, rather than an unfortunate accident. When people heard that it was suicide, they said the same about him too, that he had been *selfish*. His life was in tatters, so if he had killed himself intentionally, which could have been the case, he wouldn't have been thinking about the reasons to live, only the reasons to die. Those reasons to die would have outweighed his reasons to live, as do mine.

Considering the people that will be affected by my choice only reinforces my decision. My mother will read about my actions in the paper or on a computer-less lid. She will pour herself another gin, have a fag and move on. Just another thing that didn't quite work out, for her to tell people they don't understand. She washed her hands of me a long time ago, leaving the water dark and murky. Barney will wonder if there was more he could have done, something he could have said, but will secretly relish the fact that my ultimate dying act was to ruin The Havana Club. He has his growing family to think about now. Dylan will no doubt miss his buddies, but our demolition efforts will offer a cool story to tell his new stoner friends at university. Freddie will realise that I have lost my sense of humour.

And that is the only legacy I will leave. Reason enough to do it, before you even begin to add all the other stuff on top. Thinking about my paltry send-off only makes me wish I had decided to do this sooner. In lieu of a meaningless life, I will settle for a purposeful death.

Harley sets me the task of clearing out the car, for which I'm thankful. That I can do. I start with the suitcase and try to create an organised clutter, out of the way. As I clear out the assortment of crap in the well-lit room, I find a further four and a bit quid in loose change – too little, too late.

Being in this garage with Harley has provided me with a goal, even if it is injurious. Okay, my moral compass has never pointed due north, but nor has it been spinning round like a set of nunchucks, as it is now. I am a soulless miscreant with no future, wanting to exact revenge on everything he has ruined in his life. My moral fibre has snapped.

Once Harley has ordered our materials, he turns off his laptop and suggests that we head back inside the house. I remove a few items of clothing from my suitcase and follow him out. He sticks a log onto the fire and gives it a good prod, while I offer to make us a cup of tea. I open the cabinets, trying to find the one that contains the mugs, and happen upon the bottle of Malibu that Harley took home for Kristina. Her loss. I wonder if I can make purple drank by adding 50mgs of Fluconazole?

I tell Harley about my discovery with a worrying amount of enthusiasm and he tells me that I may as well drink it. Somewhere in between dunking the bag and adding the sugar, Harley starts to speak as he stares intensely at the flickering flames.

'I know what the hardest part is,' he begins, as if he has recently discovered his own unexpected version of coconut rum. 'Everything I considered important, no longer matters.' Another rare glimpse of candour. 'People often take their health for granted. I knew I was healthy. It was my *worries* I took for granted, if that makes any sense. Now I realise they weren't even worries at all.'

'Don't think about it,' I say, passing him his cup of tea, served black, as the milk he had has gone off. 'It's not like we're teenagers anymore, we've had a decent run,' my attempt at making him feel better, as there is no truth in what I'm saying at all. Harley is far too young to be going through this illness, not that there is a 'right' age, but no one would agree that twenty-eight was enough time to even get a momentum going, let alone run.

'I've been getting worse, but she is getting better, you know,' he says, talking positively about Kristina for the first time. 'When I met her she was pretty, but she was innocent and a little goofy maybe,' he attests, before taking a sip of his tea that I don't think he'll enjoy. 'But she's turned into this sumptuous, evocative woman, she really has.' I'm not sure he's even talking to me. He looks delirious and distant.

'You make her sound like a bottle of wine, mate,' I reply, following his uncharacteristically eloquent choice of wording, and pour myself a greedy serving of Malibu.

'She was getting better with age, and I won't be around to enjoy it,' he says, joylessly. 'Her wine has been sat in my cellar, gaining value, and I won't be uncorking it. She will make someone very happy one day, but it won't be me.' He is looking away and I know it's tearing him up inside having to talk about her being in the arms of someone else. I know the feeling all too well.

'Women aren't like wine. They're like this milk. They go off when they get old and turn sour. That's what you need to tell yourself. There's no room for thoughts like that.' I am committed to our cause, and won't be sidetracked. I will be thinking about Gemma endlessly over the next few days, or weeks, however long this plan of ours will take, but I won't be talking to Harley about it. He has his own lack of woman to trouble him. I shouldn't have contradicted him. That was a Goldschläger moment.

Gemma was truly finding herself as a person. With her college days behind her, she started to form her own opinions; her own set of beliefs and interests, which were no longer dictated by her peer group. Her new ideals just didn't include me. I rushed it. It all happened too soon. If I had kept our relationship carefree and fun and let her fully develop into an individual, maybe things would have been different, but I didn't. She went from leaving college, to leaving home, to being engaged to me. I went in too soon and Harley waited too long.

Harley and I now have our own beliefs and they haven't happened too soon. They have been lying under the surface, marinating, and even though we only decided what to do yesterday, the wheels had been set in motion long before he kicked my rear bumper.

38

The following afternoon we are in the garage again and Harley is tinkering away. I am starting to feel the effects of the two morphine pills that I double-dropped earlier. I think I am building up a tolerance, even though I'm not suffering from the kind of physical pain that they are intended to suppress. I've stopped throwing up at least. I unfold and sit on a step ladder and observe. I enjoy watching Harley work. He is definitely a measure twice, cut once kind of guy.

Neither of us knows the first thing about making bombs, even if Harley is willing to give it a good go. The very concept is preposterous, even laughable, despite there being nothing remotely humorous about it. I've played *Bomberman*, poured many bombs and bombed a Rizla full of speed, but that is where my bomb crafting experience comes to an end. What I do know is that this is what's behind door number three. We should have started with something small, like an effigy or a floating Chinese lantern.

I flick through the newspaper that Harley was reading. In the working man's *Telegraph* that is *The Sun*, I study an article: 'Man makes bombs in council flat.' It describes homemade devices constructed from aerosol canisters, nails, metal washers and fireworks, held together by packaging tape. I tear the page out for Harley, who seems too focussed on what he's doing to pay much attention.

'That sounds a bit extreme,' he says, as he continues to work on our chariot of death.

'That's because we're extremists.' I like the sound of it even though I know I shouldn't, making it all the more extreme.

Harley stops whatever it is he's doing to look over at me. He wipes his brow, which indicates he is sweating when I am sat here bloody freezing. 'I see us as the modern day Bonnie and Clyde, rather than Mohammed and Abdul,' he laughs. 'You're Bonnie though.'

'You're thinking of Thelma and Louise.'

'I wish we had something bigger than a car,' he says, looking down at my Beemer which I thought was meant to be 'perfect.'

'A van?' I suggest. I'd happily settle for being called a 'bus wanker' if it meant I could drive a double-decker through their doors. I don't care what we use, it makes no difference – either way we are driving our gondola into their gazebo.

'Not a van. A tank, or a plane even!' It's said that a bad workman blames his tools, not an exceptionally good one. I'm surprised he hasn't suggested a rickshaw yet. 'You know what they call a Chinese man flying a plane don't you?'

'What?' I ask, anticipating something funny and highly offensive.

'A pilot, you racist bastard,' he answers, laughing hysterically before slapping the boot of the car in uproar, which isn't the best of ideas, considering its potentially volatile cargo.

'I'm not racist, I have a colour TV,' I say, which is probably sitting in my landlord's front room. 'How can I be racist? Some of my best friends are white.'

Extremely stupid, more like.

'I've been looking into a few things while you've been getting spangled on morphine. We are restricted with what we can do,' he replies, meditatively.

'Well, what are we likely to end up doing?' I want to hear what we *can* do for a change, rather than all the things we can't.

'Bleve's,' he says, simply.

'Bevvies? I'm always up for getting the beers in, but I don't think that'll help, bro,' I say, even though I know he doesn't mean buying a barrel for dentist chairs and keg stands.

'Pronounced *blevys*, but spelt differently. It stands for Boiling Liquid Expanding Vapour Explosion, when a vessel containing pressurised liquid is ruptured.' It sounds like a sambuca gas chamber all over again.

'And you know how to devise something like that?' I think we'll need more than a wine glass, a lighter and a straw to get one of those going.

'Then there are fertiliser bombs, made from ANFO, Ammonium Nitrate and Fuel Oil, a widely used bulk industrial explosive mixture. Low in cost, easy to use, and common in metal mining,' he says, which is where his knowledge in filling out Barney's jiggers with molten metal must have come from.

'Sounds like something I should leave to you.' I don't want to blow myself up until we have an unwitting audience. I think Harley has been watching too much *CSI*.

'Ours would be a lot more improvised, a lot more guerrilla.' There's no way I'm hugging that.

'While you crack on, I'll get some cheesy chips on the go,' I say, wondering how we've gone from talking about colour televisions to large primates.

'There is a range of powerful explosives, like acetone peroxide – the dangerous by-product of several chemical reactions,' he replies, broadening the gap between our respective knowledge bases ever further.

'How do you know about all this stuff?'

'It's a by-product from the synthesis of MDMA. There are clinical trials testing its potential for the post-traumatic stress associated with terminal cancer,' he says, pensively. I don't know what 'terminal' means, but I sure know what 'MDMA' means, and I'm impressed. 'Someone has to put in the leg work. We can't just drive up to their doors and shout bang from your sun roof.' All I'm interested in is if he knows how to make MDMA that I can take with these morphine tabs.

'MDMA, as in the drug Mandy, yeah?' I ask, sounding like a wasteman.

'Don't trouble your pretty head. Be a dear, make yourself useful and sort us a cuppa,' he says in a girly voice, and I can't help but laugh.

'Fine, but I'm using MDMA instead of sugar in mine!'

Part of me wanted to be crucial to the construction, development and eventual destruction of our vehicle, and our plan in general. Enough has already been taken from my control. However, the other part of me, the greater part, is appreciative that everything is being taken care of. That I finally needn't worry. A bit like Dylan must feel with his dad sorting out his university application, job and accommodation for him.

Either way, I bet Ronald Benjamin couldn't synthesise MDMA.

This is the real Dead Man's Trip.

*

Later that evening, I raid Harley's cupboards looking for anything to cook up – food, rather than drugs. I may as well use it because there won't be anyone around to enjoy the tins of old tuna and the cans of oxtail soup once we're gone. Harley went for a shower some time ago, so I'd better whip this up quick. I wish I had something healthy to make him, like plain Pringles perhaps. Just as the rest of the ox has sizzled away and all we're left with is a saucepan full of tail, Harley emerges. He is fully dressed in a dark sweatshirt and jeans, rather than his dressing gown and long johns, which normally follow his showers.

'Where are you off to at this time?' I try to remember how pink the tuna was to begin with and whether or not the microwave is meant to turn it brown. I don't think I was supposed to put the metal tin in. I'm still waiting for Harley to make a joke about 'woks' and 'steaming veg.'

'We have work to do.' He picks his black coat up from the chaise longue. 'Have you fed the dog? Dish up whatever you're burning and let's go.'

'Shit, okay. This is beyond edible anyway. Yeah, Pip had her food. What we up to?' I ask, even though Harley clearly wants less talking and more walking. 'It's nearly one in the morning,' I continue, according to the oven rather than my bare wrist.

'We used to clean the club till 4am, so stop moaning. Bring the dog.' I grab Pippen's leash, put my shoes on and follow Harley out to his pickup truck.

Harley opens the door flap thing at the end of his motor and helps Pippen up before opening the window for her to amble into the back seat. It's sweet to see man's best friend so keen to ride with me and my only friend. Harley gets in, slams his door shut and presses a fob on his key ring that opens the front gates.

'Where we heading, bro?'

'To take care of a few bits,' he says ominously. As long as he doesn't plan on driving us off a cliff, then we're fine, because that wasn't part of the plan.

The roads are clear and the sky is as dark as I've ever seen it. There isn't a single star in the sky. I open the window (which actually works) and I can *feel* the country air, fresh and untainted. It is nothing like this in Hong Kong. On the weather report out there, they list the temperature, the UV Index, followed by the Pollution and Visibility Index. I've gone from living somewhere so shrouded in smog that you're told how far into the distance you can see, to somewhere so clean and green that you can sense it: yet somehow I feel dirtier now than I have my entire life.

After driving in complete silence, the radio suddenly comes on, making me jump, but Pippen and Harley don't even flinch, so they must be used to the coming and going of signal out here in Farmville. After dropping in and out of reception, the song that is playing is by Cutting Crew, and called 'I Just Died In Your Arms Tonight.' I haven't heard this in ages. I turn the volume up. Harley reaches over and turns the radio off. I don't ask why and I don't say anything. I can't imagine that Harley is in the right state of mind for power ballads involving love and death. I want to say something, but I can't bring myself to speak. Why couldn't they have been playing 'Fuck You' by Eamon? Or even a bit of Hip Hop? I intend to do for car *explosions* what Kanye West did for car crashes.

We carry on down the same road for some time and I quietly look out of the window, the side of my head pressed against the glass. I haven't seen a road sign for anywhere I recognise. We drive through a residential area and take a sharp left, tucking behind a large shed.

'Stay in the car,' he says to me sternly. I nod and slouch down in my seat. He gets out and leans through to open the back window. Pippen jumps about, eagerly waiting for Harley to lift her on to the ground, which she is desperate to explore and pee on.

They head off around the corner and I try to stick the radio back on, but he's taken the keys. Instead, I doze off, thinking about how Harley and I would be starting to get busy at the club by now. If we were still working there we would be rushing around, doing the work of six or seven, for an hour or so, before it would die down. Now it's not even 2am and I'm ready for bed. I think about the odd shift when Gemma would come behind the bar and help us and how cute she used to look serving drinks. Then I remember how she used to hate it if girls tried to talk to me over the bar, and how defiant she would get when I tried to give her any instruction, before I finally conk out.

'Time to go,' Harley instructs, as he climbs back in the car, before slamming the door.

'Cool,' I reply, as I come around from my impromptu nap. 'Was I out for long?'

'Not long,' he says, before reversing on to the road. We head back the way we came. Harley is really putting his foot down, keen for us to get wherever it is we're going. A fair few minutes pass before I realise that we are travelling light.

'Where's Pippen?' I search the back seat before looking at Harley, who seems even glummer than before. I start to panic and scan ahead to see where we can turn around.

'Pippen is gone.' I not only see, but hear, his grip tighten on the steering wheel.

'What do you mean, *gone*?' I contest. 'Where'd you go just now?'

'That was my dad's house.' His vocal chords sound like the string section in an orchestra performing something that makes the entire concert hall go still.

'Your father's looking after Pip now?' I ask, which should be a positive, but I make it sound like a definite negative. In this moment, I promise to never answer the phone with 'Battersea Dogs' Home' ever again.

'He doesn't have a choice. I put her over his fence. She'll be fine out there till the morning.' Although he would never leave her somewhere where she'd be in danger, it still sounds nothing short of barbaric. A strange notion, considering we have no issues with driving my car at potentially hundreds of partygoers. It would have been better for Pippen if Harley's father had been informed, but then we'd run the risk of rousing suspicion, unanswerable questions and intervention.

'Fuck, I'm sorry, man. She'll be well looked after,' I reply, even though I have no idea if that's the case. His dad will drive round to return Pip, and then once he realises that he isn't ever getting past the gates, may just take her to an animal shelter. As if Harley hasn't had to say goodbye to enough things he cares about. To part with Pippen must be the hardest yet, as she had unequivocal love for him. If Gemma used to cry at RSPCA adverts, she would be howling and wailing at this.

We join the motorway and it doesn't take long before I realise that we are heading to Bury. The one place I was desperate to leave, for more reasons than I care to remember. I look over at Harley for some kind of explanation, but he is concentrating on the road, doing everything he can to adjust to the decision he has made. I want to tell Harley that I have no intention of setting foot in Bury, that I was just getting used to the fact that I'd only have to visit it one final time, and that time would involve destroying it. But I don't, because I can't. Harley doesn't need my thoughts right now. He has enough in his dog bowl to contend with.

39

We pass the stretch of motorway that has the BP garage on the other side. Harley stares over at the same time as I do, and I believe we feel a mutual sense of contempt for the place. Reassuring, considering how distant he seems. After taking the Bury exit, he goes straight over at the roundabout and towards the big Tesco. Pulling up at the front door, he finally turns to me.

'I need you to get a few things,' he says, before reaching into his pocket, producing a small shopping list folded around a couple of £50 notes. 'I'll be parked down the end there after I fill up the jerry cans with petrol. They didn't consider me sick enough for a blue badge, so you'll have to walk.'

'Okay mate, I'll be right back,' I reply, relieved to be outside, considering the understandable tension in the car. Even if it does mean stepping on St Albans' sordid soil.

I look at the piece of paper he's given me and there isn't much to it. He wants forty bottles of lighter fluid (and in brackets it reads, 'not cheap stuff'). Then, in the poorest penmanship I have ever seen, it says 'fuel express fire lighter cubes,' whatever the fuck those are. I don't know if he is planning to create a murderous inferno or start a garden barbecue. Same principle, I suppose. Also on the list are doughnuts and crisps, because he is either peckish or wants the list to look a little less conspicuous. I need to do a double take on the last item, which reads 'bottle of tequila, the very cheap stuff.' If this is a gift for me, it is the most thoughtful sentiment ever. It makes me feel even worse about everything that Harley is going through and I don't quite know why.

I fetch two baskets and walk up and down the aisles until I have everything we need. The tequila doesn't look too shabby, and I can't wait to open it. If the clerk at the till recognises me from the club, she's going to think we are doing really shit, having bought only one bottle of tequila and lots of lighter fluid. Either way, her three words for me aren't going to be pleasant.

I head to the check-out as quickly as possible. I mustn't keep Harley waiting and I don't want to be recognised, even though anyone who might know me is at The Havana Club. I double bag our loot and head for the exit. If only Dylan had done the same, he could have spared Belinda some anguish. I wonder what he's up to now, probably working the glory hole circuit.

As I walk past the security guard and out of the store, I suspect that after we finish what we've started, they will use the CCTV footage from tonight on all the news reports. Someone's grieving parents are likely to put pressure on Tesco to introduce a policy on limiting the amount of lighter fluid they can sell to someone so that their child's death wasn't in vain. They'll call it Lisa's Law. How fucking sinister is that? My issues go beyond arson. I don't need counselling, I need an exorcist.

When I emerge from the sliding doors, Harley is waiting right outside for me. I am half-expecting a joke about him paying for petrol with the dog leash, but he will *never* be ready for making jokes about that, not in months, not in years, despite having neither.

'Where we off to now then, Dhalsim?' Tequila, morphine and petrol – sounds like an interesting night out.

'One last stop,' he says, checking I bought all the stuff on the list.

'Cheers for the tequila by the way, nice touch.' I manage to find it in amongst the lighter fluid and take a sharp-tasting swig. I wouldn't want to get these bottles mixed up. 'Want some?'

'The tequila's all yours, cause the doughnuts are all mine.' He reaches over for his chocolate sprinkled rings. They were half price because they expire soon, just like us.

'You could have enjoyed the nicest ox-fish tuna-tail earlier,' I say, blithely.

'Doughnuts and tequila. Perfect stakeout food.' He glances over at me to gauge my reaction.

'What do you mean *stakeout*?'

'We need to scope out the area,' he proclaims, sounding like a career criminal assassin. 'We need to assess the mark.' He casually takes a bite out of a doughnut, as if he's simply chosen which of my unreturned DVDs we're about to watch.

'So we're just going to scoot up there, are we? Why don't we pop in for a drink?' I am unsure as to whether Harley is altogether there and that perhaps Pippen was secretly the brains behind the operation.

'They don't know what my car looks like.' He raises a valid point. The windows on his Nissan Navara are tinted and there are always countless cars parked up near The Havana Club. 'Snoopy has never seen me in this and neither has Gemma.' I don't like hearing him called that, he is a Dick and should be named as such.

'So what do we do? Did you bring a telescope and those red laser pens? We need red dots on their foreheads to match your bindi.' I wonder if Harley paid for that house of his from being a professional hit man. 'If anyone sees us the game is up, you know that right?'

'No one will see us, Bamboo. We'll be fully hidden,' he says, assertively. I will savour the fact that she doesn't know I'm watching. Like a sadistic voyeur.

'There could be changes to the place.'

'That's exactly it. A new queuing system? A taxi rank? We need to see what time the police arrive and how far down they park. They might use a different entrance to account for the extra numbers since our club closed.' He's made me smile and cringe in the same sentence. He referred to it as 'our' club, proving that we are in the thick of it together, but he has reminded me that all the loyal customers we did have will now be drinking there.

'I'll get in the back,' I say, trying to avoid the petrol canisters, 'Drive slowly.' I'm in the back of Dylan's mum's Audi all over again. I wish I had Pippen hiding down here with me.

'The most crucial thing is the time.' He pulls away from the front of the supermarket. 'We need to see what time they're going to be down there. As you well know, people in this town are creatures of habit.'

'We're late though, man. We didn't leave yours until 1am.'

'They won't be there yet. Think about it. He's in charge and has Mandara and Stevie. He's now with the First Lady of the Bury clubbing scene. They'll be arriving fashionably late because they'll be getting up to…' he says, before letting the second half trail off, for which I'm thankful, even though I know what he was implying.

'I know they will. I know. Let's just get there. Hopefully they haven't arrived yet, touch wood.' I want the increase in speed to remove us from his last comment.

'Don't waste your touch woods, Kimchi. Save them for something important, like not getting recognised,' he says, after convincing me that there was no way we would be seen.

'Okay, fingers crossed then.' I try to sink down lower into the foot wells and actually cross my fingers.

'Don't forget your toes,' he says jokingly, which I try to do, but the dull pain of my foot manages to supersede the daily dosage of morphine. When I try to cross my toes I am reminded about the decimation brought to my bathroom that has led me to where I am now, in the dog's seat, surrounded by petrol and punishment.

I wish we were about to carry out the engagement proposal Dylan had always suggested: kidnapping her, bag over head. There wouldn't be a picnic at the end of this drive though. When the car stops, my heart begins to race. Harley switches the engine off and I peer over the top of the seat. We are in position. We are hidden down a dark alley, with nothing behind us apart from the forecourt of a scrap dealer and the club a mere 40ft ahead.

I climb into the front, which proves a lot harder than the climb into the back, and reach for the tequila, passing the food to Harley. The club is heaving and there are loads of people out the front smoking. Seeing the place mobbed makes me seethe. They have more people here on an average Friday night than I've ever had at mine, on my very busiest of Saturdays, *with* a Live Performance Act.

Dick is a very heavy smoker, which frustrates me because Gemma used to criticise me for lighting up (in fact she downright hated it) and I only get through a fraction of what he does. It wouldn't surprise me if she's even started smoking herself. Dick would smoke during lunch and would always say, 'Don't you hate it when people eat when you're trying to smoke?' I found it amusing then, I find it aggravating now. Dick should be the one with cancer.

I try to keep my head low, rising only to knock back some surprisingly potent tequila. I think the blend of fear and danger makes it all the more intoxicating. Despite trying to keep my breathing quiet, Harley speaks loudly. 'I get it you know,' he starts, 'I do.' He doesn't look at me. He just stares out of the windscreen, his eyes firmly fixed on our final destination. 'I know why you want to carry out this revenge of yours. Far saner men than you have been driven – excuse the pun – to do crazy things cause of a woman. I totally get that,' I can feel a 'but' coming. 'But what I don't understand is why you need to go down with them?'

There is a long silence, and I'm not even sure he's expecting an answer. This scouting mission that will hopefully gain us invaluable intelligence is the beginning of the end. He has asked me this question so many times now, there is no point in responding, but I do.

'Because I have to, Harley. I have no choice. When Gemma and I were still together, before all of this, I was fully prepared to do the till death do us part thing.' I really was. 'I even wanted to die before her so that I didn't have to live a single day without her. But that's gone now. I have nothing left. Nothing, except this,' I continue. My eyes would be tearing if I hadn't cried them all away already.

'I can drive the car, Tofu. Let me do this for you. Live out your days with lady-boys in Thailand. You don't need to be here.'

'Come on –', I begin, but he throws his crisps to the floor, pacifying my protest.

'My cancer is Advanced Stage IV. The worst kind. I didn't want to tell you,' he says, lacerating my life. A knot forms in my stomach, a difficult one like a sailor's Carrick-bend, involving larger ropes being weaved under and over. 'I have less than four months.'

'*Four…*' I start, before my voice trails off. These baleful thoughts are as baffling as drunkenly undressing a go-go dancer in Bangkok.

'You think you're the only person that has been cheated on, or lost their job? People get screwed over and made redundant every single day, and some of them even do this. Get even. Kill people. Crimes of passion they call it.' He's trying to show me that my need for revenge is a natural response to what has happened and that it doesn't have to end like this, but his words have the opposite effect. He has made something so unacceptable seem okay, because people *do* kill, all the time, and even though they might not take down half a street in the process, they do it.

'I'm not missing this for the world. I'd only live to regret it. I can't think of anyone else I'd rather burst into flames with than you, Chicken Tikka,' I say, and I mean every word. That seemed like his last ditch attempt to talk some sense into me, but I have made up my mind. 'There is *nothing* for me after this, and I already believe it, I don't need to see it.'

Harley extends his hand for me to shake and I grasp it, adamantly. Someone needs to send Steve at the Phoenix a memo to let him know that I have finally cracked too.

Two wrongs like Harley and me might not make a right, but it's the only wrong I've got.

40

Dick said to me some time ago that girls with boyfriends 'aren't off limits.' He said that in games of football there is a goalie, but that doesn't mean you can't score. I even made a throw away comment about keeping Gemma in the dug-out and off the pitch.

He said that he'd never get with a mate's missus, for two reasons. The first one being out of principle, the second one being that he knows where she's been. We all had a good long laugh at that as well, as we raised our glasses to camaraderie: our allegiance ensuring former and current conquests remain strictly off-limits.

Talk is as cheap as his drinks were. Maybe if he paid for the occasional one, we'd still be in business. I was the goalie, and he snuck past me and stuck one right in the back of her net, Rosický style. I appeal for the off-side rule, but no one cares to listen. To a Dick, every hole's a goal.

I ask Harley how long we've been sat here. *Forty minutes* and Dick still hasn't been out for a fag. This means that he's either on his way or he has the night off. I'm tired of waiting. I've been red carded and sent off with an injury.

I used to have a thing against paying the middleman, like an estate agent or a small-time drug dealer, but it turns out that's all I ever was. I gave Dick the leverage to muscle his way in on a bigger and better job, and I was the middleman that introduced him to Gemma. Now that I'm a middleman myself, I hate them all the more.

I have lost interest in staring at the entrance to The Havana. Seeing all these incredibly pissed clubbers infuriates me. To reach that level of drunkenness, they must have spent a considerable amount of money. Sammy is outrageously over-serving and he'll get away with it.

'The ceilings in the bar are low,' says Harley, analysing the head height through their front doors. 'That's a good thing, the flames will funnel.'

'The fire exit is right at the back as well, behind the bar in a separate room,' I add, which I remember from my Club Verity days.

The tequila makes me need to go for a piss and watching all these muppets smoking out the front makes me want to head across and ask them for a tailor, even though that would defeat the purpose of hiding.

I battle the need to relieve myself through urination and nicotine, and that is when I spot them – the ministers of spiritual torment. Gemma and Dick are walking up the hill, making their way past a drift of door whores, hand in hand: a sight that a few months ago, no one would have ever thought they'd see. Not in a million years. Imagine the odds if I took that one down the bookies? But I have an Arsenal of my own now.

She is simply irreplaceable. She belongs to *me*.

Looking at the pair of them swan into his busy club together is unbearable to watch, but I won't allow myself to look away. This image needs to be remembered – every last detail memorised and learnt by bleeding heart. The way their fingers are interlocked has scorched my corneas. The way their outfits are colour co-ordinated has burned through my pupils. Seeing them laugh together as they chat to the doormen, signifying how regular an occurrence this has been, has cracked my lenses. They stop to kiss in the doorway, as if they know I'm watching. Dick, the Viking chief, is near enough on tiptoes to meet her lips. Gemma has never been one for public displays of affection. I wish I had strangled her instead.

Harley turns to face me but I can't take my eyes off of them, despite how much it hurts. My retinas are throbbing and the hatred travels down my hyaloid canal and into my optic nerve. This is more painful than when I underwent laser eye surgery. It looks like they've seven-balled me off the break too. I can't bring myself to blink in case I miss it.

She clearly doesn't miss me.

Our hurtling car won't miss her.

This must be what they mean by an eye for an eye.

Maybe the reason everyone visits The Havana Club is because they *are* better than we were, an admission I've never been able to make. I've spent most of my adult life to date trying to build and develop clubs. Trying to improve them and get people in. Now I am obsessed with destroying one and keeping people away from it forever.

Fuck.

Have I a shred of decency left in me? I must have, as I know I'd forget about my vendetta if it meant that Harley would be okay. If I could make a deal with the Gods of Mercy and ask them to remove his malignant neoplasm for good, in return for calling an end to our murderous plan, then I would. In a heartbeat, I would. I wish I could make his pain go away – I wish I had saved all my touch woods.

Am I having second thoughts? Did I fail to consider my own humanity? Maybe we *can* extinguish life so quickly. I can't believe I had the audacity to call Dylan callous. All this time, my anger has been directed inwardly, but for the first time, and inevitably the last, I will be using this anger to propel and fuel something else. It feels... not good (because none of this could ever be described as 'good'), but *righteous*, somehow. How can the one person who made me the happiest I've ever been be the same person who's made me the unhappiest I've ever felt? This is power beyond measure.

Every version of my future had her in it. Even if there were the slightest of possibilities that I could win her back, every version would now be tainted. I didn't build for nearly as long as Steve at the Phoenix did, granted, but I built and I built nonetheless: a shared home, a tattoo, a beloved soft toy family. These things were tangible and actual. But what about the countless things that were yet to be? What I have lost is more than things that can be seen, but things that were envisioned. All of those are lost too. The flower will never blossom. I've lost her and every little quirk that made her, her, and that made us, us.

She used to redo high fives if they weren't good enough the first time round. She would use the internet to self-diagnose her every problem and convince herself she was dying. She would hum little songs to me if I needed cheering up. She was so many things. She has probably gained even more things, newer things, since she's been away from me. Yet, soon she will be nothing.

I've seen enough. We know what time they are likely to be here and that nothing will be stopping our tinderbox from causing maximum damage. Harley doesn't look well – in fact, he looks downright rotten.

'This *will* work, won't it?' He nods without pushing himself to speak. We need to get him off the road, safe and hidden behind his gates. 'The car will be a tight squeeze through those doors.'

'Tighter than Barney's purse strings, mate,' he replies, before coughing violently.

'Let's go man, drive,' I exclaim, as if it's being too close to The Havana that is causing him to feel ill. The Havana has Kryptonite-like properties that leave me powerless too.

I lower my head until we've joined the motorway. We travel back to Norwich without speaking, apart from swearing when we pass the BP. We listen to the radio, not a music channel, but *The World Today*, followed by *World Football* on the BBC World Service. Nothing of any interest is mentioned on this agonisingly insignificant April 3rd. This stands as a reminder that we won't be missing much when we leave this world, and seeing as there are no reports of car fires or burning clubs, chances are the world won't be missing us either.

*

Hell. We are going to Hell. The very thought strikes panic into the hearts of God-fearing suburbia with their white steeple churches and white collars, but me? I couldn't give a shit. In fact, I welcome it. At least Harley and I will get to share a cell.

There are a few ways to guarantee a first-class ticket to Hell, not that a journey to Hell would have a first-class anyway. Transport to Hell is several classes lower than Economy, in a BMW 316c with broken windows, and there are definitely ways to jump the queue.

Stealing from a charity box brings you one step closer to Lucifer, I'm sure. Rape is no doubt another. Drowning a bag of kittens makes the list. Throttling a hooker and leaving her for dead is a given. Slapping your partner and incinerating a nightclub probably doesn't help, but premeditated murder? They've already got us checked in online. Our way to Hell is most undignified indeed.

I don't think Harley cares much for the concept of Heaven and Hell, but will he really have to join me there? Surely he should serve his time, his six-month stint, and then get thrown back into Purgatory confinement, or given an appeal or something. Surely the trauma and undeserved pain of his treatments means that he has paid some dues and penance. The life he worked for has been taken from him, but taking another's life? I think that might override it.

I know what my definition of Hell would be, if I am to be damned for all of eternity. It will be an empty nightclub, lacking in stainless steel worktops with television-less walls. Lyrics from the Doris Day song will be played on loop, over and over again. I will be chained with barbed wire to a sofa with ripped arms and forced to watch Gemma and Dick make endless love on top of Harley's cancer-ridden, burnt body, to the sound of Pippen barking, locked outside, unable to get in. There will also be an endless supply of sumptuous, evocative wine, but no bottle opener. Dick is the Kil and I am the Pin.

This image is the stuff of nightmares, but my living Hell is very much real. The only secret to surviving is to attack as aggressively as possible. You throw everything you have at it. Beyond the metal, the explosive material and the other nasty things Harley has been harnessing, we are throwing our anger, our disappointment and our versions of the future at it. Four months to live. I don't know how many minutes are left, so we are making each one count.

The truth of the matter is that neither of us even wants to die. Harley and I may say to one another that we do, to claim some kind of ownership over our lives, which have spiralled out of control, but in fact we actually want nothing more than to live.

We desperately want to live. It's just that the lives we are living have become unliveable.

41

Tonight is the night. No glory or martyrdom is to be found here. I have no delusions of grandeur and there will be no positive outcome. I'm also definitely going to lose my No Claims Bonus.

One man's terrorist is another man's freedom fighter. I shall free myself from the terror my life has become at the hands of the infidels and as always, Harley is along for the ride. It remains unclear as to whether he fully comprehends the severity of his decision to help me. In my selfishness I say nothing. The life I was leading ended the day that my Giraffe lit her own match on me. My cocktail of positive change is now a Molotov cocktail.

The combination of adrenaline, desperation, morphine, testosterone and what's left of the tequila would be enough to paralyse most men, far stronger than me. But I am barren and desolate and all the Jose Cuervo in Acapulco couldn't lift the numbness of my spirit, regardless of how much spirit I consume. In Mexico, the lime wedge is placed into the top of a Corona, not for the tartness in flavour to which we have become accustomed, but to keep the hungry, soulless and diseased flies out. Well, Gemma was my lime wedge. Stemming the flow to my crisp 4.6 per cent gold: she separated what was to be cherished, from what would only perish. Now my lime wedge is absent, nestled within the bottle neck of another.

I turn to Harley as he struggles to cut the end from a long, black cable tie, which is holding together several cloths doused in paraffin or some other highly combustible liquid. The fumes are overbearing, despite the small charcoal fire burning quietly in the corner. I had asked him earlier if it was wise to have a fire crackling away in a garage full of kerosene and the likes, but he said it was to combat the smell of our solvents to reduce the risk of alerting a neighbour, even though there isn't another house for what looks like at least a half mile. His determination for discretion is fine by me. We sit in silence for what feels like too long a time, so without much thought I open my mouth in the hope that something poignant will come out.

'We really doing this, Vishnu?'

'We're going out with a bang, Hello Kitty,' he replies, setting me straight.

And with that said, it is done: signed, sealed and waiting to be delivered. Retribution is about to be served in a large, double measure, within a warm, dirty glass – no ice, no slice. It is happy hour on homemade arsonists, buy one get one free. As our grand finale beckons, my friend maintains his silent suffering.

'Harley,' I begin, 'I don't think I'll ever be able to –', but before I can start what was to be a stream of incoherent thanks and apologies all cable-tied together, he stops me by raising his hand.

'Kamikaze, tonight we go on our terms. Neither of us to be defeated. On *our* terms.' I couldn't have said it better myself. My heart swells, tears tucked away behind my eyes, stinging with the need to escape. My love for this Punjabi bastard is immense. Prepared to walk a line that Gemma couldn't prevent, and that Dylan and I couldn't snort. If only this love could fill the void.

I bring Harley a cup of tea and some biscuits. With my Malibu at the ready, I think of this as our Last Supper. With what we have in mind there would be no enjoyment taken from a final feast, so I don't bother mentioning it. We are beyond that, or at least I am. Harley has been so hardworking and industrious for a young man of twenty-eight. Only a year separates us and yet he has four houses to his name. He was about to purchase and renovate his fifth before he was diagnosed. It comes as no surprise that he has paid for all of our destructive plunder. I feel an all too familiar quiver of compassion for my dearest friend. He has been dealt a horribly unfair hand. Last night, once we got back from our reconnaissance mission, I tried to tell him just this: that it wasn't his fault, and I was astonished by what he said. He explained to me that he wished it was. He asked me why he couldn't have contracted an asbestos-related cancer, which he called 'meso' something, because at least then he'd have someone to blame and a justifiable reason.

So no, biscuits just aren't good enough. He should be dining on lobster and drinking Champagne Supernovas, but Harley is a man of simple pleasures and his brew and biscuits are good enough for him. The bottom line is I am proud of him. It would seem that pride comes *after* the fall.

I think about all the skills and expertise my friend has garnered over the years – his craftsmanship honed from a thousand tasks. What a waste it will soon be. Harley, having carried out countless jobs for me at the club, out of the goodness of his heart, has spent the last of his perfectionism on this masterfully crafted carriage of annihilation. After all his renovations and refits and revamps, this is to be his magnum opus. This menace parked before us.

In true Harley fashion, he has left nothing to chance. When I was wasting away on the couch, sleeping and taking more morphine, he worked tirelessly on this vehicle of vengeance. He told me that he had managed to weaken the crumple zone of the car to ensure that it would fold even faster on impact by removing the front cross-member. He has also fixed the headlight, removed the sensor to the airbag device and cut the cable to the emergency brake to avoid any last minute change of heart, which I knew he meant would be on my part.

As we silently wait for the clock to expire, I can tell from the look of concentration on Harley's face that he is running another mental checklist. Preparation is key. Harley has a contingency plan for every possible eventuality. There is to be no postponement.

Halfway through our dastardly plan, Harley suggested paying for a larger car that was better suited to our purpose, without the unreliability and faults that came with mine. I decided against it. As pragmatic and generous as his offer was, it has to be my car. In those last few seconds, when we are hurtling through their front doors at 40mph, I need them to know it is me. Mere hours from execution, ours and hers, Harley carefully sprays the back windows of our fiery guillotine, as dark and as black as we feel. The aerosol fills my lungs and burns my nostrils. I hope that the paint is extra flammable.

Harley has taken the back seats out to compensate for our extra load and has even removed the car radio to make way for more combustible substance, forced deep into the darkest depths of the dashboard. He said that analogue frequency can detonate forms of explosive material. I don't know how accurate this is, but it sounds bizarre enough to be true. On a psychological note, considering how susceptible I am to mood changes, his point is well made. I Will Die In Her Arms Tonight.

He has told me that I'm not allowed to bring my mobile phone, which makes no odds to me, considering I turned it off the moment I got here, to avoid calls from the Benios and Barneys. I don't even question what a phone might do because I know his reasoning will be entirely sustained by logic. I hold nothing but adulation for my very own modern day MacGyver. As we sit in the car, waiting for the closing minutes to wind down before pulling away, I have as random a thought as any.

'I didn't cancel my direct debits,' I say abruptly.

Looking rather confused, he turns to me and asks what possible difference that would make, considering my bank account would very shortly have no owner.

'I'm not paying for something I won't be using.'

'Chinese right till the end you are!' This may be the last time I ever see my best friend laugh.

As we pull away from Harley's house I am glad that we agreed that he would drive. His choice of PG Tips as opposed to my Malibu and morphine was certainly the wiser option. As Harley looks into the wing mirror, I wonder what he must be thinking. I hope that it isn't self-deprecating. He hasn't done this to himself. He hasn't caused this cancer to invade and steal from him. This intruder wasn't provoked. He has done everything up until these final moments, completely right.

We reach the end of the street at the same spot where I had to stop and call for directions when I first arrived, which feels like a lifetime ago, and Harley pulls into the side of the road.

'Why have we stopped?' I turn to face him, but he just stares straight ahead. There is nothing in front of us but empty road.

'Get out.' I don't know what I've done to deserve being told to get out of my own car on the most important and last day of my life. 'I'm not letting you do this. I can't,' he says, moving his eyes further from me still. 'Go back to the house, the gates are open. I'll carry on as planned,' he continues. 'The house and my safe are unlocked, take all that's there. Stay in the house or take my truck, up to you, but get out.'

'I'm coming with you, Harley. End of. We can talk about it after we smash through the club.' I lock the door, so that he can hear the click run through the car, signalling my remonstration.

'I'm not going to tell you again, Pak Choi. You think this is what you want, but it isn't.' He turns to look at me and there is the slightest hint of tears in his eyes.

'This is *all* I want. I don't want anything else. If you're not going to drive, I will,' I roar, raising my voice, wholly necessarily. All my commanding officers are in this shuttlecraft.

'You still get what you want either way. They'll be dealt with,' he says, boldly.

'I'm not getting out.'

'You're sure, aren't you?' he lures. The question as useless as the ones I tend to ask him.

'Of course I'm bloody sure. Now start the fucking car.' I point at the ignition like he's forgotten where it is. 'You're killing me over here.' Literally and metaphorically.

'So are you,' he says, as he wipes his eyes with his sleeve before driving on. 'Now put your seatbelt on. We wouldn't want you to get hurt.'

42

There is still so much more I should have done with my life. Places I will never get to see, people I will never get to meet and experiences left un-experienced.

Before Al Pacino planned to kill himself in *Scent of a Woman*, he wanted to travel first-class, eat 'an agreeable meal at an exclusive restaurant,' stay at a luxury hotel, visit his big brother and make love to a beautiful woman. My first-class travel is to be my ticking time-bomb of a P-reg and my meal was to be a few Malibus and a morphine tablet in a garage workshop. Harley is my big brother, and my beautiful woman is gone and is the very reason I'm off to meet my maker, to question him on his manufacturing methods.

Even Clint Eastwood wanted to enjoy a hot bath, a smoke in his house for the first time, a 'straight shave' at the barbers and a new fitted suit before he ended his life in *Gran Torino*. I am not visually impaired, I did not kill surrendering soldiers in Korea and I do not justify a bucket list. My excuse is far less worthy than theirs. My reason for ending life is not worthy of any last minute unexplored pleasures. There is no turning back.

My father died in a motor vehicle.

Soon we will share one more moment.

*

3. I must have only been six or seven: my father and I were on a Public Light minibus in Hong Kong. We were right at the back and my father had counted out our fare in what I would now consider to be far too many coins. I was only small, so perhaps coins seemed bigger, but there were loads of them.

I remember him counting them out meticulously, because it was exact tender only – you weren't getting change from a note anyhow. The minibuses in Hong Kong don't have bells, you just shout '*ting che,*' which means 'stop car,' but somewhere between the '*ting*' and the '*che*,' when it was our stop, I begged my father to let me put the coins in the driver's slot.

He told me to keep quiet and to sit still and that he would do it. I begged and begged and he told me that I would only end up dropping them. I promised him that I wouldn't and he grudgingly tipped the money into my clammy hands.

I stood up, exultant in his trust, and walked towards the driver with confidence. I dropped the lot, every last coin, and they pinged everywhere. My father swore at me and smacked me hard on my ineffectual little hands, and I can still sense to this day the embarrassment I caused him on that busy minibus.

This is the only memory I have of being on a bus with my father, similar to the one that claimed his life, making the coin dropping, the swearing, the hand smacking and the moment itself all the more significant.

2. I couldn't have been any older than nine when one summer's day my mother and father took me to Repulse Bay Beach (named after the HMS Repulse, and not the water quality), located in the south of Hong Kong Island.

It was blisteringly hot and I vividly recollect it being absolutely packed with people. I remember asking my parents if I could play in the sea and being told not to wander too far. Delighted by my independence, I went off to splash in the water, dig trenches and partake in all your usual childish beach stuff. The last thing I was expecting was for a large crashing wave to take the spectacles from my face and refuse to give them back. Nine years old with deficiently blurred vision, I recall panicking frantically at what my father would say when he saw that I'd lost my glasses.

Despite the prospect of my father's wrath, I desperately wanted to find him. I started screaming for my parents, but not only were my glasses lost to the sea, I was lost in a sea of thousands of people. I wouldn't have minded if Benio circled my parents in that edition of *Where's Wally?* I rambled around blind and crying, and without the aid of my specs, the search felt endless. No one spoke English, but eventually I got close enough for them to hear my calls and we were reunited.

I remember never having felt so happy to see my parents. They looked like nothing was wrong and couldn't understand why I was so distraught. I have spent my whole life disliking my father, to the point that I found him insufferable, but there have been times when he has been the only person who has made me feel safe, and made me feel like I was home.

1. The moment that bound my father and me together more than any was when his wife, my mother, walked out. I was angry, not just at them, but at the world. My appalling behaviour, demeanour and truancy were motivating factors in her decision to leave, and I have carried this burden throughout my adult life, even if much of it has been spent in denial.

I remember watching my mother enter a taxi with everything she could fit in a holdall. She never told me why she was leaving, or made any attempt at a farewell. She was gone in an instant. My father started showing up at my school gates to try to talk to me, but each time I pushed past and ignored him. This regret holds more weight than any other.

My father and I rarely spoke about my mother and I never had the decency to cry. We just carried on, plodding through life, going through the motions, my mother's position in our household filled by a long line of domestic helpers and a silver watch. I blocked her out, and everything that went wrong in my life after that, I categorically put down to my parents' separation.

They met at university in London in the late seventies. He was studying Engineering and she was doing something in Healthcare. I don't know much about their life before I came along. I never cared to ask. There must have been a time when things were good between them, but their dysfunctional relationship as I knew it, as I saw it, wasn't meant to be. In a world that wasn't as small as the one we live in now, it was never going to work. Their empty relationship affected the ones that I tried to forge for myself, making me appreciate what I found with Gemma all the more.

My father clawed his way up from near enough poverty, saving up enough money to move. Hong Kong being a British Colony at the time meant that he had entitlement to abode as a British National. New to the UK, my father was mesmerised by my mother's freckles and her bright blue eyes. My mother was intrigued by a gentleman from the Orient with a golden brown tan, who spoke in Ching-lish, and was in need of a tour guide (much of this is guess work). She was looking for something new-fangled and fresh, a distraction from her dreary, working-class upbringing in South London.

My mother was the first person in her entire family tree to marry someone that wasn't from England, and, similarly, my father was the first to marry someone that wasn't Cantonese. It is hard to comprehend how trailblazing this was, considering that we are only a few generations from the world becoming beige. What is seen as the norm today would have been defiant back then, the most romantic of notions and a staggering idea. But that was all it was: an idea. In practice, it just didn't work. They let things run their course for as long as they could, living separate lives, upholding contrasting principles and sleeping in separate beds.

Eventually their differences became all too glaring and my mother had had enough. The novelty of living somewhere exotic, with someone unusual, had worn off. She chose to leave, to leave him and to leave me. It was the only time I have ever seen my father shed tears, and I said nothing.

Even the most inimitable relationships are not beyond conclusion and someone as traditional as my father, who clung to his beliefs and his ideology ruthlessly, can still lose sight of what matters most. My father did everything by the book. He worked hard, fought for an education and a career and provided for his family. As far as I know, he never committed a single crime and always paid his way. He lived a noble life in an ethical sense of the word, but it still didn't pay dividends.

He tried to dissuade me from involvement with Gemma, which ultimately destroyed what was left of our father-son relationship. His instincts were right. I only wish I had listened.

This concludes my Top Ten Bomb List. Each one of the bombs, stained. The memorable moments that we experience in our lives are usually character building: graduation, getting married, having children etc, but each of mine have been character *damaging*.

I am aware that my list is remarkably different from most – undesired by many, yet preferable to some – but we all have our individual crosses to bear. My cross is worn tightly around my neck, digging into my flesh, ceaselessly strangling me. Harley would refer to it as my 'snag list' – all the problems and defects that would prevent a house from being sold at the asking price. The faults that have stopped me from being able to function properly in the way I should have done. That stopped me from being able to feel that I deserve more. Probably because I don't.

Because of this list, and the countless other things that I have seen and done, things that I either can't remember or don't want to remember, I don't deserve anything better. My snag list is too big, with too much to fix and simply beyond repair. Harley doesn't have the time or the tools to put the work in. His magic sack has been stolen and there isn't enough credit on the B&Q card.

Gemma has added so much to the snag list, I've run out of paper.

43

This isn't a reconnaissance drive or a stop for doughnuts. This is the real deal.

I wish we were in the comfy Navara, but we are in the Beemer with no radio. The car makes a heavy clunking noise as we charge down the motorway, in stark contrast to the smooth and effortless drive that is Harley's pick-up.

To distract us from the purpose of our journey (and from the overpowering smell), I turn to Harley and ask him what he will miss the most. A tough question to answer, when we've spent so much time thinking about all the things we *won't* miss.

'Bacon and egg rolls,' he says, as if that is the best life has to offer.

'Nice, good choice! For me it's music,' I say, which sounds like a dig back at him for removing the radio. 'Not the songs that remind me of her, but everything in between.'

'Like who?' Harley has never been one for listening to music.

'All sorts. Have you heard about the twenty-seven club?' I ask, recalling something else I'd read online while he was working on the car.

'Not another club opening in Bury, surely?' he replies, curiously.

'No, man – all the famous people that died at the age of twenty-seven, like us. Well, you're twenty-eight.' He looks disappointed that it isn't the 'twenty-eight club.'

'Who's on it?' he asks, wondering what distinguished company I will soon be joining.

'Amy Winehouse, for a start. Kurt Cobain.' I try to remember more. 'Janis Joplin, Jimi Hendrix, Jim Morrison from The Doors, Brian Jones from The Rolling Stones,' I continue, impressed with my usually substandard memory. 'I bet their birthdays weren't on bloody New Year's Eve.'

'Twenty-seven club!' he scoffs. 'What a load of tosh!'

'Brandon Lee died at twenty-eight though, mate. At least you've got one of my Chinese compatriots to compare yourself to!'

'You've had way too much time on your hands.' I don't think he intended it as another watch joke. 'What else are you going to miss then?'

'Tsing Tao beer has to be up there. Going bowling, maybe?' I struggle to think of anything sensible.

'Bowling? You must have something serious.' He's right. There is.

'What? Like bacon rolls?' I defend my avid interest in drunken ten-pin. 'Surely you'll miss chapatis more?'

'No, there are things I will miss, Harry.' By saying my name, I hope that means I am among them. 'Pippen, I will miss Pippen.'

'She'll be missing you too, Harley.' My heart bleeds for them both.

'Cheers, Kung Pao!' He reaches over and punches me in the arm. 'You'll miss tequila! I see you brought the rest of the bottle with you. Bet you won't be leaving any of that behind.' I want to give him a high five, one that we wouldn't need to redo.

'Call it a final nightcap!' I say light-heartedly.

Part of me doesn't want this ride to ever end. There isn't a life for me after this journey, or even outside this car, but for now, en route, I can do this. I can live this life, talking to Harley on the motorway, but there is only so much fuel and road left to go.

I feel like a passenger in all of this, which may seem obvious, considering I am sat in the passenger seat, but beyond that. Harley decided we would use my car and proceeded to fashion it to our purpose, without my assistance. I *am* a passenger, but I am thankful for it. I don't have the daring to be in the driving seat, which is why for much of my life I have been driven over. I try to take a sip from what's left of the tequila, but I can't stomach it.

'They're going to recognise your car as soon as we pull up,' says Harley, but he isn't concerned. 'There won't be enough time for them to do anything about it, beyond sidestepping, and even then, our consignment will get them.

'Good. I want them to see us. I *need* them to see us.' I will honk the horn until they come out front if I have to. They need to know it's me, even if it's only for a fleeting second.

'You understand that if they aren't there, we still have to go through with it, right?' Harley verifies, slowly and surely. 'It's now or never.'

'They'll be there,' I promise and guarantee. 'They have to be.'

'They don't have a clue that we're coming. Our arrival will be as unexpected as my fucking cancer.'

When we drive into Bury, despite being so close to death, I can't remember the last time I've felt so *alive*. It is time to be set free. Harley was my salvation, and now he is my army.

We pass the large British Sugar factory, the only sweet thing in the entire town. The weather is grim and the Heavens have started to weep. Bury has every reason to cry. We can hear the commotion before we even arrive. There are hundreds upon hundreds of people making their way up to The Havana like sheep, except this time, they go to the slaughter. I did tell Dylan that I'd fuck a sheep in a room smelling of petrol. When we reach the bottom of the road, Harley turns into the alleyway where we positioned ourselves last night.

'What are you doing?' I ask, troubled that I'm not yet sharing my tequila and turpentine with the contents of their club. 'Just do it, there's no time for bacon rolls now, son.'

'We're too early,' he says, faintly. 'No one has clocked us, so we wait.' We've made it in good time, which is bad. Harley drives down into the breaker's yard opposite the club and turns the car around. He switches the lights off and edges forward, into our favoured scouting position.

'We can wait for them to arrive now. There's no point in doing this if they aren't here.' Harley looks at me as if he's been slighted.

'There is a point. There is a very big point.' I have put my broken foot in it. 'Look at these lemmings. They're so absorbed in their bullshit.' There is still an enormous queue waiting to get into the club, despite the late hour. Barney used to try to 'build' a queue by holding customers out the front even though our bar would be empty, to give the impression that we were busy. Everyone soon sussed his sneaky tactic and took a queue as a sign that we were dead.

'When Gemma –' I start, but I stutter on her name, 'when *they* get here, everyone will get their comeuppance. Sammy Fish and his greedy club. All these people that failed to recognise what we did for them. They will all fucking get their –'

'*Forget* them, Oolong,' he says, forcefully. 'These people are puppets. Gemma and Dick are all that matter to us now,' and I have never had someone share a burden of mine so generously.

I adore him.

We are surrounded by the sound of people laughing, shouting, singing, swearing and spending. Their excited club fills me with misery. I lower my head, close my eyes and cover my ears, trying to block it out. We can feel the bass from the speakers and the repetitive movement of revellers on their dance floor. It shakes the ground and reverberates through the car. They must be hosting one of our stolen Funk'd Up nights. Big G said that if Gemma was a car, I'd have gotten rid of her a long time ago, and now I'm using my car to get rid of her. Super Fit doesn't win the derby this time. The monotonous boom, boom, boom of The Havana Club is too much. Instead of hearing the 'Booms' I hear something quite different altogether. I can hear Gemma hum one final song to me, one that she used to sing to Millie, which resounds through my head as if it were coming out of the radio-less speakers.

Zoom, zoom, zoom, We're flying to the moon. Zoom, zoom, zoom, We're going really soon.

'Is that them?'

I am brought back to the car, hands down, head up.

'Where?' I try to find the poisoned needle in the haystack of hectic crowd.

'Coming past these two, wait, wait, they're going to come past this guy here in a sec – there!' he says, pointing at the sea of bobbing heads.

'I see them. That's them,' I reply, as they cut the queue to Oblivion. Harley looks at his watch and nods, so our estimate must have been near enough correct. 'Look at her! What the fuck is that tart wearing?' It must be non-uniform day.

This is far from Holkham Bay. The waves are crashing, the wind is whirling and the world feels as though it's spinning out of control, but there is no standstill. The smirr of Scotch mist that patters off the windscreen makes it harder for me to track them. I reach over to make the wipers move faster. The raindrops turn purple and descend on us like petals plucked from a tree in winter. Here's the April showers. I have ended. Gemma is my third manhole cover.

'Get ready, Gangnam.' I'm not ready. How can anyone ever be ready for something like this? Fear prevents me from speaking and I turn cold. The hairs on my entire body stand to attention as if they are begging me to stop this. But there is no stopping this. We are no longer Law Abiding Citizens. We are both Expendables.

'Gemma,' I utter, at a whisper, 'Gemma.'

Harley waits for them to shake hands with the bouncer before he turns on the engine. As they walk inside the front doors, I can see how happy Gemma looks. How carefree she seems. She has moved on and completely forgotten what we once shared. The Florida White Trash is enjoying her new life and her new partner and hasn't spared a thought to where I am. She has no idea that I have plotted against her. She is meant to be my enemy, yet she isn't even thinking about me. I am one of those Japanese soldiers who were stuck out in the jungle, still fighting a World War because no one told them it was over. For me, it isn't over. She was to be my *wife*.

As soon as they enter the club, Harley sticks the car in reverse and carefully backs down towards the dark spares and repairs place. This is where I belong. I am spare and in dire need of repair: the scrap stripped from a totalled vehicle, to be melted down to salvage any semblance of value. I am a vigilante EHO officer, here to deal with night time noise. I will put an end to this racket once and for all, with Harley lending a hand. I'm sorry Gemma, but the internet can't diagnose this one.

'Sayonara, Five-Spice,' says Harley, but I can't say anything to him in return. I just look at him. For the first time, I really *truly* look at him. Warrior. Radiant. Kin. He is too good for all this, too pure. He has tried to dissuade me from this journey all along, but I should have been the one talking him down.

He undoubtedly wants to end his life, but he doesn't need the shame and disgrace that will tarnish his name. Maybe that's it though. Maybe he wants people to realise how they have wronged him and what they have driven him to do. He has been abandoned.

Barney, there is no such thing as bad publicity, except your own obituary.

When looking at Harley for any longer becomes intolerable, I close my eyes for the last time. I feel the car revving and sense the wheels starting to spin. Harley unclicks my seatbelt. The half-empty glass is now just empty. As much as I want to see Gemma burn in flames and witness the fear dawn across her face, I must close my eyes. Why do we close our eyes when we pray? When we cry? When we dream? Or when we kiss? Because we know that the most important things in life are not seen, but felt.

As we hurtle towards The Havana Club with my eyes fused shut, I can hear the boom, boom, boom getting louder as the zoom, zoom, zoom fades away.

My Shining Diamond Satine. 'Come what may, I will love you till my dying day.'

四十四

Cause and Effect.

Gemma, everything she meant, everything she did and everything she's become; Dick's friendship ending in deception and larceny; the club's closure, the end of an era and an income. Harley's cancer and his rapid deterioration; my father's untimely death; my mother's distance; looming eviction and possible arrest – these are the causes. This car, this is the effect.

The one final lesson from my father.

I not only hear the screams, but feel them. They are voicing what I have felt for the longest while. I let the short sharp screams wash over me as they make their way through our weak crumple zone and into my weak body. I don't want to open my eyes, I can't. I know what happens when you open your eyes. You have slapped your entire life away.

I want them to see me. I don't want to see them.

I want her to feel me, like I have felt her.

I want her to feel the burning, seething pain that I have felt and the ferocious speed at which it was all over. I want her to feel the harsh and discordant sensation that comes from losing all control. I want her to know what it feels like to have the life you love being taken from you.

All good things must come to an end. Everything does.

All the morphine in Mumbai couldn't numb this pain, however it's released.

Harley is my morphine. Dick will never have his New Year's Eve Midnight Kiss.

Goodbye, Gemma, my love, a dream that is dreamed by two, will never come true.

* * * *

I should have stolen that Enya CD instead, because I'm On My Way Home, Dad.

THE END

*'These violent delights have violent ends
And in their triumph die, like fire and powder
Which, as they kiss, consume.'*

Romeo and Juliet, Act II, Scene VI

ALTERNATE ENDING

THE

MISSING MORPHINE MEMOIRS
By HUGO TANG

For Harley

38

'There's no way I'm building a trebuchet or digging a moat,' says Harley, dismissing my suggestion to defend the fort.

'You've got high walls, an elevated vantage point, and Pippen the trusty steed – it would complete the castle,' I say, jokingly, of course – we'd need at least two catapults.

'Don't you think I have my hands full working on the car?' he says, and he has been locked away in this garage for days now. 'If *you* want to defend the castle, be my guest, Takeshi!'

The car must be near completion now.

'Let's go through the plan one more time,' I say, anxious that we haven't got long to go. 'Pay weekend starts tonight, so The Havana will be at its busiest. We leave here at midnight and strike at one, once we confirm Gemma, Dick and Sammy are inside,' I say, knowing exactly what his answer will be before I've even finished. The same answer it always is. It's as painful to hear as it is predictable.

'You're not coming, Ying Yang. Must we do this lion dance each and every time?' he replies, his own walls as hard to breach as the Great Wall itself.

'That isn't for you to –' I begin, before being struck down by a flaming trebuchet projectile.

'No. You think I'm being some kind of hero, but it goes beyond that,' he says with fury, as he loads another oil-soaked stone into his counterpoise catapult to fire at me. 'You're too important to die.'

I was the one out on my arse with no place to go, nowhere to turn, without a single option at my disposal. I've brought nothing to the Lazy Susan other than a failed MOT.

'Too *Important?* All I've done is work my way through your morphine and get in the way,' I say, and it's true. From the moment I arrived all I've done is clutter his home, eat his food, drink his Malibu, consume his medication, and, oh yeah, convince him to kill himself, taking down every young adult in Bury St Albans in the process. 'That's it, isn't it? It's the morphine I've been taking. You think it's affected my decision-making. Well it hasn't.'

'It has nothing to do with that. You've always been a state. I don't know you any different. If I saw you sober I'd be far more uncertain.'

'Uncertain of what?' I ask, sounding incredibly uncertain.

'The plan we've set in motion with the car is only the beginning. There is more in store for you once I've fulfilled my end of the bargain.' He ushers us out of his garage, no doubt in the hope that I'll stop talking about the mission.

'You expect me to continue plotting?' I protest, scared at the very prospect.

'I need someone I can trust. You need to care for Pippen; act as the executor of my estate and make sure Kristina is provided for.' I can't ensure his plants are watered and that the dishes get done. There is no way I can do any of that. I'm supposed to be an executioner, not an executor.

Harley is being deadly serious and we are running out of time. This is important to him – crucial even.

'Let's arrange these things now. Get it all tied up and out of the way.' I feel like an errant child, begging my father for something he will never agree to, and I'm in no mood for reflecting on any further father moments.

'That's just what I need you to do on my behalf. Then there is the plan I have for you,' he says secretively, and a pang of jealously hits me; that I am obliged to carry on planning, worrying, struggling and stressing, whereas he needn't concern himself past tonight. It's like he's a co-worker who has handed in his notice, or who has only got to do half a day on a Friday. But permanently.

'How deep does this rabbit hole go? You never mentioned any plan for me,' I say, suspiciously. I must sound ungrateful, but I am humbled that Harley cares enough to worry about me, when very shortly he will be hurtling towards an excruciating end.

'Never mentioned it? All I've done is explain what you need to do,' he says, angrily. 'After I've set off, there are two envelopes for you in the safe. You are to follow both to the letter.' His eyes focus on me intently.

'What the fuck is this? *P.S. I Love You*? Show me them now,' I demand, not expecting him to concede, considering his stance on hitching a lift to The Havana.

'To the letter, Harry. I don't want to talk about this again.'

Harley has gone to all this trouble to try and look after me, guide me, posthumously. But I don't want guidance, no matter how much I may need it, and in spite of how desperately I was seeking it before I arrived here. When I moved in, I found what I was searching for. My morphine, my mutt and my Mumbai mate. That was good enough for me.

If Harley didn't have to go, I could cushion myself from the harsh, unfaithful world beyond the moat. I could let Dick and Gemma get on with it. My 100mg pills of jackpot could allow me, in time, to forgive them, even if the forgiveness is artificial – an ingested illusion.

But Harley *does* have to go, and I'm not invited. I must remain while the trebuchet throws him elsewhere.

I want to sneak into the study and read these infamous letters. I want to see what all this fuss is about. To grasp what is so pressing that it should deny me my half of the tour de force. Harley has always been a joker, taking nothing seriously, so part of me expects a list of hookers (I'd only strangle them) and a plane ticket to Thailand.

From the way he's talking, without a smile or joke in sight, I can imagine it has a list of job interviews and conversational topics to cover with my mother to rebuild our relationship. It might even have Stacey's phone number.

These two letters aren't going to be Scarlett. They are black.

I don't care what the envelopes contain; only the contents of my car, and their club.

The other letter will be a list of solicitors, bank managers, account numbers and sort codes, combined with a great deal of other things that I won't be able to comprehend. Kristina's details will be in there and I won't be able to make the call. I know too much. I'd be like Big G or Dick leaving The Bomb Bar: armed with too much information and an intimate knowledge of what's taken place. How can I be responsible for making sure she's 'looked after'? The girl I have never met, who abandoned the most caring, astounding person I have ever known. My friend, whose colours shine brighter than the festival of lights.

I could tell from the photos in his study that she wanted to be cared for, and despite her departure, Harley still wants to live up to that promise. That *idea*. My partner left me and I want her dead. Harley has spent all of this time and effort creating these letters and I won't even have the strength to read them. It's only when we get back into his house from the garage and Pippen jumps up to greet me that I realise Harley is right. He worked so hard creating this home, his business and his feature wall that stands before us, representing Kristina's place in his house, like a shrine: why should it lay to waste? I don't *need* to go, even though I want to.

Harley is proving to me that he isn't being selfless, so I should at least try and prove to him that I'm not entirely selfish. If he wants me to do this for him, I should respect his wishes, honour his decision, open his envelopes, and do as I'm told.

39

'You hungry? I'm sick of your cooking, which is saying something because I'm pretty damn sick,' Harley smirks, as he wrestles with Pippen on the couch, making the most of their final hours together.

'Maybe cook Pippen?' He's made up his mind and so have I. If he wants me to stay, I'll stay. I should be making the most of my time with him too. I have asked and asked and asked. It's time to accept that he needs to do this on his own. 'Should we order a Chinese?

'Let's get an Indian. Another draw!' he replies, and I am reminded of all the fun we used to have at the bar together. 'There can't be much food left, surely?'

'Spaghetti hoops and soup.' I stare out across his patio and garden, no real desire to eat. I can't stomach very much these days as I believe at any minute, the acids contained within it are going to overcome its lining.

'Fuck it, let's order both,' he declares, his eyes lighting up at the gluttonous prospect. The thought of seeing him surrounded by countless plastic and foil containers, full of MSG and cumin, makes me smile.

This should be followed by mango lassi while I fan him with a bay leaf. Watching him work his way through the menu, tasting the food like never before, arming himself with numerous new Canto-cuisine related insults is exactly what we need to do. We definitely aren't ordering from the Golden Dragon. Big G is a Copper Lizard.

'That sounds great, bro. Pippen is saved from the wok,' I say, regretful that I don't have a single penny to put towards it. I want nothing more than to make it my treat.

'We need to lock the Indian and Chinese delivery drivers in the garage and have them fight to the death,' he says with delight.

'That would be amazing! *Gladiators* on a budget.'

Harley grabs a handful of colourful menus from a kitchen drawer and carefully selects the Indian restaurant, allowing me to choose the Chinese one. The first task on our new show that will never be aired.

I opt for 'Chopstix' and remember that I have actual chopsticks in my suitcase that I can bring out. That must gain me an extra point for authenticity. Harley would argue that we could eat with our hands, neutralising my bonus.

I listen with interest to Harley ordering his food. He is subtly taking the mick out of the poor brown bloke over the phone. He orders so much that the guy asks him if he'd be interested in the family meal deal for six. Harley tells him in amusement that we've still got the Chinese to order and that it's only for the three of us.

'Only two people and one dog. Only two person. I serious,' Harley explains slowly. The poor sod has no idea what Harley is on about, so I encourage him to speak in Punjabi.

Once his order is placed, he tells the guy to hurry up because there is a race against Chopstix to get here. A ten pound tip is to be had if he can get here first. His total came to £88, which better include the delivery. That's if they even deliver out here, Norfolk's answer to the Hebrides.

'Holy shit. There is no way we need to order any more than that,' I say, considering I'll only be picking at the odd chick-pea.

'Order now or you lose the battle. You have to match my bill, but you'll probably only get four dishes for that!' he mocks. It is comforting to see a typically cautious and sensible Harley act impulsively and to unnecessary excess.

For a laugh, I try and order my food in Cantonese but don't get very far. Unless we were to eat £88 worth of seaweed and pork chops. Harley shakes his head at me and chuckles to himself. Even Pippen brings her paw to her face in embarrassment, making Harley and me laugh all the more.

The Indian food gets here first. Tuk-Tuks travel faster than sedan chairs I suppose, and he did get a head start. If I hadn't murdered my language of origin, I might have given myself a Kung Fu Fighting chance.

Harley gives the guy his £10 tip: a month's wages to send back to his family. It is very endearing. When the Chinese guy arrives, Harley insists that I bow and thank him in Cantonese. Turns out the bloke's English is better than my own.

Pippen goes berserk at the sight and scent of all the food, hopefully not because her relatives are in amongst the stir fry. Harley lays out all the Indian food and I pull out the Chinese. The spread is vast; enough to feed a Communist army. It is reassuring to be able to receive Chinese food that I don't feel the need to throw at a door.

Harley takes a mouthful from each container and he looks so content, savouring the moment, without a care in the world. A world that gave up caring about him some while ago. I regret that I've spoiled my appetite for foil-wrapped food with grey, foil-wrapped capsules.

I want to ask him about the envelopes again and what they may contain, but I feed Pippen a shrimp instead. Very soon this poor old dog will be without her rightful owner and will be my responsibility. I'm not sure how long Pip will hold out for when she realises Harley won't be returning. I can't bear the thought of her pining. She is being really affectionate and needy today, so perhaps she senses that something is awry.

'How's your buffet?' I ask Harley, whose mouth contains a portion from every part of Pakistan, as India ran out of food.

'Tastes... rusty. Indian metal!' he says, as he sets down his fourth plastic fork, having broken the last three. 'You want to ask me about the envelopes, don't you?'

I pause for a moment, wondering if I had been thinking out loud. Harley's intuition supersedes his staffie's. Since we've been living together, he has developed an almost academic ability to read me. Unlike Dick's mind reading ability, Harley's is comforting and appreciated. I remain silent, so Harley speaks.

'They will be difficult for you to read, but entirely necessary.'

I want to tell him that he doesn't have to go through with this. That as much as I hate the Havana Hydra, with its countless fire-breathing heads, this may be one step too far. Until I realise how despicably insulting it would be: detracting from the grandness and scale of what is to be the ultimate sacrificial gift.

Outweighing all of that is that Harley is done. He's had enough and is checking out early. I don't say anything, but nod and agree.

'Now eat,' he says, with conviction. 'This is the last chance I'll get to make sure you don't starve. I bet Gemma had to spoon feed you your sweet and sour soup! Oh, and don't cook my dog.'

Harley insists on helping me clear up, even though I tell him that I can sort it. We pile the leftovers into the largest of the containers and stack them in the fridge. Harley banishes himself to the study and says that he doesn't want to be disturbed, so I take Pippen out for a walk.

Pip and I stroll into a peaceful clearing in a nearby field. It feels good to stretch my legs and I mull over what Harley must be doing and what's going through his mind. It's probably five in the evening, maybe nearer six, as the surreptitious blanket of dusk throws itself over the edges of this lonely meadow. We have four hours before he has to set off for the very last time.

When you bid someone farewell, you never presume that that will be it. It's always more of an 'until we meet again'. But I will never meet Harley again. He is off to be 'extreme' without me. Thelma can't accompany Louise, Bonnie is Clydeless and Mohammed is parting ways with Abdul. The 'Harley' tattoo on my wrist is all I'll have left.

Pippen eventually gives up on chasing after the stick I've been throwing, once she susses that our little game is both one-sided and unrewarding. I've given up on chasing sticks too, because as soon as you grab hold of it, it only gets taken away and thrown somewhere else.

I lie down on the grass and stare longingly at the sky, breathing in time with my companion's panting. It's a slumdog's life.

*

When we get back to the house the gates have shut behind us. I ask Pippen if she knows another way in, but if she does she doesn't care to share it with me. I should have given her more shrimps.

I stand under the front camera and start flailing my arms about and leaping, hoping that he'll see me on the screens. A camera is only of any use if someone is watching it, much like a windscreen approaching Gemma's face is only of use if I'm behind it.

Eventually the gates fold open as Harley buzzes us in. Pippen rushes ahead of me, already frustrated by my company and our time together has only just begun. Harley is stood in his front room and it looks like I've torn him away from something important.

'Cheers, I hadn't thought about getting back.'

'I knew you'd lock yourself out,' he says matter-of-factly, as if much like electric windows that don't open, getting locked out is such a Harry thing to do.

'You're my guardian angel, dude,' I say, which makes him tut.

'Parental guardian, more like.' He looks at me with concern. 'I've got to get back to work. Can you cover the rear windshield with the black spray paint please? Do it carefully and no fancy stencilled quotes, okay?' He disappears into his study.

This is the first time I've been asked to make any changes to the car, apart from clearing my crap from it. I jump at the chance. I close the door behind Pippen so that she doesn't get near the fumes. Harley would undoubtedly make a better job of the paint work than I would, so I imagine this is just to keep me out of his way.

The garage is cold and the air reeks of solvent and fuel. The can of spray paint is perched on the boot of the car, along with newspaper, a pair of vinyl gloves and masking tape. I notice my phone resting on his workbench, on charge. It is still switched off. Harley must want us to keep in contact on his drive, which fills me with the hope that when he heads off, at least it's only until we speak again.

I grab the spray paint and give it a good shake. I can feel the ball pinging about inside, like an unsettled morphine pill in my stomach.

A post-it note falls to the floor and it must have been stuck to the aerosol can. I bend down to pick it up, which causes a twinge of pain in my damaged foot. I turn the note over and it reads 'Don't Look Back', which probably has more meaning to it that simply blacking out his rear-view.

I shove the note into my pocket and prepare what is to be my most difficult stencil yet.

40

Harley joins me in the garage just as I pull the masking tape away.

'I couldn't have done it better myself,' he says, kindly. He seems calmer now. I want to ask him what he's been doing but I choose not to be nosy, while my nose stings from the spray.

'Since I'm in charge of the windshield project, I should be sending *you* out for KFC and Sausage McMuffins. Mind you, after that Chindian I don't think I'll ever have to eat again.'

'Why was it a Chindian? Surely it was an *Indese*,' he says, but I think I get the point for this one.

'I don't think the heat from those curries will quite prepare you for the heat of this car,' I say solemnly. I can't believe he is going through with this. He hasn't mentioned the ulcers, cramps and sleepless nights for a while now. I'm not sure if they've subsided or if he's not brought it up since his end is scheduled and booked.

'I won't feel a thing. This will seem like a holiday.'

'Some holiday. You'd need something a little stronger than factor forty. I'm glad you've come to terms but it's hardly a five-star all-inclusive,' I say, in a sulking strop. It's just too soon. I had only just acclimatised to my new surroundings. I've only recently been able to comprehend the extent of our plan, and he's completed the car. He's finished it too early.

'It has to be tonight. This is what you wanted, isn't it?'

'Yes, of course it is,' I reply sadly. What kind of person wants this? Hector from the Scarlett Black Letter, that's who.

'I'm not sure I can go on without you,' I whisper.

'Save that gay talk for Mandara. I'd make it quick though, because he's not got long.' He doesn't get the exultant reaction he was hoping for. 'Bonsai, this is happening.'

'I wish it didn't have to end this way,' I say, weakly. I don't care how pathetic I sound.

'All good things come to an end.'

'All bad things *never* end.' The look on Harley's face reminds me why we're here. 'But your suffering will be over. Finally.'

'I'm going to head out earlier than planned. I have to stop and get petrol.' The limited time we have left together is to be reduced even further.

'Stop for petrol? With all this stuff in the car?' Any early departure would have been met with resistance.

'Might stop for a bacon roll,' he says, trying to be casual, but I can see the unleaded adrenaline refilling in his eyes. 'Will you go through the route with me?'

I trace my finger along the large fold-out road map we have pinned up on the wall and describe each turning. Harley is leaning against the door of the car, his eyes closed and his hands clenched in firm fists either side of him.

I'm not sure if he's listening but I feel it may be for my benefit more than his, much like the spray painting. He's driven this route every Friday and Saturday for years. I am meticulous in my description, explaining it slowly, trying to mimic the voice of a Sat Nav. The closer my finger gets to Bury, the more drawn out and slower my voice becomes. Perhaps if I explain the journey all the way to Land's End, Harley won't have to go just yet.

When I eventually run out of motorway, roads and words, it is time for him to go. I should have explained the journey in Cantonese so maybe his pork needn't be chopped quite so soon. I think this point goes to him.

'Could you wait here while I say goodbye to Pippen?' He takes one last look at the map and instructs me to rip it down and stick it on the charcoal fire, the embers fizzling away in the corner of the garage.

I tell him to take his time. He calls me 'Chin Tu Fat' before heading out of the garage. I turn to face the map, looking at what will be the final drive of his life and am surprised that his oversized heart will even fit in my compact 316.

I tear the map to shreds. I throw the agonising ordinance survey onto the fire and watch a bin full of birthday cards burn once more. I watch the bits of paper curl up into ash and within a matter of seconds, it's like it never existed. It turns to dust and that's the end of it. Harley is about to head off to the Coliseum for his final showdown. All roads lead to Rome.

I hope Pippen understands that this is it. That she won't be able to see Harley ever again. That she sits and rolls over and hands him her paw like never before.

When Harley returns he doesn't say anything and he doesn't need to. He walks over to me slowly and his hands, no longer clenched, find themselves on each of my shoulders. He looks straight at me, into me – and I can't bear to look at him.

'It's time for me to go,' he glints, slowly, and hands float away, like cinders caught in the wind. 'Everything you need is here. When you take the dog for a walk, don't forget the key.'

'I won't. I won't forget,' I say. 'I will *never* forget.'

'Good. I know you won't,' he replies, softly. 'You'll do the right thing, Ip Man.'

'Thank you, Harley. For everything.'

'Thank me later.'

I watch Harley tuck himself into the car. He closes the car door gently, just as Gemma did when she closed the door to our house after I slapped her. I want to go back to a time when people were so mad at me that they slammed doors. I don't like this new world we live in, where people are so distraught with the things that I have done, or that I have forced them to do, that doors get closed gently.

I press the button, which opens the shutter and gate and they both move in a slow motion of respectful silence. Harley reverses out of the garage carefully, considering he can no longer see out of his rear-view. I blackened the glass like I blacken everything else. He pulls away and before I know it, he is gone. The front gates close behind him and so do I. Much like my once cherished club, I am no longer trading or open for business. I head back into the house and Pippen has no idea. Her intuition couldn't foresee this and neither did mine.

I look at my watch to see how much time there is before Harley reaches The Havana, but my wrist is naked. Pippen stares up at me, lost. The only other creature to miss master once gone. I thought Harley would have had a wealth of friends, but it would appear that much like myself, he has spent all the time that it takes to nurture friendships on his work and his woman. The falsest of economies. My mouth is dry and tastes like the bottom of a bird cage. A bird cage full of vulture shit.

The vultures have stripped the carcass clean and with no more festering meat to devour, they need Harley's flesh instead.

The envelopes.

I run to the safe, until I realise that I don't actually know where the safe is even kept. I race upstairs and I have never left the ground floor before. I settled for the new experience of the armchair and never ventured into the rest of Harley's home. When I get to the top of the flight, there are three doors that lead off the landing. I didn't like what was behind door number one, two or three, and I wish his house had a fourth. I open the door and find the bathroom. It is nice to be in a washroom that no one has destroyed or shot-up in. I check the door next to it and this must be the spare room, where I was supposed to stay.

I enter the final door and wonder what Harley's room will look like. I open the door slowly and it's another spare room. There is nothing here. No clothes, no belongings, not a thing. I don't understand. It feels like a trick or a trap – has the wolf given the green light for Kristina to sneak in and take back all her things, just like it happened to me. I pace the upper floor, unable to figure this out. Am I high?

I need to call him. It feels disconcerting to be in someone's house when they aren't in, but it doesn't look like Harley has ever been here either. I dart down the stairs, my foot hurting and my head harmed. I run out into the garage and grab my phone, scrambling to turn it on. I need to find this safe. I need to do so many things and I can't manage any of it. Harley has been gone for less than five minutes and I am an uncoordinated, confused, chaotic mess.

When my handset has fully loaded, I am saddened by the background image - a picture of me and Gemma. I don't remember this being my home screen, but many things are now a blur. This isn't the way I was meant to see her tonight. I should have been in that car.

I head to the study, scanning the room until I discover the safe under the desk. I reach down and Pippen has come to join me. Perhaps she has figured it out and demands answers too.

As the safe opens my phone begins to hum. I have received a voicemail. I don't know how old this message is likely to be, or if there are more to follow, but without giving it too much thought, I listen.

It is from Barney and it's good to hear his voice.

'Harry, where are you? Give me a call to let me know you're okay. Charis had the baby. We've named her Chardonnay. Just kidding, she's called Hope. When are you coming to meet her? Dylan is looking for you. Apparently you've borrowed his friend's cat? I think he was stoned! The main reason I'm calling is to tell you that a venue called Utopia has opened across the road from The Havana! Guess who's managing it? Stevie Mac and Man-Dem! That's karma for you! Shame we couldn't stay open long enough to see it, but what goes around, comes around. Gemma left Snoopy cause his club is dying a death. Trouble in paradise hey! Give us a bell whenever you –'

End of message.

I need to listen to that again.

I am at a loss for words. I try to ring Barney but there's no signal.

I can't believe it. I wanted to destroy them. I wanted them to witness my anger at its rawest and most vicious. I wanted them to suffer, but now I don't have to. Sammy Fish figured out that you can't buy friendship after all.

I couldn't have hoped for a better outcome yet despite Dick being dragged down, I don't feel anywhere near the level of satisfaction I had been hoping for. I don't win. My situation doesn't change. I am still sat here alone, with nothing.

Harley.

I try to call Harley to tell him to pull over, but his phone isn't on him. It's here in the safe.

I feel that I have to stop this. I don't know how, or even why, but I search my phone for Dick's number. The last time I called him was moments before my life changed irreparably. The moment I slapped her. I have fantasised at length about the downfall of Dick. I wanted a front seat in the war machine shuttling towards his club doors.

Pip begins to yap excitedly. I notice the two envelopes. The urgent compulsion to warn them subsides, and I drop to the floor, cross my legs, lift Pippen onto my lap, and run my thumb over the writing on the front of the first card.

For Harry

I turn the card over but can't bring myself to open it. I turn it over once more to read my name and despite wanting to tell him all that I now know, am painfully thankful that I can no longer reach him. How devastating a blow would that have been, to receive a call to stand down. That his services are no longer required. That seeing as my vendetta is over, he can come back for that pillow to the face while he sleeps. That all the waiting and working and prolonging, all done for me, was in vain.

I open the card. Slowly and carefully.

'I called Kristina. I told her what I intended to do. Not specifically, but she got the message. She had no time for me, Harry. But you begged to join me. I want to thank you.

For being my family. For making the pits The Ritz. For being there until the very end.

For allowing me to repay the favour –'

I drop the letter. I can't let him do this. He doesn't want to do this. He is doing this for me. I have to call Dick. I don't know what I'm supposed to say. He will think my call is to gloat. To threaten. Am I to tell him that I have planned and plotted his assassination, wanting nothing more than the destruction of his beloved Havana Club, but only now decided to warn him, when Harley is due any minute, in my car?! Pretty much.

He doesn't pick up. I call again. Not the best time to try to get through to a DJ, primetime Saturday night on a pay weekend when they are on the decks. If Utopia has taken his trade and both of his DJs, chances are he will have to DJ himself.

The phone continues to dial out and the only other person I can think of to call is Big G but even then, I'm not sure what –

'*Harry?*' says Dick, who has picked up my call.

'Where is Gemma?' I demand, frantically.

'It's over between us, alright? It's done.'

'Where is she?' I repeat, and I can hardly hear him over the noise in the background.

'She's at Utopia, but I'm guessing you already knew that,' he says, sarcastically. He thinks I *am* calling up to gloat. He sounds offended. He ruins my life, I decide to massacre him, and when I get a change of broken heart and decide to save him, this motherfucker guilt trips me. 'Surprised you haven't bought shares in the place.'

'You need to get out of there. Leave the club, now!' I shout, forcefully.

'Have a nice night, thanks for calling. I probably deserved that, so well done,' he says, proving that no bad deed, turned into a slightly good deed, goes unpunished.

'The Havana is about to get fucked up,' I exclaim, an understatement considering the heat that Harley is packing.

'Cheers, Chen. Good to know,' Dick replies, before hanging up.

I have no more time. It's done. I can't save anyone. I can't say goodbye to Harley. This letter before me is his final farewell. This single piece of paper is meant to be my closure.

With tears streaming down my cold, sunken face, I continue to read:

> '*Don't let your worries get in the way. You love her Harry, and by Shiva, you need her. You've had a change of heart, as I knew you would. You are a good person, despite your every attempt to prove otherwise.*'

The ink on the paper blots and spreads as my hot tears fall onto his beautiful writing paper and even softer and unexpected words.

> '*I haven't driven to The Havana. I've gone to get your watch back. I've reported your car stolen and you don't need to do anything. You don't need to handle my property or inform Kris. As if I'd put you in charge of anything like that! You'd sell my houses for crack and then crack onto my ex!*

Don't put metal tins in the microwave. Promise me you won't take any more morphine. And don't spend this money on booze. Sorry it's only Sterling and not Yen.

Live life for the both of us, better than we ever could have imagined.

And don't look back. Patel.'

Harley's final snag list. His generous letter has shown me how to command the full asking price. That I do deserve more and that I do deserve better.

I take the other envelope and make my way to the driveway. I am heading to Bury. I need to find her, I need to see her. Harley is absolutely right. I refuse to be alone.

I grab the keys to the Navara, throw on Harley's black coat and Pippen follows me out. I let her sit up front and hit the fob that opens the gates. Barney always said to hope for the best and plan for the worst. He was right. I planned for the worst, the very worst. Now it is time to hope for the best. He even named his daughter after it.

Hope. I'm coming to find you.

四十一

I drive to Land's End.

Deep down, I knew Harley wasn't malicious enough to go ahead with it, but I was in denial, because I wanted it so. Until of course he realised that that isn't what I wanted at all.

As I approach the motorway, I stick the light on in the car and try to open the second envelope. I have no idea what to expect. I steady the steering wheel with my knees and rip open the flap.

Photographs. I hold the first one up to the light to see. It is the picture from the clock in the study. The beautiful Christmas image of Harley, Kris and Pippen as a puppy, all sat around the tree. My heart swells at the sight of them so healthy, happy and in love.

I turn the photograph over and Harley has written:

'Harry, There are some things worth dying for.'

I look up to check on the road and I haven't driven Pippen into a ditch just yet. This car is much sturdier than mine and could probably withstand Helen and her racist petrol station. I hold up the other photo and it is a picture from a couple of years ago, taken at The Bomb Bar.

It is of an impossibly young looking Gemma, her porcelain skin and bright flowing blonde hair alongside me, with Harley in the middle, his arms around us both. Pre-cancer, pre-closure, pre-calamity. When the three words we had for one another were pure and life was good. I am so grateful he has given me this picture. I turn the picture over and on the reverse it reads:

'And there are the things worth living for.'

I tuck the photos into my new coat, Harley's favourite item of clothing. I stroke Pippen's head and put my foot down. As I approach the junction to turn off, a demonic fire engine tears down the other side of the dual carriageway. Harley gave those bastards the what for. That watch was priceless to me – as irreplaceable as the man who has immolated them for taking it.

When I arrive at Bury it is clear who has won the war. The clubs are spilling out and Utopia is doing most of the spilling, with hundreds of revellers exiting their venue. The Havana is merely squirting. I notice

Dick and Sammy on their front door smoking, with their doorman who brandishes the tasered testicles and not really anyone else.

Pippen seems startled by the number of people about, so I lift her up and cradle her in my arms, which she appreciates by way of a face lick. I pull up behind a panda car and search for my Giraffe. My Ideal Scent.

And then I see her. As if a spotlight has singled her out from the crowd of many.

My Shining Diamond Gemma.

She is with her friends. She hasn't noticed me amongst the gormless drones. She is as beautiful as I remember – a vision – but as polished and pristine as she may look, she isn't the girl in the photo. Nor is she the minister of spiritual torment that cracks lenses, scorches corneas and burns pupils. She's just a young, naïve girl, out with her pals. Her stride of pride has taken her further from me than I had ever imagined possible. She is not the donor to my rare blood type. My relationship to my bride-to-be no longer defines me.

Maybe it wasn't my notion of romance that was false, but my notion of retribution. Have I truly been seeking a way to get her back, or merely a way to make myself feel better?

The Harry Chen Show doesn't require an audience.

I am indifferent. I am not the same person and I have changed. I look down at Pip, who gives me another kiss, and I realise that perhaps, just maybe, I have changed for the better. There *are* things worth living for, but it is no longer G-Star. She is not my swan; she is not my best friend. But she isn't wishing tuberculosis upon me either.

It's Over Now. My Mystery Special Guest is Hope.

The boat I was so determined to push out to sea begins to drift back to shore. Gemma was my anchor, but it's high time I learnt to float on my own. The zoom, zoom, zoom fades away.

All the best, Gemz *x*

Four Months Later

'I'm so glad we could meet up again, dude!' says Dylan, who has finished his first term at university and is back for the break. 'It's been way too long, how you finding it here?'

'The Fox & Hound is good. Nice to be behind a bar again and they've sorted me a room upstairs. We've gone upmarket, so we're lucky to get a seat,' I reply, as I feed Harley the Labrador another pork scratching. 'Belinda has helped me out big time. She still talks about you.'

'I told you man, a hound doesn't turn into a fox for at least another six pints!' he jests, and it's good to see him again. 'I really messed up with the whole baby thing. It's a shame we didn't have my dog make puppies with Pippen. That would've been awesome.'

'I miss Pippen. I think she figured out that Harley wasn't coming back. I'm glad they're reunited,' I say, and there isn't an hour that goes by that I don't think about them.

'I miss them too.' I never thought I'd see the day where a reformed Dylan could keep his brass neck wound in long enough to share a fond memory. 'Hey, what would you rather? Be sexually attracted to fruit? Or have pork scratching dust permanently stuck to your fingers?'

'Just when I thought you could hold down an adult conversation,' I say. 'Right, I've got one for you. Would you rather watch your parents have sex every day of your life? Or join in once to stop it?'

'What a joker! That's a good one.' I don't think that was too bad for a first attempt, despite getting carried away and speaking far louder than I should. An attractive girl has heard my question and heads over in our direction. She looks familiar.

'Do you mind if I sit here?' asks random brunette. Cute. Unattainable. Solo.

'Not at all,' I reply, as I pick up Dylan's dog. Chicks love dogs.

'Thanks,' she answers, with a warm smile. She looks just as pretty as she did the day Big G failed to share her supposed taxi. I'm now really thankful that Dylan royally cock-blocked him all those months ago.

'I knew you'd join us for something to eat eventually. My charm works every time,' says Dylonius. Perhaps he is magnanimous after all.

'Here's one for you, lads. Would you rather change gender every time you sneeze? Or not be able to tell the difference between a muffin and a baby?' Cute. Attainable. Perfect.

And I don't look back.

UNTIL WE MEET AGAIN

*'Mistakes are always forgivable,
if one has the courage to admit them.'*
Bruce Lee

Acknowledgments

In loving memory of my partner in crime, Harley Etchells. Words cannot describe what you meant to me, but I hope this book was a start.

Huge thank you to Lucy Bickley, Margaret Tang, Howard Tang, Jon Bale, Charlotte Ogden, Julie Forrester, Vicki Green, Nic Chaplin, Vikki Reilly, Louise Hutcheson, Helen Johnson, The Wongs, The Bomans, The Carters, Kev Jnr, Dave Pigott, Andrew & Shanice, Matt Atkins, Schmeegz, Hannah Tang, Claire Bottomley, James Thompson and Nury Vittachi.

And a massive thank you to Don, who has never been drunk, but is often 'tired'!

I would like to thank the National Health Service for ensuring that my dear friend Mr Keyes was given the treatment and care he needed and deserved.

Finally, a tremendous thank you to YOU for reading! I really hope you enjoyed it.

Every reasonable effort has been made to contact all copyright holders, but if there are any errors or omissions the author will be pleased to insert or amend the appropriate acknowledgement in any subsequent release or update of this publication on the official website.

Original Cover Art by Brendan Smith

Copyright © Hugo Tang, 2014

Hugo Tang has asserted his right under the Copyright, Designs and Patents Act, 1988 to be identified as the author of this work. This document is also protected in the United States by Author's House.

Like it, Follow it, Watch it:
Facebook, Twitter, YouTube
@NoIceNoSlice
If you enjoyed it, please share!

Lightning Source UK Ltd.
Milton Keynes UK
UKOW03f0640161014

240181UK00001B/6/P